MOUTHLESS

By Chris Whisky

Dedication: For Anne

Books in this series

<u>No More Crime</u>

– Chris Douglas life changed after being attacked by local youths

<u>Mouthless</u>

– Second book in the series following Chris Douglas fight against crime.

Wednesday 27th October

Standing outside 24 Wainright Avenue with my wife Anne and Son Michael by my side I begin to reminisce over the last few weeks remembering the first person I attacked.

'Now what was his name? That's it, Paul Halett. I smashed his kneecap with my hammer and robbed him of a hundred and five pounds in total. He was the first one I attacked and then there was Gareth, Eric, Edward the posh lad and who was next? Oh yes, there was Philip, Joey and his mate, Neville and another Edward the suspected paedophile and of course Jenny's two lads, Brett and Alex. The last three were big Leon, John and finally Derek Pecheski. That makes fourteen in total that I've robbed and crippled in the last few weeks. So the question I need to ask myself is why am I standing outside a Police Detective Sergeant's house, not just any police detective sergeant but the very one who's leading the investigation to have me arrested?' I think to myself.

We've been invited to Pete and Jenny Norris house for dinner. They're the parents of Debbie, an eight year old girl who sits next to our own eight year old son Michael in class at school. Pete was transferred to the Merseyside Constabulary a couple of months back with his wife Jenny and his twin boys Brett and Alex from his previous marriage and Pete and Jenny's daughter Debbie. In light of the recent attacks by the 'Mouthless Maniac' Pete was promoted to Detective Sergeant and asked to lead the investigation into the local attacks.

"Are you alright Chris? You look a little faint." Anne asks.

I turn to my wife and glance back at the drive where the two Police cars are parked, then back to my wife. Seeing the two police cars parked up on Pete's drive is making me suspect that Pete knows who I am and is waiting inside the house poised to arrest me with the backup of a couple of officers as soon as we enter.

'*Why would he have two or more police officers with him unless he's just about to arrest the masked maniac?*' I think to myself.

'*If a policeman was sent round to Pete's house on Pete's day off to give him something vitally important, why would they send two cars? Surely one officer could deliver the package or message. It doesn't take two or more officers to deliver something. It just doesn't make sense that two police cars are parked in the drive of a police sergeant who's got a day off. The more I think about it the more I'm convinced that he's going to arrest me in front of my wife and child.*'

I start to feel nauseous at the thought of being caught by the police in front of my family. Anne's going to scream and faint when Pete accuses mc of being the Mouthless maniac. Michael would be upset but probably think it's the coolest thing ever that his dad is a serial attacker.

"Sorry Anne, I always feel a little nervous when I see a Police car. Ever since cheating on my maths exam at school I keep thinking someone from the school board is going to find out and send the police around to arrest me."

"What! You cheated in your maths exam?" Michael asks.

"Yes, but don't tell anyone." I whisper to my son.

"I won't." Michael replies.

"Don't listen to your father Michael, he's just joking again." Anne gives me a funny look as if to say; 'Don't put bad ideas into your son's head because he'll copy them.'

I turn back towards the front door with its brass knocker suspended from its anchor in the centre of the door. The sun is dropping low behind me causes my silhouette to rise up the door frame reminding me of our arrival at the Norris's residence. I stare at the knocker knowing as soon as I pull it out from the door and let it drop they'll know were outside. My hands feel like lead weights pulling my arms down by my sides. The more I think of the police cars in the drive and those inside the house waiting for me, the more I feel paralysed from moving.

Anne leans across me and pulls the knocker away from its cradle and lets it fall towards the door. A crashing sound echo's through the house behind the closed door. Anne lifts the knocker again and lets it drop a second time sending a repeat of the crashing sound announcing our arrival to those inside.

"You're supposed to knock or ring the bell to let them know were standing outside." My wife reminds me.

"Sorry, I was just thinking about something." I say in my defence.

I stare back at the door thinking to myself.

'They know were here now, any minute the doors going to open and a burly officer holding a set of handcuffs and a truncheon of some sort will be standing right in front of me to arrest me.'

My heart begins to pound in my chest as I feel an anxiety attack coming on. Anne notices the colour drain from my face and gives my hand a squeeze to reassure me that everything's going to be alright. She probably thinks I'm a little nervous about meeting someone new.

"Don't worry darling, Pete's really nice." She whispers in my ear.

Anne met Pete the other week when she came round to see Jenny. Anne doesn't have a clue about my night time activities so she doesn't know how petrified I am right at this moment. I squeeze her hand to reassure her that I'll be alright and we both stare at the door waiting for it to open.

We hear footfalls in the hall as someone approaches the door. The noise stops and we hear the lock turn in the door before it's pulled back and open. The sight of seeing Jenny standing in the hallway in a cream knee length dress with matching cream slip on shoes fashioned with pink bows relaxes me a little. Jenny smiles and says.

"Anne, Chris, Michael, please come on in. Wow, and look at the time, you're so punctual. That's great."

Jenny steps to the side to allow us to enter into a sizeable hallway with marble flooring and glass teardrop chandelier lighting the entrance in sparkling shimmering light.

"Nice chandelier! Has that always been there?" I ask
while trying to recall what the hall looked like when I
came around the other week to collect Michael.
Jenny giggles a little and gives me a surprised look
wondering if I'm joking or not. "It's always been
there. It was passed down from Pete's grandparents
and he loves it. I think it's a bit pretentious for our
humble home but Pete's the head of the house so I let
him have his way." Jenny explains.
"Well I was going to say how I love your décor."
Anne says.
"Thank you Anne; now that was all me." Jenny says
and smiles.
We all laugh.

We all step inside the hallway and move to the right
to allow Jenny to close the front door. The noise of
the door closing sealing my exit starts to make me
panic a little as I remember the house is full of
policemen waiting to arrest me.
My eyes dart around the room trying to see where
they're hiding but can only see an empty staircase in
front of us leading upstairs and a double doorway to
the left into the lounge.
Jenny steps away from the closed front door and pops
her head through the double doorway to the lounge
announcing our arrival.
"Pete, they're here."
I hear someone coming towards us and my heart
immediately begins to speed up again in anticipation
of seeing Pete appear through the gap. A second later
Pete appears followed by two police officers. They
stop in the doorway and Pete points to me.

"There he is!"

My heart stops in horror at being caught. I can't
believe they've worked out who the mouthless
maniac is so soon.
What gave me away?
Did Pete's sons recognise me after I attacked them
and told their dad?
Did I leave fingerprints anywhere and they've found
me on some crime database?
Did one of my victims know who I was?
It must have been Derek Pecheski; he must have put
two and two together when Angela told him that I'd
asked about the bruise on her face and that I didn't
look very happy when I left the bank the other day.
Maybe he just recognised my voice when I attacked
him.
I feel my legs give way so I reach back for the door
handle to steady myself. Blood surging through my
veins and I sense the pressure building up in the back
of my head causing my vision to blur, I blink rapidly
to clear my vision and look towards the two police
officers standing by Pete's side waiting for them to
rush forward and arrest me when I hear Pete's voice
continue.

"Chris here was the best football player in our school.
I tell you guys Chris could have played professionally
and if memory serves me well; didn't you score ten
goals in a single game?" Pete asks.
It takes me a second to compose myself from feeling
complete terror to relief at not being arrested.
Pete walks over towards me and extends his hand.

"How are you? It's been years."

I let go of the door handle and try to regain my composure as I take Pete's hand and give it a firm shake.

"Great thanks. Wow you've got a good memory." I ask while trying to recall ever scoring ten goals in a match.

"No one will forget that game Chris, we were talking about it for ages." Pete says.

"I didn't know you were that good at football." Anne asks.

I give Anne a look of surprise as I can't remember ever being that good.

"You're just being modest. When Anne told me the other day that you were in the year above me at school; I had to wrack my brains to remember who you were. Then it came to me, 'Sticky Chris!'"

"Sticky Chris?" Anne asks, looking puzzled.

"Yes, whenever Chris got the ball he never lost it; the ball seemed to stick to him like glue. The only time the ball ever left his foot it ended up in the back of the net." Pete explains.

"Wow, I haven't been called that for ages."

"Sorry, here I am keeping you at the door. Come on through to the lounge and have a seat while I just let these two officers get back to work."

Jenny escorts us into the lounge, while Pete walks with the two officers to the front door.

"Please take a seat; did anyone fancy something to drink? We have red or white wine, lager or whisky and off course some coke for Michael?" Jenny asks.

"A glass of white wine please, Jenny." Anne replies.
"A lager would be great, thanks." I say.
"Right, make yourselves comfortable and I'll be back in a moment with your drinks." Jenny says before walking through to the kitchen to get our drinks.
I take a seat on one of the arm chairs near the window while Anne and Michael sit down on the large sofa in the centre of the lounge. The room is a typical modern lounge nicely decorated in creams and magnolia with a large flat screen television mounted on the wall opposite the sofa above an artificial fire surround with decorative flowers in a crystal vase inset. The white leather opulent three piece suite looks brand new without a mark on it so I imagine it was bought when they moved into the house a few months ago with the rest of their furniture.

We here Pete close the front door behind the two officers and walks back into the lounge.
"Sorry about that, being in the police means you're never off duty. So, how are you all, has Jenny asked you what you would like to drink?" Pete asks.
"Yes thanks." I reply just as Jenny walks back through from the kitchen with all our drinks on a tray. She places the tray down on a coffee table then proceeds to hand each one of us our drinks.
"Here you go." She passes Anne her wine and hands me a pint glass filled with the chilled lager. I take a sip allowing the cool liquid to refresh my dry throat before resting the glass down on a coaster with a police helmet insignia on its face.
"Help yourself to some peanuts or crisps." Jenny says pointing to the serving bowls on the tray.

"Pete, can I get you anything?" Jenny asks.
"I think I'll have a lager as well thanks."
Jenny wanders back into the kitchen.

"So Sticky Chris how are you, what have you been
doing all these years?" Pete asks.
"Great thanks, as you can see; I'm married with no
children."
"CHRISTOPHER!" Anne calls out.
"Just kidding; we have our son, Michael." I point over
to Michael sat next to Anne on the sofa.
"Good evening young man." Pete leans over and
shakes Michael's hand before taking a seat on the
armchair opposite me next to the dining room.
"Well as you already know we have a daughter
Debbie the same age as Michael I believe!" Pete
looks around for his offspring.
"Excuse me a second." Pete gets up and walks to the
doorway and shouts up the stairs for his children to
come down.

We hear the sound of a small child's feet pounding
along the landing and down the stairs before Debbie
appears through the doorway. She stops and scans the
room before making her way over to the sofa and sits
next to Michael. A few moments later Alex and Brett
walk in on their crutches and noticing there's only
one vacant seat left on the sofa, they limp over to the
dining table and take a dining chair each and carry
them through into the lounge so they can join in the
conversation with the rest of us.

"Great! We're all here. Oh wait, Jen." Pete calls out just as Jenny walks back in with a lager for Pete and coke for Debbie.

"Here you are." She hands Pete her drink and passes a glass of coke to Debbie before sitting down on the sofa next to Debbie.

"Right, Sorry Chris and Anne this is my daughter Debbie who you've already met."

Debbie says "Hello."

"And these are our two son's Alex and Brett." Pete points over to the two boys tucked over to his left.

"Hello." They both speak out in unison.

Seeing the two lads again makes me remember the evening behind the music shop when I attacked them with a hammer and shattered both their right kneecaps. Breaking the right kneecap of my victims has become a signature of the Mouthless Maniac. I do it to all my victims as a deterrent to stop them, committing crimes in the future because I reason to myself that a thief would find it difficult to rob someone and run off when he needs a stick to walk. I remember it was one of those nights when everything seemed to go wrong. I had planned to attack just Brett and Alex, but they turned up with two other guys so I had to improvise. I tazered Alex but when Brett caught up with me I'd lost my tazer and had to resort to the old faithful; a swift boot to his family jewels. I only wanted to stop him hitting me but when I saw him black out and crumple on the ground in a heap; I knew I must have kicked him too hard. It was a few days later when my wife Anne learned from Jenny that one of her sons had lost one of his testicles.

I first met them a few days earlier when they bumped into me at Tesco's and tried to pick a fight with me. They seemed the type of young lads who were full of anger and thought the world owed them a favour. I wanted to teach them a lesson that you can't always have it your own way and that life is hard; just get on and live a good life and be nice to people along the way. That's why I wrote on their chests the message 'Bullying is a crime, be nice or I'll come back for you.' I think the message worked as they seem much nicer now.'

"Hello, so who is Alex and who is Brett?" I ask.
Alex raises his hand and says "I'm Alex."
Brett says "I'm Brett."
It nearly made me laugh when I hear Brett's voice because I immediately think his voice is a little higher than his twin brother now that he's only got one ball.
"Are you identical twins?"
They look at each other and then back at me before saying.
"Yes" in unison.
"I imagine people get you mixed up all the time, because I can't tell the difference and I've forgotten which one's which already."
"That's alright; our teacher used to demand that we wear different coloured shirts so she could remember who was who." Brett says.
"We sometimes changed during break time just to confuse her." Alex adds.
They both laugh.
"I bet you could have a lot of fun with people."

"Yes they did. They were always tricking me." Jenny says.
"So are there any differences between you to identify who is who?" I ask.
"No, were exactly the same." They both say.
'Now I know you're lying.' I think to myself.

"So I hear you were attacked recently, your mom was telling us the other day; so how are you both? I hope you've recovering alright?"
Alex says "We'll be alright, just a broken leg that's all." He reaches down and rubs the area around his right knee.
"I'm sorry to hear someone attacked you; I was attacked not long ago as well. A couple of lads hit me over the head, stabbed me in the leg and robbed me."
"Ouch, that must have hurt." Pete says.
"Yes, but as you can see, I'm all better now." I look over to the twins.

"Did the Police arrest the lads who attacked you Mr Douglas?" Brett asks.
"No, Brett they didn't, but I suppose that's the world we live in. Crime seems to be on the increase and the Police can only do what they can do."
"You're absolutely right there Chris, in recent years our workload has increased fourfold, while our manpower has remained basically the same."
"That's alright Pete, I'm not blaming anyone. I just think it's a problem we'll never resolve."
"I know what you mean. No matter how many crimes we solve, there are always plenty more that need solving."

"Yes! Its like housework, I keep working hard at it every day, but it never ends." Jenny leans over from her seat and picks up a few peanuts scattered on the floor at the base of the coffee table that Pete had dropped; Jenny gives Pete a disapproving look. "Sorry." Pete says as he notices the mess he's made. "Anyway, everyone, dinner is ready." Jenny informs us.

We all make our way through into the dining room and take a seat at the long dining table set out for eight. Pete takes the seat at the far end of the table next to the conservatory and opposite Jenny at the other end; I sit next to Pete on his left. Anne sits on the same side next to Jenny with Michael between us. Brett and Alex slide their chairs back to the left side of the table and sit next to their parents with Debbie between them facing Michael.

"Right, everyone comfortable, I'll just bring the food through." Jenny says. She stands up and wanders through into the kitchen before returning with two plates of food. She places the first plates in front of Anne and the second she hands to Michael, Pete and I get our food when Jenny returns. I look down at the beautifully presented plate of steak and prosciutto skewers, lemon and rosemary potato wedges with an Aubergine lemon and pepper salad.
Jenny returns with Alex and Brett's food before finally returning with Debbie's and her own plate. "Wow this looks and smells wonderful Jenny." I say complimenting Jenny on a well presented plate of food.

"Thank you Chris, I hope you enjoy it." Jenny takes her seat and we all tuck in.

During dinner we make small talk and enjoy the relaxed atmosphere. Michael and Debbie seem to be happy enough although they never speak to each other throughout the two courses. They do however giggle and pull funny faces at each other while they struggle to chew the large chunks of steak. I think they must be playing footsie under the table as I occasionally hear a clonking sound from a shoe catching the central wooden stem on the table. After dinner Pete and Jenny invite Anne and I to relax in the lounge; Alex and Brett ask to be excused as they need to rest their legs, while Michael and Debbie wander into the conservatory to play and read their Manga books together.

"Jenny, that was delicious, thank you very much." Anne says.
"That's alright, you're welcome. Did anyone fancy a coffee?"
"Yes please."
Jenny heads back into the kitchen to get the drinks while we all relax on the comfy chairs in the lounge.
"So Chris, do you always have a Wednesday off?" Pete asks.
"Yes, I normally work night shifts over the weekend so yes I'm off every Tuesday, Wednesday and Thursday."
"Do you work Sunday afternoons?"
"No, I'm usually off then, you know pottering around the house, why?"

"We've been playing football every Sunday afternoon for the past couple of weeks. It's mostly the lads down at the station, but we've got one or two others to make up the numbers. Just wondered if you'd be interested in playing?"

"Wow, I haven't played for ages, I do need to lose a bit of weight and the exercise would do me good, so yes, if that's OK if you don't mind having a rusty old man playing with you."

"Get away, I bet you've still got the old skills."

Jenny walks back in to the lounge carrying a tray with hot cups of coffee and a plate of chocolate mint biscuits on. She places the tray down on the coffee table and hands out the drinks to everyone.

"Jenny, Chris says he'll play football with us on Sunday." Pete informs Jenny.

"That's great; Anne you must come along with Michael to watch the game with us. Debbie and I would love to have some company to cheer our men on and after the match we usually all have a drink and something to eat at the recreation centre for a bit of socialising."

"That sounds good, I'm sure Michael would enjoy watching his dad score ten goals."

"I don't think that's going to happen. Like I say, I haven't played since school. Oh that reminds me, I found a couple of photographs you might like to see." I reach inside my jacket pocket and retrieve the four photos and hand them over to Pete and Jenny to look at.

Pete begins to laugh out load as he spots himself in the distance on one of the photos. "Look Jenny, that's me; see how much hair I had in those day's!"

"You're so young! When was this taken Chris?" Jenny asks.

"I think we were about fourteen or fifteen."

"Is this you then, with your hands in the air?" Jenny asks as she points to the picture.

"Yes, I'd just scored a goal."

"I told you Chris was good." Pete tells Jenny.

"That's great. I can't wait for Sunday's game now." Jenny replies.

I return a forced smile towards our hosts and wonder what I've got myself into.

"Right then, we play at three o'clock down at the wreck. It's best to get there a few minutes earlier so we can have a knock around." Pete informs me.

"I'll be there." I reply.

For the next hour or two the four of us play a few games of cards, mainly poker using matchsticks instead of real money. Anne and I have never played poker so we lose every game which is a good thing because it's important and good manners not to win against your hosts and as it didn't cost us a thing, we didn't mind. I expect Pete and Jenny must play a lot because they knew exactly when to bet when the kitty was big and fold when there wasn't much in the kitty. I've heard the expression 'Poker Face' before but never really understood it until now because Pete and Jenny never gave a thing away, we couldn't tell if they had good or bad hands, totally expressionless. I imagine it's something Pete was trained to do being a police officer. I gather it's to protect the officers from becoming emotionally attached to situations they face every day. It would prove to be quite embarrassing to be handed a parking ticket from a teary eyed police officer.

I check the clock on the wall and see its twenty past eight already.

"Sorry, but I think we need to take Michael home now as its school in the morning." I say looking back at the clock.

Jenny notices the time too and says. "Wow, I can't believe its twenty past eight already. Sorry for keeping you this long."

"No that's alright Jenny we've really enjoyed ourselves and thank you for a wonderful dinner, it was delicious." Anne says.

"You're welcome. It was really nice that you came over."

I call through to Michael to let him know that were about to leave. Michael and Debbie slowly immerge from the conservatory to join us.

"Thanks again Jenny the food was delicious." I repeat Anne's sentiments while making our way to the front door.

"So we'll see you at football on Sunday at three?" Pete asks.

"Definitely, I'm looking forward to it." I reply.

We say our goodbyes and head down the drive to our car.

Jenny, Pete and Debbie wave to us as we drive off in the direction of home.

We make a small detour to the corner shop and pick up a bottle of red wine to drink when we get home. I thought it would be safer not to have a second drink at Pete and Jenny's because like he said, he's never off duty and it would have been pretty embarrassing to be arrested for trying to drive home when intoxicated. Not that I ever have, but all the same; I wouldn't want him to get the wrong impression of me. Now that I'll be spending more time with police officers I really need to keep a cleaner than clean appearance so when they're looking for the Mouthless Maniac, I'd be the furthest from their minds.

Michael quickly gets ready for bed, Anne follows him up and makes sure he's alright while I get out a couple of glasses for the wine and un-cork the bottle to allow it to breath. Anne returns a few minutes later and we both relax in front of the television with a nice glass of wine, to chill out.
"Did you enjoy yourself this evening Chris?"
"Yes, I didn't think I would, but they were really nice and it was good that Pete remembered me from school."
"Yes, that was funny."
"What?"
"You having the nickname, 'Sticky Chris.'" Anne laughs.
"Careful, your false teeth might fall out!"
Anne immediately stops laughing and slaps me on the arm.
"Cheeky! These teeth are all my own, thank you very much!"
"Just kidding; love you really."

"I know you do."
We cuddle up together and watch a black and white movie on one of the sky channels.

The image of an old 'bobby' patrolling the streets of London in the movie reminds me of the two police officers at Pete's house earlier.
'Why were they there I wonder?
Had they found more evidence about this masked maniac?
Are they any closer to catching me?
I wonder what they're planning next.
I wonder if they'll be playing football with us on Sunday. If everyone's going back to the recreation centre for some food and drink, I might even overhear a couple of police officers talking about the Mouthless Maniac. Well just the thought of playing football with a bunch of policemen who are looking for me is a little ironic so whatever happens, its going to be interesting.' I think to myself.

Thursday 28th October

He's known by the police for burglary and he's been in and out of prison for most of his life so its not surprising that after being released only last week he's back to his old habits again. I see him climbing in through a side kitchen window to a house with all the curtains and blinds closed. It's late so I know he's trying to rob the place under the cover of darkness. I pick up the tazer and place it in the front pocket of my hoodie. I take out the home made gauntlets from the glove compartment and slip them on over my hands.

'I made them out of paper mache with inlaid metal strips along the outside of the gauntlets to reinforce them before covering the outside with more layers of paper mache and finally sealing them with duct tape. I clenched my right fist and punch the palm of my left hand to see if the gauntlets would hold up if I ever needed to punch someone. The pain in my left hand begins to throb from the punch and I immediately think I must have cracked a bone in my hand.'

"Ouch, that hurts" I say to myself
I step out of the car into the cold night and silently walk along the pavement to the house the burglar entered. The low garden wall and waist high entrance gate doesn't provide any cover from neighbours seeing the burglar enter the house so I wondered why he risked climbing over the low wall and crossing the small grassed garden to the side of the house. I glance back towards the houses on the opposite side of the street and notice all the curtains are tightly shut. The

sky is blanketed with dark rain clouds shielding the light from the moon providing the perfect opportunity for men dressed in black to wander the streets unnoticed. At this late hour I know people are safely tucked up in bed fast asleep.

I step over the low wall and follow the path he took to the side of the house. I reach a side window which is now wide open and notice the small round hole cut into the single glass panel of the window where the burglar gained entry.

'He must have used a compass contraption with a sucker on one end and a glass cutter on the other to make that hole. Obviously a professional' I think to myself.

I slowly ease myself through the opened window into the kitchen paying careful attention to my movement so as not to catch myself on anything. I step clear of the window and make my way around the kitchen table and towards the hallway.

A stream of light flashes across the corridor from the lounge at the far end of the house and disappears again.

'Good, I know where you are now.' I think to myself. I slowly step towards the lounge door on my tip toes making every effort not to make a sound and with a sigh of relief reach the doorway without giving myself away. I can feel my heart beating faster and faster in my chest from the stress of sneaking around in someone else's house in the dead of night. I lean my back against the side wall next to the room where

the light emerged to try and compose myself. Beads of sweat trickle down the sides of my face from my temples to my cheeks, racing each other on their way to my jaw line as I feel my body temperature rise through the roof. I take a couple of deep breaths to calm my nerves before reaching inside the hood of my hoodie top. Taking hold of the Mouthless paper mache mask with one hand, I pull the mask over my head and down onto my face. The elasticated straps holding the mask inside my hood pulls the mask tightly against my face with the plastic mouthpiece nicely inserted inside my mouth. I take out the tazer from my pocket and hold it tightly in my right hand preparing myself before rushing through the lounge door to attack the burglar.

I'm hoping the burglar is preoccupied looting the place and not notice me step inside the room. I know I need to be quick because I don't want him to have time to reach inside his sack and pull out anything heavy to hit me with. I try to imagine myself running into the room while his back is turned and quickly jab the tazer into the man's back as he faces the opposite wall. The 300,000 volts from the tazer will send his body into convulsions, contracting and extending his muscles in a synchronised dance off; violently draining his body of every ounce of energy.

I edge my head around the corner of the doorway and see the light from his torch flashes around the room in search of any valuable possessions he may want to steal. The beam of light skims across the mantelpiece and stops on a silver trophy next to a mantle clock.

Realising the light from his torch is now on the far wall with the burglar concentrating on the small white spot provides me with the perfect opportunity to rush in while his back is turned.

I take another deep breath and run into the room hoping to see the burglar in the process of loading up his bag with a silver trophy. To my surprise all the lights in the room are switched on revealing not a lone burglar helping himself but a squad of police officers standing shoulder to shoulder facing me. my eyes dart from left to right in a frantic stare trying to make sense of it all when my gaze falls on Pete standing in the centre holding our a pair of handcuffs. "NO!" I cry out and sit up in bed staring wildly in the darkened bedroom.

'Where have all the police gone?' I think to myself trying to understand what just happened when I hear Anne's voice emerge from the darkness.
"Chris! Are you alright?"
Hearing her voice brings me back to reality, realising I'd just had a nightmare. I wipe the sweat from my brow before lying back down again.
"Yes I'm fine thanks, just a nightmare that's all." I reply.
Anne snuggles up to me and strokes my chest for a few seconds before turning over and going back to sleep. The thought of becoming friends with a Detective Sergeant, who's investigating the very crimes I'm responsible for, is making me a little anxious.

I need to be really careful from now on, I can't risk saying the wrong thing in front of Pete and as I'm living a lie, it's very difficult.

The biggest problem I've got to contend with is the fact that I've created a bogus job with a local firm; if Pete asked about work, I wouldn't know what to say; I don't know what Insigna Logistics do or even know any of the employees. Luckily for me, Pete is new to the area so he won't yet know anyone who works there. Let's hope it stays that way. I really need to keep that sort of information close to my chest, maybe even keeping it from Anne too. I can just imagine Anne telling Jenny about something I told her about work and she tells Pete. Not that Pete would question it but you never know. What if Pete relates the story to another police officer and he knows everyone working at Insigna and tells Pete that no such person works there. Little mistakes like that could cause Pete to ask more questions and before you know it, I'd be found out.

I look at the clock next to the bed and see its only 2:47am. The full sensation in my bladder is telling me I need to go to the bathroom so I decide to get up and have a pee. The bed is nice and cosy but I know if I don't get up now, I'll not be able to get back to sleep for ages and I'll end up having to go to the bathroom anyway so I might as well go now. This necessity of having to visit the bathroom every night must be an age thing because I can't remember having to go every night when I was younger. I could drink three or four pints before bed and still hold out until morning. There was once that time when I drank about six or seven pints and I woke up having wet the bed but that was when I was nineteen I think. Never wet the bed since, which is a good thing now that I'm married. I think my wife would certainly insist on sleeping in separate beds if I still wet the bed and probably force me to wear incontinent pants or a large nappie. The thought of wearing a babies nappie makes me smile imagining Anne trying to wrap one around my big butt.

I ease myself out of bed and sneak along the landing to the bathroom when I hear a noise coming from downstairs. I stop dead in my tracks and strain my ears to listen out for any further sounds.
'Creeeakk.'
I can't make out exactly what it is, but it sounds like someone scraping the glass with a sharp object. I silently make my way down the stairs in the dark. Having lived in a house for many years is an advantage, because you know where everything is even with the lights off. I reach the bottom of the stairs and stop to listen again to get an indication where the sound is coming from.

Looking through the lounge door in the darkness, I don't see anything but suddenly hear the same sound again of cloth scraping over a sharp edge coming from the back of the house. It sounds like it's coming from the kitchen; so I make my way across the lounge to the kitchen door and position myself next to the door frame with my back against the lounge wall. I close my eyes, endeavouring to identify exactly what the sound is; but can only hear total silence.

'Do we have mice? Has a cat or vermin found its way into the house?' I wonder to myself.
In the silence of the room, I begin hearing pounding sounds in my ears; boom, boom, boom, boom. Getting louder and louder when I realise it's the sound of my heart beating in my chest.

'*Come on Chris, calm yourself*' I think to myself.
'Boom, boom, boom' the sound continues in my chest. I look down at my chest and physically see my ribcage being pushed out every time my heart beats; it's as if my heart is trying to get out.
'I can't believe how nervous I am; considering all the practice I've had at attacking people during the past few weeks this should be easy, so why do I feel a little panicky?'
'Maybe it's because when I normally go out to work at night, I'm prepared to attack criminals and I have my protective clothing and tazer with me. I don't have any weapon with me now and as I'm only wearing my pyjamas and in my bare feet, I feel a little vulnerable.'

'Clonk!'
I hear the window being opened and my heart starts to beat faster and faster to the point of making me panic.
'I need to calm down,' I think to myself.
'*I've dealt with worse criminals than this before, now take a deep breath.*'
I breathe in deeply and allow the air to exhale slowly. The breathing has a calming effect on me and I start to feel better; I sense my own heartbeat start to subside as I continue to breathe in and out to calm my

nerves. I slowly tilt my head round the corner of the door frame and peer into the kitchen to see if I can see who's breaking in. I see an object being pushed into the kitchen through the opened back window from the outside. Staring at the object, I notice a couple of handles on the top and realise it's a holdall bag. *'Is that the bag the burglar hopes to fill? We don't have much of value so he'd be lucky if he could half fill that.'* I think to myself.

I take another deep breath before stepping around the door frame and into the kitchen. I quickly make my way around to the right alongside the kitchen worktops towards the open window, as I watch the holdall being pushed further into the kitchen and along the draining board next to the sink. I'm two metres away now as I see the man wearing a woollen beanie hat start to climb into the room. Holding the window sill with one hand while his other hand reaches into the kitchen and holds the cold tap to use to pull himself into the room, I see his head and shoulders emerge from the darkness outside above the sink. I quickly pick up the heavy, oak, chopping board with both hands and swing it at the man's head. 'Crack!'

The flat side of the chopping board makes contact with the side of his head just as he looks up; the speed of my swing combined with the weight of the board knocks the man's head to the side, sending the burglars false teeth flying through the air, crashing against the far wall of the kitchen. His head drops down towards the sink before the weight from his dangling body pulls his head and shoulders back out of the window and disappears.

"What! I don't believe it!" I exclaim.
I put the chopping board back on the worktop and rush round to the back door and turn the key in the lock. I open the door and step out onto the paved walkway along the rear of the house and look towards the rear window to see if I can see the burglar on the ground; nothing! I can't see a thing. I flick the light switch on in the kitchen and step back out onto the paved walkway to see if the light from the kitchen has made any difference. It has, I notice a crumpled heap on the ground a few metres away from me.

'What am I going to do with him?
I don't want to call the police because they'll ask why I hit the man, then it would all be on record and the burglar would probably sue me for GBH or something because of his human rights malarkey and I would be arrested for using excessive force, blah blah blah.
It makes me sick just thinking how wrong the law is today. I think I'll just have to deal with this myself. It'll be far safer and easier that way.'

I run through to the front hallway and retrieve my coat and shoes and put them on before making my way back to the rear garden. The man is still crumpled on the ground so I walk over to him and lay him down along the paved walkway. The limited amount of light shining from inside the kitchen allows me to focus on his face which seems to be swollen on the left side of his head; it wouldn't surprise me if he's got a broken jaw or something from the whack I gave him. His eyes are still closed and I notice his chest is slowly rising and falling so he's still alive. I reach down and feel inside his pockets for any kind of identification. His right hand pocket has two keys in; one must be to his van and the other must be for his house. I put the keys in my pocket and continue checking his other pockets where I find his wallet.

I need to identify who this man is so I can make a call on him in the near future to repay him for his visit. I step back into the kitchen and grab a notepad and pen to write down his details. Inside the wallet I find his driving licence, debit card and thirty pounds in cash. I jot down the information I need and replace the wallet back where I found it.

'Right what to do with him now?' I think to myself. *'He must have a vehicle parked in our street to transport all his swag home as it's not practical or safe to be carrying a large bag of goodies through the streets at night around Liverpool. He looks like he's out for the count at the moment so I'll see if I can carry him back to his car.'*

'I've seen firemen carrying victims out of burning houses before with the person on their shoulder in what is termed the 'Firemans Lift.' I think I'll try and use that method to transport him.'
Bending down I grab hold of his right wrist with my left hand and pull him up into a seated position, I tuck

my head under his arm pit and grab the inside of his leg in the attempt at lifting him onto my shoulders. "Urghhhhhhh"

I find myself straining with the effort that's needed to pull the man up and position him across my shoulders. It takes all my effort but eventually he slides into place while I'm crouched low to the ground. I try to stand up with the man flopped over my back but carrying the extra weight; I find I can't move an inch.

'You've got to be kidding me. How do firemen lift heavy lumps like this?' I wonder as I don't seem to be moving while the weight of the man is crushing my body already in its crouched position.

'This is ridiculous! How on earth am I going to carry the man out of the garden when I can't stand?' I think to myself when I notice the wooden garden bench only two metres away from me.

'Maybe I could use that as leverage to get up.'

I shuffle my feet towards the bench with the man still on my shoulders, looking like a troll carrying a large sack. I reach the bench and lean my arms on the seat to give myself leverage to get up; transferring the weight forward over my shoulders, I push out with my legs whilst walking my hands up the back of the bench into a standing position. I turn and begin to stagger forward towards the side gate which has been left open by the burglar.

I make it out of the gate and turn left towards the main road; each step I take is short and laboured due to the extra weight I'm carrying making me walk look like an old man. I eventually arrive at the top of the side road and stand at the edge of the pavement. The road is quiet and full of parked cars and vans belonging to all the residents, I look left and right hoping to identify the man's car which I assume would be one that I've not seen before. It's too dark to see the make and model of all the cars in the street so I'm finding it a little more difficult than I thought when I suddenly remember the keys in my pocket. I manage to take the keys out and press the fob unlocking his vehicle; I see the orange flash of light from a Ford Transit Connect van parked ten metres away.

'There you are; I'm glad your van's not too far away.' I think to myself feeling the strain of carrying a dead weight on my shoulders and wondering if my legs will hold out till I reach his van.

I stagger the short distance and prop the man down against the passenger door. I take out the keys I took from him and slip them back inside his pocket when I remember I'd forgotten his holdall bag which is still in my kitchen.

Luckily for me, the man is still out cold so I turn and run back to the house to collect his bag. I grab the bag which feels weighty like it may contain some heavy items. *'Probably the glass cutting implement, and possibly a screwdriver and hammer'* I think to myself.

I make my way back out of the kitchen and up the side road to our street where I'd left the man. As I reach the kerb and look towards the man next to his van, I see him move.

'Crap! What to do?' I think to myself.

I don't want him to notice me and if I carry his bag back to him, he would. If I keep the bag, he'd miss it and come back for it which I don't want. On the positive side, I'm hoping he's feeling a little disorientated and a little worse for wear so he'll decide to go home instead, but I still need to give him his bag back.

I think of the next best thing and hoist the bag in the air towards him, hoping it would land near where he's sat. The bag flips over and over on its journey high above him and for a second disappears in the dim light. I see it reappear just above him as the heavy object smashes down on his battered face.

"Oops! Sorry." I say quietly as I make my way back down the side road leading to the garages at the back of the houses and right through my neighbour's garden to my house.

I reckon the man feels pretty bad at the moment with a sore face from being smacked with the chopping board and now being hit on the head with a bag of spanners or something. He's no doubt suffering with a splitting headache so I expect the first thing on his mind will be painkillers and maybe a shot of whisky; so I don't think I'll be seeing him again tonight. I'm hoping he randomly called at my house as most opportunists do and so won't remember where he'd got clobbered. Which means with any luck, he won't return. If he does remember he'll probably be too scared as he wouldn't want to be bashed around again.

I walk into the house and lock the back door; the window is still open so I pull it shut and lock it before making my way to the front of the house, where I take off my shoes and coat before heading back upstairs to finish off what I intended doing ten minutes ago. I climb into bed and snuggle up to Anne; I close my eyes and try to think of soft, fluffy sheep jumping over styles. I relax and drift off into a peaceful, sound sleep.

"CHRRRIIIIISSSSSS!"
My eyes fly open as I try to determine if the sound I heard was from a dream or was it real. Then I hear it again.
"CHRRRIIIISSS."
Recognising Anne's voice calling from downstairs instantly sends me into action.
I leap out of bed and dash down the stairs, jumping down three steps at a time. I run through the lounge and into the kitchen where I see Anne staring down at the floor.
"What's wrong, what's happened?" I call out.
Anne points towards the corner of the kitchen floor with her right hand, holding her left hand over her mouth to prevent her from being sick.

I look down and see a broken set of dentures on the floor.

"Eeeeyuck!"

"Where the hell did those come from?" Anne asks.

I can't think of an excuse so I just come out with the truth.

"A burglar tried to rob us last night when I went to the loo, so I hit him with the chopping board, he must have lost his teeth!"

"Chris that's disgusting! He's probably left drool all over my chopping board. Now that can go straight in the bin!"

Anne walks over to the worktop and picks up the chopping board with just her index finger and thumb on each hand as though she's removing something repulsive. She steps on the lever of the pedal bin to open the lid and proceeds to drop the board straight in at arms length.

"You owe me a new chopping board!" she says glaring straight at me.

"Sorry, it was the first thing handy that I could use to stop him from robbing us blind."

"What happened to the window? There's a hole in it." Anne exclaims as she points at the small circular hole.

"That's where he tried to break in."

"So whatever happened to calling the Police then?" Anne asks.

"There was no time. He stuck his head through the window so I hit him with the board, then he scarpered! End of story."

Anne thinks for a moment, before replying.

"I'm sorry Chris, I was just a little shocked that's all; we've never been robbed before and I wasn't thinking straight. You did the right thing."

I walk over to her and give her a hug.

"That's alright darling, he won't be coming back; I can assure you of that."

"That's good." She replies.

"So you can get rid of those teeth on the floor." Anne demands.

After breakfast I telephone a glazier and arrange for him to pop round and give us an estimate to replace the pane of glass. Luckily for us, the firm is only half a mile away so the workman turns up just after Anne leaves with Michael for school.

I show the young man around to the kitchen window where he takes some measurements and jots down several notes on a pad. He rubs his head again with his carpenters pencil and re-measures the window a second time before adjusting the notes in his pad. Then he turns to me and says.

"To remove the existing glass and beading, clean and prepare the frame and fit a new easy clean pane with replacement sealant and new beading will come to…."

He continues scribbling on his pad before saying.

"Eighty six pounds fifty and that also cover the cost of labour sir and we could do that straight away as we have that exact size of glass on the van."

"Eighty six pounds fifty!" I exclaim.

"It would normally cost you a hundred and fifteen for any call out, but as we're in your area today we can do it much cheaper for you."

'I can't believe its going to cost me nearly ninety quid to have one pane of glass fitted. Now this is daylight robbery.' I think to myself.

'If it's going to cost me that much, I'm going to make sure that burglar pays me back for the cost of the window plus interest!'

"OK; go on then." I tell the glazier.

It takes the guy about twenty five minutes to complete his work and I never offered him a single drink.

'Eighty six pounds and fifty pence.' I keep thinking. *'Maybe I should become a glazier. I could pay a young lad five quid to throw a stone through someone's window and then charge them eighty six quid to fix it. It's taken this guy twenty five minutes and he's earned eighty six pounds fifty pence for his trouble. I would only have to fix one window in the morning and one in the afternoon Monday to Friday and I've earned an honest wage! These guys are the criminals. Maybe I should attack him and get my money back! Well that's a thought I might consider, sorting out cowboy builders and tradesmen; maybe I should remind them of the need to be honest.'*

I pay the man and he makes his way out of the house.

I telephone the polling station and ask to speak to information.

"Good morning, my name is Mr George Peterson and I've not received a notification of any sort so I can vote." I inform the lady on the other end of the line.

"One moment please Mr Peterson. I'll just find your details on the computer."

I hear the lady clicking away on a keyboard for a few seconds as she enters my name into the database.

"Mister Peterson, can I ask for your date of birth."

"Yes, my date of birth is the sixth of July nineteen sixty; I was just thinking as I've not long moved house, you may have my old address? I ask. *"

'I'm hoping she won't ask me for my old address as I don't know it.'

She asks "Mr Peterson, we have you residing at 34 Linacre Road, Bootle. Is that now your old address?'

"No, that's the right address; oh, hold on a second my son is calling me!"

I wait a few seconds before continuing our conversation.

"Sorry, my son's just told me that we did get a polling card and he put it away in one of our drawers when we were away on holiday, sorry to bother you."

I hang up the phone and jot down the address for Mr Peterson on a notepad.

"So my friendly neighbourhood burglar, what do you think to me giving you a friendly call one evening." I say to myself.

Anne arrives home at twelve twenty five so we have a late lunch together consisting of quiche, potato salad and coleslaw with a glass of orange juice.

'I think Anne is worried about my weight so she's trying to encourage me to eat healthier meals. I don't know what she's worried about because I'm sure I'm burning off plenty of calories with my new work

schedule so I think I'm in pretty good shape for a forty nine year old.'

"How was your morning at work?" I ask.

"Great thanks, what about you?"

"Good; as you can see the glazier came round and fixed the window for us."

Anne looks over at the window.

"Wow, that's great. He's done a good job there."

"Yes, but expensive." I say.

"How much was it?"

"Eighty six pounds fifty!"

"What! You've got to be kidding; eighty six pounds fifty; that's daylight robbery, we should go round to that burglar's house and get the money off him, if we knew where he lived."

"That's exactly what I was thinking when I was given the bill. And I know where he lives." I look into Anne's eyes to see what response I get.

"Do you really know where he lives?" Anne asks; looking at me intently.

"Yes."

"So what are you going to do?"

"I think I'll go and give him a visit later tonight."

"Are you really? Is that wise? Do you want me to come with you?" Anne asks.

"No that's alright; I think the sight of you screaming at him would cause him to have a heart attack."

"What time were you thinking of going?"

"I don't know, probably after seven as I expect he'll be home from work by then. That's if he does any honest work."

We both relax during the early afternoon watching a bit of television before its time to collect Michael from school.

"Anne; do you think we should give Jenny and Pete a thank you card?" I ask.

"That's a good idea; I think I have a card in the drawer."

Anne takes out a card from the drawer in the sideboard and proceeds to write a thank you note. I tend to leave the writing of cards and letters to Anne as she has a much nicer handwriting style than I do and an eloquent way with expressing words. I know if it was left up to me to write a card, I would have just written 'Thanks for the grub.'

"Here you are." She hands me the completed card nicely sealed in a white envelope with Pete and Jenny's name written on the front.

"Well done darling, you're the best." I grab the car keys and head out the door and make my way down towards the car.

I drive to the school and park in the usual spot about a hundred metres down from the school's main entrance. I assume all those who manage to get a parking space closer to the main entrance must have arrived at least half an hour ago and to be honest, I've got more important things to do than wait in the car outside school for forty minutes before the children come out. We usually park here and allow Michael to walk the short distance along the pavement to the car but today I want to catch Jenny and Debbie to give them the card. I step out of the car and depress the auto lock on the key fob before making my way towards the school entrance where I spot Jenny standing next to the school gate.

"Hi Jenny." I wave to her hoping she'll see my hand above the crowd of parents waiting for their own children.

"Hello Chris I thought you usually stay in your car for Michael?" she asks.

"I would normally but I wanted to give you this." I hand Jenny the card.

"Oh you didn't have to."

"We just wanted to thank you again for a great evening, we really enjoyed ourselves."

"Oh, that's really nice of you, thank you for the card. We enjoyed your company too and Pete was really pleased to meet someone from school, after you left he was telling me all about your football skills. I think he's really looking forward to playing football with you on Sunday."

"Talk about pressure! I think I'd better get some practice in before then, just so I don't show myself up."

"I'm sure you'll be brilliant."

Debbie and Michael walk out of school together and wander over to us.

"Hi dad."

We say our goodbyes and Michael and I head home in the car.

"Did you have a nice time at school?" I ask.

"It was OK." Michael replies.

I realise it's no good trying to have a conversation with my eight year old son when they're not socially aware and don't possess the interactive skills of a grown up person so I just keep quiet and head in the direction of Linacre Road.

"You're going the wrong way dad!" Michael pipes up as he doesn't recognise any of the houses along the route.

"That's alright son, I just wanted to find out where someone lives."

"Is he a friend of yours dad?"

"No! It's someone I just met, but I would like to pay him a visit later."

"Why?"

"You know I just thought it would be nice."

"But why?"

"Because I just decided, that's all."

"But why?"

I start to think to myself what a bad idea it was telling Michael about my detour.

"It's a grown up thing, you'll understand when you're older, much older." I say.

"OK dad." Michael continues to stare out of the car window at the houses going bye.

We drive along Linacre Road and pass the burglars house on the corner of Violet Street opposite a playing field.

'Perfect!' I think to myself.

'There's somewhere to park outside the house out of view from everyone and with an open field opposite, couldn't be any better.'

We arrive home ten minutes later and Michael makes his way up to his bedroom to do his homework while

Anne and I relax in the lounge before its time to start the dinner. Anne wanders into the kitchen to start preparing dinner which gives me a few moments by myself to think through a plan of action for when I go and visit Mr Peterson.

'I think the best thing to do would be, to park on Violet Street right next to Mr Peterson's back door. Its far enough back from the main road so as not to be noticed by passing traffic and with the field opposite, no one will see me park there so the car won't be reported to the police. I just need to work out how to get him out of his house.'

I mull over a couple of ideas in my head before deciding on one that should work.

Anne cooks spaghetti bolognaise with garlic bread for dinner which always does the trick in filling up her two hungry lads. We all clean our plates with the last of the garlic bread before Michael and I head into the kitchen to do the washing up.

"Thank you boys!" Anne shouts through from the lounge as she relaxes in front of the television.

"Just need a glass of wine one thinks!" she calls through.

"Yes me lady, we menials working hard in the kitchen recognise you must be royalty?"

"You could say that; when one has royal blood in their lineage then it's only natural to recognise our true purpose in life."

"That's funny because I definitely feel like I'm a ruler of a country."

"Why?" Anne asks.

"Because I'm A'King all over from doing all this washing up."

"Very funny, you'll never make it as a comedian, so I suggest you stick to your day job."

Anne and I relax in the lounge and watch a little television until ten to seven.

"Right! I think I'll make a move and go and visit our burglar." I say.

"Are you sure you don't want me to come along with you?" Anne asks.

"No that's alright; why don't you start on the wine in the kitchen and I'll join you when I get back. I might be a couple of hours, you know, as I may have to take him to the cash point to get our money."

"Don't do anything stupid or illegal." Anne instructs me.

"Would I do anything illegal?" I ask, as I stare at her innocently.

"Love you! And be careful." Anne calls out as I grab my coat and car keys before heading out of the door into the darkness.

George Peterson

I walk down the side road to the row of garages and make my way to the second garage on the right which backs onto my garden. I use the keys to unlock the garage door and open it to reveal the Renault Master Transit van nicely parked inside. I hired the van from Budget Van Leasing Company on Wallbeck Road. They needed details of my business and details of someone we were trading with so I made up a fictitious letter from Bullwark Timber in Derbyshire who supposedly agreed to supply us with timber for the coming year. It did the trick and the van only cost me a hundred and ninety four pounds a month. The nice thing about it, I paid with cash and gave a bogus address so there are no comebacks providing I continue paying the rental.

I unlock the van door and climb into the cab. It's quite tight parking the transit van inside a residential garage that's designed for normal vehicles; the van only just fits with just enough room on the left hand side to squeeze in the driver's door. I need to keep the van out of sight during the day because I know the police are checking any vans in the area. They believe a van is being used in connection with the local mouthless crimes, where petty criminals have been attacked and robbed by this assailant. So to be on the safe side, I thought it would be best to keep the van out of sight from everyone, as I don't want any unwanted attention from the police. I turn the engine over and pull the van out of the garage and park up near the entrance road leading to the main road.

After closing and locking the garage door, I open the side door to the van to check everything is all in place. The back of the van has been boarded out and has a six foot ladder fixed lengthways along the centre of the floor in the back. Lying across it in the centre, also fixed to the floor is my workbench forming a cross with the ladder. I usually carry my victims inside the back of the van and attach a couple of plastic ties around their wrists and ankles. I sit them on the workbench and hook a karabiners attached to one end of a rope around their ankles to hold their feet down against the ladder. The rope has been threaded through under the rungs of the ladder under the workbench so the other end is attached to another karabiner which is hooked over their wrists restraints. To finish securing the victims in the back, I just step out of the van and pull on the end of the rope which pulls the victim into a back breaking arched position over the workbench so their feet and hands are secured by the rungs of the ladder. I just tie off the end of the rope and their restrained for the night.

I look down at the box secured to the floor of the van which contains duct tape, plastic ties, a hammer, bin liners, matches, scissors and a bottle of water. I check the small plastic petrol can next to the box, which is now half full of unleaded petrol.
"That should be plenty." I say to myself while gently shaking the can.
I use the petrol to burn my victim's clothes once I've finished with them. Not only does removing the clothes from my victims make them feel more vulnerable and less likely to try to escape but it also

removes any evidence the police could use in their attempt to track me down.

I replace the petrol can back down next to the box and pick up my protective gear which comprises a pair of long johns and top with rubber guards glued onto the forearms and shins to give me the needed protection. I've sewn strips of metal rods along the guards and covered them with duct tape to stop the sharp edges of the metal rods from snagging on any clothing over the top. Finally I have my wife's corset, now covered with metal brackets stitched to the material, to protect my chest, sides and back. Anne made it easier for me to put the corset on by sewing eyelets into the fabric at the back and lacing up with a length of string. All I now have to do is slip the corset over my head and pull on the ends of the string at the base of my spine to pull it tight around me. She modified it a few weeks ago as I told her that I injured myself at work, catching myself on a heavy object. Anne doesn't know anything about what I really get up to when I go to 'work' and I would like to keep it that way.

I glance around the garages to check the coast is clear before climbing into the back of the van and undressing down to my boxers and socks. I pick up the long john bottoms and slip them on. The thick rubber guards with the sewn in metal rods, fit snugly over my shins from ankle to knee providing an impenetrable defence against being kicked or hit with a stick or bat; the rods fixed on the front are quite effective for kicking people between the legs as Brett Norris can verify after losing a testicle from one of my kicks. I secure the guards in position by tying the laces at the back of my calf and ankle. Cold air whistles into the van and onto my naked chest, causing me to shiver.

"Brrreeeerrr! That's cold." I say to myself.

I rub the goosebumps out of my arms then reach for the long john top with the forearm guards glued in place and quickly slip it over my head to help keep the night chill out.

"That's better." I say out loud to myself before tying the strings around my forearms.

To finish off dressing, I lift up Anne's corset and slip it over my head to protect my chest and back; after pulling the strings at the back and tying them off I slip my trousers back on and finally my black hoodie with the mouthless mask sewn inside the hood section which now rests out of sight between my shoulder blades.

I figure that when I need to walk in public, having the mask out of sight won't draw any attention from onlookers; I'll just look like a normal guy wearing a hoodie. When I need to put the mask on, I can reach behind me and grab the mask and pull it over my head and into place. When I made the mask out of paper mache I secured a folded piece of plastic inside the mask where the mouth should be so I had something to bite on and keep the mask in position; since then I've improved the fitting of the mask by attaching two elastic strips either side of the mask and stitching the other ends of the strips inside the hoodie. When I now pull the mask over my head, the hood part of my top comes with it. The hood protects the side and back of my head from view while the mask covers my face.

I slip my shoes back on to finish off dressing then look inside the cardboard box for a couple of items I'll need to carry with me. I pick out a couple of plastic ties, duct tape and marker pen and slip them inside the large pocket at the front of my hoodie. I pick up the hammer and climb out of the van and close the back door. I open the passenger side door and place the hammer down in the foot well before climbing in; closing the door behind me I slide over to the driver's seat and turn the engine on. I now feel ready to pay a visit to Mr George Peterson.

I make a small detour and call into the supermarket to pick up a football before continuing on my journey to number thirty four Linacre Road. I'm aware that the police are on the lookout for the masked assailant but with all the attacks so far; usually on a Friday, Saturday or Sunday night, I expect they're not concerned this evening on stopping every van in the area. I pull into Violet Street around seven forty and drive down the street past the house on my right until I reach a railway bridge at the end of the street where I turn the van around and head back along Violet Street and park the van next to the kerb just down from the back door to number thirty four. At this time of night Linacre Road is fairly busy, with traffic streaming left and right past the end of Violet Street. To my right is a large, grassed area with a low border wall around its boundary; I imagine children playing football during the summer months, kicking a ball to and fro, from one end of the field to the other with a stray ball occasionally flying off into the path of oncoming vehicles along the main road.

I turn the engine off and look at the brand new football in its packaging. The last time I bought a ball was years ago when Michael was only five. Other children at his school were playing football and obviously Michael wanted to join in. I think it's about the right age to teach a young lad. This ball however was bought not as a present for Michael but for a completely different purpose.

I un-wrap the ball from its protective packaging which takes me a minute or two to remove the plastic and corrugated cardboard that's covering the ball. "Why on earth do you need protective packaging for a football?" I ask myself.
'This is ridiculous. Look at all this plastic and card board. I understand some things need to be protected against damage but why put protective packaging on everything. Talk about overkill, I tell you its damaging the environment using all this cardboard. No wonder our forests are disappearing at an alarming rate!'
I open the glove compartment and take out the tazer and place it in the front pocket to my hoodie.

In my previous job I was lucky enough to travel to America on a security seminar where I was presented with the latest self defence aid; a Tazer that delivers 300,000 volts into any potential attacker. It's been an essential part of my armour in tackling criminals in

the area and helping me re-educate them to live honest lives. I pick up the gauntlet gloves I made out of papier mache card and strips of metal and slip them on over my hands. Finally picking up the hammer, I hook it under my belt at the base of my spine.
"OK, all ready to party." I say to myself.
I pick up the ball, lock the van and walk along the pavement to the side of number thirty four.

There's a window on the side of the house with frosted glass, so I assume it's a window to the downstairs bathroom. The rest of the building is mainly brick facia with a three foot retaining wall at the back of the house around a small paved yard and back door. I drop the ball on the ground four metres away from the side of the building and step back ready to have a kick of the ball. The window to the bathroom is probably forty centimetres by sixty centimetres in diameter so it's a small target to hit. I step forward and kick the ball; it bounces off the brickwork surrounding the window and bounces back towards me. I kick it again on the volley and again I miss my target.

I imagine Mr Peterson inside the house hearing the sound of the ball hitting the side of his house fuming at the thought of kids playing ball against his wall. The ball bounces back to me and again I kick the ball against the side of the house where Mister Peterson is now probably thinking its time to come outside and give those annoying kids a piece of his mind. The ball bounces back towards me and I catch it just right with my right foot. I watch the ball fly through the air directly at the window.

'Crash!'

The ball disappears into the small, darkened room beyond.

I quickly dash round to the back door of the house and pull my mask down over my face. I notice a light flash on from inside the bathroom as Peterson investigates the noise. I knock loudly on the back door and wait a few seconds until I know Mr Peterson has heard the knocking and is making his way to the back door. With a highest pitched voice I can muster, I call out.

"Can we have our ball back mister?" It surprises me how realistic my voice sounds, just like a twelve year old when his voice is just about to break.

Holding my tazer in hand, I ready myself to pounce at the man as soon as the door opens.

"What the…." Mr Peterson exclaims as he opens the door, ready to have a go at the youth waiting for his ball. I throw my shoulder at the door, smashing it against Mr Peterson's chest and sending him flying backwards stopping him in mid sentence. The football held in his left hand, flies up in the air and over my shoulder as it heads out of the back door and bounces down Violet Street along the pavement. I step into the kitchen in pursuit of Mr Peterson as he stumbles backwards. My left shoulder makes contact with his chest pushing him backwards as a rugby player would take out one of the opposing team players. His body lifting slightly as he's transported across the kitchen when he comes to a halt against the freestanding washing machine. His upper body is pushed back against the wall while his bottom is sat on the washing machine. My tazer finds his chest and sends the 300,000 volts surging through him. His body spasms and jerks as his muscles tense and relax violently. I use my right hand to hold him upright as the charge takes its effect, his face contorting and relaxing then grimacing in a kind of speed gurning competition. His eyes close and his head falls to one side as he blacks out.

I remove the tazer from his chest and slip it back inside my hoodie pocket while holding on to Mr Peterson with my left hand. Realising the back door is still open and not wanting anyone to see me with my mask on inside Mr Peterson's house; I quickly try and position Mr Peterson against the kitchen wall. His slumped body remains still for a few seconds so I quickly turn around and close the back door to stop anyone seeing us. Mr Peterson's starts to slide sideways and would have fallen off the washing machine except for my quick reactions; I grab his shoulders and prop him back up into his seated position against the wall.

I hold his body steady while I listen out for any other sounds from inside the house. All I can hear is silence, no noise from the adjacent room and no sounds from upstairs on the first floor so I gather the house is empty. Looking around the kitchen, I notice the room is small with the usual base and wall mounted cabinets on the left of the room while the washing machine on the right side is tucked against the external wall with a doorway on my left leading to the remainder of the house. His body, now drained of all energy, starts to flop over to the left side of the washing machine.

I look at the washing machine and realise it's a perfect base to lay him down so I swing his legs around to the opposite side of the washing machine allowing his body to lie across the top with his head and shoulders hanging over to the left while his legs are now neatly over to the right.

When I've caught criminals in the past, I usually tie them up in an arched position over a workbench in the back of my van. I do this to inflict the greatest amount of discomfort to my victims because I want them to suffer for the short period they're with me in the hope that they would never want to experience it ever again in the future. I know if you leave someone in the same position for a long period, the strain on the muscles brings on severe cramp which can be excruciating and being positioned in a back breaking arch can add to their suffering. I step back and look at Mr Peterson's already in a perfect arched position over the washing machine.

'That's handy' I think to myself.
'I don't have to move him.'

I take out a couple of plastic ties from the pocket of my hoodie and attach the first tie around his right ankle and around the right hand front foot of the washing machine. I do the same with the other ankle and attach it to the right hand back foot of the machine. His body naturally wants to slide off to the right where his feet are attached so I have to quickly grab hold of his right wrist and pull it down towards the front left foot of the washing machine and secure it. I tie his left wrist to the left back foot before tearing off two strips of duct tape and applying them over his eyes and mouth. '*All done*' I think to myself as I step back to admire my work.

Mr Peterson starts to stir as his body is slowly regaining its strength. He moans under his mouth restraint as he contends with being arched over his washing machine. I decide to leave him for a while as I want to explore the remainder of his house. The first thing I notice as I step through from the kitchen into the hallway is the amount of clutter. I see radio's, TV's, Laptops, Camera's, Guitars and Keyboards piled high along one wall of the hallway leading into the front of the house that turns out to be a second hand shop, full of goods which may all be stolen. I look around at the plethora of items and realise how busy Mr Peterson's been to accumulate all this gear.

'*How many houses has he burgled?*
How many lives has he ruined, stealing valuable,
sentimental items from unsuspecting people who
could never replace what they've lost?
If he's really nicked all this stuff, then he's a bad man
and needs to be stopped.' I think to myself.

I take a quick look upstairs and see much of the same; TV's, bikes, phones and ornaments. The place is literally full of bric and brac. I see his bedside cabinet stacked high with wallets and purses probably from unsuspecting people lying in bed at night when this lowlife breaks in and steals from them. I pick up a wallet from the top of the stack and open it. The driving licence tucked inside the front sleeve has the name 'Peter Wentworth' and the photo shows someone in his late twenties. I pick up another wallet and the licence inside says it belongs to 'Simon Shepherd.' I return the wallet to the stack.

'He must go out at night to steal stuff, then try and sell it in his shop the next day. He probably has a quick nap in the evening before heading out again to ruin someone else's life. The more I think about it the more I dislike this guy. I remember the day I was attacked by two youths and the sleepless nights and the worry it caused my family went on for weeks. I can't imagine how much pain and suffering this man has caused other and by the looks of things, he's hurt a lot of people. This is why I like doing what I do. Stopping this type of person from hurting others makes me feel better about myself; not only does it clean up the streets we live in but it makes it a safer place to live.'

"I think it's time to teach Mr Peterson a lesson." I say to myself as I make my way downstairs and back into the kitchen.

As I enter the kitchen I find Mr Peterson still arched over the washing machine; I suppose it would have been a miracle if he had moved; bearing in mind his wrists and ankles are securely tied down. I open a kitchen drawer in search of a pair of scissors, as I had left my pair in the van. I usually cut off all of my victim's clothes to make them feel vulnerable and to be blindfolded and tied up at the same time contributes to his susceptibility and cooperation. I find a pair of scissors in the second drawer and carry them back over to my victim.

Mr Peterson senses that I'm next to him and tries to free himself from his restraints by jerking and twisting. I place the scissors down on a small window ledge and take out my hammer, holding it tightly in my right hand I swing the metal head down at Mr Peterson's right knee cap. The hammer head smashes against his patella causing the bone to shatters and immediately causes the tissue around the knee to fill up with blood as the joint swells to twice its size in seconds. Mr Peterson screams under his mouth restraints and his whole body tenses with the sharp injection of pain cascading through his body; his breathing becomes rushed as air is quickly breathed in and out of his nostrils in rapid spurts.

I don't like hurting people and hitting someone with a hammer makes me want to throw up. The feeling of nausea sweeps over me but I fight back against the feeling and crouch down with my head between my legs, breathing deeply to get the blood and oxygen back to my head. It's good that my victim can't see what a wimp I am because that would contradict the persona of the Mouthless Maniac that I'm trying to portrait. I want them to fear me and dread the thought of ever seeing me again so they do as I tell them and start living a good and clean life. It's worked so far with all my other victims and I don't see the need to change, although if I could find an alternative method to break their right leg without using a hammer, I would.

My head clears enough for me to carry on so I stand up and hook the hammer back under my belt at the back and take out my tazer. Mr Peterson's body still arched over the washing machine seems to be covered in sweat from the assault to his kneecap.

'If that hurt, then you're not going to like this.' I think to myself as I jab the tazer into his chest allowing the electric charge to work its magic.

His body jerks violently for a few seconds until he passes out, unable to remain conscious from the physical attack on his body. I wait a few seconds until I know he's out for the count before removing the tazer from his chest and tucking it away inside my hoodie pocket.

"Right, time to find that money you owe me for the window." I say to myself.

I begin to search his pockets which are empty except for a leather bound wallet in his back pocket. I examine the contents One hundred and fifteen pounds in cash, a drivers licence and debit card and a photograph of what appears to be a younger pretty woman in a portrait style picture. I assume it must be his daughter as she's far too young for him. I pocket the cash and the debit card and drivers licence and drop the empty wallet and photograph into the half full waste bin near the back door. Picking up the scissors, I slowly and methodically remove all of his clothes and drop the cut up material inside the waste bin alongside his empty wallet.

I step back and place the scissors back inside the kitchen drawer after wiping them clean of fingerprints. Mr Peterson is now naked and arched over the washing machine with his right kneecap swollen and discoloured from receiving a blow from my hammer. I pour some water from the cold tap into a cup and walk over to Mr Peterson. His head is arched right back over the left side of the washing machine with the duct tape securely over his eyes and mouth leaving his nose free to allow him to breath. I hold the cup of water over his head and tip the cold water over his upturned face.

His body jolts and jerks from the shock of the cold water freezing his face and restricting his airway. His head twists to the side to prevent the liquid from running into his nostrils and he snorts out the excess water from his airway. The stream of water dousing his face lasted but a second and accomplished what I wanted. Mr Peterson's head turns towards where he senses I'm standing while his body stiffens in anticipation of what to follow giving me his full attention.

I crouch down close to his ear and after removing my facemask I allow my breath to fall on the side of his face. Mr Peterson senses I'm close and tries to speak from under his mouth covering. I wait a few seconds before speaking.

"Mr Peterson, George, you're a naughty boy stealing from people so I've had to punish you, do you understand?"

Mr Peterson nods, while the rest of his body remains still.

"I don't like people who commit crimes so I want you to stop, and that means now! Do you understand me?"

He nods again, as he strains his ear to hear what I have to say.

"Now listen to me, coming round to see you, has cost me money, so I want you to reimburse me for my expenses. I'm going to remove the tape from your mouth and I want you to tell me the pin number to your debit card. I just want to hear only and I mean ONLY those four numbers. If you tell me the truth, I'll leave you alone; if you lie to me, I'll let my hammer continue what it started; do I need to say anymore? Do you understand me George?"

George nods again.

I grab hold of the edge of the tape and begin to peel it back and away from George's mouth until he's able to speak.

"YOU'RE DEAD...." George screams out at me, before I manage to press the tape back over his mouth.

"Naughty, naughty, naughty! You didn't pay attention to my instructions so I'm going to punish you again." I tell George.

I stand up and step back thinking of how best to punish him further when seeing George's body arched over the washing machine gives me an idea.

'That can't be very comfortable being arched over a washing machine with a broken leg. I remember when I had a stab wound to the back of my leg and any kind of movement was really painful so moving with a broken leg would be excruciating. Maybe thirty seconds on a fast spin will persuade him to tell me his pin number.' I think to myself.

I lean forward and turn the dial on the washing machine to spin and press the on button. The machine immediately kicks into life with the sound of the motor making a whirring sound. I step away from the machine and lean on the kitchen cabinets to watch my subject suffer for a while. The central drum inside the washing machine begins to rotate at a slow speed while the spin cycle begins its program.

'This is going to be interesting. I've got a machine to do my dirty work and I don't have to lift a finger. He'll be pleading with me to stop any second now.'

I watch the drum continue on its steady rotating cycle and then I hear a click and the machine leaps into a one thousand two hundred spin cycle vibrating violently from side to side causing George's penis to flop over and over and over.

'NOOOOOOOO! That's disgusting.' I think to myself not knowing where to look.
Covering my eyes with my left hand to shield myself from his flapping manhood, I dash forward and turn the machine off. The washing machine immediately

comes to a stop with George screaming under his mouth restraint before blacking out.

"Well I won't be doing that again, that was horrendous." I say to myself.

I look at George's unconscious body arched over the machine and think.

'If he blacked out, then maybe the machine did work. It was horrible to look at but if it caused George to faint then maybe he won't want to experience that again. Let me wake him up again and find out just what he thought of his shaking experience.'

I make my way back to the sink and refill the cup with cold water again and tip the contents over George's face. He immediately comes round and snorts the excess water out from his nostrils and turns his head towards me.

I crouch down again and whisper into George's ear. "George, did you enjoy that? I could do that again and again all night, or I could use my hammer again. In fact I think I'll use the hammer next as he's feeling a little left out. But let me clarify one thing for you. You probably know who I am and you may be aware of the people I've attacked; but know this, I'm a man of my word. If you tell me the pin number to your debit card so I can be paid for my trouble, you'll be a free man and no further injury will befall you. If you don't tell me the pin number, you will suffer, and I mean suffer all….. night…… long, do you understand me?"

George nods and tries to speak, as I hear a muffled sound trying to break free.

"OK George, this is your last chance, tell me ONLY those four numbers and you'll be a free man after I've been paid."

I take hold of the tape and pull it away from George's mouth.

"8, 9, 6, 6." George calls out.

I place the tape back over his mouth.

"George, I'm going to check your bank now and if I find out that you've lied to me, I'll be back, so I am going to ask you one last time; is that the correct number for your debit card?"

George nods.

I pick up the tazer and zap him in the chest until he blacks out.

I don't like returning to someone's house as you can't guarantee everything would be the same as you left it. Maybe someone might call round while I'm at the cash point collecting my money and calls the police or maybe George manages to escape his bonds and called the police himself. Either way, I don't want to risk being caught. I think the best plan would be to make him think that I'll be calling back either to release him if I manage to collect some money or to punish him if he's lied to me. If I were in his shoes knowing what I've just endured in the company of the masked maniac, I'd tell him the truth. So I think I'll just leave and not come back, but I need to do something first.

I take out the marker pen and write on his bare chest.

'Burglary is a crime, steal again and I'll be back.'
I pick up Georges mobile phone from off the kitchen
worktop and take a photograph of George, showing
the message on his chest and send it to a news
reporter I admire named Jackie McQueen at the
Liverpool Echo. I've sent her other pictures of
criminals I've attacked in the past, as I know she
writes an accurate column in the paper and tells it as it
is. I slip the phone inside my hoodie pocket to dispose
of later and pick up the bin bag full of Georges cut up
clothes and exit the house.

The van is parked in the same place next to the kerb
on Violet Street so I make my way over to the side
door of the van and open it. I place the big bag of
clothes inside the van and notice the storm drain
between the van and the kerb, central between my
feet.
'*How perfect is that.*' I think to myself.
I pull out George's mobile from my hoodie pocket
and drop it through the gap in the drain cover. I slide
the back door of the van shut and make my way
around to the cab and climb in.

I realise the news desk will inform the police so I
don't expect Mr Peterson to be left strapped over the
washing machine for long, which also means, I have a
limited amount of time to get any cash out of his bank
before he rings them and puts a stop on his account. I
start the engine to the van I pull out onto the main
road in search of a cash point. Within ten minutes I
notice a cash point next to a petrol station on the main
road to my left. I continue driving for another

hundred metres before pulling over. I don't want anyone to see me get out of the van and walk to the cash point outside the petrol station because it would be easy enough to find out the time money was paid out of Georges account and cross check it with the CCTV camera's from the petrol station. If the van was parked in view of the camera I'd be arrested in no time.

I get out of the cab and wander down to the petrol station, which seems to be busy at this time of night as one car pulls in for petrol, one car leaves having filled up. I walk up to the cash point and insert Mr Peterson's card, the screen flashes as it changes to the prompt screen asking me to enter the pin number. I enter the four digits 8, 9, 6, 6 and press the enter button, immediately the amount of six hundred and sixty seven pounds and ninety eight pence appears on the screen showing the balance of George's account.

"Very nice George, I think I'll take out the maximum daily withdrawal of three hundred for now, thank you very much." I say to myself as I depress the numbers three followed by zero and another zero before pressing the Enter button and wait for the card and cash.

'Screeech' the sound of screeching tyres and a noisy exhaust from a car accelerating quickly behind me catches me off guard for a moment and I find myself jumping out of my skin.
"What the…." I exclaim as I quickly turn to see a Blue Renault Clio with two lads in it speed out of the

petrol station and accelerate down the road when I notice a small object fall from the car as it clips the corner of the kerb. I take a mental note of the registration as I assume they've either robbed the petrol station or took off without paying for petrol. I collect my cash and card and make my way towards the object lying in the road. The oblong metal shape is easy enough to identify; I pick up the false registration plate and continue on towards where I left the van.

I find another cash machine a mile down the road next to a corner shop. I park on the side street and make my way to the cash point where I take out another three hundred pounds from George's account, I cant be bothered with the sixty seven pounds and ninety eight pence he has left in his account so I tuck the three hundred inside my trouser pocket with the debit card and make my way inside the corner shop for some refreshments. It takes another twenty minutes to park the van back inside my garage and change back into my normal clothes.

"Hello Anne, I'm home." I call out as I walk through the front door.
"Hi darling, how did it go?"
"Good, good." I say.
Anne walks into the lounge from the kitchen and immediately notice's the full carrier bag in my hand.
"What's in the bag?" She asks.
"Well that's the good thing I was about to tell you."
I walk over to the coffee table and place the bag in the centre.

"Now look at what I've picked up. Red wine for my wife and a bottle of coke for Michael and a nice bottle of Glenfiddich 12 year old Malt Whisky for me, and of course Crisps and Peanuts."

"Where did that all come from?"

I sit down on the sofa and indicate for Anne to fetch a couple of glasses for our drinks. She wanders into the kitchen and returns with the glasses and a couple of bowls to put the crisps and peanuts in.

"Well then, tell me all about it." Anne asks.

Michael walks into the room from cleaning his teeth ready for bed.

"Ah Crisps, can I have some dad?"

"OK son, but you'll have to brush your teeth again before you go to bed."

"Thanks dad." He quickly grabs a packet of crisps and sits down to eat them as Anne pours Michael some coke to wash the crisps down.

I pour the wine for Anne and a nice shot of whisky for myself. Anne takes a seat beside me and looks attentively into my eyes.

"I called round to the guy's house and you should have seen his face, he was really shocked to see me."

"I'm not surprised." Anne agrees.

"Anyway, I told him about the cost of replacing the window and he apologised for what he did; I think he thought I would tell the police where he lived so he gave me the money for the windows and an extra fifty quid. So I thought I'd use some of it for our drinks."

"Well now, if burglars compensate people with fifty quid every time they try to burgle you, then keep them coming."

"That would be nice, but I don't fancy having to come down every night to bash them around the face with your chopping board, I need my eight hours sleep."
"Oh yes, that reminds me, you owe me a new chopping board." Anne says.
"I'll try and pick one up tomorrow but for now, here's to our burglar. Thanks for the wine and whisky."
We all clink our glasses together in a toast for the man who paid for our drinks.

Friday 29th October

"Good morning, did you sleep alright?" Anne asks as she places a cup of tea down on my bedside cabinet.
"Good morning, what time is it?" I ask.
"Eight fifteen, I thought I would let you sleep in a bit longer this morning as you had quite a bit of whisky last night."
I take a sip of my tea and try to remember last night……. total blank. I put the cup back down on the bedside cabinet and ask Anne.
"So just remind. How did I get to bed last night?"
"Don't you remember anything?"
"No why?"
"Can you remember doing your seductive dance before you managed to get into bed last night?"
A vague image jumps into my head of me dancing at the base of the bed and a sudden sharp pain stabbing around the top of my thighs surges through me.

"Arghh, my legs hurt." I call out
I pull back the covers and notice both my legs through one leg hole of my boxers; cutting the circulation off both legs.
"Ouch, I wondered what was hurting."
Anne starts to giggle as she looks down at my over stretched boxers acting like a tourniquet wrapped around my thighs.

I sit myself up and try to pull the boxers down past my knees but having no feelings in my legs I cant bend my knees.

"Anne! Help, I can't move my legs and I've got pins and needles now."

Anne bends down and pulls the boxers off before gently massaging my numb legs.

"I think I'm going to have to limit my consumption of whisky to only two shot glasses a night from now one; I feel like a cripple."

Anne opens my underwear drawer and passes me a clean, un-stretched pair of boxers to put on.

"I think that's a wise decision Chris. It can get pretty costly having to replace boxer shorts every time you have a drink."

I manage to pull the clean pair of boxers on with Anne's help and relax back against my pillows as Anne walks out with my damaged underwear to deposit them in the bin.

I get washed and dressed fifteen minutes later once my legs feel normal and make my way down stairs to join Anne and Michael for breakfast. Anne is busy in the kitchen preparing our cooked breakfast of bacon, eggs, sausages and mushrooms so I take a seat at the dining table.

"Morning Chris, your breakfast is just about ready." Anne calls through from the kitchen.

"That's great, I'm starving."

I notice Michael has already finished his cereal and is sat in one of the armchairs reading a Manga book he borrowed from Debbie.

"Good morning Michael."

"Hi dad."

Anne walks through from the kitchen carrying a large plate piled high with food for me and a slightly smaller portion of food for her self and places them down on the table.

"Are you feeling better now Chris?"

"Yes thanks, I don't know what happened there; and I'll thank you not to remind me."

Anne giggles to herself.

"OK darling. So what are your plans for the rest of the day?"

"Not sure, I thought I would go for a drive after dropping Michael off, what about you?"

"Oh, I though I would pop round to Maria's after work if that's alright."

"Yes, of course; say hi to Mario if you see him for me."

Maria is Anne's best friend; she's married to Mario an Italian entrepreneur. They met about ten years ago when she was on holiday in Italy. He imports wine from a family vineyard and has a few shops dotted around the country so they're pretty well off if you ask me.

After breakfast we all drive into town where I drop Michael off at school and continue to the supermarket to drop Anne off for work.

"Have a nice time at work."

"Thanks, you enjoy your drive." Anne says as she closes the car door and walks along the pavement towards the supermarket. She stops at the entrance and waves to me before entering through the door and disappearing inside. Just beyond the supermarket I notice the front end of a police car pulling out from a side street. The sight of a police vehicle reminds me of the increased efforts the police are making to catch the Mouthless maniac; me! Last weekend the police set up a sting operation in an all out attempt to catch me. They stopped every van in the area and I only managed to avoid them by the skin of my teeth.

'The police obviously know that I drive round in a van of some sort but don't know the registration, make or colour because from what I can remember, they stopped every kind of van in the area. From what I can gather; none of the victims have spoken to the police about the description of the masked man except that he uses a van and that his mask doesn't have a mouth, hence the 'Mouthless Maniac signature name that's been given to me.' I think to myself.

I watch the police car drive past before I pull out and drive in the opposite direction.
'Would it be foolish of me to take the van out tonight? What if they continue with their sting operation again this weekend, the chances of avoiding the police would be nigh on impossible. It would be like playing Russian roulette, eventually its inevitable I'd be caught and I just can't take that risk.'

I'm in the process of renting a unit in the city of Birmingham but that's going to take a few more weeks before I can relocate and stop criminals there. So in the meantime I have to find another way to attack criminals around Liverpool without using the van.
'How can I catch a victim and transport him if I can't use the van?' I think to myself. *'What if I use my car,*

I've used it before when I first started; I remember transporting Paul Halett in the boot of the car. No, that won't do, Paul wasn't that big and I did have a garage to take him and hide him out of sight from people. I couldn't keep someone in my boot for hours during the night; someone would surely see a body stashed in the boot of my Skoda Fabia and report me to the police.'

'I can't afford to get another vehicle as I don't have anywhere to park it during the night, so for the time being, I'll have to keep using the car.'

I glance over at the shop fronts looking for inspiration when I notice just what I need in a home store shop window. I pull the car into a vacant parking space just up ahead and walk back towards the shop.

I put the back seats down in my Skoda Fabia car and slide the Samsonite 120 litre black suitcase down inside the back. While I was in the store, I crouched down next to the suitcase pretending to tie my shoe laces as I needed to work out if the case was big enough to fit a person inside. Bending forward, I surreptitiously glanced to the side to see if I could fit, in a crouched position. The case seemed to be about the right size, but I won't really know until I get it home and try it out for real. I did think of climbing inside the case in the shop but then decided it would have been too risky and probably bad taste. If a shop assistant saw me they would automatically assume I wanted the case to transport a body and as I need to keep a low profile it's probably best to wait until later when I'm not overlooked. I close the boot and climb back into the driver's seat; I check that I can still see through my rear view mirror and pleased to see that I can. The suitcase fits nicely in the back without impeding my view.

"Perfect!" I say to myself, as I start the car and drive off in the direction of home.

The garages at the back of our house are empty as most people are at work at this time of day so I'm able to park my car easily enough on the spacious tarmac between the two rows of garages. I open my garage door to reveal the Renault Transit van I've leased parked neatly inside. I squeeze myself down the side of the van and the garage wall to the back of the garage where I've a toolbox tucked in the corner. I open the lid and scan the inside for a metal eyelet and base plate; usually used to hang heavy objects from ceilings. I find what I need and carry the eyelet outside with my hand drill and drill bits. I open the back of the car and lift out the suitcase and place it on the ground next to my car.

'So how am I going to do this?' I think to myself staring at the large black suitcase at my feet.
'I need to fix the metal eyelet inside the case near the handle positioned about central on the side wall of the case. As the case is made out of toughened plastic, I'll have to drill a small hole through the outer casing so I can slot the eyelet though from the inside. I could then slot a small metal plate on the outside and inside of the suitcase with a small nut on the outside to secure the eyelet in place. That should do it.' I think to myself.

I find the right drill bit for the size of hole I need and quickly drill a hole through from the outside of the suitcase, after removing the rough edges, I slot the eyelet bolt through the base plate on the inside and the hole in the suitcase leaving about 30mm of the bolt protruding through the outside of the case. I slip over the end of the bolt another base plate and the locking nut to hold it in place; I tighten the nut on the outside which holds the eyelet rock solid on the inside. I put the spanner back inside my toolbox and lay the drill on top.

"Right, that looks good. I hope I've fixed the eyelet in the right place." I say to myself.

I look around at the empty garages and down at the suitcase before thinking.

'I need to know if a person could fit in the suitcase with his hands and feet secured to the eyelet in a crouched position and I won't know if I've put the eyelet in the right place unless I try it.'

I glance around the garages again and see the coast is clear so I step inside the opened suitcase and lay down in a crouched position with my feet tucked behind me so my bottom is resting on my feet. I slip my hands behind my back so they're touching my ankles.

I cant believe I fit in this small space, I glance over my shoulder and see that my ankles and wrists are approximately in the right place to be secured to the metal eyelet. I just need to find out if the suitcase will close properly with someone inside; I reach up and pull the lid allowing it to drop in place while I quickly tuck my hand back behind me.

'Bang' the lid closes in place.

"Wow, that's brilliant." I say to myself as I realise how perfect this suitcase will be for transporting my victims in. I push against the lid of the suitcase and realise its locked.

"HELP! HELP!" I scream out.

I know it's futile to do so as there's no chance of anyone hearing me, but as I'm stuck inside a suitcase behind a row of garages, I think I'm just a little panicky.

"HELP! HELP!"

I try to bang on the side of the suitcase to make some noise, but the restricted space is preventing me from swinging my arm and so the sound of my fist against the wall of the suitcase is more like a tap than a bang.

"I don't believe it, how stupid am I?" I scream at myself.

"They should give me an award for being the biggest idiot in the world."

I scream at myself inside the enclosed space. Laying scrunched up in a confined space in the dark is making me feel claustrophobic and hysterical; all I can think about is dying in my own makeshift coffin when the lid suddenly flies open and bright light explodes into view.

"Are you alright?" a voice calls out to me.

I try to focus at the figure standing beside me but all I can make out is a darkened silhouette. I blink rapidly to help re-focus when the image becomes a lot clearer and I see an elderly gentleman looking bemused as he stares at me.

"I heard a noise coming from inside the suitcase so I thought you needed help." The man says.

"Yes! Thank you very much." My mind quickly tries to work out a rational explanation to why I was locked in a suitcase so as not to appear to be a lunatic. I slowly climb out of the enclosure and stand up next to the man, brushing myself down when I continue.

"The funny thing was, I lifted the suitcase out of the car and just wanted to check it was empty, when I tripped and fell inside, and the lid fell closed on top of me! What's the chance of that ever happening?" I ask the man.

He looks at me shaking his head; I don't know whether he just thought I was a nutter or he was agreeing with me when he replies.

"I was just about to collect my car from number twelve, when I noticed the suitcase on the ground and heard the noise, so that's why I opened the lid."

"Anyway, thank you very much for helping me get out; I shan't do that again."

The elderly gentleman makes his way over to his garage.

I close the lid of the suitcase and carry it over to the garage and slot it down the side between the van and the outer wall. After collecting the remainder of the tools and putting them back in the garage; I lock up everything and make my way home for a well earned cup of tea.

Before picking Michael up from school I make a quick call round to the DIY store to pick up a short length of barbed wire; the attendant looked at me funny when I purchased only three metres. He probably thought; that's not enough to go around anything. I told him I needed it to go on top of my garden gate as we've been burgled in the past. He seemed to accept my plausible story. When we arrive home, Michael makes his way up to his bedroom to carry on reading his Manga book; Anne arrives home a few minutes later from Maria's.

"Hi, did you have a nice time with Maria?"
"Yes thanks." Anne replies although I notice she looked and sounded a little upset.
"What's wrong? Has something happened?" I ask.
"Oh, its nothing really I'm just being silly."
I walk over and put my arms around her and give her a hug. She buries her head in my chest and I sense she's not happy. I lean back from her to look at her face and ask.
"Come on; tell me what happened? Did Mario upset you? Shall I go round there and punch him in the nose for you?"
Anne looks up at me and smiles. "No, it's nothing really darling. It's just that Mario and Maria are going away again on holiday and we've not had a holiday for ages."

I remembered telling Anne that we were all going to get a bonus from work the other week so we could go on holiday soon. Having earned about ten grand from the people I've attacked means for the first time in ages, we've actually got the money to go on holiday for once.

"I tell you what. How about we book our holiday now?"

"Are you sure, do you really mean it?"

"Of course there's no time like the present; so let's get something booked."

Anne gives me the biggest smile which makes me so happy.

"I could get the brochures out again. The ones I collected the other day." She says.

"Great; you find the brochures and I'll put the kettle on for a cuppa."

"I do fancy Lanzerote." Anne says as she collects the brochures from the drawer of the side cabinet.

"Great! Lanzerote it is then." I reply as I take out two cups and place them down on the kitchen worktop and switch on the kettle to boil.

"Here they are darling" Anne walks through from the lounge holding the brochures up.

I finish making the tea while Anne puts a few biscuits on a plate and we carry them through to the office.

We take a seat next to the computer so we can look up the holiday resort online.

Anne turns over the pages of the brochure to the right place advertising the Hotel Natura Palace in the resort of Playa Blanca.

"How about this one, the hotel looks nice and it's right on the southern coast of Lanzerote?" She points to the picture of the swimming pool and sun loungers.

"Looks nice; let me just check the website and see if it's available."

I turn on the computer and wait for it to do its usual checks on startup.

"So when would you like to go?" I ask.

"Argghhhh I don't know." Anne replies sounding all excited.

"My boss says I can take my holiday anytime. Everyone in the factory has already taken their holidays this year so whenever suits you should be alright with me; are you able to get time off before Christmas?" I ask.

"Yes, I've not taken any holiday this year so it should be alright, when were you thinking?"

The computer finishes its checks and I click onto the internet and bring up the holiday website for the brochure. After selecting the resort and the number of people the screen churns away before returning with the availability for the next month.

"Look! They've got a family room available from Monday 8th November to 22nd November. What do you think?"

"Wow that's only a week away."

"I know, that's why it's reduced in price, it must be the last room available, so shall I book it?"

"OK."

I realise I don't have the money in the bank to pay for the holiday.

"I'll tell you what; the travel agents in town could confirm everything for us today. If I drive into town now, I could book and confirm everything including the flights and hotel with the travel agents and then it's all done. At least if we've forgotten anything, they would know and sort it out for us. What do you think?"

"OK if you think that's that best way of booking it?"
"Anyway, I don't like booking things over the internet. At least when you do it with a travel agent you can ask them other questions."
"Did you want me to come with you?"
"No that's alright, don't really want to drag Michael out and I thought it would be a nice surprise for him when we tell him later together when everything is booked."
"OK, that's a good idea. He will be surprised." Anne smiles to me as I pick up my car keys.
"See you later." Anne says as I step out of the front door.

I leave the house and make my way down to the garage where I've stashed all the money from the people I've attacked. The small router box tucked in the corner of the garage holds nearly ten thousand pounds. I take out a bundle of cash and count out enough for the holiday and flights before locking up the garage and making my way into town in my skoda. After paying for our return flights and hotel from Monday 8th November for two weeks at the Hotel Natura Palace in the resort of Playa Blanca, Lanzerote I climb back in the car and head for home.

The petrol gauge light flashes on as I notice the tank is nearly empty so I decide to pick up some fuel before I break down. The petrol station up ahead is empty so I pull in and fill up the tank with unleaded petrol.

As I return the hose back into its slot, I notice a blue Renault Cleo pull in behind me next to a vacant pump. I wander into the shop and pay for my petrol before returning to my car. The lad filling up behind me is wearing a blue hoodie. I look over at him and wonder why these youths nowadays have to walk around with hats on and hoodies covering their heads when it's a sunny day; are they allergic to the sunlight or something? I open my car door to get in and glance at the registration number of the Renault which seems familiar for some reason. I can't quite place it, but I've seen it before but can't recall where. I turn the engine on and make my way out of the petrol station and head on down the road, when it hits me.

"That's it!" I remember seeing the car the other day when they stole petrol using false plates. I notice a gap between two parked cars up ahead where I manage to pull in and park while I wait for the two lads to speed off out of the garage. I check my rear view mirror but can only see the vehicle parked behind me; the inside mirror displays the pavement leading back towards the petrol station with a couple of people walking along blocking my view slightly. I look to my right at the driver side wing mirror and can see clearly the road behind me.

'I'm hoping if it's the same lads, they'll speed off out of the petrol station and drive in this direction so they can make a quick escape. If they were to drive in the opposite direction; they would have to negotiate cutting across the traffic.'

'The problem with doing that at this time of day means having to wait for a gap to appear, which could take ages. If they're not bothered about upsetting one or two drivers then they may well just speed out in front of oncoming cars but that could be risky. They may even cause an accident and have their precious Renault with the sports exhaust get smashed. No, I think I've chosen the right place to wait for them. They won't risk damaging their car; so I should see them any second now.' I think to myself.

I stare in my rear view mirror as I wait for the car to speed out from the garage. Moments later the car does exactly as I thought, the flash of blue flying out of the exit and up the road towards me; engines roaring and tyres screeching, no doubt leaving half his tread on the tarmac. I wonder if it's all worth it, the relatively small amount of petrol they've stuck in their small car compared to burning off all his tread from the four low profile tyres would certainly cost the lads more money to replace than the fuel they've just nicked.

I start my engine and indicate to pull out as the blue Renault passes me. Because they've sped along the main road away from the petrol station in the attempt to flee the crime scene as quickly as possible, they've created a large enough gap for me to pull out onto the main road behind them. I continue following them at a distance as I'm hoping they'll lead me to wherever they live. After turning left and left again at the end of the street, they're now heading in the opposite direction parallel to the petrol station; I assume it was a tactical choice to head in one direction so the petrol station owner would notify the police that you're heading in that direction when in fact you're going in totally the opposite direction away from any police cars on the look out for a blue Renault.

The car slows down to a normal speed as it continues along the road, I gather they're more relaxed now that they've avoided detection and no doubt laughing to themselves at yet again stealing from the unsuspected petrol station. They indicate right and head into a housing estate and I follow in pursuit. As I turn into the street I notice they've already pulled up outside a terraced house and the two lads get out and make their way to the front door to a house with a green door. I drive past at a normal speed hoping they don't notice me. They're laughing and patting each other on the back as they walk into the house. I notice a space further up ahead on the left so I pull in to the gap and turn the engine off. The house numbers are the usual odds on one side of the road and even on the other; the houses on my left are all even so I assume the house they've gone in is odd.

My eyesight isn't brilliant but I can see to my right the house opposite is number twenty seven and the house next to that is twenty nine; I continue counting the front doors to the right incrementing the number by two each time so I can arrive at the house with the green door with the right number. From my calculations, the number the two lads live at is number thirty five. I enter the number on my phone for reference later on before driving off. I make a note of the name of the street and get my bearings so I can return here when it's dark.

Using the Suitcase

Anne cooks Spaghetti Bolognese for dinner which is not the easiest of foods to eat. I watch Michael leaning over his plate suck a strand of spaghetti into his mouth. The strand full of sauce quickly disappears inside his pursed lips before the end of spaghetti full of sauces whips across his face flicking sauce across the table and onto his shirt and face. I laugh at what a mess he's making and in the process do exactly the same.

"Christopher! Look at the mess you're making." Anne exclaims.
"Sorry, I'm trying to eat it carefully." I respond.
By the end of the meal Michael and I have covered ourselves in sauce while Anne hasn't a mark on her.
"For making such a mess, you two can wash and clean up." Anne demands.
Michael and I carry the plates through to the kitchen to wash up, grinning at each other from being told off. Anne sits in the lounge in front of the television with a glass of wine to relax.

We finish the washing up and clearing away before Michael heads upstairs to his room to read. I check the time and see it's nearly six o'clock.
"Anne, I think I'll head off to bed for a couple of hours sleep."
"OK darling, shall I wake you at nine with a cuppa?"
"Yes thanks." I reply.
I give Anne a kiss on the forehead and make my way upstairs for a sleep. I snuggle down under the duvet

and try to fall asleep but can't because my mind is a little preoccupied with what I'm going to do with the two lads who stole petrol. I haven't got a plan at the moment and I'm not sure what I'm going to do but I know I usually come up with something when I need to act. I try to clear my mind and imagine fluffy white sheep jumping over a fence when I hear Anne's voice.

"Wakey wakey." Anne walks into the room with my cup of tea and places it down on the bedside cabinet. I glance up at the clock not believing its nine o'clock already, when the clock display confirms it is. I turn over and sit up in bed and rub the sleep from my eyes. "Hello."
Anne kisses me on the forehead and says.
"Did you want me to make you a sandwich for your midnight snack?"
"Yes thanks." I reply. I pick up my hot cup of tea and take a sip.

It seems strange starting your working week on a Friday night, when most people are planning to go out and party. It just feels like a Monday morning to me and I don't fancy going to work.
'If I had a real job, I could ring in sick and take the night off.' I think to myself.

'I wonder if I'll ever get used to going to work when the majority of others are chilling out at the pub with their friends, It's not fair.' I think to myself feeling unmotivated and despondent.

I look over at my wife stretching to put a couple of clean tee shirts away on the top shelf of the wardrobe. Seeing her beautiful feminine outline reminds me of how much I love her and want to take care of her. *'Now that's the best reason for going to work and earning a living.'* I think to myself. I throw back the duvet and jump out of bed.

Anne makes her way down stairs to prepare my sandwiches while I finish getting dressed.

"Are you looking forward to getting back to work with your work buddies?" Anne asks as I walk through into the kitchen with my empty cup.

"You could say that, although I don't speak to many people at work; I think I only ever talk to one or two people during the whole night." I place my cup in the empty sink.

"You poor thing, well I hope it doesn't get too boring for you?"

"Boring I don't think so; I usually keep myself busy with this and that. You know me; I can always find something to do."

"Well if you don't speak to many people tonight, you could always think of me tucked up in bed." Anne kisses me on the cheek and hands me my snack.

"Thank you." I grab hold of my sandwiches and drink while Anne walks over to the front door and opens it.

"Well, I see you're desperate for me to get to work then?"

"No, not really; it's just that there's a good film on in about ten minutes." She looks at her watch and then back at me sheepishly.

"OK, I get the hint, enjoy the film and I'll see you in the morning." I step out onto the pavement and make my way down to the garages to change.

I unlock the side door to the van and climb in to the back to change into my protective gear. I haven't decided exactly what I plan to do with the two lads as I don't know where they'll be this evening. I think the best thing for me is to drive around to where they live to see if they're still at home. The chances are at this time of night they should be at their local pub chatting up women and getting drunk. I know the car and registration so it shouldn't be a problem finding them if they're parked up in a pub car park; I've just got to work out which one. From what I can remember of the area, the Red Lion is just around the corner from where they live so unless they've been banned from the Red Lion; that should be their local and the place to find them.

I finish off putting my protective clothes on and slip my black hoodie over my head with the mouthless mask tucked inside the hood. I fold down the back seats to the skoda and put the suitcase in the back of the car with a couple of plastic ties, duct tape, scissors and an empty bin liner. I check the petrol can and notice it's just over a quarter full, so that should do me for tonight; I place it in the foot well behind the passenger seat before checking the tazer. I depress the on button and watch the blue electric charge jump from one probe to the next; I place the tazer inside the glove compartment.

"OK, I think I'm ready to go." I say to myself.

I lock the van and close the garage doors before driving off in the skoda in the direction of Woodbine Street; I want to check if the two lads are still at home or if they've ventured out to their local. It takes me about fifteen minutes to get to Woodbine Street and I notice the car is gone so I carry on driving to the Red Lion. As I pull into the car park of the pub, I see the Renault Cleo parked towards one corner of the car park; luckily for me there's a space right next to the Renault. I pull in with the front of my car facing the pub with my driver's door next to the passenger door of the Renault. I turn the engine off and sit in the dark looking at the back door of the pub.

The car park hold about twenty four cars; a row of eight vehicles right next to the pub with a second row along the centre of the car park and finally the last row of eight cars up against the border fence where I'm parked. Usually the early visitors to the pub generally park right next to the pub while the late comers take up the spaces being left which usually are the furthest away. I'm quite pleased that the Renault is parked towards the farthest point as it suits my purpose and gives me some protection from onlookers.

I check the time and see its nine minutes to eleven. There's been several people coming out and going in to the pub, but no sign of my two lads. I rest my head back against the head rest and close my eyes for a moment as I try to formulate a plan of action in my mind.

'As soon as I see the two lads come out of the back door and start walking across the car park to their car, I'll pull out and drive to their house so I can prepare myself to attack them once they get home. I don't imagine they'll put up much of a fight as at least one of them may be drunk so a swift punch to the face would take him out while I tazer the other in the chest. I couldn't attack them here because there are too many people about that could see me and maybe come to their aid; but outside their home would be a different matter, it's quiet so I think that would be a better plan.'

I check the time again and see it's only just turned eleven when one of the lads walks out of the back door and makes his way over towards the car. I recognise the guy straight away because he has the same clothes on that he was wearing earlier today with his baseball cap tilted slightly over to the side of his head and his hoodie covering the baseball cap. His jeans are pulled down with the waistband just clinging on to the lower part of his buttocks leaving his crotch around his knees. I giggle to myself at the stupid fashion of today.

'Why would anyone in their right mind buy clothes that are just too small for them, it doesn't make any sense to me.'

The first lad is half across the car park when I spot his mate walking out of the pub with his arm around a pretty brunette girl.
'This is not good' I think to myself.

'There's no point in driving off now to where they live as I'm not sure on what's going to happen with this girl. Will they be taking her home and dropping her off or will the driver drop his mate off with the girl at the girl's house? I don't know. I think I'll just hang around for a minute to see what transpires.'

I notice the lad with the girl has the identical stupid fashion outfit as his mate, which doesn't surprise me, what does surprise me is why any girl with an ounce of sense would ever think of hooking up with such a loser dressed like a clown. The two of them stop just outside the door to the pub and sidle up to the side wall, kissing and feeling each other up in a kind of romantic embrace.

My eyes dart back to the first lad as he arrives at the car and opens the driver's door; after stopping for a second he looks back over the roofs of other parked vehicles and sees his mate still snogging the girl against the wall. He decides to give them their privacy and climbs into the car to wait. I glance over at the lad outside the pub and see he's committed to his romantic endeavours and won't be coming back to his car for a little while. I look back at his mate sat in the car and back to the lad kissing the girl while thinking.

'If I'm going to do something, this is the perfect opportunity to make my move.'

I pull the mask up and over my head and slip the mouthpiece into my mouth. The hood is quickly pulled into position covering the rest of my head. I grab the tazer and tuck it into the front pocket of my hoodie before glancing over to my right at the lad sitting in the driver's seat of the Renault. His head is down, looking at his mobile phone.

I don't know why I'm nervous, but I am. I can feel my heart beating faster and faster in my chest while the sound of my heart pounds like a base drum in my ears.

'*Come on Chris, calm yourself. I've done this plenty of times.*' I think to myself.

I realise I don't have much time to waste as his mate will be heading towards the car any second. I take a deep breath and open the door and step out between the two cars. The lad kissing the girl is in full on mode and oblivious to anything. I hold the tazer in my right hand and in one fluid movement; I open the passenger door to the Renault with my left hand and slide into the seat beside the lad behind the wheel. He glances left towards me expecting to see his mate as I jab the tazer into the lad's side.

Seeing a total stranger climb into your car could give you the shock of your life when you least expect it. Having that person jab a tazer into your side that delivers a charge of 300,000 volts surging through your body could prove to be your worst nightmare. The look on the lads face portraits that very expression of shock, anger, pain and horror all in one. His body jerks and writhes in his seat, legs kicking and head twisting, teeth clenching and relaxing as the charge permeates his whole body. The lads head drops to the side as his eyes close from shear exhaustion; he drops his phone in his lap. I quickly pocket the tazer and his mobile and slip back out of the passenger seat. I look over at his mate who's still busy. I open the boot of my car and open the lid to the suitcase; the lid just about opens in the restricted space as I slide the case nearer the edge of the boot to make it easier to put my victim in. I check his mate again, still busy.

I reach into the Renault and grab the lad by his arm as he's flopped over towards me; I drag his body out and onto the gravel between our two cars. I haven't quite worked this scene out in my mind as it was a spur of the moment thing; so I drag him around to the back of the Skoda ready to lift him up into the back of the car and into the suitcase.

I rush back to the passenger door of the Renault and close the door quietly before returning back where I left the lad on the ground below the boot of my car. Holding the lad under both armpits, I lift his upper body up but can't quite work out how to fold him inside the suitcase when I can't quite see past his baseball cap and hoodie which are now pulled up blocking my view.

My mind starts to panic as I realise I haven't got a lot of time as anyone could walk out of the pub at any moment or his mate might just finish off with the girlfriend and decide to walk over. I stare all around for a solution, when I realise its going to be much easier if I put the suitcase on the floor and then put him in.

I quickly lay him down to one side and pull the suitcase out of the boot and place it next to him. He starts to move his arms, only gradual as his energy levels are coming back. I grab his wrists and secure them together with a plastic tie and do the same with his feet before tearing off two strips of duct tape and placing them over his eyes and mouth.

I tazer him again, just to make sure he's not going to resist. His body jerks for a few seconds before I pocket the tazer and lift him into the empty suitcase. It's a bit of a squeeze as I have to push his head forward and shove his feet back so his wrists and feet are near the hook fitted on the inside of the case. I take out another tie and loop it around his wrists and ankles to secure them to the hook.

"Great, all done." I say to myself as I close the lid and lock the clasps in place. I take off my mask and slip it over my head back into the hoodie so it's out of sight and stand up. I glance over to the other lad whose now said goodbye to his girlfriend and is making his way over towards the car.

'*What am I going to do?*' I think to myself.
'*I can't lift the suitcase into the back of the car, its going to look suspicious. He's going to want to know where his mate is, and why is the Renault empty with the keys in the ignition.*'

I crouch down and push the suitcase under a four by four car parked to my left as the suitcase is too fat to slide under my car. I close the boot of my car and step around the side pressing the key fob to lock the doors as I casually walk towards the pub.

"They still serving beer?" I ask the lad as he approaches.
"Yeah mate." He replies as he steps up to his car and looks in for his friend.
I continue walking towards the pub.
"Hay mister, you seen my mate in the blue Renault parked next to ya?"
I turn round towards him.
"Yes! He saw someone walking down the road and ran over to him; it's probably someone he knows." I point down the road to my right.
"Thanks." He replies before climbing into the driver's seat and driving off in the direction I was pointing.

An elderly gentleman and his wife walk out of the back doors and head over to their car parked next to mine.
'WHAT I DON'T BELIEVE IT!' I think to myself.
As I watch them unlock the doors to the four by four parked on top of the suitcase with the lad in it.
'What am I going to do? Please don't run over the lad in the suitcase.' I think to myself while watching the couple climb into their vehicle and start the engine.
'They're going to pull out and squash the lad or at least get the suitcase trapped under their vehicle and have to call the police and all hell is going to break

*loose. I just don't believe it. Why doesn't anything
ever go right for me?'*

I watch in horror as the four by four slowly drives out
from its parking space and out of the car park without
touching the suitcase or noticing there's a large
suitcase left in the gap they've just exited.
"Wow that was lucky." I say to myself while jogging
back to my car.

I unlock my car and open the boot. looking round to
double check the coast is clear, I walk over to the
suitcase and drag it back around to the rear of my car
and stand it up on its side. The weight inside the
suitcase would normally take two men to lift so I
know it's going to be difficult to get it inside the boot.
It's one thing lifting another person when you can
reach around them and get a firm hold, but lifting a
large oblong dead weight is another thing.

I bend down and push the suitcase up against the boot
of the car; holding the handle on the top of the
suitcase, I rotate the case into its upright position
which is probably better for the lad inside because
he's now in the correct position with his head
uppermost.
I position my feet either side of the suitcase as a
weigh lifter would stand before attempting to lift a
heavy weight. I remember to keep my back straight as
I bend down with my knees either side of the suitcase;
holding the bottom of the suitcase at each corner I
press my body up against the case with my cheek
pressed against the side of the case to keep my centre

of gravity as close to the weight as possible in the hope of avoiding a back injury.

'OK a few deep breaths before lifting'

I breathe in and out and in again before holding my breath.

"Argghhhhhhh"

I cry out at the shear exertion needed to lift the weight off the floor. My knees begin to shake at the strain as the case slowly moves up and over the lip of the car.

'Bang.'

The case drops inside the boot.

I stand up and look down at the large suitcase laying flat inside my boot and think to myself. *'I'm not lifting that sort of weight again. I thought I was going to get a hernia. I'll have to re-think my strategy of loading people into the car. I can't afford to get a back injury and I don't want to collapse and have the suitcase fall on top of me.'*

I close the boot and make my way back around to the driver's door now walking like an elderly man in his nineties due to my stiff aching joints. I realise the lad's mate might be coming back soon when he cant find his friend so I try to speed up a little so I can get out of the car park before he returns. I climb in behind the wheel and start the car and drive out in search of a lonely spot to continue my plan.

I drive north out of Liverpool and past Maghull on the Northway looking for a quiet location when I spot a turning on the right along Springfield Road. I pull into the turning and stop the car on a small tarmac area just off to the right. We're far enough away from any residential areas and equally as far from the main road so as not to disturb anyone while I persuade the young man in my boot not to steal anymore. I turn the engine off and rest back into my seat to relax a little and to compose myself. I look out of the windscreen of the car towards a pocket of houses in the distance across the far side of a field in front of me. The small silhouetted houses with their bedroom lights reflecting back towards me remind me of nights when I've sat up in bed with the wife watching television.

The sky is brimming with visionary luminaries lighting up the landscape making it possible to see all around without the aid of street lights which is handy as there aren't any in our locality.

My relaxation is disturbed when I hear a moan coming from the suitcase in the back.
'He's awake then.' I think to myself.
'I suppose I'd better go and see him. Thinking about it, I wonder if he's got enough oxygen cooped up in that suitcase.'

The thought of the lad dying inside the suitcase is a little disconcerting and I find myself climbing out of the car a little more hastily than normal. I make my way around to the back of the car and open the boot. I check the time on my watch and see it's a quarter to twelve.
'That's good, there shouldn't be many people driving around at this time so I wouldn't expect anyone

seeing the interior light to my car and wonder what
were up to.'

I glance around just to make sure but can only see
empty roads.

The lad inside the suitcase moans again. I imagine
he's just heard the boot open and is expecting
something to happen.

I reach in and grab hold of the suitcase by its handle
and pull it towards me so I can have easy access to
the inside. The sound of moaning starts again from
inside the suitcase and gets louder as I open the lid.
The lad is jerking inside the case in an attempt at
trying to escape with his ankles and wrists secured to
the hook located central near the handle. His face is
all sweaty from the exhaustion and cramped condition
within the small enclosure. He body stops for a
moment as the cold air from outside washes over his
face. I don't want him to struggle while I cut away his
clothes so I take out the tazer from inside my hoodie
pocket and zap the lad in his side for a few seconds.
He shakes for a moment as the 300,000 volts drain his
body of energy leaving him still and listless in his
crouched position.

The lad is tightly packed inside the suitcase like a
sardine so I know it's not going to be easy to remove
his clothes. I reach in and pull out the man's wallet
from his back pocket which was easy enough as half
the wallet was already hanging out. I tuck the wallet
inside my hoodie pocket and then check his front
pockets for anything else. I find a packet of cigarettes
and two pounds thirty six in change in his right hand

pocket. I keep hold of the change and toss aside the packet of cigarettes as I don't smoke. I pick up the scissors and begin to cut away his clothes in small strips until I've removed most of the top layer of clothes covering his body. The remainder of his clothes are tucked under him and difficult to get at with a pair of scissors. I decide to try and pull out the rest of his clothes from under him. I put the scissors down and grab hold of the ends of the fabric with both hands and with a couple of sharp tugs, the material comes free. I roll some of the rags up and tuck them in between the lad's legs to prop his right knee up clear of the suitcase so I can break his kneecap with my hammer.

I pick the hammer up and take a swing at the lads kneecap. The hammer head swings round in a perfect arc from behind me around from right to left heading for his knee when I hear a 'Bang.'
The head of the hammer catches on the rear side panel of my Skoda and flies out of my hand narrowly missing my face and hitting the lad in the side of his head before coming to rest inside the suitcase.
"Damn it!" I cry out, looking at the damage to my car. I reach in and pick up the hammer next to the lads head, when I notice the cut on the lad's cheekbone. Within seconds his face begins to swell and more blood oozes out from the cut and trickles down his face onto the duct tape across his mouth.
'I'm impressed, the lad didn't make a sound and that must have hurt. Ouch.'

Looking at the position of the lad inside the suitcase and the position of the suitcase inside the boot of the car, I immediately realise that I should have angled the suitcase a little more towards the back of the car to get a good swing at his knee. I grab the right edge of the case and give it a tug, pulling the suitcase so it rotates clockwise towards me. I step back from the car and reassess the positioning, which looks good to me.

"OK, here goes for a clean hit." I say to myself as I swing the hammer once more at his naked protruding kneecap.
'Crack.'
The sound of metal on bone causes the bone to shatter within the knee; his knee changes colour from pinky white to crimson and blue as the joint swells quickly to double its size. The lad screams under his mouth restraint from the assault to his knee, his body tenses and shakes for a second before becoming still as the lad blacks out.

I place the hammer back down in the boot of the car and grab hold of the bundle of rolled up clothes between the lads knees. I pull the material out allowing the lads knee to drop down back inside the suitcase against his left leg. I place all the cut up clothes inside a bin liner and stuff the bag inside the suitcase near his head before closing the lid.
'I think I'll leave you for a little while so you can think about your hopeless situation you're in.'

I push the suitcase back inside the boot cavity of the car before closing the boot and climbing back behind the wheel.

'Time to chill out for a while I think.'
I hear the lad moaning in the back as he's woken from his unconscious state and is probably feeling the extreme agony from his cramped position and now his broken leg to add to his pains.
I insert a music CD into the car audio player to help me relax and to make my victim feel a little more nervous. The first track on the disc begins with a Frank Sinatra song. I close my eyes and rest my head back into the car seat as I'm soothed to the silky voice of Frank singing.
'And now, the end is near, and so I face, the final curtain.'
It makes me smile, thinking.
'I wonder what that lad is thinking right now'

Saturday 30th October

The music CD finishes playing so I open my eyes to
check on the time and see it's now well past midnight.
*'The lads spent enough time on his own so I think its
time to have a chat with him and get paid.'* I think to
myself.

I realise I hadn't checked his wallet yet, so I take out
the slim wallet from my hoodie pocket and open it up
to inspect its contents. I find forty five pound in notes
in the side flap and a membership card to a snooker
club, driving licence and debit card. I look at the face
on the licence and see it belongs to a David Wood. I
place the contents back inside my pocket and step out
of the car and walk back around to the boot. After
opening the boot and lid to the suitcase, I see the
naked scrunched up body of the man curled up inside
the suitcase shivering in the midnight air.

"David, David, you've been a naughty boy haven't
you?" I say.
David remains rigid in his crouched position
expecting to be attacked again.
"David, you've been stealing and you're old enough
to realise that stealing is a crime and you must know
that people who commit crimes must be punished."
David begins to whimper.
"Listen to me David, I only punish people who
commit crimes and as I've already punished you
tonight I'm happy to let you go home providing you
do something for me."

I see David's head turn slightly towards me as he endeavours to listen to what I'm about to say next.

"David, I've been working very hard tonight so I need to be paid for all my hard work. Do you understand what I'm saying?"
David's head remains still as he tries to understand the implications of what I've just asked.
"David, it's very simple. I want you to tell me the pin number to your debit card so I can get paid. If you tell me what I want, you'll be free very soon. But I've got a word of caution for you. If you lie to me or refuse to tell me the pin number, I'll be forced to continue using my hammer which won't be very nice for you. So the choice is yours. If you tell me what I want, you'll be free and I promise not to punish you anymore but if you refuse or lie to me, well, I wouldn't want to be in your shoes. So this is what's going to happen, I'm going to remove the tape from your mouth and I want you to tell me the four numbers to your debit card. I don't want to hear anything else, just those four numbers. Do you understand?"

I lean over and peel back the tape from David's mouth.
"4, 4, 7, 1" David calls out with a dry crackly voice.
I put back the tape across his mouth and close the case and boot before climbing back into the car and driving off in search of a cash point.

It doesn't take me long to spot a cash point at a large supermarket. I'm a little wary about using the cash point at large supermarkets because they tend to have security cameras in store. If the police can identify when money was taken out of an account and check the surveillance camera's from the store; they could possibly link the person taking out the money to his vehicle parked in the car park. I decide not to take the risk of parking inside the supermarket car park so I pull in to a side street within walking distance of the store.

I notice a sign to the entrance to the street tells me that all the residents in the street have permits to park. Cars are neatly parked inside their respective bays outside their houses. I drive along looking for an empty space and find a space at the very end of the street.

'That's unusual to find a parking space as every house has one allocated space so I assume the people living on the end are either on holiday or don't own a car.'

I'm not concerned about being in a permit only parking space as I don't expect traffic wardens to be working at this time of night and if a resident saw me park up; I wont be long even if they did report me to the police. I'm sure the police have better things to worry about than making a special trip to give someone a ticking off for parking illegally. I lock the car and wander back along the pavement to the end of the street and then across the road towards the supermarket which happens to be a 24 hour supermarket.

The three cash machines are vacant so I walk up to the nearest one and insert David's debit card into the slot. The information on the screen disappears for a second then reappears with the instructions to enter the pin number. I press the numbers 4, 4, 7, 1 and depress the enter button. The screen goes blank for a second as it gathers the information to the lads account.

'Your account balance is £63.27' the screen informs me and asks me if I would like another service. I press the option to withdraw money and enter the amount of sixty pounds when I hear the sound of a car pull into the car park and accelerate towards me. I press the enter button on the display and wait for the debit card to be ejected. The car stops just behind me and I hear the sound of two car doors open and close as two people climb out and walk towards me which makes me nervous considering the late hour.

I don't want to turn around because whoever they are would know that I'm nervous because I felt the urge to turn around. They may well be just a young couple just after some money from the cash point to pay for petrol or a bottle of wine to finish their night off. I try to keep calm and listen out for any indications as to who they are and what they want. One of them walks right up behind me and stops within a foot of me which I'm not happy about. I feel their breath on the back of my neck which makes my heart beat a little quicker. I catch sight of the second person with my peripheral vision just to my right. I look closely at the display on the cash point which shows me the outline of the man behind me to my left.

'*What are they up to?*' I wonder.
'*Why are they standing right behind me? Am I just about to be robbed?*'

All these thoughts rush through my mind in an instant. I glance back over my shoulder to my left and see a heavy set lad with deep set eyes and a protruding brow looking a little like a Neanderthal but a few inches taller, looking over my shoulder at the cash point. He's got a stupid grin on his face and I can smell beer on his breath.

"Do you mind!" I say to him hoping he'd get the hint and step back to allow me room. I turn the opposite way and see his mate doing the same to my right. He's about the same height but not so stocky and wearing a flat cap. I notice a can of lager in his left hand, leaving his right hand free to snatch any cash that comes out of the machine. Both of them ignore me, which confirms my suspicions as I turn back towards the cash point in time to retrieve the debit card. I quickly grab it and tuck it in my trouser pocket as I don't want to lose it at this moment because it has my fingerprints on it and I don't want the police using it to convict me.
I think about the protective equipment I'm still wearing.

'*My chest and back is protected by my corset with the metal brackets sewn on and my forearms and shins*' *are protected with the rubber matting with metal rods attached which can be useful for blocking kicks or punches and even being hit with a large stick or baseball bat. My only vulnerable area would be my head and groin. I didn't see the guys holding any sticks or bats so I assume I'm not going to be beaten to death. If they were going to stab me, I would have thought they would have done it by now so I assume they're just here for the money.'* I think to myself.

'So what's their plan I wander? As there's two of them, maybe, one of them will shove me while the other grabs the money. I think the one to my right holding the can of beer in his left hand must be the one who's going to make a grab for the money, which leaves the guy on my left just behind me the one to give me a shove as both his hands are free.'

I've literally got seconds before the money comes out and I'm attacked. I try to work out my plan in my head.
'Maybe I can turn and punch the chunky lad in the face then kick the other one and try and make a run for it?' I hurriedly try to formulate a plan.
Just then; the money is ejected from the slot. I reach out for the money with my left hand when I feel the force of the Neanderthal push me against the cash point. Instinctively I place both hands on the wall to stop my face crashing into the brickwork. I turn my head to the right and catch sight of the thin lad reaching around me for the cash from the machine when I hear the Neanderthal cry out.

"Arghhhhhhh."
I quickly turn round to see him clutching his right
hand with his left and it suddenly dawns on me that
he hadn't shoved me at all, but punched me in the
kidneys to incapacitate me while his mate snatches
the money. Luckily for me, the full force of his fist
smashing against the reinforced corset has broken his
right hand.

The thinner guy is already at the car and about to
open the passenger door while the bigger lad still
clutching his hand tries to run round his car to the
driver's door without passing out.

The thinner lad bends down to open the car door but
realises he has both hands full; cash in his right hand
and a beer in his left. He sacrifices the beer and drops
it on the ground. The tin rolls under the car out of
sight; he uses his now free left land to open the car
door; he bends down forward to duck his head inside
the car as I step up behind him. With the same effort
our rugby players use to do a drop kick from the half
way line, I launch my right leg up between his legs.

My foot catches him in his lower stomach while my
shin with the metal rods over protective rubber
matting makes contact with his manhood. His feet are
lifted up off the ground with the force of my leg
destroying any chance of him ever having kids
naturally in the future. He squeals out a sound that
I've only ever heard from sopranos as the
excruciating pain in his loins causes him to black out
and collapse half inside his car. His head and chest

falls flat on the car seat while his legs and feet lying outside the car on the ground next to the money he stole from me.

The bigger lad struggles to open the door with his broken hand and has to revert to using his left hand. He jumps into the driver's seat and puts the car in gear. He looks at his mate and then at me and decides on the safer option. Pressing his foot to the floor; the wheels begin to screech and the car speeds away across the car park dragging his mate for a good hundred metres before coming to a stop. The figure behind the wheel leans over and drags his mate's body back into the passenger seat before speeding off again. I reach down and pick up the sixty pounds. "Idiots!" I call out to them as they disappear down the main road. I make my way back to my car.

I don't like being in a permit only parking space for too long as I wouldn't want one of the residents to notice the car and wander out and take the registration to report to the police the following day so I drive out of the street in search of a quieter location. It doesn't take long before I see another side road with a couple of shops all locked up for the night. I drive down the street and find a quiet spot next to a boarded out shop which is located far enough from the main road as not to be overlooked. I check my mirrors for anyone wandering about but can't see anyone.
"Looks OK to me" I say to myself.

I always feel better in myself when I deposit the victims somewhere rather than cooped up inside my vehicle. It makes it easier to deny everything to the police if they catch you when the persons not tied up in your car.

I step out and walk around to the boot. I glance around again just to make sure the coast is clear before opening the boot; David moans as he hears the car open. I notice the shop we're parked next to is an old disused business premises that looks as if its not been used for many years with the windows boarded out downstairs. I decide its safe enough to let David go. The suitcase has slipped forward in the boot compartment so I have to pull it towards me a little so the lid will open.

David makes another noise from within the enclosed space as I drag the suitcase towards the end of the boot. I flip open the catches and open the lid to reveal a scrunched up young man covered in perspiration. I remember my trademark is not yet complete so I make my way round to the front passenger door and take out of the glove compartment the black permanent marker pen before making my way back to the boot area.

I lean in towards David and whisper into his ear.
"David!"
He body stiffens in anticipation of what's to come next.
"David, I'm going to let you go now but I want you to remember something. If you ever commit another crime, I'll come back for you. I know who you are and I know were you live, so I want you to be a good

boy from now on. If you're nice to people and live an honest life, you'll be safe. If you ignore my advice, I'll get you and finish what I started. Do you understand me?"

David nods and says yes from what I can make out from his muffled response.

"Good lad." I reply.

I tazer David in the chest until his body comes to rest as he blacks out. I don't want him to try and retaliate as I let him go, so having him unconscious makes it easier for me. I tuck the tazer away inside my pocket and take hold of the scissors by the side of the suitcase and cut off David's restraints. I grab him under his arms and lift him out of the boot and shuffle backwards with his body towards the doorway of the disused shop. Standing just outside the shop entrance, I twist round ready to lay David down inside the doorway when I notice a figure in the corner.

My heart must have skipped a beat at the thought of being caught out. I stare down in the darkness at the figure in the doorway and realise it's a homeless man beneath what appears to be a bundle of rags and a holdall bag; half his right arm hanging out from his covers holding on tightly to a half bottle of whisky; now three quarters empty. I realise he's probably well away in the land of nod so I relax a little. I lay David down next to the man and take out my marker pen. 'IF YOU COMMIT A CRIME YOU WILL BE PUNISHED' I write on his chest. I use David's mobile to take a picture of his naked body lying next to the homeless man before I tear off the tape from his eyes and mouth and step back towards the car to retrieve the bag with David's clothes and the petrol can.

I drop the clothes on the pavement about two metres from the sleeping bodies in the doorway and douse the fabric with accelerant from the petrol can in the foot well before igniting the bundle. The flames quickly lick up into the air as the petrol burns generating a small amount of heat and light. The homeless man in the doorway now clearly seen from the light of the fire starts to turn away from the light. He turns on to his side towards David and with his right arm still clutching his bottle reaches across the naked man beside him. I smile as I make my way to the car; Imagining a romantic encounter between the two of them. I put the petrol can back in the foot well of the car and close the rear door. I climb into the driver's seat and drive off before anyone sees me.

A few minutes later I see a lay-by on the side of the road where I pull in. I want to notify the newspaper as I've done before. It would help them get the true story of what the lad did, also it would allow the police to find him quickly as I don't want the lad to die of pneumonia as the nights are getting colder now that the winters drawing in. I send the photo to Jackie McQueen at the Liverpool Echo Newspapers with an explanation to what he did and where he is now; I wait for the message to go before I open the car passenger door and look down at the grill to a storm drain, I drop the phone through the gap into the depths below.

"All done, time for a rest I think." I say to myself as I close the passenger door. Turning the engine back on, I pull out onto the road and head south in the direction of Wrexham and my favourite lay-by near Cefn-Y-Bedd.

I find the lay-by empty as usual and pull in for the night. The sky is clear and full of stars illuminating the landscape around the countryside, I step out of the car to bask in the tranquil night and to enjoy the world as it should be. The peacefulness of my surroundings make me yearn for a life in the country, I can hear the hooting sounds of a nearby owl and see bats dart across the sky in search of food, the rustle of the bushes as badgers wander through on their night trek makes you start to appreciate our wildlife. I try to think back to the days when I went camping with my brothers as young lads. It was great fun and exciting to venture out into the country for a lad who was brought up in the city.

I climb back into the car and set my alarm for five o'clock in the morning and place my mobile on the dashboard so that the vibration of the alarm against the plastic would definitely wake me at five. I wind the car seat back fully to allow myself to recline back into a near horizontal position and lay back in the seat until I feel comfortable. I quickly recall the money I've made this evening and calculate that I've earned about a hundred and seven pounds so far.
'I really need to earn at least five hundred pounds to cover the cost of the van rental and my salary. Maybe I should focus of someone with a little more money

tonight so I don't have to go to work Sunday as I'm playing football with the police.' I think to myself before closing my eyes and drifting off to sleep.

The alarm on my phone wakes me up at five o'clock with a loud vibrating sound causing me to jump. It's funny how your dreams incorporate the last thing you hear or do before you wake up. I remember in my dream, chasing a car that had stolen from a petrol station. The car speeds down the road trying to escape and I find myself chasing after them on foot. That's where I should have known it was a dream because I must have been running at fifty miles per hour after this car. I run alongside the driver's door and shout at the driver to pull over when he looks back at me and then points forward to an oncoming car just about to hit me. I look towards where he's pointing when I hear the sound of a horn; but in reality it was my alarm going off.

I reach forward and turn the alarm off on my phone and adjust the chair so it's back in the upright position. The sky is still dark so it takes me a moment or two to wake up properly. I rub my eyes and allow my body to shake out the cold of the night before turning the engine on. I turn the car around and drive back towards home. Its nice driving at that hour because most people are still in bed so the roads are fairly clear. I drive down the slip road leading onto the motorway towards home when I notice a box van up ahead driving in the centre lane. It's not uncommon for cars to remain in the centre lane when there are other vehicles up ahead on the left hand lane travelling slower than they are. In this case; there are no other vehicles on the road and the van driver seems to be weaving from left to right inside the centre lane.

"What on earth are you doing, get over to the left you numpty." I call out as I gradually catch up with the van. I pull out into the right hand lane to start my overtaking manoeuvre as he's doing 60mph and I'm driving at a constant 70mph. As I pull level with the driver, I glance over at him and can't believe my eyes. The driver is holding a Tupperware tray with one hand while using a spoon to eat food out of it with the other. I can only imagine he's steering the van with his knees.

'*What a plonker*' I think to myself.
I'm not having this. I beep my horn to show my annoyance that he's driving recklessly. The sound of my horn must have startled him because I notice his body jerk spilling the food out and onto his lap. He immediately screams out in pain as I see his mouth wide open and his eyes tightly shut. He tries to stand and brush the hot food down and away from his groin area as the van careers off to the left and onto the hard shoulder before ploughing into the barrier.

"Idiot!" I shout out in the general direction of the crashed van.
I start to feel a little guilty that I could have caused a serious accident, but as there were no other vehicle involved; I smile to myself thinking.
'It served him right.'

I arrive outside the garage in plenty of time and quickly change back into my normal clothes whilst storing my protective gear in the back of the van. I put the money I made back into the router box with the rest of my earnings and close up the garage before making my way up the side road towards my house. Anne has timed it perfectly as usual with a cup of tea all ready for me just as I walk in through the front door.

"Morning darling, how was your night?" Anne asks.
"Good, good, what about you, did you sleep alright?"
Anne walks over and puts the cup of tea down on the coffee table in the lounge before giving me a kiss.
"Yes, I had a really good sleep thanks. I bet you're looking forward to getting some sleep, you look tired?" Anne asks.
'*Tired*' I think to myself.

'*I shouldn't look tired as I've slept most of the night.*'
I look in the mirror and notice my puffy eyes.
'*It's probably from not fully being awake that's why my eyes are puffy but I can't tell Anne so I think its best that I just agree with her.*'
"I am a bit tired; maybe I'll take my cuppa upstairs and have it in bed before getting some shuteye."
"OK Darling, shall I wake you at the usual time."
"Yes thanks." I pick up my drink and head upstairs.

It takes me a little while to drink my tea as it was piping hot and didn't have much milk in; Anne doesn't like milk so she thinks everyone else doesn't like milk either. I finish off the last dregs from the bottom of my cup and snuggle down under the duvet before glancing at the time on the alarm clock. Below the digital display time display is the date '30th October.'

'Thirtieth of October.' I think to myself.
'It's Halloween tomorrow night, but as tomorrow is a Sunday. Everyone will be out tonight celebrating Halloween in costumes, dressed as ghosts and ghouls, freaks and monsters. That means I could stay in my protective outfit and no one would know the difference because I would blend in with everyone else. I may have to modify my outfit a little, maybe a bit of fake blood or something to make myself look a little more ghoulish. I'll think about it some more when I wake up.'
I close my eyes and fall asleep thinking of a plan for later on tonight.

Anne walks into the bedroom with a cup of tea for me and places it down on the bedside cabinet before pulling the curtains to allow the afternoon sun to stream into the room.
"Wakey, wakey, its two o'clock." She says.
"Thanks." I reply, scrunching up my face to blot out the bright sunlight. Anne picks up my dirty clothes from off the floor and carries them out to the laundry basket.
"The Laundry baskets out here you know." She says.
"What?"
"The laundry basket, you know, the basket that has all the dirty washing in. If you put your dirty clothes in it, I would know they need washing. My clothes and

Michael's are in the basket but not yours, you could always put your own clothes in yourself you know."
"Sorry, I was waiting for my clothes to be so dirty; they'd make their own way to the basket."
"Very funny!" Anne says while shaking her head. She turns around and makes her way down stairs again.

I sit up in bed and take a drink of my tea.
'Now how does a masked man fit in with a crowd of people dressed as 'the living dead' I wonder?'
I start to remember the old horror film 'Halloween with Jamie Lee Curtis and the character Michael Myers with his white face mask holding up a large kitchen knife.

'Now that would be perfect, I wouldn't need to do much to change my disguise. I could find myself a large kitchen knife and go as Mike Myers. Wait a minute; I don't suppose the night clubs would let me enter with a ten inch kitchen knife in my hand, I'd be arrested in no time. What I need is a plastic fake knife from a toy shop. If I pop into town this afternoon I could see if I can find something suitable. If I can't find anything, I could always make one with a piece of card and some duct tape.' I think to myself.
I finish off my drink and get dressed and washed before heading down stairs.

"I thought I would nip into town, did you need anything?" I ask Anne as she's ironing some shirts for me.

"We do need some milk and potatoes and maybe a new pair of tights for me as I have a ladder in my old pair."

"I'm not buying tights; that's girlie stuff. Maybe you should come with me so you can buy them yourself."
"OK, let me just finish this shirt."
"Dad, can I go round Paul's house?" Michael asks from the corner of the sofa.
"Is that alright with him, is he expecting you?" I ask.
"Yes, I told him yesterday that I would ask you today."
"OK, we'll drop you off at his before we go shopping, so you'd better text him and let him know we'll be there in about fifteen minutes."
Michael immediately jumps on his phone and texts his best friend.

"So what was it you needed from town?" Anne asks as she puts away the ironing board and iron.
"Oh, there's going to be a kind of fancy dress thing at work tonight, the managers said we could all dress up in costume as its Halloween weekend."
"That's nice, so do you know what costume you wanted?"
"I thought I would use that white mask I made the other week and maybe get a toy knife so I could play the character from the film Halloween."
"That's a good idea, there's that toy shop on Wilson Street that sells gimmicky stuff; maybe we should take a look in there?"
"OK; that sounds like a good idea, thanks Anne."

"I've told him dad, he knows we'll be there in fifteen minutes." Michael shouts as he slips on his shoes.
"Great! So are we all ready, let's go."
We all head out of the door and down to the car.

I don't know what it is about women, but they don't miss a trick. As we walk round the garages towards where the car is parked, Anne spots something at the rear of the car.
"What's that?" pointing at the boot of the car.
"What?"
"Someone's bashed the back of the car."
I quickly remember when I swung the hammer at David Wood's knee and hit the side of the car. I make out that I haven't seen it.
"Where?" I ask.
"There! Look." Anne points her finger right at the dent.

"Someone's tried to break in to our car!" she adds.
"No! I tell you, the kids living around here have no respect for anything." I feel the dent with my hand showing some concern while shaking my head.
"This is terrible; it's going to cost me at least a hundred quid to get that fixed." I say.
"Darling from now on you must keep the car in the garage when you're not using it." Anne suggests.
"I know I'll try to remember." I reply knowing quite well that I can't park the car in the garage during the day because the vans in there. If I leave the van out, our neighbours would soon realise the van doesn't belong to anyone in the street and report it to the

police. That would cause me a big problem. I decide
to ignore it for the time being.

We climb into the car and head into town.
We pull up outside Paul's house just as Paul opens his
front door and runs over to the car.
"Hi." He says as he opens the back door to let
Michael out.
Paul's mom Sally wanders over and leans into the car
as Michael makes his way into the house with Paul.
"Hi, Paul wanted me to ask if Michael could stay for
dinner, I could drop him off later on this evening if
that's alright with you?"
"Thanks Sally that would be great." Anne replies.
"OK, shall we say around eight o'clock for me to
drop him off?"
"If that's alright with you, then it's fine with us." I
reply.
"Yes that's fine, so see you later." Sally closes the
rear door and waves as we drive off.

I find a space in the multi-storey car park and we
make our way down the high street towards the toy
shop on Wilson Street. The shop is quiet so were able
to spend plenty of time looking at the fake fangs and
fake blood on sale in the shop. I expect as most
people will be out in their Halloween costumes
tonight, the shop would have brought in plenty of
disgusting things for people to buy and wear for
tonight. I find just what I need on one of the shelves.

"Anne, look at this!" I call out while holding the knife up in the air before making stabbing swings forward and down.

"Psycho! Do you fancy taking a shower tonight so I can practice?"

"CHRISTOPHER! Stop being stupid." Anne shouts at me across an aisle as two elderly women stare in shock.

"Sorry ladies, were rehearsing a scene from a movie were making."

The two ladies scurry past nattering together about people doing things in bad taste.

I look over at Anne.

"OOPS!"

I take the fake knife to the counter and pay the three pounds and sixty pence for the plastic ten inch kitchen knife.

We pop into the chemist to buy Anne's tights and shampoo before making a brief stop at the grocers to buy potatoes, broccoli and onions. I carry the bags back to the car and load everything in the boot. We drive out of the multi-storey car park and down past a nightclub which is popular with young ones. A large billboard outside the club is advertising a Halloween party tonight with a banner across the bottom stating. 'Half price Alcohol to anyone in fancy dress.'

'Well that's going to get the club packed out tonight, selling alcohol at half price will surely draw in the young clubbers wanting to get smashed on cheap beer. I remember reading about this club in the newspaper the other week. I'm sure it had something

to do with drugs although I imagine most clubs nowadays must have a problem with people buying and selling drugs to drunken youths. Maybe I should give the club a visit tonight? I don't want to arrive too early as it's usual for people nowadays to frequent a pub for a couple of drinks before they make their way to the nightclub around about eleven. I suppose they do it to meet girls in the pub first and then take them to the nightclub to get high and make out. The nightclub has limited parking so I'll need to get there a little earlier so I can park the car in the best location before everyone else gets there.'

I formulate a plan in my head as I drive home.

Halloween Night

"So what's everyone else at work going to be wearing tonight?" Anne asks.

"Not sure, probably the usual cut two holes in a bed sheet for the eyes and pretend to be ghosts."

"That would be funny if everyone at work turned up with sheets over their heads."

"Yes it would, but I doubt it as it's not very practical; driving a fork lift truck with a sheet over your head then the sheet gets caught under the wheels pulling the sheet across your eyes and you end up forking someone."

"How romantic." Anne replies sarcastically.

"You know what I mean."

"I know, I was only joking. Well you'd better tell me all about it in the morning."

We hear a car pull up outside and two doors open and close.

"That must be Michael." I say.

Anne stands up and makes her way to the front door. I glance at the clock and see its 8.03pm. The front door opens and Michael walks in.

"Hi mom, hi dad."

Anne speaks to Sally at the door as Michael disappears into the kitchen and I hear the lid of the biscuit tin open and close.

"Did you have a nice time then?"

"Yes dad….crunch….we played……crunch, crunch… 'World Rally Cars'….crunch… which was really cool."

"So did you win, or did you let Paul win a race?"

"Erm we raced together in a team, oh yes and Paul did this really cool jump, and his car did a somersault and landed back on the road and he bashed the car in front and knocked him off the road and…"

"That's good; it sounds like you really enjoyed it at Paul's house."

"Yes, it was fun. Can I go around his tomorrow please dad?"

"No not tomorrow, maybe you could go round later on next week. What if we invite Paul to come over here on Monday to have Chinese with us again and maybe he could bring over his game."

"OK thanks dad."

"Off you go now upstairs and get ready for bed as its way past your bedtime."

Michael dashes upstairs as Anne closes the door to Sally and sits back down next to me.

"Sally's really nice, we must invite her over one evening. Did you know her husband works abroad, he travels a lot for work and I think he's working in Germany at the moment. Sally says he left about three weeks ago and he's due back in one more week."
"Oh, I was just saying to Michael about inviting Paul over on Monday to have Chinese with us, maybe we could ask Sally to come too."
"That would be great; I'll give her a quick call in a few minutes to allow her time to get back home."
I check on Michael while Anne rings Sally.

"Chris it's 9:30!"
"OK, just finishing shaving, I'll be down in a minute."
I examine my butchered face and notice several nicks around my chin and neck as I'd cut myself with a wet razor. I grab the aftershave and splash a good amount into my left palm ready to apply to my face. I put the bottle back down on the shelf and rub my hands together to distribute the perfumed liquid and to warm it up a little before patting the aftershave over my face and neck.

"Ouuuuch! That hurts." I say to myself.
'Why do men do it? Why do we put on aftershave which feels like someone slapping you round the face everyday because it sting's. It's not usual to want to feel the burning sensation across your face everyday so why do we do it? What would happen if we didn't have aftershave, would we ask our wives to give us a good slap so we don't miss out on that feeling men put up with every day, NO!'

I stare at my reflection in the mirror for a moment as the burning sensation from the aftershave slowly subsides.

'OK enough of being a grumpy old man, let's get to work.' I think to myself.

I tear off a small piece's of tissue and apply them to the small cuts on my face before heading downstairs.

Anne is waiting at the front door for me with my usual pack up for the night.

"It looks like you've crawled through a thorn bush, what happened to your face?" she asks.

I glance back in the mirror again and notice the small pieces of tissue I'd placed over my wounds have already absorbed the blood from my wounds and look like small red circles blotches dotted over my face. I count six in total.

"I think I need a new razor?" I say looking at Anne.

"You think you need a new razor! NO, you will get a new razor before you shave again; it's got to be cheaper to buy a new razor than to use up all the toilet roll to stop the bleeding." Anne grins at me.

"OK, so see you in the morning."

I take my midnight snack and give Anne a quick kiss on the forehead. I step back to walk out the door and notice one bit of read circular tissue has stuck to Anne's forehead, just between her eyebrows. I step outside the door and walk along the pavement thinking how shocked she'll be when she looks in a mirror; she looks like an Indian woman with a bindi which makes me laugh.

I change into my protective gear inside the van and put my hoodie over the top with the mask neatly sown inside the hood. I tuck the fake kitchen knife inside the front pocket of the hoodie with my tazer and climb out of the van. I hear faint cries of laughter in the distance as party goers make their way from one pub to the next looking to scare other individuals with their ghoulish outfits. I smile to myself when I try to imagine the outlandish costumes some of the youths will be wearing tonight.

'It's definitely going to feel different tonight to be wandering around in the midst of people. I wonder if anyone would recognise me dressed as the Mouthless Maniac or would they just think I'm Mike Myers from Halloween? I'm hoping with all the other people wearing costumes, I'll just blend in.'

I try to push aside any feeling of nervousness because I'm doing something different from my normal routine and focus on the job in hand. I take out the large suitcase and place it in the back of the car along with some plastic ties, scissors, duct tape, bin bag and the remaining petrol in the petrol can which I tuck down behind the passenger seat as I've done before.

"OK, I think I'm ready." I say to myself as I look round for anything I may have missed. I don't see anything else I need so I close the back of the van and lock the garage before getting in the car ready for my ghoulish night at work.

It takes me only about ten minutes to arrive at the nightclub car park and luckily for me there are only a handful of cars already parked up. I expect most of the cars belong to the staff inside the club as they would need to get home once they finish work. One or two other vehicles may belong to a customer inside the nightclub; no doubt some party goers have drawn straws to see who's going to be the designated chauffer for the night while their friends enjoy themselves and get blotto. I find a space about ten feet from the back door on the far side of an industrial bin which works out well for me as I didn't want people to stare inside my car wondering what's in the big suitcase.

I step out of the car and walk around the bin to the path that runs along the side of the building to the front door. I notice a group of girls and boys walk past the front of the building towards the entrance of the nightclub all dressed in fancy dress.

'I wonder if I could tag along with that group as they enter the club, it would definitely look better if I was part of a group and not on my own.' I think to myself as I quicken my pace to catch up with them before the reach the front entrance.

One of the lads in front of me is dressed like Frankenstein; his mate has his hair greased back and is wearing fangs and a cape so I gather he's Dracula. The three girls following behind are all dressed in maid's outfits with ripped stockings and black eye and lip makeup with the faint trickle of blood from their mouths. I can't remember the name of their characters but they look effective as Dracula's daughters or something. I catch them up just as the Frankenstein reaches the front door. The bouncer on the door looks like a wrestler with a bald head and big arms and chest.

"Evening ladies…….. and gentlemen." He says while eyeing up the girls in their short uniforms. He steps aside to allow us to enter the lobby.

The small lobby area is dimly lit with a compact kiosk located off to the right next to a doorway leading to the main auditorium. The sign above the doorway indicates the tariff for entry to the night club; the five people in front of me individually pay the lady behind the glass screen the appropriate amount and continue through the narrow passageway towards the sound of music cascading along the murky tunnel. I reach the kiosk and slide a couple of notes through the hatch to the lady. She takes the money and begins to hand back the change.

"I love that film and you look really scary." She says as I collect my change.

I hold up the ten inch kitchen knife and make stabbing thrust towards the glass.

The lady holds her hand over her heart and says.

"I'd hate to see you down a dark alley; you'd give me a heart attack."

"Thanks." I say while putting the change in my pocket. I head down the corridor towards the main auditorium thinking.

'That's good to know, if I look scary in here, maybe I really look terrifying in a dark alley.'

The large dance club has the usual main floor to dance which is now occupied with about ten or twelve girls dancing to Michael Jackson's song Thriller. The perimeter of the floor is a mish mash of boys and girls standing holding their drinks and chatting, some are gently moving to the beat of the music from the DJ on his tape deck tucked over to the left behind massive speakers. On the right is a large bar area surrounded by people buying drinks with a speckling of tables throughout the floor area with stools and chairs either two or four to a table.

I make my way over to the bar area to order a drink. Not everyone in the club is in costumes; some girls have really worked hard to make themselves look ghastly with dark lipstick and thick eyeliner and mascara with red lipstick drawn as drips of blood from the corner of their mouths and eyes. Hair shaped and styled with possibly a mass of hair products to produce dagger like protrusions from their heads in all directions. Some with veils and one girl with what appears to be a skull stuck on the side of her head as you would wear a fascinator.

The barman brings me my pint of lager and only charges me the promotional half price for being in costume.
"Great outfit mate." He compliments me on making the effort. "Mike Myers, right." He asks.

I hold up my rubber knife in a menacing manner. He smiles and says.

"Scary."

"Thanks" I say as I take my drink in my other hand. I squeeze through the now growing number of people wanting to get to the bar and make my way around the dance floor in search of an empty table.

Most people at clubs either want to be seated near the edge of the dance floor or near the bar area so they have easy access for dancing or drinking. I find a small table tucked in the corner away from the main group of people. I notice a group of girls off to the right sat around a small table all in ghoulish outfits with fishnet stockings and low cut bodices revealing ample cleavages chatting away and sipping on what appears to be black and red cocktails. They stop talking and watch me as I casually walk over towards the vacant table.

I don't know what it is but it's very complimentary to be eyed up by young women at a night club. I'm very happy and contented with my married life and wouldn't dream of straying although having someone pay you a compliment by eyeing you up gave me an exhilarated feeling of contentment.

'Wow, these girls really fancy me. I haven't lost that sex appeal even at my age.' I think to myself. I start to swagger a little and wobble my head from side to side like I'm someone of importance as I step up to the small table. I turn casually to look at the girls before lifting up my face mask enough to take a large swig from my pint of lager. I swallow the cool liquid and replace the mask over my face before sitting down on the low chair next to the small square table, trying to look confident and nonchalant.

I slide back in the chair and lean forward to rest my pint on the table when a blinding light sears through my body sending excruciating surging pains throughout my extremities, easing and griping in rapid succession as I watch the pint in front of me shake violently within my grasp. The lager within the glass is shaken abruptly from side to side sending sprays of liquid and froth in copious amounts across the table top. Lager spills over the end of the table and onto the floor around my feet as the pint glass empties itself in front of me while my body contends with the uncontrollably spasms electrifying my muscles into debilitating bouts of pain that seems to last forever.

The girls stare at me for a few seconds before turning away and giggling at the idiot in the face mask having a fit. My body stops shaking and I find myself with my face and chest flopped on top of the table covered in lager. I know what's happened and I know I need to sit up but my body feels exhausted from being tazered in the abdomen from my own tazer. I sit there looking through the small eye holes in my mask with my head resting on a pool of lager as people continue to enjoy themselves. A young couple walk past the table and I see the girl glance down at me looking concerned before turning to her partner who tells her. "It's alright, he's drunk."

They carry on towards the bar and disappear into the throng of people gathered there.

The pain slowly dissipates and my energy gradually returns over the next few minutes as I slowly move my head from off the table top. Drips of lager run off my face mask and chin as I ease myself back upright into the chair. I'm only too aware that the tazer must have activated itself when I leant forward, squashing the on button against the table top. I begin to pray to myself that it doesn't go off again as I don't know what I would do. Having endured it once is enough for me, suffering the same pain again would be worse than hell.

I lean back in the chair and reach inside the pocket of the hoodie to feel for the tazer. The fabric is twisted around the machine so when I sat down and leant against the table, the machine had nowhere to go when it was squashed against the hard surface. I release the tazer from its tourniquet and lay it flat against my stomach to prevent it from re-activating. The pain in my head is probably the same as having a bad headache while my joints feel as though they've been hit with a cricket bat. I reach forward for what remains of my pint, and with one mouthful down the small amount of liquid that was left in the glass.

'That was horrible' I think to myself.
'boy o'boy that was like the worst experience of my life. I wouldn't want to go through that again for a million pounds. I suppose looking on the positive side

of being tazered is that I know now how my victims feel after being zapped.'

I decide just to relax and enjoy the surroundings until my body returns to normal and my brain starts to work again. The club gradually fills up with people until all the tables are taken and most of the available floor space is filled with clubbers rocking with the music. I decide to stand among the throngs of people to watch for any activity. I notice a strange character in the corner next to the fire exit dressed as a Mummy out of ancient Egypt. People wander over to him and after a short exchange they make their way to the toilets. I can only assume they've bought some illegal drug from the man before taken it to the toilets to either inject themselves or smoke what they've bought. I watch for a few more minutes just to make certain my assumptions are correct when another lad ventures over to the mummy and then leaves and heads for the toilet; I follow.

"Did you get the stuff Mal?" One of his mates calls out as Malcolm walks in through the toilet door.
"Yeah mate, its here."
Malcolm's friend sees me walk in to the toilets behind Malcolm and immediately stops talking. Malcolm senses someone's behind him so he heads straight for one of the cubicles. I casually walk over to the urinals and pretend to relieve myself from only drinking less than half a pint of lager.
The other lad joins Malcolm in the cubicle and they close the door. I can hear whispers as Malcolm must be sharing out whatever he's bought with his mate. I

finish off at the urinal and tip toe over towards the cubicle to listen out to what he boys are saying.

"So how many did he give you." One of them whispers.

"He only gave me two for twenty quid, one for you and one for me."

"That's great, come on give me mine I wanna get high." Malcolm's friend says.

I decide I've heard enough so I tip toe over to the wash basin and wash my hands and dry them on the hand rail before making my way back into the main auditorium. I make my way over to the area where I can watch the mummy.

I position myself next to a central supporting brick column at the corner of the dance floor. The dance floor is heaving with revellers and the bar is equally packed so from my vantage point at the far side of the bar next to the column, I've got a clear view of the mummy in one corner of the night club and the entrance to the toilets at the other end.

There are plenty of people milling around in the empty spaces between tables between me and the mummy so I know I won't be spotted staring in his direction. I notice another person make his way over to the mummy and take a seat next to him. The man says something to the mummy and I see the mummy mouth 'Twenty' to the man. He reaches down inside a sports bag and retrieves the drugs and an exchange is made. The man slowly stands and makes his way to the toilets.

'So that's how it's done.' I think to myself.
I hear shouting above the sound of music and look behind me to see where the noise is coming from. Two men are standing toe to toe in the middle of the dance floor and appear to be punching each other. They're holding each others collars with their left hands and swinging their right fists towards the other persons face but yet to make contact.

'Are they fighting or dancing?' I wonder to myself. Just then the taller lad makes contact and within seconds the bouncers are all over them. I look around and notice everyone in the club staring at the fracas. *'I think it's time to make my move while everyone's distracted.'*

I step over towards the mummy and take a seat next to him.
"Ecstasy man, how much?" I ask the mummy.
"Twenty."
He reaches down inside his sports bag and pulls out a small white paper packet with the tablets wrapped securely inside and holds out his other hand for payment. I reach inside the front pocket of my hoodie to make it appears that I'm getting the money. I grab hold of the tazer tightly in my right hand and in one fluid movement, pull my hand out and thrust the tazer into the mummy's chest while pushing him back with my other hand against the emergency exit door.

His body crashes against the doors emergency handle and the door quickly opens allowing us to disappear into the darkness outside. The mummy collapses on the ground landing on his back and I land across his chest still pressing down on the tazer. His body shakes and jerks for a few seconds while the 300,000 volts drain his body of all energy leaving him exhausted underneath me. His head flops to the side telling me he's had his fill so I release the tazer and tuck it back inside my hoodie pocket. Just then I hear a loud bang behind me as the emergency door closes.

The noise from the door draws the attention of a young couple making their way towards the front entrance door some fifteen or twenty feet from us. I know it must look suspicious seeing one man on the ground and another standing astride him so I look towards the young couple and say.
"Sorry, he's drank too much again, he does this every week." I hold both my arms out to the side in a kind of 'I give up gesture' while shaking my head.
They still seem a little concerned so I turn towards the mummy on the ground and reach for his hand to help him up.

"Come on Rodney, don't be a plonker! Grab my hand."
I reach down and grab both his hands and pull him up into a seated position.
"Now don't be sick in the car when I drive you home." I say looking back at the young couple who smile back at me.
"Don't worry about us, we'll be alright."
They both smile again and continue on towards the main entrance and out of sight.

'I know I need to move him as quickly as possible just in case more people spot us down the alleyway and wonder what we're doing. Having to explain myself to every passer bye will become very tedious and tiresome.'

I crouch down and tuck my head under his arm right arm and stand up while supporting his waist with my left hand. We both stand up together. I know he hasn't got the energy to walk so with his right arm around the back of my neck and holding on tightly to his waistband, I half carry him towards my parked car tucked in the corner behind the rubbish bin. Luckily for me, his head is flopped back as he hasn't got the strength to hold his head up so all he sees is clouds and sky.

We shuffle our way around the metal industrial bin and to the back of my Skoda Fabia car where I proceed to lay him down on his side so he's turned away from the car. I don't want him to recognise the make or model of the car or the registration plate. Opening up the boot, I reach in and take hold of a couple of plastic ties and secure the mummy's hands and feet. I tear off two small strips from the roll of duct tape and apply one strip across his mouth and the other across his eyes. I look around over the rooftops of the other parked cars in the car park to see if anyone has just arrived and making their way towards the alley past where we're parked. I can't see anyone.

I remember the trouble I had with loading the last victim into my car and decide the best and easiest way would be to sit him on the back of the car and then shove him backwards in to the suitcase. I open the lid to the suitcase and position it a foot back from the edge of the boot. The mummy is probably five foot ten inches in height and maybe slightly lighter than me, so I don't imagine he's going to be too much trouble to lift or fit inside the suitcase as I fitted inside quite easily the other day.

I step either side of the mummy on the ground and bending forward, I tuck my hands under his armpits while keeping my legs bent, I pull him up into a seated position on the ground and drag his body around so his back is resting against my registration plate on the Skoda.

'OK, I just need to lift him up now, so he's sat on the back of the boot compartment.' I think to myself. Keeping my feet firmly positioned either side of him; I crouch down into a full squat so I can wrap my arms around his chest and pull him close to me.

'I remember hurting my back a few years ago lifting something not really heavy into the car. The bag of shopping was easy enough to carry, but when I extended my arm to place the bag on the far passenger seat of the car, I ripped the muscles in my back. It all had to do with keeping the centre of gravity as close to me as possible, as soon as you extend the weight further away from you. The muscles that are needed to support the weight change, when the weight distribution changes; it's kind of like a set of scales, when you transfer weight from one side to

the other; the scales become unbalanced. It's a little more technical than that but I do remember the pain in my back which kept me awake for days, so it's something I don't want to experience again if I can help it.'

I pull the mummy tightly towards me as someone would embrace another person and push down with both my legs until were in a standing position. I slowly ease him down so he's sat on the back of the car while remembering to keep my back straight. "Now that wasn't too bad." I say to myself as the boot of the car takes the weight of my victim.
I glance over the mummy's shoulder inside the boot on the car and notice the suitcase is nicely positioned directly behind him.

'Cool that looks good.' I think to myself.
I let go of the mummy and allow his body to flop backwards inside the suitcase which seemed like a good idea at the time. His upper body falls backwards over the side walls of the suitcase and down inside the case which naturally lifts his dangling legs up right between my legs squashing my manhood.

"Arghhh I don't believe it." I cry out.
The pain rushes through me in waves making me feel nauseous from the blow to my testicles. I push my backside out away from the car sliding my manhood off his knees and immediately grab hold of my groin to ease the pain while my head and chest flop forward onto the mummy's lap.

I hear giggling sounds behind me so I quickly turn around to investigate where the sound is coming from when I see two young lads holding hands quickly scurry past me heading up the alley towards the club. It suddenly dawns on me why they were giggling because from what they could see; I had my face buried into someone else's groin while holding onto my own certainly paints a telling story.

'I'm so glad they weren't from the newspaper.' I think to myself.

I could just imagine it, front page news. 'Mouthless maniac is a homosexual.' Not that I have anything against homosexuals but it would be difficult to explain with everything else to my wife and son.

The pain quickly subsides and I'm able to push the mummy inside the suitcase. It takes a few minutes to position him correctly within the enclosed space before I close the lid of the suitcase and shut the boot. The coast is clear so I make my way around to the driver's door and get in. I sit quietly for a few minutes to compose myself.

Sunday 31st October

I look at the clock on the dashboard which informs me it's Sunday already as the time is three minutes past midnight.
'It's Sunday already.' I think to myself.
I remember the conversation I had with Pete Norris on Wednesday about playing football with all the police this afternoon in less than fifteen hours. Just thinking about it sends chills down my spine.

'Here I am having just kidnapped someone and soon to rob him and break his leg and later on today, I'll be hob knobbing with the police after playing football. This has got to be the strangest day of my life. If only the police new the truth. 'Oh hi, this is Chris he'll be playing football with us today. He's the one we've all been searching for. You know the Mouthless maniac who's been attacking all the criminals in the area.'
I giggle to myself, thinking what a crazy world we live in. I start the engine to my Skoda and reverse the car out into an empty gap behind before driving forward and out of the car park in search of a quiet location to have a chat with my victim.

I find an old playing field with wooden goal posts and a pitch mostly comprising of mud with the odd patch of grass. It's situated at the back of a housing estate and next to a large factory on the opposite side. I park the car against an eight foot wall bordering the field and the factory and turn the engine off. The lights from the factory shines over the wall and illuminates most of the field so it's clear enough for me to see what I'm doing. I make my way out of the car and around to the boot. I look around just to be certain that were not overlooked and nobody is in sight, the coast is clear, so I open the boot and pull the suitcase towards me. I hear the faint moans from inside the case and know the mummy is alive. I laugh to myself because that sounded like the title of a movie. 'The Mummy is Alive.'

I open the lid to see the mummy jerking and twisting in an attempt to escape as he pulls at the plastic ties around his wrists. Just then one hand comes free and quickly moves towards his face to remove the tape from his eyes and mouth.
'CRAP! If he uncovers his eyes, he'll see who I am and if he manages to remove the tape from his mouth he could scream.' I think to myself as I quickly reach forward with my left had to try and grab his free right arm while my right hand reaches inside my hoodie for the tazer.

I grab his sleeve with my left hand and pull his right hand away from his face. Luckily for me, he's not been able to remove the tape but his right arm is proving to be stronger than my left arm and I see his hand moving closer towards his face. I strain with my left arm at this tug of war match, his hand moves closer to his face then I exert myself some more and his hand comes away. Back towards his face then away again as I lean back to get leverage. He moans as he pushes himself to the limit in his attempt to reach for the tape across his face when the sweat on my now strained hand slips and my grip is gone. The effort in trying to pull his hand towards his face when it's been pulled away then suddenly being released, results in the guy punching himself in the face; which makes me smile.

I fly backwards and fall towards the ground as I watch his hand reach across his face to remove the duct tape. I decide its best to cover my face just in case he frees his blindfold so I pull my mask over my head and into position covering my face and quickly clamber up. The mummy at this point is pulling the duct tape off his eyes when he stops and moans.

'Why has he stopped I wonder?' I think to myself. I move closer to him and see the reason why. The adhesive on the tape is so strong across his eyes that when he was tugging on the tape to remove it. The tape was ripping out most of his eyebrows from their roots and nearly tearing off his eyelids causing me to grimace under my mask.
'Ouch that's got to hurt.'

I use this pause in events to dive forward and do the only thing I can think of to stop the mummy from continuing. My tazer finds his side and delivers the 300,000 volts into him once more. I watch his muscles contract and relax in his confined space for a few seconds until his freed arm drops down by his side and I know he's too exhausted to do anything. "That's better." I say to myself as I pocket the tazer.

Taking hold of another plastic tie, I secure his hand back behind his back and attach it to the locking hook. I open the bin bag and using the scissors I start to remove his clothes as I've done many times before and place the rags inside the bin bag. I notice his eyes are still uncovered, so I re-apply another strip of duct tape across the original strip and press it down firmly over his eyes before continuing on with removing all of his clothes. I find a wad of cash in his pockets with a plastic flip card holder and a mobile phone.

I open the wallet and inspect the contents; two hundred and sixty pounds in cash, a credit and debit card and drivers licence in the name of Leroy Knibbs. I pocket the cash, cards, mobile phone and driving licence and drop the plastic flip wallet in the bin with his clothes. I roll up the bag with his clothes in and tuck the bag between his knees to elevate his right knee up out of the suitcase. Leroy is still out of it for the time being so I close the boot and make my way back round to the driver's side and climb in behind the wheel.

I sit quietly in the dark waiting for Leroy to regain his strength. I look out at the midnight sky and watch the clouds move gracefully across from left to right as the wind transports them to other locations inland. I see a glimmer of light as the moon appears from behind a thick cloud only to disappear again and then to emerge at the other side of the ever changing shape of rain molecules and vapours. The light from an international commercial flight makes its way across the sky no doubt heading for warmer climates, taking holiday makers to some exotic beaches. My mind drifts off to imagining my holiday not to far off now in Lanzerote with my wife and son. I can just imagine myself drinking a nice chilled beer lazing by the pool as the sun gently warms my body till its golden brown.

I watch a young buxom blonde wearing the smallest bikini edge her way into the pool, first her toe is dipped into the water and her body shivers as the temperature is cooler than she anticipated but then everyone is watching, so she commits herself as she doesn't want to appear chicken. Stepping down into the water down the shallow ramp, her body slowly moves lower and lower into the cool water when the water level now reaches her naval.

Her arms stretched out to her sides she stops, uncertain whether to continue or just to remain where she is and maybe splash the water onto her flat stomach in the hope of acclimatising her body to the water temperature. She scoops up some of the water in her cupped palms and rubs it over her chest, allowing the water to run down through her cleavage and past her stomach on its way back to the pool.
"Aarmmmmmmmmhhhh."
'*That's a funny sound.*' I think to myself.
"Aarmmmmmmmmhhhh." The noise comes again and I realise it's not the beautiful blonde performing some amazing images in my mind, but the mummy laid down behind me.
"Well thank you very much for spoiling my daydream." I shout out my annoyance at having my dream interrupted.

I open the driver's door and make my way back around to the boot not happy in the slightest.

I open the boot and reach for my hammer. Leroy's knee is nicely protruding up out of the suitcase ready for being bashed with my hammer. I step to the side so I don't hit the side of the car again and swing the hammer down at Leroy's knee.
'Crack.'
"Arghhhhhhh." Leroy screams under his mouth restraints and blacks out.
I put the hammer back down by the side of the suitcase and close the boot before making my way back to the driver's seat.
"Now where was I?" I ask myself.
I close my eyes and try to imagine the image of the beautiful buxom blonde again. NO! Not a hope, I try again. NO!

'Typical, when you want to return to a dream you were enjoying, you can't' I think to myself. I look out of the windscreen and see some movement up ahead.

'What's that?' I wonder. Two figures are moving towards me, they're about a hundred metres away at the moment and heading in my direction.
"Crap. What to do, what to do" I ask myself as I watch them get closer and closer. *'What if they're they police doing a search of the area, they would want to know what I'm doing in a field late at night.'*
I turn around and look over my shoulder at the opened suitcase and realise I've made a big mistake.

'I don't believe it, they're bound to see Leroy all naked and curled up in my suitcase, I should have closed the lid, at least then I could have blagged my way out of it, if I had to. I can't actually say anything in my defence now that the evidence is clearly in view.'

I stare at the advancing figures in the distance trying to think of a solution, looking left and right.

'If I start the car and try and turn around in this short strip of field to the left of the football pitches it would take me for ever. I don't have room to do a u-turn so I'd have to try a three point turn which may turn out to be a nine point turn given the space. Surely they'd catch up with me half way through my manoeuvres and arrest me for having a body tied up in the back and for bad driving. I could always attempt a u-turn and drive to my right across the football pitch but that would surely attract attention and they'd radio in with my registration plates and have me arrested for destruction of property as well as kidnapping and anything else they could pin on me.'

My heart begins to race inside my chest causing me to panic a little as I try to think of the best options available to me.

Looking at the dark silhouetted figures approaching, I notice the one on the right seems to be holding something in his hand.

'Why would he be swinging his truncheon around when there's no one in front of them?' I think to myself.

I stare at the figure as they get closer and closer when I realise it's not a baton but a bottle of wine or spirits. "You're not the police." I say to myself. Realising they're a couple of lads probably coming home from a party.

The lad takes a swig from the bottle and hands it to his mate who takes it and also drinks. They both stop as the one who was drinking must have finished what was left in the bottle; they both turn toward the car. They must be about fifty metres away at this point when one of the lads throws the bottle directly at the car. I can just make out the glass container rotating through the air as the image gets larger and larger as it's propelled through the air towards me. It drops down and hits the ground just in front of the bonnet of the car and bounces underneath smashing against the axle. Now that's really annoyed me.

The car is mostly in shadow from the eight foot wall so I don't imagine the two lads can see inside the car; maybe they think the car is empty and abandoned as I watch them giggle to themselves. I hear one say to the other.
"That was rubbish; I could have hit the car, easy, hic"
"No you couldn't."
"I could."

They continue walking towards me. I reach up and turn the interior light switch off so when I open the door, they won't be able to see me sat behind the wheel. I pull the door handle very slowly and open my drivers door just enough so it's off the catch before positioning my foot against the inside panel of the door ready to kick the door open as the lads approach.

"Is there someone in the car?" One of the lads says to the other as they get nearer to the bonnet. They stop and lean forward while frowning trying to focus on the dark interior and decide to take a closer look. They walk around to the driver's door and bend down to press their faces against the glass to peer in.

I kick the door open with all my might against the squashed faces of my predators. The impact of the glass hitting them in the faces causes their noses to take the full impact. I see their squashed faces being forced back by the glass just as a spray of blood spurts out across their faces. The speed of the door being kicked out sends our two friends flying backwards and into a backwards roll in unison across the grass.

The combination of the cold air and a sharp bash to the faces must have revived the lads from their drunken stupor to one of being alert and focused. Within seconds they're back on their feet standing side by side with clenched fists facing the opened door of the car.

I realise there's no time to waste so I launch myself out of the door towards them when the hem of my trousers gets caught on the seat adjustment lever prohibiting my movement forward. My body drops to the ground in mid dive landing flat on my stomach just in front of the two lads knocking the wind out of me for a few seconds.

The two lads can't believe their luck seeing their attacker lying helpless on the ground at their feet. With both lads holding their noses to stem the flow of blood they both take a swing with their right legs to simultaneously kick me in the head and stomach. Remembering my shin and forearm guards with sown in metal bars; I pull my knees up to protect my stomach and push my forearms together in front of my face to defend myself from the incoming kicks.

'Crack, Crack'
"Arghhhhhh, Arghhhhh."
I feel the impact of the kicks directly on my shins and forearms as the shin bones break against the metal bars. I look up at the two lads hopping in front of me holding their noses with one hand while their other hand holding their injured legs.

I slowly stand up and reach in to my hoodie pocket to retrieve the tazer. I zap the nearest lad in his chest while holding onto his shirt to prevent him from hopping away from me. He squeals for a second as his body shakes and collapses in a heap at my feet.

"No! No, sorry mate" his friend tries to appease the situation, knowing his fate is soon to befall him like his friend. He hops back, before trying to run; his body falls to the ground as he's unable to support his body weight on his broken leg. I catch him up and tazer him in the back of the neck. His body jerks and shakes in his prone position as the 300,000 volts drains his energy leaving him motionless on the ground within seconds. I put the tazer back inside my hoodie.

"Drunks! They think they're so brave when they've had a drink." I say to myself. I don't particularly want to hurt the lads as they've already suffered enough and they've not committed any crimes except for being drunk and stupid. I decide the best punishment would be to cause them a little inconvenience instead.

I pull one of the lads over to the other and quickly remove their belts. I sit them up so they're propped against each other with their legs outstretched in a seated position with their backs together. Using their own belts, I tie both their wrists on one side of their bodies and with the other belt; I do the same on the other side of them. I imagine their going to struggle to stand with both of their right legs broken and both arms tied together. I cover their eyes and mouths with duct tape as I don't want them to see what's going on, while I interrogate Leroy.

Interrogate Leroy

Leroy is wide awake when I open the boot of the car and I can see him tense as he no doubt heard what was going on with the other guys.

"Leroy, Leroy, you're a bad man selling drugs, do you know that?"

Leroy body stiffens with the anticipation of being attacked again.

"Leroy, if you do as I ask, you may go free without any further injury to yourself. Do you understand?" I look closely at Leroy's face and see him nod in agreement.

"Good, now listen very carefully; I'm going to remove the tape from your mouth and I want you to tell me the pin number to your debit card and credit card. If you tell me anything else or if you lie to me I'll start breaking other parts of your body and you will wish you were dead. Do you understand?" I ask.

Leroy nods in his confined space.

I reach over and start to peel back the duct tape from off Leroy's mouth.

"I'm gonna kill….."

I replace the tape quickly and lift up my hammer.

"Naughty naughty naughty, you didn't listen to my instructions properly, did you? I said I only wanted to hear the numbers to your debit and credit cards, nothing else and here you are, telling me you want to kill something. I didn't quite get the last words so I assume you must be hungry and you could kill a burger and fries. Well talking of food, I think I'm quite hungry myself. But listen; because you didn't tell me what I asked, I guess you must really want me to break something else and I'm not one for not doing what I've been asked, so here goes."

Leroy tenses and moans at the thought of being hit again as I swing the hammer down against Leroy's shin.

"Crack!"

His tibia shatters under the impact of the hammer head splintering small shards of bone through the skin around the mid section of his shin. His skin splits around the impact area causing contusion and lesions allowing the dark red capillary blood to oozes out from the wound drawing a red line down around the calf muscle and onto the bin bag now propping up his leg. Leroy faints.

I decide its time to eat. I remove the bag of clothes from between his legs and stuff it in the small gap between his feet and backside before closing the suitcase and boot of the car. The two guys have gained consciousness sat some ten feet from us still tied together in their seated position which gives me an idea. I walk over to them and reach inside their pockets in search of a mobile phone which I find straight away. I turn the phone on to camera and take a picture of these muppets tied up. I connect the phone to the internet and send the picture to the guy's social media page with the comments.

'I've been stupid by getting drunk and I'll not do it again because if I do, this kind crime prevention officer will break my other leg.'
I use the man's tee shirt to wipe the phone of any finger prints and deposit the phone back inside his pocket.

The clock inside my car tells me it's a quarter to one so I start the car and drive in search of some food. It's not long before I'm on the motorway and driving towards a service station signposted just three miles away. I pull in and park up at the furthest point away from the shop and dining area as I don't want anyone looking inside the car at the huge suitcase and possibly hearing Leroy making any noise.
The car park is fairly empty as its now Sunday morning and not many people work at this hour so I'm quite relaxed with leaving my car loaded with a body in the car park as I have my midnight snack.

"Quarter pound cheeseburger, fries and a strawberry smoothie please" I place my order at the kiosk. The guy behind the counter takes my money and proceeds to gather together the individual items before placing them on a tray for me to carry to the table. The dining area only has three other people sat down, all on separate tables and all in work uniforms; maybe from construction or road maintenance of some sort. I take a seat equidistant from the others with two of them in view in front of me while the third person sat just out of view to my right. I open the burger box and tuck in with biting a large chunk out of the burger while stuffing a couple of fries in the small gap left within my mouth. The taste is heavenly and I close my eyes for a moment as I enjoy the flavours and textures from this simple food.

I open my eyes and take a second bite of my burger while repeating the format of shoving a couple of fries into my mouth when I spot two police officers making their way over towards my table. The shock of seeing them suddenly appear causes some of the burger to lodge against my epiglottis sending me into a convulsion of simulated retching and going blue in the face. The officers notice me straight away and hesitantly speed up their pace to give me some assistance.

'Crap' I think to myself.
'I don't want them near me.'
I hold up my left hand in a kind of 'STOP' I'm alright signal while I take a big swig of my ice cold smoothie. Big mistake! The feeling of choking and then having brain freeze turns my face from blue to red with eyes bulging and a croaky voice I call out. "I'm alright thanks…brain freeze!" pointing to the smoothie.

The officers acknowledge they're happy that I'm alright and make their way to a table off to the side with their food. I sense their laughing to themselves as I quickly finish my food and exit the building to save embarrassment.

I climb back into my car and drive off in search of an industrial estate. It's easier to park up at this hour in an industrial estate as most business premises are empty which leaves the area quiet and not overlooked. I see a sign up ahead with the directions to an industrial estate just two miles away and soon find the entrance to turn in. The estate is fair to middling in size which means I'm able to find a quiet space to park up well away from any residential housing and the main road. I turn the engine off and sit in the quite for a few moments to compose myself. Leroy moans from inside the suitcase so I take this as a sign he wants to talk. I climb out and make my way around to the boot again. After opening the boot and the lid to the suitcase I notice the scrunched up body is covered in perspiration.

Being tied in a small cramped space with your feet tucked up behind you can bring on severe cramp which I imagine can be excruciating. Having a broken knee and shin bone certainly adds to the discomfort Leroy is experiencing at the moment so I know he's suffering right now. I know Leroy knows I'm looking at him because the cold air sweeping across his naked body would have told him that the lid of the suitcase has been opened. Leroy begins to moan. I lean in to the back of the car and speak quietly into his ear.

"Leroy, have you had time to think about the situation you're in?" I ask.
Leroy nods.
"Good, I'm glad to hear it. So here's how I see it. If you cooperate with me and tell me what I ask, you'll be a free man in no time. If you don't, well you know

my hammer likes to break things, so the choice is
yours."

Leroy makes a sound indicating his
acknowledgement. So I continue.

"Now listen Leroy, I'm going to take the tape off your
mouth and I want you to tell me the pin number to
your debit card followed by the pin number to your
credit card in that order. I don't want to hear anything
else except those numbers, first your debit and then
your credit card. If you lie to me I'll not give you
another chance. Do you understand?"

Leroy nods.

"Good lad." I peel back the tape off his mouth.

"2,4,2,3" Leroy chokes back the sobs. "7,3,8,9."

I quickly replace the tape.

"Good lad, now I'm just going to take a small
payment for all my hard work this evening and then
I'll let you go."

I close the lid of the suitcase and close the boot.

I climb back in the driver's seat and start the car. I'm
not too sure of the area so I decide just to drive along
the main road in the hope of finding a cash point. It's
not long before I see one next to a convenience store
so I turn the car into the next street and decide to walk
the short distance to the ATM. I insert the debit card
into the slot and enter the pin number 2, 4, 2, 3 and
watch as the screen goes blank while the machine
acknowledges the card. The screen re-appearing with
the options to check the balance or perform some
other function, I press the option for the balance.
£435.90 is displayed.

"Good man Leroy, I think I will pay myself three hundred from your current account for starters."
I enter the amount of three hundred into the keypad and press enter. The mechanism churns away for a few seconds as it counts out the number of notes while the debit card is ejected. I take the card and wait for the money to be dispensed. I hear a girl giggling somewhere behind me and I glance over my shoulder to see a red headed young girl dressed in a white vest top and short knee length frilled skirt and high heels staggering towards me with what appears to be her boyfriend.

The notes appear in the slot, so I take them quickly and put the money in my pocket with the debit card. I'm not too concerned about the two youngsters walking towards me as they seem nice enough so I insert the credit card into the slot and enter 7, 3, 8, 9 and await for the option to withdraw cash. I enter the numbers 3, 0, 0 and press enter.

"Cor that's a lot of money mister?" The girl behind me says.
I look round and see the young girl looking over my shoulder with her boyfriend standing behind. The boyfriend looked a little worse for wear with his spaced out look.
"Give us some money for a taxi home mate?" She asks.
I smile to the girl and return my attention to the ATM as I watch the credit card appear in the slot. I pocket the card and wait for the cash to be dispensed.

"Go on mister, give us some money?"
The money appears so I quickly grab hold of the cash
and turn around. The girl looks at the money and then
stares into my eyes. She's very pretty probably early
twenties with large breasts and slim waist. I take a
twenty out of the wad and hand it over to her.
"There you go, that should pay for a taxi for you."
"Thanks mister." She takes the cash and leans
forward and kisses me. It takes me by surprise to be
kissed by a young girl which is very nice considering
the awkward situation with her boyfriend standing
right behind her. She steps back and tucks the twenty
down inside her brassiere which is bursting already.

"Oye wot do you think you're doin."
The boyfriend suddenly returns to the land of the
living when the realisation eventually dawns on him
that I've just kissed his girlfriend. He steps around his
girlfriend to face me although he seems to be very
unsteady on his feet. I see his right fist clench at his
side before swinging back and around in a large arc
towards my face. The effect of alcohol and a long
night dancing has taken its toll on the lad as his
movements are tired and slow. I step back to avoid
the incoming swing and watch the clench fist pass in
front of my eyes as he misses my face and continues
on in its path hitting his girlfriend on the top of her
forehead.

"Arghhhhhh, wot are you doing, that hurt."
She turns to her boyfriend and delivers the biggest
slap across his face in retaliation to being hit. His
head twists to the side as his cheek takes the full force

before his eyes close and his body falls backwards like a fallen tree after being chopped down.
'Timmmmmbbbeeerrr' I think to myself as he crashes onto the pavement. She holds her left hand to her forehead rubbing the reddish area while staring down at her, now to be ex-boyfriend.
"Screw you!" She screams at him before turning away and walking off towards a taxi parked further down the road.

"Interesting evening." I say to myself.
I look at the lad on the pavement and decide he'll be alright in a little while when he comes round with a sore head and face. I make my way back to the car.

Leroy moans as I sit back in the driver's seat, obviously aware that I've returned.
"Good lad Leroy, you've paid me now so I'll let you go soon."
I start the car and drive off along the main road past the sleeping young man on the pavement in search of somewhere I can drop Leroy off. A few miles down the road I spot a temporary Police Station where the front desk is not manned twenty four hours but only during the day.

"Perfect" I say to myself.
I pull up just past the station and walk round to boot. The Police Station is basically a small brick building with one main door and a side entrance to a car park for two vehicles. I imagine it's basically used for a couple of hours a day to deal with local enquiries

whereas the main police station in town deals with the majority of crime in the area.

I open the boot and lid of the suitcase to see Leroy scrunched up tightly; the strain from being attacked and tied up is obviously taking its toll on Leroy as his body is shaking.

"Leroy, Leroy, I'm going to let you go now but I want you to remember something."

Leroy turns his head to listen to what I'm about to say.

"Leroy, if you ever commit another crime, either by selling drugs, stealing, or just being horrible to anyone. I'll come back for you and punish you further, do you understand me?"

Leroy nods.

"So I'm warning you now, live a good life and you'll be safe. Do anything horrible and I'll be back for you."

Leroy continues to nod in his confined space.

I lean over and tazer Leroy in the side; his body shakes and a small scream projects out from his covered mouth until he blacks out from the shear pain and exhaustion.

I pocket the tazer and cut his restraints freeing his arms and legs inside the suitcase. It makes it a little easier to lift him when I can pull his body out by his arms and legs. His upper body is dragged over the lip of the suitcase and towards the rear of the car until I can hook my hands under his armpits and drag him out. The front doors to the police station are about four metres back from my parked car so it takes a good ten seconds to drag him to the doors walking backwards. I prop him up against the front door of the Police Station and take out the marker pen to write my message across his chest which takes me a little longer that normal because his chest is so hairy.

'I hope this message shows up on the camera, it's like writing on a carpet.' I think to myself as the marker pen gets knotted in his body hair.
'This is ridiculous. I think next time I'm going to have to bring a wet razor with me.'

I pocket the marker pen and step back to take the photograph using Leroy's phone. I tuck the phone in my pocket and jog back to the car to retrieve the bag of rags and the petrol can. When I return, Leroy's body is slumped over to the side with his head nearly touching floor so I prop him back up again but this time tuck him in the corner of the doorway. I empty his clothes from the bin bag a few feet away and dousing the rags with petrol before finally jogging back to the car to collect the matches and put the petrol can back inside the car.

I'm all to aware that I need to get a move on before Leroy comes around but as he still has the tape across his mouth and eyes, I know he wouldn't see me if he did wake up.
I haven't seen any headlights from any other vehicles so far so I gather the road isn't a main through road so I relax a little knowing I've got time to ignite his clothes and remove the tape from his face. I strike a

match and drop it on the bundle of rags which ignite immediately lighting up the area and the entrance to a Primary school appears in view across the street which is reassuring as I know nobody there at this time of night so no-one would notice the flames outside the police station.

I step towards Leroy and pull off the two remaining pieces of duct tape from his face and drop them into the burning clothes. Leroy's propped in the right hand corner of the doorway facing the opposite direction, if he does come round in the next few seconds he'll only see the empty road ahead of him. I make my way off to the right past the burning clothes and to my car. I climb in and drive off in the opposite direction.

I continue along the road for about a quarter of a mile just to get away from the police station and the naked man in the doorway before pulling in to the left and parking against the kerb alongside a storm drain. I take out Leroy's mobile phone from my pocket and look at the photograph I took earlier to see if I can read the message I wrote across his chest.

I must have pressed something else on his phone because another picture pops up on the screen of what appears to be a model in lacy underwear. I press the arrow key to the left of the screen to get back to the photo I took when another woman appears wearing skimpy underwear.
'What! Who are all these women?' I think to myself as I press the arrow again to the left when another woman appears wearing similar attire.

"So, apart from selling drugs; are you a pimp as well? Either that or you have a lot of girlfriends willing to be photographed in sexy underwear?" I ask myself. "Well, I think the newspaper should know all about what you've been up to young man and I'm just the person to tell them."

I use the phone to upload the picture of Leroy naked outside the police station onto the internet before sending the pictures of Leroy and the girls to Jackie at the Liverpool echo newspapers with a brief message explaining what I think.
"Done." I say to myself.
I slide myself across onto the passenger seat and open the car door. I look down at the storm drain positioned right between the car and the kerb and drop the phone through the wrought iron grill into the depths below before closing the door again.

The clock in the car tells me its two seventeen so I drive off to my favourite rest location near Wrexham for a couple of hours sleep. I pull up in the remote lay-by and set the alarm on my phone to go off at five thirty so I can get home on time. Reclining my seat as far back as I can; which is nearly horizontal. I close my eyes and try to get some sleep. My mind quickly calculates the sum of money I've earned so far this week and I smile at the thought of having another one thousand six hundred pounds to add to the rest of my takings as the Mouthless Maniac. I drift off into a restful sleep.

I arrive home just after seven o'clock after packing everything away.

"Good morning Anne did you sleep well."

"Yes thanks, how was your night shift?"

"Not too back thanks."

She carries through to the lounge my cup of tea and places it down on the coffee table.

"So are you looking forward to the big game later?"

"What big game?" I ask.

"You know; the football game with Pete and all his policemen colleagues."

"Oh, I'd forgotten about that for a moment, thanks for reminding me."

I pick up my tea and take a sip.

'I don't believe it. Why am I going to play football with policemen who are trying to arrest me? This surely has to be the most idiotic thing in the world for me to do.
Have I lost the plot or something?' I think to myself.

"Michael's really looking forward to seeing his dad score a goal." Anne says.

I look up at Anne sat next to me and smile back. I don't know if she can see the panic in my eyes so I lift up my cup again and take another drink to break eye contact.

'Come on Chris, just relax. Nothings going to happen and it's going to be fine.' I think to myself trying to calm my nerves.

I place my cup back down on the coffee table.

"It would be great if I did score a goal but as I've not played for years, I'll probably miss kick the ball and give a goal away to the opposition." I say trying to smile.

Anne senses I'm nervous and grabs my hand to reassure me.

"Don't worry darling, I'm sure you'll be fine. They say it's like riding a bike. You never forget. Anyway Sticky Chris, I was informed by Pete that you were the best player at school so you should be able to run rings around these clowns." She says.

"I though I was going to play with police officers, not clown's"

"There you are; feeling more confident now are we?"

"Yes thanks."

"Great, now finish your tea and get off to bed for a rest. I want my man fit for his game of football." Anne says.

I down the last of my tea and make my way upstairs for a sleep until two o'clock.

Football with the Police

"Wakey wakey." Anne calls out over the sound of my alarm going off. I reach out from under the duvet and switch the alarm off just as Anne places a hot cup of tea down on the bedside cabinet.
"Did you have a nice sleep?" She asks.
"Yes thanks." I reply while rubbing the sleep from my eyes.

"What time do we need to leave here for your big game with Pete?" Anne asks.
The mention of the 'big game' revives my senses and I immediately sit up in bed with my back against the headboard. I pick up the hot cup of tea and take a drink before answering.
"It only takes about ten minutes to get to the wreck and the game is at three so if we allow a bit of time for traffic and getting changed, I think maybe twenty to three."

"I've packed some biscuits, crisps and lemonade for Michael and Debbie to have while you're playing and a flask of coffee for Jenny and me, just in case it's cold. Is there anything you might want, maybe at half time?"
"Have we got any still water as I think I'll be dehydrated by half time and maybe a chocolate energy bar to see me through to full time?" I ask.
"I'll pack a couple bottles of water and a chocolate bar now while I remember."
"Thank you."

Anne leans over and kisses me on the forehead before heading down stairs.

I slowly finish off my cuppa before dressing in my football gear.

"Well, don't you look the part all togged up in your football gear?" Anne asks as I walk into the kitchen to return my cup.

"Don't be fooled, I may look the part but can I kick a ball?" I ask.

"I'm sure you'll be fine." Anne says while taking my empty cup and putting it in the sink to be washed up later. She carries the cooler bag with the food and drink in through to the lounge and calls Michael.

"Come on Michael, we've got to go."

"OK mom, coming." Michael calls back from his bedroom.

We hear clonking and banging coming from Michael's bedroom before Michael appears at the top of the stairs with his coat and gloves and heads down to join us at the front door.

We all climb into the car and drive off towards the wreck. The traffic is fairly light so we arrive at the wreck ten minutes before kick off. I park up next to Jenny and Pete's car and we all wander over to the crowd of people milling around the recreation centre. As we get closer we hear Jenny voice call out to us.

"Chris, Anne."

Jenny appears from the crowd and wanders down towards us with Debbie at her side.

"Chris, Anne, we're so glad you made it, I was getting worried."

I quickly check my watch thinking we were late.

"The game starts at three doesn't it?" I ask.

"Yes, but they're just about to pick the sides for the game."

Jenny points towards the group of players on the pitch. I look towards the group and notice they're regrouping themselves into a straight line.

"Oops I'd better get a move on then." I quickly jog past the girls towards the pitch. One of the players sees me running towards them and tells Pete who turns around and beckons me over.

"Guy's this is Chris." Pete introduces me to the other players.

"Hello." I say feeling a little embarrassed, not knowing anyone.

They all say hi in reply and I quickly join the line of players as the selection take place. Pete and someone named Stewart stand to one side as the team captains to choose who'll be in their teams. Pete tosses a coin in the air while Stewart calls.

"Heads."

The coin rotates high in the air before falling to the soft grassed area at their feet and both men bend down to see how it landed.

"Tails, my first selection." Pete says as he picks up the coin and stands up.

"Right, I'll have Chris on my side."

I don't know whether it's because he doesn't want to embarrass me or he really thinks I can still play football. All the same I'm grateful. I make my way over to where Pete is standing and Stewart picks his first player. Once all the players are selected, Pete hands out to his team green tabards to put on over our tee shirts while Stewart hands his team yellow tabards.

"OK everyone lets get the game started." John Moore informs everyone.
Pete told me that John used to play semi professional football before he was injured and retired from the game. He now works at a local Junior School as a PE teacher. John is the brother of Robert Moore a Police Sergeant in charge of the police desk who is playing on our team in goal.

I nervously jog onto the pitch and look back towards Anne, Michael, Jenny and Debbie waiting on the side line eagerly waiting for the game to start. They all wave frantically towards us when Anne calls out.
"Come on Chris."
I take up my position on the left wing as they didn't have a natural left footer. Pete thought I'd be most effective up front as I can kick the ball with either foot, from what he could remember. I really don't want to embarrass myself or my family so I try to concentrate on reading the game and playing well.

John blows the whistle to start the game and Pete quickly passes to Dave playing just behind him. I make a dash forward past a midfield player in yellow and dart across towards the central penalty kick spot in front of their goal. I turn and look back towards Dave who still has the ball.

"Dave." I call out.

Dave spots my run and kicks the ball diagonally across towards me past two players. I step quickly to the left catching the ball between my feet; stepping left and right in front of the last defender before tapping the ball through his legs. I run round to his left and strike the ball hard with my left foot towards the right of the goalkeeper. The ball speeds across the pitch passing the goalkeepers outstretched hand, hitting the back of the net in the lower right hand corner.

"GOAL"

I hear John Moore call out. I turn to see the rest of my team members all rushing towards me to congratulate me on scoring. Anne, Jenny, Michael and Debbie are all jumping up and down on the side line cheering away. I give them a brief wave before the rest of my team members surround me.

"Well played Sticky." Pete calls out while patting me on the back.

"Cheers mate." I reply.

Other team members join in and pat me on the back.

"Well done Chris."

We all make our way back to our positions for the yellow team to kick off. The ball is quickly passed back to a midfield player while all the forwards make a dash forward towards our goal. The ball is kicked long and high past the front line of defence and one of their forwards collects the ball and makes a run for goal. One of our defenders makes a tackle on him and collects the ball; he passes the ball to a free player who makes a run into space. Seeing that we have the ball back, I start my run past a midfielder in a diagonal direction towards the corner flag glancing back hoping our player notices my run.

I see the ball being kicked in my direction from our defender and change my directional run to intercept the ball. I collect the ball with my right foot and with a diagonal tap with my left foot, head towards their goal again. Two defenders run at me heads down locked on the ball, they both jump in with a sliding tackle but I'm too quick for them. I lift the ball up and forward past them and make a dash towards goal.

The goalie comes out towards me and crouches to block any direct shot at goal. I fake a move to the right, my natural shooting foot and the goalie follows as he leans over to block the shot. Quickly taping the ball to the left I kick the ball past the goalie and into the net.
"GOAL." John calls out again.
Further screams echo out from my remaining team members as they rush towards me to congratulate me once more.

I'm not that good at football especially at my age, but I'm a lot better than these amateur footballers. I start to relax, knowing I'm not going to make a fool of myself now that I've seen the standard of football. I smile and wave to Anne and Michael as I walk back to my position ready for the yellow team to kick off again.

"Well done Chris, let's see if we can win big time. Just another eight goals and they'll be totally humiliated." I hear Pete call over to me.
I give him a smile and take my position. I don't know what it is, but I notice their team captain Stewart glaring at me from the central midfield position. I look away and watch the ball being placed on the spot for the yellow team to kick off. I glance back at Stewart who's still staring at me, which makes me feel a little uneasy.

The yellow team quickly kicks off and passes the ball back to Stewart in the central midfield position; he sees one of his strikers making a run down the wing behind me and kicks the ball high and long towards the player. I watch the ball float through the air over my head and quickly turn and give chase.

The man in yellow collects the ball and heads down the wing dribbling the ball past Dave in midfield and carries on towards our defender at left back, he slows up a little as our defender slides in with a tackle. He dribbles the ball past our last man and heads in towards goal as I catch up with him. He takes his eyes off the ball for a second to see where the goal which gives me the opportunity to snatch the ball from under his feet. I turn quickly and head back in the opposite direction towards their goal dribbling past two of their player's.

I pass the halfway line when three more players in yellow tabards merge on me from the front. I slow up a little looking for support from my team members when I see Pete making a run through the centre into the space left by Stewart who's also running in towards me from the right. I know I could dribble past Stewart if I wanted but as Pete's making a run for goal I kick the ball hard and straight to the left of Stewart into the space Pete's running into. A second later Pete collects the ball and with his right foot and after taking two more strides he blasts the ball past the goalie and into the back of the net.

"GOAL." John calls out.

Just then I notice a figure to my right leaping through the air towards me.

Stewart running at full speed jumps through the air towards me with both feet.

In that split second of seeing someone about to hit me, I try to jump back out of the way just as the studs on the bottom of his football boots crash into the side of my left knee. The force of the impact sends my left leg splaying out to the side rotating my body through the air as Stewart slides underneath me taking me out like a bowling ball against a lone pin.

"Arghhhhhhh" I hear myself scream as my body crashes down onto the grass.

The burning sensation and rush of pain is excruciating. I role over on to my side and pull my injured knee into my chest as the pain pulsates through me in waves. I force my eyes open and stare at the player in yellow next to me slowly get back on his feet. Stewart turns and looks down at me and smiles.

"What the hell was that?" Pete yells at Stewart.
"What! It's not my fault." Stewart walks away unperturbed by his dangerous tackle.
I see Anne and Jenny run to my side looking concerned followed by Michael and Debbie.
"Chris Darling, are you alright?" Anne crouches down and holds my hand.
"I'm alright." I reply through gritted teeth, holding my injured knee.
"I hope nothings broken." Anne says looking concerned.
"Let me through." I hear John Moore call out as he pushes through the crowd of spectators.
He kneels down beside me and examines my leg which is now red and bruised with grazed skin across my upper calf and knee. John feels around the joint and says.
"The good news is there's nothing broken; I don't think you'll be able to continue playing though."

Two team members help me up and carry me in a kind of chair lift over to the side line; they lower me down on a park bench while someone fetches an ice pack from the recreation centre.
"Here you go, put this ice bag on your knee. It'll keep the swelling down." One of the police officers with a yellow tabard says as he places a bag of ice over my knee. The freezing bag of ice quickly cools my burning knee joint giving me some relief from the pain and discomfort. He takes out of his pocket a

bandage and quickly wraps it around the ice bag and my knee to keep the bag in place.

"Just keep that on until all the ice melts and we'll check it at the end of the game." The officer says.

"Thanks." I tell him as he runs back to his team players standing in a group on the pitch.

Anne rolls up a coat and places it under my knee to elevate the injury as I sit sideways along the bench.

Jenny returns from her car carrying a cushion so I've got something to lean against to make myself more comfortable.

"How are you feeling?" Anne asks.

"Not too bad thanks; I'm just pleased that nothings broken."

"So am I, it really looked like he'd broken your leg." Michael and Debbie are staring at my bandaged knee looking concerned.

"It's alright Michael I'll be fine, really, don't worry about it." I give them a reassuring smile.

Michael smiles back.

Edward Pickles one of the yellow team players makes his way over to where we are sitting and sits down on the bench next to me.

"Hello, how are you?" he asks.

"A little sore, but I'll be alright."

"That's good. I'm sitting the rest of the game out to even up the sides as we don't have any spare players." He informs us.

"Sorry." I apologise thinking I've spoilt the game for him.

"No that's alright, I was getting tired anyway and I think I ate too much for breakfast which was making me feel a little sick. It can be a little embarrassing throwing up in front of your sergeant."
We all smile.

"Why didn't that player get sent off?" Anne asks.
"The one who tackled Chris, you mean?" Edward asks.
"Yes, I don't know all the rules but surely jumping two footed at another player must be a sending off offence?" Anne asks.
"You're right, it was a vicious tackle and in a normal game he would have." Edward says.
"So why is he still playing?" Anne asks.
"Because he's our sergeant and he can do as he pleases."
We hear the whistle blow to restart the game so we all turn around to watch the rest of the game from the side line.

I didn't really see what exactly happened because I was watching Pete make his run for goal but I get the impression that Stewart tried to take me out on purpose. If it wasn't for my quick reactions, he may have broken my leg for sure. I look over at Stewart as he runs past; he returns my look and smiles.

We continue watching the game and see Pete score another goal; the yellow team manage to get two goals back but the match finishes 4:2 to Pete's team.
"How are you doing Chris?" Pete asks looking concerned.

"Not too bad thanks Pete, well done on scoring two goals."

"You too, but I think if you'd stayed on for the whole match you would have certainly scored at least five or six." Pete says.

"Ten, I think" I reply.

"You're probably right. Anyway sorry for that tackle, Stewart normally plays pretty well."

"Don't worry mate, this ice pack is doing a grand job. I'll be up and running in no time."

"We're all going to get showered and changed and then a couple of pints in the bar, if you're up for it, and your drinks are on me." Pete offers.

"Thanks Pete, we'll meet you in the bar."

Pete follows the other players into the changing rooms while Anne, Jenny, Debbie and Michael help me hobble over into the bar. We find a table in the corner and I manage to prop my foot up on a vacant chair.

Pete comes in to the bar after getting showered and changed and joins up at the table.

"How's it going Chris?"

"Not too bad thanks; I think the pains slowing getting less and less now."

"Well you deserve a nice drink, I think. What can I get everyone?"

We all give Pete our order and he makes his way over to the bar.

Other police officers return from the changing rooms and ask how I'm doing to show their concern.

"I'm fine thanks." I tell everyone.

Stewart Grimm walks in and totally ignores me which really winds me up.

"Are you alright Chris?" Anne asks as she notices my strained expression.

I don't want anyone to sense I have a grievance against Stewart so I quickly smile back at Anne.

"Sorry, I just got a twinge in my knee, that's all. It's eased off now."

Pete arrives back carrying a tray of drinks.

"Here you are." He places the tray down on the table and hands out the drinks.

"Pint of lager for you Chris, a white wine for you Anne, red wine for my lovely wife and a couple of cokes for Michael and Debs."

"Thanks Pete I think I need this." I take a mouthful of chilled lager.

Pete lifts up his pint of bitter to make a toast.

"To Sticky Chris, most definitely the man of the match."

We all lift up our glasses and clink them together in the centre of the table before drinking to the man of the match.

"So, apart from getting injured, did you enjoy the game?" Pete asks.

"I did thanks and thanks for inviting me to join you."

"No, it was great, and you played really well."

"It must be, about thirty odd years before I played last, so I suppose I didn't do too badly."

"You played brilliantly Chris, we thought you we're great; didn't we Debs." Jenny pipes up.

"Thanks Jenny."

"You was the best player dad." Michael chirps up.
"Thanks son."
"Well, if you're fit, you could always play for us again next week?" Pete asks.
"Thanks Pete, if my leg feels up to it, I think I will play."

Pete and I talk about who's going to win the Premiership this season while I overhear Anne telling Jenny about our holiday plans.
"Pete, Chris and Anne are going on holiday in a week's time. You must be due some holiday by now; you've been working for ever without a break?" Jenny asks.
Pete looks to his wife and then to us.

"I'm currently working on something important at the moment Jen but as soon as we catch this criminal, we'll be free to take a holiday then."
"Well try and catch him quickly so we can go on holiday, and Lanzerote sounds really nice." Jenny says.
"It does sound nice and as soon as we can book a holiday, we'll go." Pete says.
"You could come with us; I think the hotel has a couple of rooms still available. We could all sit around the pool drinking martinis and get tanned together." Anne suggests to Jenny.
"That would be lovely, wouldn't it Pete?"
"Well let's see what happens, I still need to catch this criminal before we think of a holiday."
"Go on then Pete, get back to work and catch him." Anne says.

"I would do if it was that easy."

Pete helps me to my car and waits till I'm strapped in to the passenger seat. Anne climbs in behind the wheel while Michael sits in the back. We say our goodbyes and Anne drives out onto the main road heading for home. It's not easy hobbling from the car to the front door while leaning on your wife and an eight year old boy but we all make it in to the lounge. I hobble over to the armchair to rest my leg while Anne goes upstairs to run a hot bath for me to soak away the pain from my injury.

'I'd better pretend to ring in sick as I don't want Anne ringing Insigna Logistics later telling them that I cant make it into work tonight.'

I pick up the phone from the side table and hold it to my ear and in a slightly raised voice so Anne can hear me, I say into the handset.

"Hello is that Linda, its Chris Douglas here."

I wait a few seconds so it sounds like I'm having a real conversation.

"Sorry, but I'm ringing to say that I wont be in work tonight as I've injured my leg."

I pause for a moment before continuing.

"Yes, I should be back to work tomorrow."

Anne walks into the lounge from running my bath and waits for me to finish my telephone call.

"OK thanks, yes see you tomorrow night." I put the phone down.

"Your bath is ready for you darling, how did it go with work; were they alright about you not going in tonight?"

"Yes, they're fine. I spoke to Linda Harris who works in the office and she passed the message on to the gaffa. I could hear his voice in the background, he sends his regards and hopes I recover in time for tomorrow but said not to worry if I cant."

"That's brilliant, it's really nice of them to allow you time off sick as you haven't worked there long."

"They obviously think I'm worth it."

"Well I'm pleased you can rest up tonight; now let me help you upstairs so you can relax in the bath."

Anne puts her arm around me and assists me upstairs and into the bathroom.

"Do you need a hand undressing?"

"You're always trying to ogle my naked body aren't you, we'll I don't need help and you're not going to stare at my handsome physique." I jokingly say.

"Whatever!" Anne walks out of the bathroom and heads downstairs.

The water in the bath relaxes my aching body and soothes my painful knee. I try to relax in the water but my mind replays the tackle from Stewart over and over. I can clearly see him running at full pelt towards me with no intention of getting the ball. I remember kicking the ball straight through to Pete who was making his run, and in my peripheral vision I could make out Stewart jumping in the air towards me. If I'd waited a second later, he could have broken both my legs. How can anyone be so violent and aggressive; especially a law enforcement officer? It's just wrong. How can someone whose profession is the prevention of injustice do such a thing? The more I think of what happened, the more I become angrier and angrier. I wonder if he's one of those rotten apples in a barrel. I wonder if he joined the police just to abuse his authority. If he's as bad as I think he is, then maybe others know about him. Before I decide to take vengeance against him, I think I'll do a little bit of investigation myself.

I finish soaking in the bath and ease myself out. The water has done wonders for my injured knee; although my joint feels a little weak at the moment so I decide to keep the bandage on for support. It takes me a few minutes to wrap the two inch dressing around my joint and secure it with a safety pin. It brings back memories getting dressed with a bandaged leg from my stabbing so having to slip my jeans on with one leg straight doesn't cause me any trouble as I'm well practiced at getting dressed. I hop down the stairs to the smell of spaghetti Bolognese wafting through from the kitchen.

"Hi dad." Michael calls out.
"Hello son, dinner smells nice."
Anne walks through with a serving dish full of spaghetti and another full with Bolognese meatballs and sauce and places them down in the centre of the table.
"Hi darling, you're just in time."
I join Michael at the table while Anne fetches the garlic bread and a chilled bottle of wine.

"I thought as you don't have to work tonight, we could share some wine together."

"I don't like wine." Michael replies.

"Not you dopey, mom was referring to me."

"Sorry dad; mom, can I have some coke?"

"No problem, I'll just get you some." Anne walks back in the kitchen and brings Michael his drink.

"I gave Dave Smith a call while you were having your bath to let him know you've been injured at football. He said he would pop round later to cheer you up as you're not working. I hope that's alright? I just thought you could do with a bit of cheering up."

"No that's great; I haven't seen Dave for a while, so it'll be nice to catch up with him. What time did he say he was calling round?"

"He said around about eight."

We finish our dinner and relax in front of the television; Michael decides to play in his room instead of watching 'rubbish' as he calls it with his parents.

We hear a knock at the door exactly at eight o'clock. Anne opens the door to reveal Maria and Mario standing there holding a box of chocolates and an expensive bottle of champagne.

"Maria, Mario what brings you round our neck of the woods?" Anne asks.

"Hi Anne, we heard about Chris so we thought of popping round bearing gifts to cheer him up." They hold up the gifts.

"Come on in, Chris is resting on the sofa."

"Hi Chris, how are you doing?" Maria makes her way round the sofa and leans down to give me a kiss. I can say one thing about Maria; she does always look and smell nice.

"Ouch, that looks painful mate." Mario leans forward and shakes my hand.

"Take a seat everyone; I'll get some more glasses. Did you want the champagne Mario or would you prefer a lager?"

"Yes, a lager would be nice thanks."

"What about you Maria, did you want to stick with the champagne?" Anne knows she will, but poses the question all the same.

"Yes, thank you, the champers will be perfect."

"I expect you'll want a beer too Chris."

"Yes thanks, I'll join Mario in drinking a man's drink and let you girls enjoy the champagne."

Anne wanders into the kitchen with Maria to fetch the drinks.

"I can't believe it mate, you're in the wars again; what bad luck you're having."

"I know Mario, it seems that way. But to be honest, this wasn't an accident."

"What! Someone did this on purpose?"

"Yes, one of the policemen did it. I could see it in his eyes as he ran for me."

"That's terrible mate; did you upset him or something?"

"No, well I don't think so. I scored two goals against their side and before I knew it. Here he was charging at me like a bull in a china shop and jumped two footed on to my leg."

A knock at the front door interrupts our conversation. "Anne, Anne can you get the door for us." I call through to the kitchen.
Anne walks in with our drinks and places them down on the coffee table. She opens the door to Dave and Susan standing with flowers and a six pack of beer.
"Dave, Susan, come on in. Chris, Dave and Susan are here." Anne announces.

"Hi mate, oh hi Mario we didn't know you were here as well." Dave says.
"Hi Dave, Hi Susan." Mario greets our new visitors.
"We thought we would come round and cheer Chris up." Dave holds up the beer while Susan hands Anne the flowers.
"So what would you like to drink?" Anne asks.
Susan joins the girls in drinking champagne while Dave joins the men with a lager. Mario and I sit on the single arm chairs while the three girls and Dave squeeze on the three seater sofa.

"Chris was just telling me that one of the policemen jumped on his leg on purpose." Mario informs Dave and Susan.
"That's terrible mate; I hope you reported him to the chief constable at the station?" Dave suggests.
"That's alright Dave; I don't think it would make any difference as we were playing a friendly game."
"I don't call it a friendly game when someone tries to break your leg." Anne adds.

"Did you see who did it?" Dave asks.

"Yes, it was a desk sergeant named Stewart…"

"Grimm!" Mario calls out.

"Yes that's him. Why, do you know him then?" I ask.

Maria shakes her head in disgust and says.

"He's the pig that caused us grief when one of our shops was broken into a couple of years ago. He was just a constable at the time, but he's bad news."

"Wait a minute, I know that name…Grimm…that's it. I remember someone crashing their car into mine a while ago and this officer, I'm sure it was Grimm said it was my fault and made me pay the other guy money to get their car fixed. Do you remember Sue?"

"Yes that was about three years ago. We were parked on the side of the road when the car on the other side of the road careered into us. The woman in the other car said she would ring her insurance company and within minutes this copper appeared and tried to charge us with reckless driving. We could only get off if we paid for the damage to the other car."

"I don't remember that. When did that happen?" I ask.

"It was about the time you were made redundant and we didn't want to tell you about it as you had enough problems yourself." Dave replies.

"It sounds like the same dirty cop we've both encountered. If you want my advice; I'd keep my distance from him, he's bad news." Mario suggests.

"Thanks guys, I think I will. So who wants another drink?" I ask.

Anne fetches some more beers for the guys and champagne for the girls.

We change the conversation to something light hearted for the next hour or so before they all make a move for the door.

"Thanks for coming round, you've really cheered me up. I feel much better now."

"Not a problem, now you get better and stop injuring yourself. Talk about being accident prone." Dave says as he shakes my hand.

Sue and Maria give me a kiss and Mario pats me on the back.

"Rest up mate, and I hope you get better soon." They all make their way out of the front door at exactly ten o'clock.

"Well that was nice, having your friends call round, wasn't it?"

"Yes thanks for telling them. It was nice." I reply.

'*I thought it was interesting too that both my friends knew about Stewart and knew what sort of guy he was. Learning all about Stewart being a bad cop has definitely made my mind up. Dirty cops are worse than criminals. They exploit their trusted positions in society and need to be exposed for what they really are.*

I think Stewart has over stepped the mark more than once and need to be punished and I'm just the person to do it. We can't have dirty cops in positions of authority anymore. Its wrong and it needs to be sorted as quickly as possible.' I think to myself.

I start to formulate a plan in my mind.

"Hi darling, are you ready to go to bed?"
"Yes." I reply.
Anne helps me up the stairs to bed.

Monday 1st November

The sun shines through the curtain and wakes me up at eight o'clock. I see Anne still asleep beside me so I decide to make a cup of tea. I pull back the duvet from off my legs and slide both legs off the end of the bed and allow them to naturally drop until my feet touch the carpet. I rub the injured part of my leg which doesn't feel too bad; a little stiff but no undue pain to worry about.

'*That's a good sign*' I think to myself.
I ease myself up on both feet and slowly step forward on my left leg while steadying myself holding the window sill for support. I transfer my weight fully on my bad leg; which supports my body weight well enough and doesn't give me any pain.

'*Not bad.*' I continue to walk out of the bedroom to the top of the stairs.
'*Now here's the big challenge, will I fall down the stairs is the question.*' I think to myself.
Holding tightly on to the banister rail in case I fall; I step down the stairs concentrating on every step; I reach the bottom feeling very relieved not to have any serious problems with my legs. I walk into the kitchen and put the kettle on.

Waiting for the kettle to boil gives me a few moments to think.
'*So what shall I do today? I need to pop into town and pay some money into the bank and I need to find out where Stewart Grimm lives as I don't think it*

*would be easy to attack him while he's at work. If he
was a normal copper walking the beat, perhaps I
could plan something. But this guy works behind the
desk at the station; I couldn't exactly walk into the
main entrance and zap him behind the counter, the
rest of the police would be on me in seconds. There is
the problem of security camera's, I'm sure they've
some inside the station filming people who walk in
and out, so that's not going to work. So how am I
going to find out where he lives?*

*I suppose the other problem I could be presented
with; what if he lives with a large family or does he
live alone? I really need to get some more
information. That's it! If he's the desk sergeant,
surely he works regular hours each day, so his day
must start at nine and maybe finishes at five. If I can
get to the station before nine, maybe I'll spot him
coming into work in his car. Once I know what car he
drives, I could follow him home when he finishes
work and then I'd know where he lives. That's what
I'll do.*' I think to myself.

I finish making the tea and carry the two cups
upstairs.
"Wakey wakey sleepy head."
I place Anne's cuppa down on the bedside cabinet
and walk back around to my side of the bed and put
my cup down. I don't have much time so I decide to
quickly get washed and dressed. I take a slurp of tea
before heading into the bathroom for my usual
ablutions. When I return to the bedroom, Anne is sat
up in bed drinking her tea.

"Hi darling, you're up early." She asks.
"Good morning. I need to pop into town this morning before nine, if that's alright with you."
"Yes, that's alright
I quickly get dressed and finish my tea.
"As I'm back to work tonight I thought I'd have a sleep for a couple of hours after dinner tonight, so see you later."

I give Anne a quick kiss and make my way downstairs. After grabbing my car keys and keys to the garage, I step outside into the morning air. There's a slight nip in the air as the sun hasn't broken though the clouds yet. Breaking into a slight jog, I make my way down to the garages to fetch some money to put in the bank. I take out of the router box the four hundred and twenty pounds for my wages and lock up the garage before driving the short distance into town.

I find a parking space across the road from the Police Station so I can see the front entrance and the side entrance to the car park. I'm not sure whether Stewart will walk in to work or drive, so I need to keep my eyes on both entrances to the police station. I check the time and see its 8:27am.

'Not bad, I think I've made it in time.'
If Stewart starts work at nine, then he'll either arrive ten minutes earlier, or if he is very keen, I'd imagine him arriving no earlier than eight thirty. I look at the stream of traffic travelling along the main road; luckily for me, the traffic isn't too heavy at the moment so I'm able to see the drivers of each car

quite clearly as they approach the station. No, no, no not him. I can't see him in any of the vehicles.

I spot a figure walking on the opposite side of the road walking along the pavement in the distance. I try to focus on the face of the man, but can't quite make out who he is as he's too far away at the moment. Another car comes from the right; I turn my head to look at the driver; no, it's a woman. I look back at the man walking and notice he's walking in a slow leisurely fashion that gives me the impression he's a police officer.

He has that distinctive gait in his walk that only the police are trained to walk in so he could be Stewart; but I can't be sure at the moment. A lorry turns into the road in the distance and drives towards us heading in the direction of the police station. Quickly calculating the speed of the lorry and the pace of the policeman walking, I imagine they'll arrive outside the police station about the same time. I try to focus again on the walkers face but can't see him clearly as he has his head down looking at the pavement.

"Come on hold up you're head, you muppet." I call out.
The man carries on walking still looking at the pavement. I see the lorry catching up with him. I know if the lorry drives past him as he reaches the front door to the station; the lorry will block my view and prevent me from seeing who he is.
"Come on, come on dopey. Lift up your head, will you." I call out.

The lorry gets nearer and nearer. He's still got his head down. I'm willing him to lift up his head. He's maybe ten feet from the front door now and the lorry is twenty feet from him travelling at speed. I don't want to miss this opportunity as I could be sat here all day if it's really him.

The lorry drives between us blocking my vision just as he turns towards the front door of the station.

"NO!" I cry out.

I quickly open the door of the car and step out on the side street trying to see if I can see him as the lorry passes. It seems like forever waiting for the lorry to pass, then suddenly he's in view but I can only see his back as he reaches for the front door.

"STEWART" I shout out.

Oops; I don't want him to see me if it is him, so I quickly jump back in the car and close the door behind me.

Stewart turns around and looks down the street towards the person who called his name; he looks to the right and left but can't see anyone he recognises. I pick up the A to Z road atlas from the door panel and hold it up in front of my face to hide myself from view. I see Stewart look left and right again, before turning back to the main entrance and walking into the police station.

"Great, so you walk to work." I say to myself.

'*That's going to be easy to follow you home. I need to make some sort of excuse to Anne so I can return here for five o'clock tonight.*' I think to myself as I start the car and pull out of the side street and head for the town centre so I can do my banking.

I see Angela Green behind the desk dealing with a customer just ahead of me. She's a nice girl who was in a bad relationship with an idiot called Derek Pecheski. He punched her in the face the other week so I had to sort him out. I don't imagine he will be horrible to women anymore after I broke his right knee. The lady at the counter moves away leaving a space for me to do my banking; I walk forward towards the vacant counter where Angela is sat. Angela sees me and smiles.

"Hi Chris how are you?" Angela asks.
"Good thanks, what about you?"
"Fine thanks, so how's the new job going. Are they still paying you cash?"
"Yes the job's good thanks and yes." I hold up the wad of money.
Angela laughs a little but tries to hide it.
"Sorry, they could pay your money directly into your bank, you know?"

"I know, I think there's been some sort of hiccup on their accounts department or something. The person who normally does the accounts has just left and the new person doesn't quite know the procedure yet, so it looks like I'll have to bring in cash every Monday until they get their act together, sorry."
"No, that's alright; anyway its nice seeing you. How's the leg?"

"Great thanks." I hand her my money with the paying in slip.

"So have you seen much of Derek lately?" I ask.
"No not a peep. Why have you seen him?"
"No." I reply.
I'm glad Derek hasn't been round to see Angela as he was an idiot and as he hasn't been around proves the warning I gave him must have worked.

"Anyway, I've got a new boyfriend now." Angela says.
"That's nice; I hope he treats you well."
"He does, and he wouldn't dream of ever hitting me." She stamps my completed paying in slip and passes it back towards me.
"That's great, anyone I know?" I ask while picking up the slip.
"I don't think so; he's in the police actually. His name's Edward Pickles."

"Edward; is he tall about six foot three with blonde hair and plays football?" I ask.
"Yes, wow, do you know him then?"
"We played football together the other day. Did you not see me at the game on Sunday?" I ask.
"No sorry, I had to cook a roast dinner, cos my mom and dad came over to visit. I can't believe that I missed you playing football with Eddy. Did you score?"
"Two. And then someone took me out with a dangerous tackle, nearly broke my leg."
"No! It wasn't my Eddy was it?"

"No, it was someone else."

"Will you be playing next Sunday?"

"I should be, why?"

"I'll be there so I can cheer you on providing your not playing against my eddy."

"Hopefully we'll be on the same side."

"That's great, so I'll see you on Sunday."

"Definitely, see you at the game." I fold the paying in slip in half and took it inside my wallet before heading out of the bank.

'That's interesting, Angela going out with a policeman. There's another link to knowing what the police are up to if I can make friends with Edward as well as Pete. They say; you should keep your friends close and your enemies closer. There's a lot to be said about those words of advice. I don't imagine the police would tell me what they're up to, but they may let slip when they have to work late on a Friday or Saturday night. If I'm aware of a potential sting operation going into action, I could easily avoid going into town and so avoid being caught.

The last time they made a concerted effort to catch the Mouthless Maniac, they literally stopped every van they could see in town so I could just take my car out instead or even avoid the area by driving out to my lay-by in the country and rest up for the night. The important thing is not to take risks.'

I make my way back home and arrive after Anne has left with Michael. There's nothing I can do at the moment regarding Stewart as I don't know where he lives, so I make myself a cup of tea and rest in the armchair and think of a plan.

'*Before I could formulate a perfect plan, I'd need to know where he lives. If I follow him home, I could look for somewhere I could hide to catch him. It would need to be somewhere not overlooked and I imagine he's not going to go down easy, being a policeman. I really need to find somewhere where I could maybe attack him from behind so he's not pre-warned. If his house has a small wall or fence, I could hide behind that and get him when he enters his gate. What if he's got a big family, they would surely see me crouching in their garden. What if I used a wire to trip him up somewhere on his route; if I could do that where we're not overlooked, I could pounce on him while he's on the floor. I think that would be my best opportunity; hopefully, if he falls over, he would be too concerned about breaking his fall than thinking about defending himself. OK that's what I'll do. I need to get things ready first.*'

I make my way out of the back door and head towards my garden shed. I know the shed is crammed full of stuff; paint pots, lawn mower, deck chairs, old lamps, boxes old records and books stacked high on base cabinets along the right hand wall. Luckily for me the thing I need should be tucked away in a base cabinet near the front of the shed. I remember buying fence wire on a role a few years ago and I'm sure I didn't use all of it. I open the shed door wide so I can see what I'm doing. Crouching down I reach for the door to the cabinet when I notice something run across the top of the cabinet above my hand; I snatch my hand back.

'What was that?' I think to myself as the black object scuttles under a shopping bag containing paint tins resting on the top of the cabinet. I'm not really frightened of spiders, but this thing I saw scurrying across the top of the cabinet had a saddle on it; it was massive. Well maybe I was exaggerating a little, it wasn't that big, but it was the biggest spider I've ever seen.

My heart begins to pound inside my chest as I build up the nerve to reach forward and open the cabinet drawer. I stare at the base of the shopping bag for any black object to appear while reaching forward and grabbing hold of the handle. The spider reappears now at the base of the cabinet which make me jump. I pull my hand away while still holding the drawer handle; the cabinet shifts forward as I pull out the drawer. Paint pots tumble out of the shopping bag crashing down; one hits me on the back of my hand while another tin lands directly on top of the spider squashing it flat.

Still holding the drawer in my left hand; I stare down at the paint pot squashing the spider; imagining the spider to push the paint pot off him and run at me baring his fangs. The pot doesn't move.

"That was lucky." I say to myself.

I still feel a little uneasy, as I know there are more spiders in the shed, hiding away somewhere. I quickly reach inside the cabinet drawer and pull out the role of wire.

'I really need to tidy up that shed sometime.' I think
to myself as I place the drawer on top of the cabinet
and shut the shed door to keep the spiders inside. I
head back into the house and pick up my car keys. I
decide to put the wire directly inside the car as I don't
want Anne to wonder why I've got some wire with
me when I leave later on. I tuck the wire in the glove
compartment and return to the house for a rest.

Anne walks through the door at a quarter to one while
I'm napping on the sofa.
"Hello, I'm home."
"Oh hi, how was work?" I ask.
"Good, good. Jenny popped in this morning doing her
food shop so we had a bit of a chat. She sends her
love and hopes your leg gets better."
"That's nice."
"Anyway, Pete is off again on Wednesday so I've
invited them over for dinner if that's alright with
you."
"OK, will the boys be coming as well?" I ask.
"I don't think so; they're still finding it a little
difficult to get around with their knee injuries, so it'll
be Pete, Jenny and Debbie."
"So what were you thinking of cooking?"
"I thought of doing pork in cream mustard sauce, new
potatoes and asparagus tips and maybe baked
cheesecake, strawberries and cream."
"Sounds nice; you're making me feel hungry now."
"Have you not eaten yet?" Anne asks.
"I wanted to eat with my beautiful wife."

"Whatever! I think you just didn't want to make anything as it means getting out of the chair, you lazy sod." Anne smiles as she says it.

We pick up Michael from school and pop round to the supermarket to pick up the food we need for Wednesday. Anne buys extra ingredients for the cheesecake as she's never made one before and wanted to practice tonight.
"Don't forget we've invited Sally and Paul around tonight for a Chinese. I thought we could have cheesecake for afters."
"Oh yes, I nearly forgot about Sally coming over. What time did you invite them?"
"I told Sally to come round about six so we can eat at six thirty if that's alright with you?" Anne asks.
"Yes that's OK with me." it actually suits me fine because it gives me time to catch Stewart leaving work around five so I should be back home before six when Paul and Sally turn up. We both walk into the kitchen, I put the kettle on for a quick cup of tea and Anne takes out the ingredients to start making the cheesecake for tonight.

I start thinking what time I should leave to catch Stewart when he finishes his day shift.
'*I don't imagine Stewart will leave early as he arrived early. Running a busy desk at the police station would mean passing on all the important information and incident reports to the next person taking over from you, so I don't imagine it's a five minute job. If Stewart's shift finishes at five o'clock, I imagine the handover would take at least ten minutes so I don't*

expect on seeing Stewart leave the building until at least ten past five. If that's the case, I really need to leave home by five o'clock so I don't miss him.'

I give Anne her cup of tea while I walk back into the lounge to drink mine. I need an excuse to get back into town which in normal circumstances wouldn't be a problem. But having to leave at dinner time is going to be a little bit difficult as we're expecting guests this evening. I try to rack my brain on a plausible excuse to leave the house but can't think of anything. I look at the time and see its four twenty five already.

'What can I say? I could pretend my mother has called and has asked me to fix something. No, that won't work. Anne would tell me to do it later. What if I say my work has phoned and they need me urgently to organise something? No, that's pushing it, to expect me to call in at the drop of a hat and as they found cover for me when I couldn't make it last night; wouldn't make sense.' I start pacing the lounge trying to think of something to say when I get an idea.

Anne is still in the kitchen baking; so I make my way to the fuse box tucked in the corner of the lounge and open the cover to reveal the electrical panel with several fuses along a bank of connectors along the front of the panel. Underneath each fuse is a label indicating what part of the house that particular circuit is providing electricity to. Kitchen: Lounge: Bedrooms: shower: cooker etcetera. I don't want to disconnect the cooker or the kitchen as Anne would be furious; I remove one of the fuses and close the cover.

"Anne! The television's not working." I walk through into the kitchen as Anne puts the cheesecake into the hot oven. Standing in the doorway, I reach back into the lounge and flick the light switch on and off.
"Anne the powers gone off everywhere, is the cooker still on?" I ask looking concerned.
"Yes. Everything's working in here."
"I'll just check the fuses." I say.
I make my way back over to the fuse box and pretend to inspect the inside.

"Can you see anything?" Anne calls through.
I walk back through to the kitchen holding up the fuse. This fuse is blown and we don't have another. I could pick one up tomorrow but that would mean being without the lights in the lounge for tonight."
"We can't sit round chatting with Sally with candles everywhere. You'd better go somewhere and pick up a fuse before they get here." Anne suggests.
"I'll be as quick as I can, just order our usual from the Chinese and get them to deliver at six thirty to give me time to get back."
"OK darling, drive safely."
I grab the car keys and head for the door.

Stewart Grimm

There's nothing wrong with the fuse so I just keep it tucked inside my pocket. Anne won't notice that the fuse I replace is the same as the old one, so I don't bother going to the shop for a new one. I head directly to the parking space opposite the police station. I arrive about two minutes past five and park up with the car positioned as before so I can see the front and side entrance to the police station. I don't know if he'll walk out of the front entrance or decide to exit the building through the back door so I keep an eye on both just in case. It's not long before I see a policeman exit the building from the front door; I look closely to see if it's Stewart but realise he's wearing a different coloured coat. A few minutes later two more policemen walk out and I can tell neither one is him because they're too fat.

'I don't know how policemen can be fat; surely they must lose weight chasing after criminals all the time. When I think about it; I can't remember ever seeing a policeman run; they're usually walking or driving, so I'm not surprised to see a couple of fatties in the force.' I think to myself.

I quickly glance at the time and see its just about a quarter past five when a dark figure walks out of the main entrance of the police station and turns right. I recognise Stewart immediately wearing the same clothes that I saw him wearing this morning.

I start the car and pull out of the parking space and drive to the junction of the main road. I can see Stewart walking in the distance along the pavement before turning right just past a corner shop. The traffic is quite busy at this time as most people are heading home from work. A gap appears in the traffic and I quickly pull out and slot into the gap as I drive forward towards the turning on the right that Stewart had walked down. I indicate and slow up before the turning.

Stewart has crossed over the road and is now walking down the left hand side along the pavement away from me. I turn into the street and continue driving towards him when I realise what an idiot I am. I'm in a queue of traffic that's moving quicker than Stewart and I'll pass him in a few seconds which means losing sight of him. I desperately try to look for somewhere to pull over before I drive past him. I spot a vacant gap just ahead of Stewart on the left so I slow up a little and indicate to pull in. Stewart is leisurely walking towards the vacant gap and I'm catching him up quickly.

"COME ON, WALK A BIT QUICKER!" I shout out. I don't want to pull into the gap ahead of Stewart as he may recognise my car so I slow down to nearly a walking pace.
"COME ON, COME ON, GET A MOVE ON!" I continue to shout at Stewart while the stream of traffic travelling behind me crawl along bumper to bumper.

'Please don't beep your horns.' I think to myself as I
know Stewart would turn around at the queue of
traffic and surely notice me driving so slowly.
Stewart reaches the gap and paces along the pavement
as I turn in just behind him.
'BEEP, BEEP' a car horn sounds from the vehicle
just behind me now passing Stewart. Stewart looks
towards the passing car and waves; obviously
thinking it was someone who knew him. He carries
on along the pavement not breaking stride as I quickly
turn off the engine and apply the hand break.

By the time I can safely climb out of the car with
traffic passing next to my driver's door, Stewart is
about fifty metres in front of me and increasing the
gap with every step. I lock the car and jog around the
front of my car onto the pavement and follow Stewart
as he walks down the street. I know I need to stay
behind him at a safe distance; not too far away that I
lose sight of him and not too close that he may notice
me if he turns around. I expect he lives fairly close
bye as he walks to work so I need to keep my eye on
him just in case he stops and enters his house.

The street we're walking along is a typical city street
comprising of mostly shops, from furniture shops,
clothes shops, estate agents and takeaways so there's
several people already on the pavement making their
way home from work or just browsing the shop fronts
before they all close. I can see Stewart up ahead
walking past the estate agents so I quickly look back
towards my car just to get my bearing so I can

remember the route we're taking. When I look
forward again; Stewart has disappeared.
'What! Where has he gone?" I ask myself.
My eyes search along the street looking at everyone
on the pavement, checking the doorways and alcoves
to see where he may have turned off but can't see
him. *The street is really long with no side roads so
where are you? There's no place to go, unless he's
popped into one of the shops.'* I think to myself.

I speed up my pace to see if I can spot him. He was
about fifty metres ahead so I walk to where I last saw
him taking particular attention to the shop fronts on
my left in case he entered one of them. I pass an
Indian restaurant and estate agents and stop at the
bargain booze shop with the furniture shop just up
ahead.

*'I don't imagine he would go in there for alcohol and
I don't think he wants to buy furniture so where could
he be?'*
Looking further along the street staring at every
figure along the pavement hoping to identify Stewart
among the handful of pedestrians and not recognising
him; I notice the line of business beyond the bargain
booze shop are all set back.
'I wonder if there's a gap between the buildings.'

I sprint towards the furniture shop and see a gap
appear between the two buildings. I reach the corner
of the alleyway between the bargain booze and the
furniture shop leading to the next street and look
down through the gap. I see a figure in the distance

reaching the end of the alleyway before turning right and disappearing out of view.

"Great, found you." I say to myself.

I quickly jog down the alleyway to the far end and look to my right for Stewart. The street is mainly residential houses on either side and from what I can tell, there's no one in sight.

"Crap! Where the hell did he go?" I ask myself.

I stare up and down the pavements on either side of the street but can't see anyone.

"He must live in one of these houses on the right."

I don't want to aimlessly wander up and down the street just in case Stewart sees me and wonders why I'm walking outside his home. So if he lives on the right I'll avoid going in that direction. Looking back down the alley, I realise this could be the perfect place to get him.

'If I park my car at this end of the alley, I could attack him in the alley and drag him to the car under the cover of dusk.' I think to myself.

I make my way back along the alleyway to see if there's anywhere I could set up a trap to catch Stewart. The alleyway is probably four metres wide with bricked walls the length of the alleyway on either side. The bargain booze shop on one side and furniture shop on the other side of the alleyway have mainly brick fascia sides with a wooden door entrance to the rear of the buildings. The residential properties at the other end of the alleyway adjoining the backs of the commercial premises are again brick fascia with a doorway to the rear of their houses. There are a couple of plastic industrial bins butted up to the side of the building on the left and right of the alleyway.

'This looks good, it looks like the alley is not overlooked at all except from people walking past the entrance at either end. It's fairly dark along here so unless someone walks through the alley at the same time, they're not going to see anything.' I think to myself.

I look at the two commercial bins located half way through the alley and wonder if they're big enough to hide behind. They certainly look big enough. I walk over to them and crouch down behind one of them. *'This is perfect. I just need to find somewhere to set up a trip wire.'*

The bins are made of a hardened plastic with small trolley type wheels for legs so they could be pushed or pulled.
'I wonder if I could position one of the bins against the wall on the other side of the alley and one on this side, I could tie a wire around the legs of the bins to trip Stewart.' I think to myself.
I grab hold of the handle to one of the bins and push it against the wall; the bin moves very easily which concerns me.
'What if Stewart tripped over the wire and pulled the bins over? The sound of the bins toppling over could cause people to look in this direction which would be

dangerous. I really need something like a fixed anchor to be on the safe side.'

Looking down the length of the alleyway I spot a drain pipe running down the wall mid way down the alleyway just two metres from where the bins are located. I look over to the opposite wall and can't believe my luck; another drain pipe affixed to the wall almost opposite.

"I don't believe it, that's perfect." I say to myself. *'If I position the bins next to the drain pipes on either side, I could tie one end of the wire around one of the pipes at the right height and leave the wire on the floor ready to attach to the other pipe as soon as Stewart walks into the alley.'*

I walk back towards the end of the alleyway where Stewart disappeared and look left and right to see where I could park the van. Just to my left is a zebra crossing with chevron markings either side of it preventing me from parking next to the alleyway. I look past the zebra crossing and see the nearest place to park being about thirty feet away.

'That's a long way to carry or drag Stewart to the van and at five o'clock while people are making their way home, it's too risky. I've got to think of another way to get him inside the van without drawing attention to ourselves.' I think to myself.
"Right, I'm happy about the location, just need to decide on how to transport him." I say to myself as I

make my way to the other end of the alleyway and towards my car.

I reach the car having no more idea's how I'm going to get Stewart into the van without carrying him. I pull out into traffic and drive along Bridge Street to the end, turning left on Lower Road I pass Connaught Street on my left where Stewart lives and make a mental note of the name of street for when I have to return to park the van tomorrow. A few hundred metres further along Lower Road I see a sign for the hospital which gives me an idea. I turn towards the hospital and park up as close to the Accident and Emergency department as I possibly can in the drop off and collect parking area.

Climbing out of the car, I make my way around to the boot and collect a woollen blanket before heading off towards the main entrance to the A and E department. As with most A and E departments; they're thriving with people coming in and out. Some, holding towels to their heads, others limping being helped in by a relative, some in a wheelchair while others arrive in ambulances. I step through the main entrance door and immediately notice a waiting area to my right with around fifty or more seats for injured newcomers to wait until they can be assessed by triage. A small queue of people stand next to a glass partitioned room for those who need to be booked in by an elderly lady sat behind her desk.

I walk past the queue and sit down in the waiting area with many others who haven't yet been seen. I remember seeing people pushed around in wheelchairs belonging to the hospital in the past, so I'd assume there are empty wheelchairs stored somewhere for people who need them and I need one. A few seconds later I notice a young man walking through the main entrance pushing an empty wheelchair. He makes his way over to the far corner and deposits the chair alongside two other wheelchairs I hadn't noticed.

'Perfect' I think to myself.
Most people are bored in the waiting area having sat for at least forty minutes to be seen by someone. Some are reading magazines or talking to friends while some are staring at the walls trying to read the mass of information displayed on posters or leaflets.

'I need to pick up one of those wheelchairs without being noticed.' I think to myself.
There has to be at least twenty people in the waiting area so I'm sure someone would notice if I walked over and grabbed one of the chairs. I remember being told once that people generally notice other people who look confused or act strange or peculiar. If you don't want anyone to notice you, just act with confidence and authority. OK, here goes.'
I stand up and walk around the chairs in the waiting area and head over to the wheelchairs in the corner.

I lay my blanket across the seat and pull the wheelchair out from the corner. I look towards the exit doors I push the chair towards the doors trying to look as confident as possible while praying that nobody calls out that I'm stealing a chair. The automatic doors open ahead of me and I quickly walk through with the chair onto the paved walkway leading towards where I parked my car. The main doors close behind me and I haven't heard anyone screaming at me so I begin to feel a little better. Now that I'm outside, I'm hoping if anyone sees me now they would just assume I'm pushing an empty wheelchair to collect someone from a parked vehicle.

I stop the wheelchair at the side of my car and look around to see if anyone had noticed me. I can't see anyone at all, the area is clear. I open the boot and lay the blanket inside. It takes me a few minutes to work out how to dismantle the wheelchair, but eventually manage it and tuck the chair inside the car. I close the boot and climb in behind the wheel before pulling out from the drop and collect area and head home.

"Hello, we thought you got lost or something, it's been like ages since you left. What took you so long?" Anne asks.

"Sorry, there was a bit of road rage incident outside the hardware store, a guy reversed out of his space and bumped his car into another car just about to park. There wasn't a lot of damage, but the two guys were having a bit of a fight."

"That's terrible." Sally says.

"Oh hi Sally, have you been here long?" I ask.

"No, we got here about five minutes ago. Paul is upstairs with Michael. So what happened with the accident? Did the police turn up?" Sally asks

"No, they were shouting at each other for a while before they resorted to fisticuffs and then if finished when their wife's came out of their cars and persuaded them to stop."

"Well thank goodness for their sensible wives." Anne replies.

"I suppose so; it was funny thou. One woman was hitting her husband with her handbag to get him to stop."

"That's all very interesting but we've still got no light in the lounge. Did you get the fuse?" Anne asks.

"Yes, got it here," I take out the fuse from my pocket and walk over to the fuse box before Anne has a chance to see.

"Great, I'll call the boys down so we can have dinner now." Anne says.

I plug in the fuse and immediately the light comes on in the lounge.

"Voila!"

Anne fetches the Chinese food she had ordered from the Chinese out of the oven.

"Sorry everyone if the food is a little dry as we had to keep it warm in the oven while my husband took his time shopping."

"Sorry Sally. We're not that disorganised usually, its just one of those moments when things go wrong when you least expect it." I say.

"It's no problem really. Anyway thank you for inviting me, its nice to have the opportunity to have an adult conversation with someone." Sally says.

"Would you like a glass of wine with your food?" Anne asks Sally.

"Some white wine please, Anne, if you have it."

Anne brings two wine glasses through from the kitchen and places them on the table before fetching the wine and a bottle of coke for the boys.

"You don't want anything alcoholic Chris do you?"

"No, I'm fine thanks. I'll just have some coke with the boys."

We all tuck in to the Chinese food neatly laid out on a hot serving dish from the oven.

So what did you think of the cheesecake?" Anne asks me.

I take a big bite of the baked cheesecake, strawberries and cream.

"Mmmmm nice, this is delicious. Is there anymore?"

"Sorry guests first. Sally and Paul would either of you like another piece of cheesecake?"

"Not for me thanks Anne I'm full." Sally replies.

"Yes please Missus Douglas." Paul says.

"What about you Michael, would you like another piece of cheesecake?" Anne asks,

"Thanks mum."

Anne serves the boys another slice of cake and looks over at me.

"Well darling you're in luck. There's one piece left. The question is. Do you really want another slice as you're putting on weight around your stomach?"

"Excuse me! I do burn my calories off while I'm at work. Not like someone in this house chubby."

Sally looks a little shocked at how the conversation is going.

"Sorry Sally. We do have this banter going on all the time. He insults me and I do the same. We don't mean it really. We're a couple of jokers aren't we Michael?" Anne asks.

"What?" Michael looks at his mum with a mouthful of cheesecake.

"You had me worried there for a minute." Sally says.

"That's alright, you'll get used to us. Were quite normal; really."

"I'm normal, I'm not too sure about my wife. I think she's lost the plot if you ask me." I say.

Anne places the last slice of cheesecake on my plate and kisses me on the forehead.

"There you go honey."

After dinner we relax in the lounge for a while before I explain to Sally that I have to go to bed for a while as I'm working tonight. I thank her for coming over and make my way upstairs for a sleep while the boys go downstairs to join the adults. As I climb into bed and lay down; my mind immediately focuses on my planned future liaison with Stewart tomorrow.

'I should park on Bridge Street and wait for Stewart to arrive before heading down the alleyway to set up the trap. I don't want to set it up too early in case someone else comes down the alley before Stewart and trips on the wire. If I watch for Stewart to turn the corner, I should have about two minutes before he reaches the alley. That should give me enough time to attach the wires and hide behind the bins.'

I start to relax now that I've got my plan worked out in my head. I close my eyes and slowly drift off into a restful sleep.

The alarm wakes me at nine o'clock and I immediately reach out from under the duvet and switch it off. Anne walks in with a hot cup of tea for me and places it down on the bedside cabinet.
"Hello darling, did you sleep well?"
"Yes thanks." I quickly take a sip of tea.
"Sally and Paul really enjoyed themselves. She thanked us again when she left at eight and thought we were a little crazy but really liked us. She's so sweet."
"Yes, she seems a really nice lady. I'm glad she likes us."
"So, it's your last night at work and then you've got three days off."
I look round at Anne and give her a smile while thinking.

'I still need an excuse to leave the house tomorrow at five so I can attack Stewart. As I've just woken up, my mind is still half asleep so I can't think straight. Maybe I should forget about it for the moment, I've got all night to think of something.'
Anne leaves me to finish my tea and get dressed and heads downstairs to make a pack up for tonight.

I sit up and relax for a few minutes as I finish my cup of tea in bed.
'I've already made enough money for this week so I don't need to go out and attack anyone tonight. I'm

not sure on what to do while I'm at work, I could even afford to book myself into a hotel and sleep in a comfy bed. The problem would be when I arrive home in the morning looking wide awake; Anne would surely suspect something. I look at the time and notice it's already twenty past nine.

"Right, I'd better get a move on." I say to myself as I climb out of bed and dash into the bathroom to get washed.

I head down stairs after getting dressed and collect my midnight snack before heading out of the door and down to the garage to collect the van.

'I know the police have made a concerted effort to catch me on a Friday and Saturday night as most of my attacks have happened on a weekend. As it's a Monday night I don't imagine they're going to bother as it's a week day so I think it'll be safe enough to take the van out tonight.'

I open the garage and pull the van out before parking the car back inside the empty garage space. I open the side door to the van and climb in to the back to quickly change into my night time protective clothing. Having had to change most nights into my corset and shin and forearm guards, I've managed to get the time down to just three minutes which is pretty good considering the confined space I have to change in. I step out fully dressed and climb into the cab ready for my nights work.

'I suppose as I'm all dressed for action, I may as well take a drive around to see if there's anything dodgy

going on. I know Mondays are fairly quiet as most
people have been out over the weekend partying so I
don't expect to see anyone tonight. If the police stop
me, I could use the excuse that I'm looking for a place
to rest up for a while before moving on to my next
customer. I could open the back doors again to show
them the two rows of crisps boxes stacked in the back
of the van to prove I was legitimate.' I start the engine
and pull out from the row of garages and make my
way up the side road to our street. I turn right and
head for the town centre.

I drive up and down streets around Liverpool looking
for anything suspicious but as I expected, I don't see
anyone around. It might just be that I'm not altogether
focussed on catching anyone as my mind is still on
tomorrow and my meeting with Stewart. I pull over to
the side of the road and switch the engine off for a
while. I look up and down the street and realise I'm
parked in a more affluent part of town. The houses are
Georgian three storey town houses with wrought iron
railings at the front bordering pristine trimmed
gardens. I imagine the residents are all professional
men and women probably in their senior years now
all tucked up in bed. I close my eyes and dose off for
a while with my head against the side window.

<u>Tuesday 2nd November</u>

The sharp pain in my neck wakes me up and I look at my watch in the darkness of the cab to check on the time. '2:18am' the light from my watch face reflects back at me. I pull my head away from the window and rub the side of my neck to ease the pain and stiffness. I notice a wet patch on my shoulder from the line of drool hanging from the side of my mouth; I quickly wipe the dribble with my sleeve to dry my face. My mouth feels as dry as a bone and I find it difficult to swallow as my tongue seems to be stuck to the right side of my mouth.

'I need something to drink.' I think to myself when I remember the lunchbox Anne gave me containing the can of coke. I open the box and take out the can of coke.

The cold fizzy liquid revives my dry mouth as I swallow half the can in one gulp. I place the can down on the dashboard and pick up the ham and mustard sandwich. The last time Anne made me a ham and mustard sandwich she must have put half the jar of mustard on the bread because it nearly blew my head off. As a precaution, I lift off the top layer of bread to examine the contents.
"That's better." The underside of the bread has just a smear of mustard so I deem it safe to eat. I take a bite and glance out of the window while eating my midnight snack.

I look up and down the streets but don't see a single person. The pavements on either side of the streets are lined with cars parked outside their respective houses. There's something tranquil about looking at a city in the dead of night; lights reflect the outline of the streets while the houses mostly in darkness are peaceful. I look over to my right down a side street and see a figure all in black climb over a railing into the front garden to one of the Georgian terraced houses.

"That's not right." I say to myself.
"Why would you climb over a fence in the middle of the night, I wonder?" I ask myself.
I put the remainder of my sandwich down and finish off what's left in the can of coke.

'Now what should I do about this night time mystery figure.'
I'm probably twenty metres away from where the figure disappeared into one of the houses. So I decide to amble over there and investigate just in case they're up to no good. I grab my tazer from the glove compartment and step out onto the pavement. I slide the back door open and pick up the role of duct tape and two plastic ties from the box inside the door and tuck them inside my hoodie pocket just in case I need them. I don't imagine I'll need my gauntlet gloves so I'll leave them in the cab as I have my tazer with me. I close the side door and lock the van before crossing the road into Pearl Street where I saw the mystery figure.

I glance over the small privet hedgerows of each house as I pass in the hope of seeing where the mystery man climbed over the fence. I expect they would have damaged part of the hedge as they clambered through so all I need to do is look for a damaged hedge. I continue walking along the pavement examining each hedgerow when I reach the end of the street having not noticed a thing.

'Well that was more difficult that I imagined. Maybe I should look at each house as I pass and listen out for any noise.' I think to myself.
I start to make my way back along the pavement paying particular attention to the outline of each house; stopping for a moment to listen before moving onto the next house in the row.

I reach house number five and stop to examine the dark outline of the house in the hope of seeing something like a person moving or a flash of light from a torch. My eyes scan along both sides of the house as I've done with the previous houses. I don't see anything so I start to walk on when I hear a faint clatter.

'What was that? I'm sure it came from the back of number five.' I think to myself.
I listen again and stare towards the right of the house to see if I can catch the faintest of noises when I see a flicker of light escape from around the back of number five. It was only for a brief second but it was enough to persuade me to investigate.

I decide to follow my instinct and climb over the
fence where I can see a small gap in the hedgerow.
The top of the fence has small bayonet spikes spaced
out along its length sticking up two inches above the
top rail; with the fence mounted on a low brick wall
about waist height. I step up onto the base wall and
comfortably step over the low fence into the garden
while paying particular attention to the protruding
spikes. The thought of snagging my trousers on top of
the spikes could prove to be very painful for a man
and highly embarrassing having to explain to the
police why I'm straddling a stranger's garden fence in
the middle of the night.

I step through the gap in the hedgerow to find my foot
land on a paving slab. I look down and notice a bright
yellow paved walkway that runs around from the
entrance gate to my left to the back of the house
around to the right.
'That's handy. I can see where I'm going now.' I
think to myself admiring the illuminated pathway in
the moonlight.
*'This reminds me of the yellow brick road in the
Wizard of Oz. Oh were off to see the Wizard the
wonderful wizard of oz.....'* I begin singing the song
in my mind.

I make my way around to the back of the house
paying attention to the path and any overhanging
branches from a couple of Apple and Plum trees
nicely spaced in the garden. The trees block out most
of the view to the back of the house from the roadside
which is handy in this instance as I don't want to be

seen by any cars that may turn into the street. I turn a corner around the back of the house and immediately spot an opened sash window. I crouch down quickly so as not to be seen by whoever has broken into the house and focus my gaze at the opened window hoping to see evidence that someone has actually broken in and that the owner hasn't just left the window open.

I stare at the upper part of the window as burglars tend to break the glass near the locking mechanism so they don't have to reach in too far to unlock the window. It only takes me a second to see a small circular hole in one of the panes that has been cut with some sort of glass cutter and suction contraption allowing the burglar to reach in through the hole and unlock the window.
'Very professional' I think to myself.

I don't want to risk climbing into the house as I'm wearing my corset with the metal brackets sewn into it. The metal rods fixed on my shins and forearms could also easily catch against something giving my arrival away to the burglar. Looking through the window, I notice a faint light flicker across a hallway at the far side of the house.
'I wonder if the burglar has finished looting the house and is making their way back towards the opened window. If he is, I need to do something and fast.'

The light starts to get brighter as he gets closer and closer to his exit.

'What to do, I wonder? I don't want him to spot me as soon as he reaches the open window and as I'm crouched down on the pathway right in front of his exit he's bound to notice me straight away when he pops his head out of the window to see if the coast is clear. I really need to be on the other side of the window at the back of the house. I don't suppose he'll look in that direction as he'll probably go out the same route he came in.' I think to myself.

Staying in a crouched position, I sneak along the path towards the back of the house and position myself just out of sight two metres away from the opened window. I turn around and wait for the man to exit the building. I notice the light from his torch flash across the opened window, lighting up the fruit tree to the left of the path for a second before the torch is immediately switched off as he nears his exit. I quickly grab hold of my mask and pull it over my head and into position covering my face while taking hold of my tazer in readiness. I'm starting to feel a little anxious so I take a deep breath and calmly breathe out to settle my nerves.

'I imagine the burglar will pop his head out first to check the coast is clear before maybe passing out his swag bag and then climbing out himself so I'll wait for the sound of him climbing out before I make my move.' I think to myself.
I listen intently to any sound coming from the opened window and imagine the burglar looking out about now as I hear a faint brushing sound maybe from his gloves on the paintwork as he pops his head out. The

sound stops for a few seconds before I hear a rustling sound possibly from his clothes catching on the window frame as he steps out onto the pathway. I slowly edge my head around the corner until I can see the space outside the window.

A large black holdall bag is slowly being passed through the opened window when two arms appear holding the bag and lowers the bag down onto the path. The burglar's arms disappear back inside the room before his left leg reappears through the gap and steps down onto the pavement next to his bag. I don't want to move too early and catch him half in and half out of the window as he may collapse as I zap him and if he falls back inside the kitchen he could make too much noise. I decide to wait for the right opportunity.

I watch his upper body appear through the open window followed by his other leg. He crouches down to pick up the holdall bag with his left hand.
'Right, let's get going.' I think to myself.
I quickly step forward from behind the corner of the house and lunge myself towards the crouched burglar with my tazer outstretched in front of me. The tazer finds his left side as he's turned away from me and my left hand pushes on his left shoulder blade forcing him forward and down into a prone position. The burglar falls flat against the path still holding his swag bag in his left hand down by his side. The 300,000 volts quickly surge through him and I feel his body shake and jerk like a frantic fish trying to get back into water. I continue to press the tazer into his side

until his body becomes limp and motionless. I stand up and look down at the man still clutching his bag and think to myself.
'That went well'

I tuck the tazer back inside my hoodie pocket and take out the two plastic ties. I use one to tie the burglar's hands behind his back and the other to secure his ankles together before tearing off a strip of duct tape to cover his eyes. The burglar is wearing a black beanie hat that covers his hair and ears so it's easily enough to place the strip of tape across his eyes just under the hat. I tear of a second strip and place it over his mouth before putting the tape back inside my pocket. Looking down at the body on the ground, I think to myself.

'The van's at the end of the street and I need to put him in the back of the van. It's going to be too risky to carry him all that way so my best option would be to bring the van closer. I don't suppose he's going anywhere at the moment with his hands and feet secured so I think it would be easier just to drive the van down the street and park outside.'

I put the mask back inside the hood of my hoodie and walk back around the pavement to the front gate. The gate opens smoothly which I'm happy about as I step down onto the pavement. The street is quiet and all the lights to the buildings are off so I assume all the residents are still asleep. I walk the short distance to the end of the street and cross over to the van.

I didn't see anyone as I walked back to the van so I consider the area to be safe enough to drive the van to the front gate of number five.

'I know elderly men and women tend to frequent the bathroom all hours of the night so it wouldn't surprise me if the residents in at least one of the houses in the street are using the bathroom right at this moment. If I drove into the street while an elderly resident is wandering through his house, no doubt in the nude and I don't want to even go there, imagining a naked old person. But now that I've thought about it, it's difficult to get rid of the images in my mind.

Arghhhhh. Anyway, if they see the light from a vehicle drive into their street at this hour, they would automatically look out and notice me double parked. I just think it would be wise to keep the revs low and the lights off to avoid anyone seeing me.'

I start the engine and drive the van towards the entrance to the street before taking the engine out of gear and freewheeling the short distance to number five. I stop the van between two parked cars so the side door is accessible between the parked vehicles. I apply the hand break and make sure the interior light is switched off before quietly opening the door to the cab and climbing out. I walk around the van and open the side door as quietly as possible before walking through the front gate to number five and making my way around the house to the burglar still motionless next to his bag.
'*What to do*' I think to myself.

'It's wrong to take the bag with me as I expect most of the contents would belong to the owners of the house.'

I pick the bag up and pass it back through the opened window and drop it on the floor next to a washing machine.

"There you go, you've got yourself a new bag with some equipment inside as compensation for your window." I say quietly.

I grab the burglar under his armpits and rotate his body over onto his side and then onto his bottom as I lift his upper body into a seated position. I crouch down beside him and wrap my right arm around his back while my left hand grabs his belt around his waist. In one swift movement I lift him up and throw his upper body over my right shoulder so he's nicely positioned in a shoulder lift. The man doesn't seem to be too heavy and from his youthful skin only seems to be in his early twenties. I carry him along the path to the front gate and out onto the pavement. I turn quickly to check the coast is still clear before stepping through the gap in the parked cars to the side door of the van where I lay him down in the back of the van.

I look again down the street checking for any movement but can't see anyone. I start to feel a little better now that I'm back at the van but I know I'll feel much better once we've driven away from here. I step inside the van and lift the burglar up so he's sat on the workbench. I attach his feet to the karabiner positioned by his ankles and quickly step around him and attach the other karabiner to his wrists on the opposite side of the workbench. I step out of the van and pull on the end of the rope which stretches the burglar over the workbench into an agonising arched position. I tie off the rope securely and close the side door concealing my victim inside.

I make my way around the van to the drivers door and climb in. The engines still running at a tickover pace so I put the van in gear and pull away forward along Pearl Street at a crawl until I feel were at a safe distance away before turning the lights back on. I reach the main road again and see a sign for an industrial estate a few miles from here so I head in that direction as I need somewhere quiet and secluded to teach my burglar a lesson. It's not long before I turn into the industrial estate on my right and I drive deeper into the estate in search of somewhere to pull over. I stop outside a pallet manufacturer on my left and what appears to be a scrap metal merchant on the right with no other businesses in sight.
'This looks a good enough place to stop.' I think to myself.

The clock in the van tells me it's nearly three o'clock in the morning.
"I think its time to re-educate this guy about changing his occupation to something honest." I say to myself.
I open the door and climb out into the cold night air. I stop and listen for any other sounds but can only hear the faint sound of the occasional car travelling along the main road in the distance. I notice the street lights on the industrial estate are spaced out quite a bit, looking left I see one light about a hundred metres

away and to my right the next street lamp about eighty metres away leaving me parked up in a relatively dimly lit area. Not that it matters to me as I don't need a lot of light to do what I need to do anyway.

I slide open the door to the back of the van and notice my burglar friend wriggling from side to side trying to free themselves from the plastic tie restraints. I step inside the van and pick up the hammer. "Naughty naughty naughty; you know its wrong to steal from others and because you've committed a crime you're going to be punished." I say to the man arched over the bench. His body stops for a second as he listens to my voice.
I lift the hammer up and smash it down on his right knee.
'Crack' the kneecap shatters from the blow of the hammer and the guy squeals under his restraint and blacks out. I put the hammer back inside the box and feel inside his pockets for his wallet.

I find his car keys in his front right pocket and nothing in his left hand pocket so I reach around him and check his back pockets which are also empty.
'That's unusual, he's got no ID or Drivers licence, no credit or debit card; nothing except his car keys.' I think to myself.
"This is not good, how are you going to pay me when you don't have any money or bank cards on you." I say to myself.
'What if he's left his money and bank cards in his car? I could try and persuade him to tell me what car

he's driving and go back and retrieve a bank card or money later. So as he's out cold and not wriggling around, I'll use this time to cut his clothes off.'

I open a bin liner and hang it on the internal handle of the door to put his clothes in for burning later. I pick up the scissors from the box and slip one leg of the scissors inside the hem of his trousers and begin to cut all the way up the side of his trousers to his waist band. I continue cutting though the left side of his jumper and straight down his left arm to his wrist.

'*Great, that's one side done*' I think to myself. I step around him and repeat the process of cutting up his right leg past his waste band and down the length of his right arm to his wrist. The bottom half of his clothes fall away from his body and dangles down over the work bench. I grab a hold of the clothes with both hands; I pull them out from under the burglar lying across his clothes.

I roll the rags up into a ball and drop them inside the bin liner and turn back towards the burglar who's still unconscious. I grab the top layer of clothes and pull them off his body, bundling them up and dropping them inside the bin liner with the bottom half of his clothes when something strange catches my eye.

I stare at the guy's chest in amazement at seeing a white lacy bra.
'*Why would someone be wearing girl's underwear? He must be gay or a cross dresser or something. Not*

*that I'm bothered what people do but it's the first time
I've actually seen one in person.'* I think to myself.
*'I do find it a little strange for a burglar to wear
women's underwear while they're out robbing other
people's houses. It's kind of perverted if you ask me.
What's the world coming to, when we not only have to
contend with regular burglars but now perverted
burglars as well.'*

I cut the two vertical straps over the shoulders and
slide the scissors under the bra strap between the cups
and cut the fabric. The brassiere drops to the floor of
the van revealing small fleshy mounds with erect
nipples.

I still can't believe what I'm seeing. The light in the
van is subdued from its small internal light source and
is not helped from the darkness outside the van. I lean
down towards the perfectly formed white mounds
wondering if they're real or not.

*'They look like breasts but then again they may well
be pecs from someone who works out in the gym.'* I
think to myself.
I notice he's still got his beany hat on so I crouch
down beside him and pull off the hat hoping it would
tell me something. The man's short dark hair hangs
down from his head.
I stand up and stare back at his pecs.
*'If they're breasts they'd be soft and not firm like a
man's chest.'*

I reach out my hand and feel one of the breasts and immediately snatch back my hand realising how soft the flesh felt.

'You've got to be kidding, this cant be right. Wait a minute, what if these are man boobs? That would explain everything.' I think to myself.
'Normally man boobs are found on people who are overweight or elderly and as this guy is neither he must be a woman.'

I know the only way to definitely confirm whether a person is a man or woman would be to check to see if they have a penis or not. The idea of staring at a man's penis does not appeal to me but I know I have to do it to be a hundred percent sure.

As the burglar is arched over the workbench with his groin area positioned low down over to the left near the front of the van it's a bit difficult to see. I step around him and lean over to see the top of his legs and notice the small white cotton briefs lying over the small raised mound between her legs. The confirmation of not seeing a penis knocks me for six causing me to stumble against the side panel in the van.

'Crap! Crap! Crap!' I think to myself.
'There's one thing attacking a man, but attacking a woman is just not right.'
I step out of the van and slide the side door closed before climbing back into the cab.
"What the hell am I going to do now?" I ask myself.

I feel guilty enough with breaking her leg and now that she's nearly totally naked arched over the workbench in the back of the van is causing a deep feeling of remorse to wash over me.

'This is so wrong. This is so, so wrong' I keep thinking to myself.

I close my eyes and bury my head in my hands thinking.

'Please be a dream; please let me wake up next to my wife.'

Suddenly the reality of the situation dawns on me.

"Wait a minute, I'm thinking about this all wrong." I say to myself.

'She's a woman but that shouldn't matter? When I decided to stop crime in the area; I didn't decide only to attack men. My intentions were to stop all criminals. If woman commit a crime; they're just as bad as a man committing a crime; both should be taught a lesson. It's the same in the judicial system; just because someone is male or female, shouldn't matter.

Burglary is burglary whether it's been performed by a man, woman or child, it's all the same so I shouldn't feel bad about re-educating a woman just because she's a woman. I don't like hurting anyone but if I want them to stop committing crimes, I have to teach them a lesson no matter who they are.

'The reality of it all is I just don't like hurting women.' I think to myself.

'I wouldn't ever dream of hurting a woman and the fact is; I've never hurt a woman in my life; until now.'
The realisation that I've got an injured woman tied up in the back of the van is making me feel physically sick.
"Come on Chris, stop dwelling on what I can't change." I say to myself.
'So let me think this through.' I think to myself.
'What am I to do, now that I've destroyed almost all her clothes?'

"She can't wear them now and I can't exactly give her my clothes." I say to myself trying to talk through a plan.
"I can't exactly reverse what I've already done, so that's not an option."
'I think the first thing I need to do is to purchase some clothes for her so she's warm and decent. And then what?'

"I'm not prepared to hurt her anymore so there's no point in trying to locate her car to get payment out of her as I originally intended. So that just leaves me with one option to let her go; but how do I go about it?" I ask myself.

'I don't like the idea of dropping her off naked like my other victims because she would be defenceless against perverts living in the area and I would hate to leave her vulnerable and susceptible for abuse. So that just leaves dropping her off somewhere safe'.
"Before I do any of that, I just need to do one thing first before I forget." I say to myself.

I step back out of the van and walk around to the side door again and open it. I climb into the back and pick up the marker pen from the box.
'You're still a burglar and the police need to know who you are' I think to myself.

I look down at her white fleshy mounds with my marker pen poised. Its one thing to write on a flat surface; but when the surface is undulating; it takes you a second to decide where and how to start so that your writing is legible. I press the tip of the marker pen down on the left side of her right breast and begin to write across the upper part of her breasts just above the nipples.

'Steal again and I will come back for.' I realise I've run out of space when I reach the right side of her left breast.
'I didn't do that very well and it doesn't look right without the word 'You' at the end' I think to myself.
I can't exactly rub permanent marker pen ink out; so I decide to fit the word 'You' in between her cleavage so the sentence is grammatically correct.
I put the permanent marker pen back in the box and close the back up.

I need to get some clothes for her before I release her so I decide to drive in search of a Tesco's twenty four hour store. I find one and park up near the entrance but far enough away from other vehicles so no one would hear moans coming from the back of the van. I head into the store and pick up a track suit top and a pair of football shorts and pay for the items at the checkout. The checkout girl gives me a strange look as it's an odd time to buy clothes.

"Playing football tomorrow and cant find my kit; couldn't sleep!" I say to her.

The lady smiles at my explanation and takes the cash for the items.

I drive to the nearest hospital and pull into the car park near the Accident and Emergency. I open the back door to the van and climb in with the shorts and top. I lean forward to the girls face and breathe in her ear. She squirms and moans in anticipation of what could happen to her.

"I'm going to let you go now but if you ever commit another crime, I'll come back for you and break something else; do you understand me?" I ask.

The girl nods.

I tazer her in her side and watch her body shake as the 300,000 volts rush through her causing her muscles to contract and relax in quick succession. I hate doing this to this vulnerable girl but I can't think of any other way. I hold the tazer to her side until she passes out.

I need to be quick before she gains consciousness so I cut her restraints and lower her down on the floor of the van. I slip each foot through the leg holes in the short and pull the shorts up around her waist. I lift up her head and shoulder into a seated position and slip the tracksuit top over her head; after feeding her arms through the sleeves, I pull the waist down to cover her upper body. I pull off the tape from her mouth and eyes and carry her towards the A and E department where I prop her up next to the doors before quickly heading back to the van and drive off.

I'm hoping someone will see the girl quickly and if not, she should be able to crawl through the front doors to the A and E to get assistance once she regains consciousness. I'm sure the hospital staff would notice the writing on her chest and notify the police, so she should be caught for all the burglaries she's committed in the past. Hopefully too, my little warning might persuade her to live a good life from now on.

I drive the van away from Liverpool towards my favourite lay-by near Wrexham when I remember the bag of cut up clothes in the back. I pull over in the next available lay-by and burn her clothes at the side of the road before continuing on to Wrexham.
I pull in to the lay-by and turn the engine off as I've done in the past. The quiet tranquil surroundings of the countryside eases away the stress and strains of the night making me feel totally relaxed. I pick up my half eaten sandwich and finish it off alongside the chocolate bar Anne gave me. I set the alarm for my return home in the morning and lie down in the cab with my feet up on the passenger door arm rest. I close my eyes and drift off dreaming of the girl naked arched over my workbench.

Attacking a Police Officer

My alarm wakes me up in the darkness of the countryside. I sit up and rub my eyes to clear away any sleep left in them. The condensation on the glass forms a curtain of mist closing off the outside from view. I wipe away a small patch of glass so I can look out at the sky. A faint hue shimmers across the sky as the morning sun tries to appear far below the horizon. I think back to the last few hours and my encounter with a female burglar; the very thought of hurting a woman is totally alien to me and I wish never to experience it again. Maybe the news of a female burglar being apprehended by the mouthless maniac might even deter other women from breaking the law in the future; I really hope so.

I turn the engine on and wait for the heater in the van to clear the windscreen of moisture before driving off out of the lay-by heading for home. Driving along the single country roads affords me time to think of the opportunity I'll have to get my revenge on Stewart later on today. When I recall to mind, the moments after I passed the ball to Pete and seeing Stewart's shadowy figure running at me from the side fully determined in causing me the greatest of injuries makes me so angry.

'Why would a so called law enforcement officer do such a thing? The way he refused to apologise and totally ignored me when others apologised for his bad behaviour just confirms to me what a bad person he is. He deserves to be punished and I'm not going to

feel any regret about hurting you Mister Stewart Grimm.' I think to myself.

I run through in my mind what I hope to achieve later on when I catch him down the alleyway. I try to imagine where I need to be while I wait for him to arrive and where I should hide myself behind the industrial bins. I imagine tying off the wire across the alleyway so that it's positioned just at the right height to cause Stewart to stumble to the ground. I see myself rushing out from behind the bins and jumping onto Stewarts back pinning him to the ground as I jab the tazer into his neck. It all sounds like a perfect plan and I start to feel a little more confident knowing that I've covered all the bases. I smile to myself feeling much better now that I know what I'm going to be doing later. I turn the radio on in the cab and tune in to classic fm to chill out.

I park the van next to my garage and change back into my normal clothes before driving my car out of the garage and parking the van back inside out of view from others. I lock up everything and make my way up the side road for home.

"Good morning Anne, I'm home."

Anne walks through from the kitchen with a cup of tea for me and places it down on the dining table.

"How was your night?" she asks.

"Good thanks, what about yourself, did you sleep well without me?"

"Yes, I did; I do like it when you're at work as I sleep very well having the bed all to myself. But I do like it when you're home because you keep me safe and warm at night."

"Well I'm glad to hear it. So you don't miss me for anything else then?" I ask.

"You are good at fixing things."

"And?"

"Oh yes, you're good in bed."

"That's what I like to hear"

"Yes, you don't snore. So you don't wake me up like some husbands."

"What do you mean; some husbands. How many husbands have you had?"

"Oh I was just reading about it in this free magazine that was posted through the letterbox"

"Well that can go straight in the bin."

"No it's good; anyway it describes you as a perfect husband."

"OK you can keep it then."

"So what do you want to do today as you've finished your shifts for the week?"

"I don't know. I thought I'd have a couple of hours sleep until lunchtime if that's alright, then spend the afternoon with my beautiful wife when she gets back from work."

"That sounds nice. I love you." Anne says.

I finish drinking my cup of tea before heading upstairs for a couple of hours sleep. It takes me a little while to relax because my mind is preoccupied with my plan to attack Stewart. I hear the front door slam shut as Anne leaves the house with Michael; which distracts my thoughts from thinking of Stewart.

Eventually I manage to drop off into a restful sleep within the hour.

I hear the bang of the door again as Anne walks in after returning from work.

"Hello I'm home." Anne calls up the stairs to me.

I quickly jump out of bed and slip my trousers and tee shirt on before wandering down the stairs to meet her.

"Hello darling, did you sleep in?" Anne asks.

"No, no I've been awake for ages."

"Sure you have; so why is your tee shirt on inside out and back to front?"

I look down at the label sticking out just under my chin.

"It's the new fashion don't you know."

"Of course it is." Anne shakes her head and looks up to the heavens.

"OK you sussed me out, I must have been tired. Anyway so what's for lunch?" I ask.

Anne and I relax during the afternoon watching television before I need to set off and collect Michael from school. A cooking program comes on television where two celebrities have to bake a cake in a bake off challenge. One of them tries a chocolate orange and brandy sponge cake while the other bakes a lime and lemon cheesecake. While watching them prepare their cakes; an idea pops into my head of what I could say to Anne later when I need to leave the house. I check the time and see its time to pick up Michael from school.

"I'll go and collect Michael if you want; you may as well stay here and rest." I say to Anne.

"Well thank you, so see you in a little while."
I collect the car keys and head out of the door.

I drive the car to the school and notice Jenny standing near the school gates for Debbie to appear so I decide to join her. I park the car in my usual spot and wander down towards the main entrance.
"Hi Jenny."
"Hi Chris how are you, how's your leg after the football?"
"It's alright thanks."
"We were really worried when we saw what happened, I thought Stewart had broken your leg."
"I did too at the time; but hey, as you can see I'm all better now. Anyway that's what you get when you play a contact sport like football. It's all part and parcel of the game."

I want Jenny to think I don't have a problem with Stewart because when I do sort him out, I don't want anyone saying.
'Oh yes, Chris was really angry at Stewart for trying to break his leg.'
It's much better to appear not to hold a grudge so when the police start looking for whoever attacked Stewart. They won't be looking in my direction.

"It looks a bit too rough for me, but if you guy's like playing then that's good. So will you be playing next week?" Jenny asks me.
"Too right, I really enjoyed it."
"That's great; Pete really enjoyed having you play with him again after all these years. The problem is;

next week the other team will want you to play for them now that they know how good you are."
We both laugh.
"So what's Anne cooking for us tomorrow?" Jenny asks.
"I can't remember, but whatever it is. I'm sure it'll be edible; I think."
"Chris you're terrible, I'm sure it will be lovely."
Debbie and Michael walk out together and head over to us.
We say our goodbyes to Jenny and Debbie before heading back to the car.

'I'm glad I had the opportunity to see Jenny today; seeing me fit and well will add credulous to my amicable relationship with Stewart. I know at some point Jenny may mention it to Pete that she saw me and he's bound to ask how I was. I definitely don't want Pete to think that I have a grievance with Stewart especially just before I attack him.'

"So did you have a nice time at school Michael?"
"Yes dad."
"Did you do anything interesting?"
"We learnt about what happens to criminals.
"That's interesting, so what did you learn?"
"The Government has Laws that we have to keep and if we don't we could go to prison and we'd be criminals."
"Well it's kind of like that; the Government have put in place laws to keep the peace and to provide security for the people. If you break any of the laws,

then you could go to prison if you've done something really bad."

"How do we know what's really bad? I don't want to go to prison." Michael asks.

"That's alright son. You haven't done anything bad. Whereas some people have no respect for others, they take things that don't belong to them and other people hurt others for no reason. They're the ones who do bad things and should go to prison."

"Have you done anything bad dad?"

"Oh look; is that your teacher just walking out of the school gate?" I point to a young female in smart clothes.

"Yes, that's Miss Clarke; I think she's a new teacher."

"She's pretty; she looks like your mom."

I needed to change the subject quickly so I just said whatever came into my head. I look across at Michael in the passenger seat as his expression changes to a confused look.

"Mom's got dark hair and Miss Clarke has blonde hair." Michael tells me.

"Oh yes, I forgot." I pull a funny face at Michael to show that I was joking.

Michael smiles at me. I carry on driving towards home.

Michael makes his way upstairs to play on his game while Anne heads into the kitchen to start preparing dinner. She likes to get organised so she prepares the vegetables and potatoes in plenty of time before having to actually cook the food. I think she thinks preparing all the vegetables in advance is less stressful when it comes to cooking the dinner; I think I have to agree with her. There's nothing worse than having food nearly cooked and suddenly realise you've not done any brussel sprouts; not that that would be a tragedy.

"I just thought of nipping down to the garage for a tinker around if that's alright?"
"Yes that's fine."
"What time were you planning on eating?" I ask.
"The usual time, five o'clock, why?"
'Five o'clock is going to be too late for me as I need to be outside the police station at five or just before five. How can I get Anne to prepare the dinner earlier?' I think to myself.

"Can we eat a bit earlier today? I don't know what it is, but I seem to be starving by four o'clock recently."
"OK, I could get the dinner ready for four thirty if that's any better. Or you could eat a biscuit or something to appease your appetite." Anne suggests.
"I don't want to spoil my dinner by eating biscuits and four thirty would be great thanks. So see you in a little while."

I grab the car keys and head out of the house. If I'm going to use the excuse of wanting to bake a cake later, I really need to collect the things I need before hand so I don't forget when I'm sorting Stewart out. I climb in the car and drive around to the supermarket to collect the brandy, cooking chocolate, flour, oranges and eggs. It takes me a little while because of the queues but I eventually make it back to the garage at quarter past four. I drop off the items inside the garage before locking up and walking home.

"That smells nice." I say as I walk in the front door.

"You're just in time; I'm just about to serve up."

I call Michael down from his room and we all tuck in to marinated chicken with boiled potatoes and mixed vegetables for dinner.

"What's for pudding?" I ask.

"We've only got yoghurts at the moment."

"I'll tell you what I fancy. Did you see that chocolate orange and brandy sponge cake they made on television earlier. I just fancy that; what do you think Michael. Do you fancy a Chocolate Orange Brandy Sponge Cake with custard?"

"Mmmm nice, I like chocolate."

"We haven't got any chocolate or brandy Chris." Anne exclaims.

"That's alright, I'll just nip out and get the ingredients and I'll make the cake so we can have it later."

"What! You bake a cake. Now that's going to be interesting. What do you think Michael, will your dads baking be edible?" Anne asks.

"What's eddibul mean?" Michael asks.

"Don't worry son, your moms trying to be funny; which she isn't."

I pick up the car keys and head to the front door.

"You'll be eating your words later when I prove you wrong young lady." I say staring at Anne looking smug at the dining table.

"I may have to eat yoghurt as I think it'll be the only thing edible for pudding." Anne says.
"We'll see. Humble pie is what you'll be eating. See you in a little while." I say as I step out into the street.

I quickly make my way down to the garages and climb inside the cab. I decide not to bother with changing into my protective clothing because I don't have a lot of time but I do put my hoodie on as it has my mask sown inside the hood. I drive out towards Connaught Street which only takes me a few minutes and park up just past the no parking area with the back of the van facing towards the alleyway. I unlock the side door to the van and take out the wheelchair which I had stored. Locking the van up I quickly check I have everything I need. '*Mask?*' I think to myself. I feel the mask tucked inside my hoodie.

"Good."
'*Tazer,*' I feel the tazer inside the pocket of my hoodie.
"Got it."
'*Wire.*'
I reach inside the left of my hoodie pocket and feel the wire coiled up neatly.
"Got it."
'*Ready.*' I think to myself. I grab hold of the handles on the wheelchair and make my way along the pavement past the zebra crossing before turning right into the alleyway.

I look at the time on my watch which tells me its seven minutes past five. I realise Stewart must be on his way by now so I've only got a few minutes to get ready. I park the wheelchair behind the plastic industrial bins hidden from view next to the drain pipes. I make sure the industrial bins are positioned in such a way to obscure the lower part of the drain pipes so Stewart won't see the wire attached to the pipes as he walks past. I bend down and tie one end of the wire on the opposite side of the alley from the bins and leave the coil on the ground ready for when I need to tie it to the opposite side behind the bins. I jog down the alleyway towards Bridge Street so I can take a look up the street to see if I can see Stewart walking into the street from Station Road. I reach the end of the alley way and step out onto the pavement to look.

The end of the road where Stewart will appear is approximately a thousand metres away so I strain my eyes to look for him in the distance as he walks into the street. A lady walks into the street, followed by two lads far off in the distance. There are a couple of cars parked sporadically along the street towards Station Road which partially obscures my vision but all and all; I can just manage to see the far corner where Stewart will appear between a parked box van and a Mercedes parked just behind it.

I stare at the far corner of the street between the two parked vehicles when Stewart walks into view between the two parked vehicles parked fifty metres away from me.
"Crap, Crap" I say to myself.

I was hoping to see him at the far end of the street to give me time to set everything up but now he's thirty seconds away. I'd better get a move on. I quickly turn back towards the alleyway and sprint towards the parked bins. I bend down and collect the end of the wire before darting across the alleyway and jumping behind the bins just as Stewart walks into the alleyway. My heart is pounding from the short sprint, having to run in my protective outfit. I can feel the sweat start to pour down my face and neck as I wrap the end of the wire around the metal drain pipe and pull the wire tight so it's secured around the pipe about thirty centimetres about the ground; I tie off the end of the wire around the suspended wire so it's properly secured.

Stewart is only three metres away and I can hear him talking to himself.
"Whoo das ee thank hees tellin mee ta…"
I see him come into view from my hidden vantage point behind the bins as he steps towards the wire.
"I'll gee me oon back on heem one o these deys. Jus wait…arghhh."

Stewart right foot catches on the wire as he tries to step forward. The wire pulls his foot back behind him as his upper body starts to tumble. Instinctively he tries to bring his left foot forward to save himself but that also catches on the wire causing him to fall forward. Stewart tries to lift out his hands from his pockets in an attempt at breaking his fall but everything happens too quickly for him and he crashes down hard on the ground.

'Thud'
The hollow sound of his chest and face smashing into the tarmac knocks the air from his lungs leaving Stewart's motionless in his prone position.

I quickly slip my mask down over my face and dive on top of him pressing my left knee into his back to prevent him from moving while pushing the tazer into the side of his neck.
"Argh" Stewart tries to scream out but the 300,000 volts quickly prevent his vocal chords from working correctly. His body violently jerks as his muscles tense and relax in quick succession until all his energy is dissolved leaving Stewart motionless once more on the ground. I stare at his face watching his eyes flicker for a moment before his eyelids slowly close.

I look around to see if anyone else had turned into the alleyway from either end but don't see anyone. I quickly pocket the tazer and take out the plastic ties from my hoodie pocket and tie one around Stewarts wrists held behind his back. The wheelchair is only a few feet away so I wheel it over and position it by the side of Stewart's motionless body.

Tearing off a strip of duct tape; I place the strip over his eyes and affix another strip of tape across his mouth. I tuck the tape back inside my hoodie pocket and take off my mask so it's stored back inside my hood. Stewart is still out for the count so I crouch down and lift him up so he's sat on the wheelchair. I position his feet on the foot rests. Stewart is wearing a coat with a hood attached so I lift up his hood and pull it over his head to prevent anyone else seeing the tape across his eyes and mouth; Stewarts head flops to the side. I grab the handles on the wheelchair and slowly push him along the alleyway towards Connaught Street and my parked van.

The street is getting busier by the second as residents return home from work in their cars. Parked cars are slowly filling all the gaps along the street and I notice several cars have already parked next to the van and have made their way indoors. A car pulls into another vacant gap further along the road but I'm not concerned about them as they're far enough away not to notice what I'm doing.

I lift Stewart into the back of the van and lay him down on the floor next to the workbench. I take out another plastic tie and fix it around his ankles before lifting the wheelchair into the back and closing the side door. I start to walk around the van to climb into the cab when I hear a voice behind me say.
"Good evening sir, did you know you're not allowed to park there?"

My heart nearly leapt out of my chest as I turn to see a policeman standing a few feet away. My mind is screaming at me to run. My knees begin to buckle as I steady myself on the van door.
'What am I going to do? Did he see me load Stewart into the van? Is he going to arrest me?' I stare wildly at the officer.
"Sorry." It's all I can think of to say.

He points to the back of the van which is a foot over the diagonal chevrons.

"I could give you a ticket for parking illegally." He says.

I look back at the rear of the van and see it's clearly over the end of the chevrons.

"Sorry officer, I thought I'd left enough space at the back."

"It's Chris isn't it?" The officer says.

'*How does he know my name, I don't recognise him.*' I think to myself.

"You played football with us on Wednesday; how are you?" He asks.

My mind is desperately trying to think who he is, when a name pops into my head.

"Edward. Edward Pickles! Sorry I didn't recognise you in uniform."

"Yes, same here. I thought I recognised you. You played brilliantly the other day. How's your leg. Is it better now?"

"Yes thanks." I slap my thigh indicating that everything's alright.

"I hear you're going out with Angela Green?" I ask.

"Yes I am; how do you know Angie?"

"We used to go to school together and I also do my banking with her; well not exactly her, but the bank she works at."

"Wow what a small world. So will you be playing football with us again on Sunday?"

"Definitely, that's if it's alright with everyone else. Why?"

"Just so I know to play in your team as I want to be on the winning side for once."
We both have a giggle together.
I look at the back of the van and the illegal parking then back at Edward.
"Oh forget about it, so see you Sunday and drive safely."
"Thanks officer, and give my regards to Angela."
Edward makes his way back around the van and walks on along Connaught Street on his beat.

I climb into the cab and start the engine.
'I can't believe how lucky I've been. If it wasn't for me playing football with all the police the other day; I may have been given a ticket or even arrested if he decided to check the insides of the van. I realise how fortunate I've been to be able to play football with the local bobby's. Maybe keeping friends with the police will help me greatly in the future.' I think to myself.

I put the van in gear and pull out into traffic heading for home. I pull up outside my garage and jump out of the van. I open the door to my garage and pull my car out so I can re-park the van back inside out of view of everyone. I reverse the van inside the empty garage space and turn the engine off when I hear a noise from inside the back of the van.
'Stewart must be awake then, I'd better just check on him.' I think to myself.

Climbing out of the cab, I make my way around to the side door and slide it open. Stewart is still lying on the floor of the van with the wheelchair lying next to his back. I notice Stewart's arms behind his back moving up and down as he's scraping the plastic tie around his wrists on a metal lever at the base of the wheelchair.

"No you don't." I shout at him while stepping inside the van to stop him from trying to free himself. Just then, Stewart's hands break free from his restraints and he reaches up with his left hand to uncover the tape from his eyes and mouth.

I reach over and grab his wrist as his hand reaches his face to remove the tape. Fortunately for me, he's still lying on his right side so he's unable to use his right hand. Holding his wrist with my left hand, I tazer him again with my right.
His left hand tries to push away the object of torture from his chest but within seconds his body is drained of energy and his left arm drops down by his side.

I pocket the tazer and lift him up onto the workbench. I take out another plastic tie and fix it around his wrists before securing them to a karabiner behind him. I step around and secure his ankles to the anchor points on the ladder and step back out of the van.

Stewart's body begins to fall backwards but is pulled into position arched over the workbench when I pull on the end of the rope securing him in place; I tie off the end and quickly step back inside the van and pick up my hammer.

'I'm not a vengeful man but in this case smashing Stewart's right knee makes me feel good about myself.'

I swing the hammer down hard onto his right knee and hear the sound of bone breaking under the impact of the hammer head. Stewart's out for the count at the moment so I don't hear a sound from him.

"That's alright, it's going to hurt like hell when you gain consciousness, I can assure you." I replace the hammer inside the box and step out of the van. I take off the hoodie and leave it in the cab before locking everything up.

I collect the food items from the boot of the car and make my way back up the side road for home. I don't mind leaving Stewart for the night as I know he's not going anywhere and to be honest; I haven't got the time at the moment to do anything more.

"Hi I'm home." I make my way straight into the kitchen to start baking my cake.

Anne walks through from the lounge.

"Did you manage to get everything?" She asks.

"Yes thanks. Can you turn the oven on for me to warm up while I mix all this stuff together for our cake?"

"Mix all this stuff; you don't sound like you know what you're doing." Anne asks as she walks over to the cooker.

"Trust me; I know what I'm doing."

An hour later, we all tuck in to a slice of Chocolate orange and brandy sponge with custard.

"Mmmm this is really nice dad." Michael says in approval.

"Thanks son," I look over at Anne to see what she thinks of my baking.

She nods her head and continues chewing her mouthful of sponge pudding.

"Well it was my first attempt at baking, so I think I did pretty well don't you think?" I ask.

"It's a bit chewy." Anne says while giving me a big smile with her teeth plastered in chocolate orange pudding.

"Nice." I reply.

Anne washes up the dirty dishes before we relax in front of the television for the evening. I try to concentrate on the film but all I can think of is Stewart tied up in my van inside the garage. I only hope no-one hears him and that he doesn't escape. I realise he cant escape but all the same, I feel a little anxious about the whole situation of having a police officer tied up. Anne helps herself to a glass of wine which is left over from one of her bottles and I pour myself a nice full measure of whisky to calm my nerves and help me relax. We make our way up to bed around ten thirty and I find myself falling asleep within minutes of my head hitting the pillow.

<u>Wednesday 3rd November</u>

I hear the alarm going off as I open my eyes to see streams of sunlight breaking through the gap in the curtain, reflecting across the wall above my bed. Anne stirs too and throws back the duvet before sliding her feet out over the edge of the bed and slowly down to the floor. She sits up on the edge of the bed and turns the alarm off.

"Morning Chris, do you fancy a cup of tea?" she asks. *'I don't know why she asks if I'd like a cup of tea as we always have a cup of tea first thing in the morning; so why the need to ask? I suppose she may think I might change my mind one day and fancy something else for a change. In any case; wouldn't it be easier just to assume your partner wants what they've always had unless they tell you different. I decide not to mention it as it would probably end up as an argument'*
"Yes please." I answer.

Anne stands up in front of the curtains and stretches with her hands in the air. I notice the sunlight penetrate through her pyjamas outlining her natural shape.

'I don't understand how women are never happy with the way they look. They seem to hate the size of their breasts; their bottom is too big or they've put on too much weight around their hips or stomach. They don't like having grey hair or wrinkles; their legs are too short or too hairy; they've got kankles, which I

*think means fat ankles but I'm not sure. They
constantly cover themselves with moisturising cream
to smooth away the natural aging process. I look at
the outline of my wife and my heart sours. This
woman is gorgeous; who cares if she has a couple of
grey hairs and she's put on a few pounds. All I care
about is that she's mine and she loves me and I love
her.'*

I watch Anne as she wanders off out of the bedroom
and heads downstairs to make the tea when I hear a
scream.
"Argggggggggggg"
I throw back the duvet and dash out of the bedroom to
the top of the stairs looking for some disaster which
has caused my wife to scream. Anne is frozen
stationary at the bottom of the stairs.
"What! What is it?" I ask.
"Spider! There's a spider."
I make my way down the stairs and stand to the side
of her looking for the huge spider that's preventing
my wife from making it to the kitchen.
"Where is it?"

"There." Anne points to a small dot on the floor near
the bottom step.
The spider must be the side of a pound coin; and that
includes its legs so it's not that big really. I don't like
big spiders but little ones this size, don't bother me. I
step past her and crouch down towards the shivering
spider. Obviously more terrified of us than we are of
him. I cup my hands around it and pick the thing up.
"Don't come near me." Anne screams.

I wander over to the front door and after opening it; I throw the spider out onto the pavement and close the door locking the spider out.

"OK all gone now."

I walk back upstairs and climb back into bed to wait for my cuppa and a thank you kiss from my wife.

A few minutes later Anne walks back in the bedroom carrying two cups of tea and places her cup down on the bedside cabinet by her side of the bed before walking around the bed and putting my cup down. She leans forward and kisses me.

"Thank you; you're my knight in shining armour."

"That's alright; I did promise to protect you and that spider looked devilishly aggressive."

"I know. He was horrible wasn't he?"

I realise Anne hadn't noticed I was being sarcastic so I just continued with our conversation.

"He was a nasty looking beast." I confirm.

"No..no stop talking about it. Arghhh" she lifts up her hands to her face and shivers in her attempt to shake off every thought of the spider from her imagination. She walks back around to her side of the bed and sits down to take a drink from her cup of tea.

"That's better." She swallows the hot liquid and smiles at me.

"So are you looking forward to tonight?" I ask.

"Yes, are you?"

"Sure, Pete and I can talk about tactics for our game of football. Oh yes did you know I saw Edward Pickles yesterday."

"Edward Pickles. Who's he?"

"You know the police man that sat next to me at the game, the one on the other team."

"Oh, I didn't know you knew him that well."

"No, I don't its just that he's going out with the girl from the bank, Angela Green."

"Oh wow, didn't Angela go to your school?"

"She was the first girl I had a crush on."

"Well I never knew that. So do you still have a crush on her?"

"No. I only have eyes for one girl." I look into Anne's eyes and smile.

Anne smiles back at me.

"Her name is Philippa Dwight! Only kidding it's you really."

We finish our drinks and get dressed. Michael is already downstairs in his school uniform eating breakfast.

"Good morning Michael did you sleep well last night?"

"Yes dad."

"So are you looking forward to having Debbie come over later?"

"Yes."

I realise its hard work trying to have a conversation with an eight year old first thing in the morning so I take a seat next to him while Anne cooks the eggs and bacon for breakfast.

"Here you are, eat up." Anne puts my plate of food down on the table in front of me and sits down with her food. I grab the brown sauce and saturate the bacon and eggs in the brown liquid.

"I'm surprised you can taste the eggs and bacon with all that sauce."

"You know me. I like my brown sauce. So did you want me to prepare anything for tonight while you're at work?"

"No thank you I think I've got everything sorted. Oh you could pick up two bottles of wine and maybe a six pack of beer in case Pete and Jenny want something to drink."

"OK, I'll grab something after I drop you two off this morning."

We finish our breakfast and head out of the door to the car. The sun is shining in the morning sky as we drive along the street and stop at the junction ready to turn left towards Michael's school. I look right and see the coast is clear when I start to pull out onto the main road. Suddenly an artic lorry speeds past us narrowly missing the front wing of my car as I slam the brakes on; Anne screams.

"Stupid idiot!" I call out towards the driver.

"He could have killed us! People like that shouldn't be on the roads." Anne cries out.

"I know darling. I don't think he even noticed us as he was travelling far too fast."

I watch the lorry continue on down the road focussing my attention on his registration and the name on the back of the lorry.

'Pinchford'

I pick up my phone and quickly enter the registration into my notes.

"Are you alright Michael?" Anne asks.

"I'm OK mom."

"Well done Chris. If it wasn't for your fast reactions; we'd all be in hospital."

"Don't concern yourself Anne; people driving like that sooner or later get caught by the police and end up losing their licence."

"I hope he gets his licence taken off him before he hurts someone." Anne says.

"I don't expect he'll be driving for much longer." I say as I finish inputting the information on my phone.

We drop Michael off and quickly say hi to Jenny and Debbie before heading to the supermarket to drop Anne off. I pull up outside the front door to the shop and Anne gets out.

"So don't forget the wine and beer?" she reminds me.

"Don't worry; I'll pick them up now."

It may seem ironic that my wife works in a supermarket and asks me to purchase wine from somewhere else when they sell exactly what we want right there in front of her. The truth is, everything is more expensive where Anne works and there's more choice at a larger superstore just around the corner.

Anne closes the car door and blows me a kiss through the glass before entering the supermarket. I pull out into traffic and drive the short distance to Tesco's around the corner.

I pick up the wine and beer and climb back in the car ready for my drive home when I see a police car drive past. My mind quickly jumps to Stewart who's still tied up in my garage. I'd forgotten all about him for the moment. I need to get back as quick as I can and sort him out. It's actually the perfect time because most people are now at work and the kids are all at school so the garages will all be empty. I drive home and drop off the beer and wine before wandering down to the garage to check on Stewart.

Lifting up the garage door allowing the light to penetrate the covered enclosure announces my arrival. I hear Stewart moan from inside the back of the van. I slide the door open allowing the light to stream into the van. Stewart arched over the workbench showing a tear in his trousers around his right knee with dried blood clotted between the fabric. To the casual onlooker, the tear wouldn't be obvious and neither would the dried blood as the dark blue material blends in with the dark red of the blood; I noticed straight away, because it was the last thing I did to Stewart last night. I step inside the van and Stewart senses I'm close.

"Mnnnmmmmhhg" he moans something unrecognisable beneath his taped mouth. I ignore his attempt to communicate at this moment because I'm more concerned with the short amount of time I have and the schedule of things I need to do. Taking out the tazer; I jab it into his side until he passes out again. I put the tazer back inside my pocket and reach for the scissors from inside the box on the floor and begin to cut away all of Stewarts clothes. I place each piece of material inside a bin bag and any other items inside the box on the floor which includes a bunch of keys, a wallet, a warrant card, mobile phone and a packet of cigarettes. Once all his clothes have been removed; I put away the scissors and pick up his wallet for further inspection.

His driving licence reveals a much younger photo of Stewart; one where he still has hair. He obviously resents the fact that his head is mostly bald now with; only short curly hair around his ears and the back of the head while the top of his head is smooth and shiny.

"Stewart Orville Noone Grimm, that's funny the Acronym of your name spells 'SONG' did your parents not think about your name before they named you?" I ask. Not expecting any reply from Stewart as he's out cold.

"Oy Stewey giz us a song" I say in a Scottish accent. '*Maybe old Stewart is musical*' I think to myself. '*Maybe he sings to himself in the bathroom.*' "I've just come down from the isle of sky, I'm no very big and I'm awful shy, the lassies shout when I go by, Donald where's your troosers" I sing out and giggle to myself.

I take out his credit and debit card from the wallet together with the seventy five pounds in cash. I put the money and cards in my pocket before dumping the empty wallet in the bin bag.

Stewart begins to stir. His body tenses as he tries to manoeuvre himself into a comfortable position but the pain in his knee reminds him where he is.

"Mnnnnnngghh" he cries out. His whole body seems to shiver in a kind of nervous response to being arched over a workbench and tied down to anchor points on the ladder. I notice his jaws are clenched tight fighting off the pain from his knee and the agonising cramp that must be screaming throughout his joints. I decide its time to speak to him so I lean forward closer to his ear.

"Stewart! Stewart. I don't like bent coppers like you. People put their trust in the police because they're supposed to represent the law, that is, they should be ambassadors, law abiding, honest people; worthy of wearing the uniform. I'm afraid you've let yourself down. From what I've been told; you've been abusing your respected position within society. Taking backhanders; breaking the law and just being a nasty piece of work. This sort of behaviour is going to stop, and I mean stop right now."

I wait a few seconds for Stewart to take in what I've just said before continuing. "Because you've been dishonest; I'm going to fine you. So this is what's going to happen. I'm going to take the tape off your mouth and I want you to tell me the pin number to your debit card and your credit card; I don't want to hear anything else except those numbers. If you try to say anything different or you lie to me; I'll start

breaking other parts of your body. Do you understand
me Stewart?"
Stewart doesn't flinch. I realise being a cop; he's
going to fight me all the way.

I can't be bothered to repeat myself so I just reach
forward and pull away the tape from off his mouth.
"You're noo goin ta hurt me any more, we noo ya
MO sonny. Yoo oonly ever breek ya victim's reet leg.
Noo tha ya've brooken me reet leg, yoo'l nea do
anythin else soo why noo be a good laddy an let me
goo. Ye know we'll catch ye an I promise ya this. I'm
goin ta beat …."

I put the tape back over his mouth and reach down for
my hammer. Stewart shakes his head to try and free
the tape so he can carry on his rant when I swing the
hammer head down hard on his left knee.
'Crack'

"Arghhhhhhhh. Arggghhhhhh" Stewart screams out. I
can hear his breathing become more rapid as his body
tries to cope with the new injection of pain.
"Stewart, Stewart isn't this fun?" I whisper in his ear.
Stewart turns his head towards the sound of my voice.

"Stewart, my hammer is having a smashing time and
wants to continue. You see I don't like upsetting my
hammer by stopping him when he's having so much
fun but as I don't have anything else to do at the
moment. Wait a minute, I could go off and get some
money from your bank; but I can't do that because I
don't have your pin number. So what should I do, I

wonder? I'll tell you what. I'll remove the tape once more. If you tell me the number to your debit card, I'll go and collect my fee and leave you in peace for a while."

"Fiinnnnhh" Stewart tries to say something.
"Now listen carefully Stewart; I'm a man of my word. If you tell me the number to your debit card and your credit card, I'll take out what you owe me in the way of a fine and let you go. You know I've let others go and I'll do the same to you provided you tell me those numbers so think about it. If you tell me the truth, you could be free very soon. If you lie to me; I promise you it's not going to work out very well for you."

I step back to give Stewart a moment to think about the situation he's in. I can see the furrows on his forehead squash together as his mind deliberates the options open to him. Does he want to be totally crippled and suffer the consequences of spending however long in the company of a maniac or does he want to pay the fine and be free very soon. I step forward again and lean in closer to his ear.

"Stewart, times up. I'm going to remove the tape again and I want to hear only the pin numbers; first the debit card and then your credit card. Do you understand?"
Stewart nods in agreement.
I reach forward and remove the tape.
"2,2,4,1."
"9,9,1,2."

I pick up the bottle of water from the box in the van and remove the lid.

"Drink some water." I instruct Stewart as I place the nozzle of the bottle to his lips. Stewart swallows some of the liquid as I pour the water into his mouth. I replace the lid before covering his mouth again with the duct tape; I drop the half empty bottle of water inside the box and step out of the van and close the sliding door behind me.

I take a quick drive to the other side of Liverpool in search of a cash point. I'm always conscious of not repeating anything I've previously done in the past as I don't want the police to find a pattern in my movements. I park round the corner to a cash point next to a convenient store and wander around to the hole in the wall.

The street is fairly quiet, which doesn't surprise me as it's a week day and most people are hard at work. I insert Stewart's debit card into the slot and wait for the prompt to enter the pin number. 2,2,4,1 I enter into the keypad and wait for my options. The screen returns with the options 'View Balance on screen, View Balance on slip, Withdrawal or Other' I press the option 'View Balance on screen.' The screen goes blank for a second before it returns displaying 'Balance of Account £2766.98'

"Very nice Stewart I think I'll withdraw some money today, thank you very much" I say to myself as I depress the numbers 3, 0, 0 on the keypad.

The machine returns the card to me followed by the three hundred pounds. I pocket the money and card and head off in search of another cash point. I find three more cash points and withdraw three hundred from each before I realise the time.

"Crap! Anne's going to kill me" I say to myself. I know she stresses out when she needs to prepare a meal and tidy the house before guests arrive, so I'd better get back home before she does and give her a hand. I climb back behind the wheel and drive home quicker than usual as I don't want to be late; I'm mindful of not getting caught by the police so I keep the speed to the maximum allowed all the way home. I pull in and park up outside the garage door while checking the time on the analogue display in the car '12:23.' I realise I've just got time to stash the one thousand two hundred and seventy five pounds in the router box in the garage.

Anne walks through the door exactly at twelve thirty and I carry through to her a hot cup of tea from the kitchen.
"This is nice, thanks" she says as she puts her handbag down and takes a sip.
"So what do you fancy for lunch?" I ask.
"I think I'll just have a cheese and pickle sandwich, I don't want to eat too much as we've got a big meal to enjoy tonight."
"Oh yes, I'm looking forward to it." I say to Anne although I'm thinking
'I'm really looking forward to hearing what Pete has to say about Stewart being missing.'

I wander back into the kitchen to prepare our lunch as Anne takes off her coat.

After lunch, I relax in front of the television as Anne prepares the food for tonight. The BBC news is on reporting on the usual; problems in the Middle East and the increased prices at the pumps for fuel. I kind of zone out when the news is on because its brain numbing; you can only take so much bad news and the news reports tend to go on and on and on with more and more bad news. Don't get me wrong; I want to hear what's going on in the world, but my head can only take a little at a time. The main news finishes and moves on to the local regional news. The anchor news reporter appears on screen.

"The so called mouthless maniac has finally been caught; two hundred and fifty jobs have been created with the new Ultimer Limited moving into town and bad news for Angela Peters as she runs the Liverpool marathon."

I turn my focus fully on the television as the news reporter mentioned 'mouthless maniac' and wait for the full report.

"The vigilante called the mouthless maniac has finally been caught by the local police late last night; the man was caught red handed outside O'Flannighans holding his hammer as he attempted to attack a police officer in plain clothes. Let's go to our local reporter Kerry Fischer; Kerry what can you tell us about the incident last night?"

The screen changes to a blonde reporter standing outside O'Flannighans.

"Thank you Tony; it was around eleven thirty last night when the masked maniac tried to attack an off duty police officer walking through the alleyway around the side of O'Flannighans. The masked man jumped out from behind the industrial bins wielding a hammer and confronted PC Williams. From the information we've gathered so far, PC Williams managed to disarm the masked man with the help from a passing member of the public. Mister Roger Fouler the nightclub owner heard shouting from the alley and on seeing the off duty police officer making an arrest, telephoned the police for further assistance."

"So what do we know about this masked man Kerry?" Tony asks.
"The man is believed to be in his forties and is local to the area; the police are not saying much more than that at this time while they question the masked man. One thing is for sure; the masked maniac won't be attacking anyone else in the near future while he's behind bars."

"Thank you Kerry."
Tony swivels round in his chair and faces another camera.
"Good news for the unemployed; Ultimer Limited have moved their business into town creating a hundred and fifty new jobs. Our business reporter Dennis Whitman has the full report."

I turn the television off and rest back in the chair.

'I can't believe it; the police think they've caught the masked maniac.'

'What was that guy thinking? Dressing up like me, he's obviously got a screw loose.'

I begin rubbing my eyes and temples as I consider the eventuality of this new situation.

'So they've made a mistake. Do I care that they've arrested the wrong man? Not really. I expect they'll know soon anyway when they find Stewart and realise they've got the wrong man. Maybe this'll take the pressure off me for a little while if they think they've got the masked maniac.' I think to myself.

I give Anne a hand in the kitchen for a while before returning to my usual spot on the comfy arm chair in the lounge. Anne seems happy enough preparing the food so I decide to take a nap in the chair to rejuvenate myself. It feels about five minutes later when I open my eyes and see the wall clock telling me its time to pick Michael up from school.

I stand up and arch my back reaching up with my hands to see if I can touch the ceiling; my fingertips hover a few centimetres below the surface just out of reach. I know I'll never do it; but I try all the same. I can hear Anne still pottering around in the kitchen so I wander over and pop my head around the corner.

"Anne, I'm just off to collect Michael. Did you need anything from the shops?"

"No I'm fine thanks. So see you in a little while." She says.

I pick up the car keys and head out of the front door.

I manage to park in my usual spot a hundred metres away from the main gate and wait for Michael to walk down to me. It's quite a nice place to park because it's far enough away from the bustle of waiting parents chatting outside the main gate while being near enough to see Michael exit the main gate and walk towards the car. I watch the first stream of children with their parents walk past me making their way along the pavement. I spot Jenny and Debbie walking towards me with Michael walking just in front. He walks up to the passenger side door of the Skoda and opens the door.

"Dad can Debbie come home with us now, she's got a new manga book we want to read?"
I look up at Jenny who's smiling.
"Hi Chris what time did you want us over later?"
"I think Anne's cooking for about six so you could come over say five thirty if that's not too early"
"No that would be great. Did you want us to bring anything; maybe some wine?"
"Wine's good thanks but you don't have to bring anything really; just yourselves. So did you want us to take Debbie home with us so they can read their book together and we'll see you and Pete later?" I ask.
"Yes if that's alright with you."
"Of course it's alright."
Michael and Debbie quickly climb in the back and Jenny closes the door behind them.
"So see you later Debbie." Jenny says to her daughter and blows her a kiss.

"OK mum."
We pull out into traffic and head home.
Pete and Jenny for dinner

Michael and Debbie rush upstairs into Michael's
room to read Debbie's book while I wander into the
kitchen to see about giving Anne a hand with
anything.

"You could finish washing up for me and maybe lay
the table." Anne suggests.
There's only the mixing bowl and wooden spoon left
in the sink to wash up so it only takes me a minute to
finish that. I open the cutlery drawer and take out the
correct number of knives and fork to lay the table and
carry them through to the dining table.

"Is this alright?" I ask Anne as I look down at the
table settings.
Anne wanders in from the kitchen and immediately
notices something wrong.
"The knife and forks should be the other way around
dopey."
"I knew that, I knew that, I was just testing you." I
quickly rearrange the table with the forks placed on
the left of the table mat and the knives on the right.

"What if Pete's left handed and wants his fork on the
other side?" I ask.
"He does have a pair of hands so he could swap them
round if he wants."
"So why do we have to set the table this way, why
can't we just leave it with the forks on the right?"

"It's just the way it is. There are certain things you have to do when having a dinner party and laying the table correctly is one of them. Now come in here and whisk the cream for me."

The aroma wafting through the kitchen from the pork in cream mustard sauce is getting my gastric juices flowing.
"Can I taste it?" I ask Anne.
"Christopher, no you can't." Anne says in her authoritative voice.

"Pete and Jenny should be arriving anytime now and I need the cream whipped." She continues.
I grab the double cream out of the fridge and pour it into a mixing bowl ready to be whisked. Anne checks on the new potatoes and asparagus tips as they're slowly cooking on the hob.

"Right they're looking just about right. Should be all done in ten minutes so I'm just going to dash upstairs and change. Make sure nothing burns."
Anne heads out of the kitchen leaving me in charge.
"I don't believe it. Whisk the cream, check on the potatoes, stir the pork, set the table." I say to myself feeling a little stressed at being put under pressure when I hear a knock at the door.
"It's the door, they're here." I shout through from the kitchen.

"Hello can someone get the door?" I call out again.
I hear the knock again a little louder.

I look at the food on the hob simmering away nicely and decide everything looks OK.

Laying the whisk down next to the mixing bowl; I make a dash for the front door.
"Hello Pete, Hi Jenny, come on in." I step back to allow Pete and Jenny to enter the lounge. I shake Pete's hand and give Jenny a kiss on the cheek.
"Can I take your coats?"
"Thank you very much, and thanks for inviting us." Pete says as he hands me his black leather jacket to hang up. I hook it on the coat hook in the hall and turn to take Jenny's coat.

"Please take a seat in the lounge, Anne will be down any second. I just need to finish …..."
"Whisking the cream?" Jenny finishes my sentence.
"Yes, how did you know?" I ask.
Jenny points to the few dollops of cream on my trousers.
"Oops, I know why aprons were invented now." I say. We all giggle to ourselves.
We hear Anne and the children making their way down the stairs to join us.

"Jenny, Pete, its lovely to see you again and thanks for coming." Anne says as she leans over and kisses Pete and gives Jenny a hug."
"Thank you for inviting us." Pete says.
"Look at the time; you're so punctual which is perfect as the dinners just about ready."
"Yes Pete insists on punctuality. It must be a police thing as he's always on time." Jenny replies.

"You should work for the train company Pete. They need a kick up the backside about keeping time."
"I know what you mean Anne, I needed to take a train to London the other week for a course and the train was twenty minutes late which meant I missed the connection at Kings Cross Station. The Super wasn't impressed that we had to start later than expected so I was flavour of the day." Pete explains.

"What, you have to go on training courses in the police?" Anne asks.
"We've all got to go on courses from time to time; you know with updates on new procedures and techniques."
"What's that smell?" Anne asks. "CHRISTOPHER!" Anne dashes through to the kitchen to rescue the pork. I look at Pete and Jenny.
"I'm always getting in trouble and being told off." I say.
They both giggle and look a little embarrassed.
"Don't worry, everything will be alright. So what would you like to drink?"

Pete hands me the bottle of wine they've brought and asks for a lager.
"Jenny what would you like to drink?" I ask.
"I'll have a glass of that wine if that's alright."
"Coming up; now have a seat in the lounge." I point to the sofa and make my way into the kitchen to fetch the drinks.
"Is everything alright?" I ask Anne as she transfers the pork and cream sauce into a new frying pan.

"Yes darling, as always I've saved the day. I could do with a large glass of wine about now."

I take the hint and pour my wife a large glass. I pour a glass of wine for Jenny and grab a beer from the fridge for Pete and carry them through into the lounge.

"I like the picture on your wall Chris; where is that, it looks familiar?" Pete asks.

"That's Malham Cove, I used to rock climb many years ago." I hand Pete his drink and give Jenny hers.

"So Debbie, did you want some coke?" I ask.

"Yes please." Debbie says still reading the Manga book on the window seat with Michael.

I walk back through into the kitchen and fetch two glasses of coke for the kids. I return to the kitchen and collect my beer from the fridge.

"Tell them dinner will be ready in a minute, so you can all take a seat at the table." Anne informs me.

I follow Anne's instructions and inform everyone that dinner's about to be served. Jenny and Pete take the seats opposite Anne and I while the children sit on the ends of the table facing each other. Anne walks through with the main course and hands Pete and Jenny their plate of food. She quickly returns to the kitchen and brings out the children's plates and finally ours before taking a seat next to me.

"I hope you all like it. I won't be offended if there's something you don't like; just leave it on the side of your plate"

"No Anne this looks delicious." Jenny says.

"Yes Anne it looks and smells really nice." Pete concurs

We all tuck in and the conversation stops while we enjoy to food.

We all finish our main course about the same time so I help Anne take the plates out and place them in the sink ready to be washed up later.

"Does everyone want to try my cheesecake with strawberries and cream?" Anne asks.

"Yes please, sounds delicious" Pete calls out followed by.

"Yes thanks" from Jenny and Debbie in unison.

We know Michael will eat anything so Anne portions the cheesecake into six slices and plates them up with strawberry halves surrounding the slice of cheesecake and double cream spooned across the top. We take the plates through and take our seats to enjoy the dessert.

"Mmmmm this is lovely Anne; I've never baked a cheesecake before and this tastes delicious." Jenny compliments the food.

"Its quite easy really; I'll have to give you the recipe."

"So Chris I hear you've recovered from last weeks game; are you up to playing this Sunday?" Pete asks.

"Of course, I really enjoyed it."

"That's good because I'll arrange for you to play on my side again. Don't want the opposition nicking our best player."

"I don't think I was your best player. You played a great game too Pete."

"Now let's not be modest about this. You were brilliant. You haven't lost it then after all these years."

"I'm not as fit as I used to be, but hopefully I'll get fitter each time I play"

"If you improve that much, you'll be unstoppable. You may have to play professionally."

"I don't think so; I'm far too old for that. Oh, I nearly forgot to say; I won't be able to play the week after because Anne and I are on holiday."

Jenny and Pete start grinning as they stare back at us then Jenny looks at Pete and says.

"Go on, you tell them."

"Tell us what?" Anne asks looking a little concerned.

"I can't play either that week because we're on holiday too."

"That's nice. So where are you going?" I ask.

"LANZEROTE" Jenny and Pete call out together.

"Lanzerote! Wow that's great. That means we'll be on holiday all together. So what hotel are you staying at?" Anne asks.

"The same as yours, the Hotel Natura Palace" Jenny says all excited.

"Wow, that's brilliant news, isn't it Chris?" Anne says.

'They'll be at the same hotel. I don't believe it.' I think to myself.

My heart begins to beat faster as I consider the repercussions involved in having a police officer stay with us.

'How am I going to relax and enjoy my holiday when Pete will be watching me every minute of the day?

What if I mess up and say the wrong thing; it's going to be impossible to keep my guard up for the whole time. This is a nightmare.'

"I thought you couldn't get any time off work?" I ask.
"I couldn't while we were still trying to track down this masked maniac. But as you may have heard; we caught him last night in town. So I'm free to take my holiday now."
Pete looks at Jenny brimming with excitement and continues.

"Jenny suggested we look at going to Lanzerote and we looked at the Late Cancellation website and someone had cancelled in the very hotel you're staying at. We hope you don't mind?" Pete asks.
"Of course not, this is brilliant news. Chris and Pete could explore the sites while Jenny and I could sit around the pool with a gin and tonic and look at all the bronzed Adonis men walk bye." Jenny giggles at the thought while Pete gives her a disapproving look.

Anne raises her glass of wine and makes a toast.
"Here's to a great holiday with our friends."
Pete grabs his beer and Jenny her wine glass as we all toast to our holiday in less than a weeks time.
'I wonder if letting Stewart go would spoil their holiday plans; surely finding out that the masked maniac they have in custody has just attacked a long serving police officer would surely prove they've arrested the wrong man and the search would go on. Pete would be called back on duty while Anne and I could carry on enjoying our well earned holiday in

total peace without the eyes of the police watching
every move we make. I don't like the thought of Jenny
and Debbie not having a holiday; I just don't like
them having one with us with Pete alongside. Its hard
enough keeping up my persona while at work; but to
keep it up on holiday seems a little more difficult. It
only takes a second to say the wrong thing and I know
how easy that could happen once you've had a drink
or two and I refuse to go on holiday and not drink just
because Pete's with us.' I think to myself.

'*I begin to wonder why Pete hasn't mentioned*
Stewart yet; they must know that something's wrong
because he didn't turn up for work today as he's tied
up in my garage. Maybe I should ask Pete.'
"So, that means we've only got one football game
before we go on holiday. I'd better score a lot of goals
then." I say.
"That would be good; maybe we could score at least
ten goals together for our side." Pete adds.
"That would really upset Stewarts team; losing ten,
nil?"

"It would; but sadly Stewart's on holiday and won't
be back until after we go to Lanzerote. So you won't
be playing against him for at least three weeks now."
Pete replies.
'*That explains it. I wondered why he hadn't*
mentioned Stewart not being in work today when he's
on holiday. That was bad timing; but then again if I
hadn't have attacked him when I did, he wouldn't
have gone back to work and I would have missed him

completely. So I suppose it was fortunate that I caught him when I did.' I think to myself.

"Well here's to a great game on Sunday." I raise my glass of beer and Pete does the same.
"To a great game with me old footie partner." We clink our glasses together and take a large swig of lager.
"So as long as you both don't get injured. We don't want you two limping along on crutches while were on holiday." Jenny adds.
"We should be alright now that bruiser Sergeant Grimm is not playing." Pete says.

We adjourn to the lounge and relax on the comfy sofa. Pete takes out a couple of Photo's he found from our school days to show me which gives Anne and Jenny a laugh at seeing me in the school play dressed as a dwarf walking around on stage on my knees wearing a beard made out of cotton wool.
"Chris, you really suit a beard." Jenny says holding a cheeky grin.

"No thanks. I don't mind a short beard. But one that big; you've got to be joking. Maybe Pete could grow one if you like beards that much?"
"Not likely! The force has strict policies regarding beards." Pete replies.
"So if Pete's not allowed and I don't want to; it's down to you girls to grow a beard?" I say.
"Now that would look strange. Two beautiful women with beards; we don't think so." Anne comments.

"Thank you Anne." Jenny replies before noticing the time.

"Pete it's gone past eight and it's a school night, we'd better be going."

We all stand and head towards the front door.

"Thank you so much for a lovely evening and delicious food" Jenny says as she gives Anne a hug and a kiss.

"Yes thanks Chris, it's been really nice and thanks Anne, the food was great." Pete shakes my hand and leans over to give Anne a kiss.

I give Jenny a hug and kiss before they put their coats on.

"So will you be coming to watch the match on Sunday Anne?" Pete asks.

"Yes, are you going Jenny?" Anne asks.

"Yes we are. So we can all have a drink after and talk about what were going to do on holiday"

"Great, so we'll see you all on Sunday. Thanks again." Pete says as they all walk out of the door.

"Goodnight" we call out to them before closing the door.

"Right Michael go and get ready for bed, its past your bedtime." Anne instructs Michael.

"OK" he runs upstairs to his bedroom.

"That was nice and I can't believe they're going on holiday with us to LANZEROTE!" Anne cries out.

"Yes I know." I try to sound excited as I don't want Anne to suspect anything.

"I'll just make sure Michaels got in bed; can you pour me another glass of wine?"

"OK, I think I'll have a whisky."

Anne heads upstairs while I venture into the kitchen to pour myself a stiff drink to calm my nerves.

I take our drinks into the lounge and sit down on the armchair.

I think to myself.

'*I can't believe what's happened within the last 24 hours. I catch Stewart, the news report they've caught the masked maniac and Pete and Jenny are coming on holiday with us in a few days. When I think about my situation; it would be safer for me if the police and the media think they've caught the masked maniac. At least they won't be looking for me which affords me relative freedom for the next few days.*

The problem I do have is Stewart tied up in my garage. I need to release him soon but as soon as I do; the police will concentrate their efforts in catching me which means not being able to move at night without the police stopping every car or van. So the decision I need to make; is when do I release him and where? It's Wednesday today and I don't go on holiday until Monday so that leaves me four days with two of those nights working.' I take a sip of whisky.

'*If I release him in the morning, the police will have a search party out for me by the afternoon which means for the next few days, life would be very stressful which is not what I want before going on holiday. It would also mean work on Friday and Saturday night would be too risky; the police would surely catch me driving around in a van. I suppose I could just go to a hotel and sleep in a comfortable room for two nights; I wouldn't get caught then, but what would happen when I got home; Anne would expect me to sleep during the day. That's not going to work, she would surely know something was wrong; like noticing that I don't look tired or stressed from a nights work.'*

'What if I keep Stewart locked up until Sunday and then set him free. The problem then would be the risk of someone finding out that he's tied up in my garage inside a van. There is the other problem of keeping him fed and watered for the next three days. It would definitely look suspicious taking food to the garage every couple of hours; someone would notice my strange behaviour and report me to the police. So what should I do?

What if I release him somewhere remote tomorrow; somewhere where he wouldn't be found straight away, than it would give me a few days grace and relieve me of the undue anxiety of keeping him locked up on my premises. I think that's definitely the best option available to me.' I pick up my glass of whisky and stare at the amber liquid swaying gently in the glass while I wait for Anne to join me.

Thursday 4th November

The alarm goes off breaking through the silence in the room telling me it's a new day. I open my eyes and try to focus on the illuminated digital display but my pupils take a few seconds to focus in on the clock just a foot away. The digits reflecting back at me shine brightly bringing shape into the room. I see the corner of the bedside cabinet and lampshade as its reflective edges sketch the shape and position allowing me to reach across and turn the alarm off. Anne's arm reaches across me under the duvet as her hand strokes my chest; she snuggles up to my side pressing her breasts into my back.

"What time is it?" she whispers.
"Seven thirty." I give her my reply.
"Ten more minutes." She says.
I stroke her arm with my hand and give her forearm a gentle squeeze to acknowledge my approval of staying in bed while we enjoy the moment together. I look at the gap between the curtains in anticipation of seeing the first rays of sunlight stream through but to no avail. I check back with the clock and watch the digits change every minute until the ten minutes are up.

"I'll make a cup of tea." I throw back the covers and ease myself out of bed. The cold air is a definite reminder that we're fast approaching winter; I reach for my dressing gown and slip it on. Anne remains tucked under the duvet; burying her eyes into her pillow to block out any resemblance of light entering the room. I walk out of the bedroom and head downstairs. On occasions Anne finds it difficult to get out of bed; in this instance I think it's because she had a little bit too much to drink last night. Maybe it was because she was excited about going on holiday with Pete and Jenny so I'm not too surprised. I walk into the kitchen and put the kettle on for a drink.

Anne stirs when she hears the clinking sound coming from the two cups of freshly brewed tea as I walk back into the bedroom; I turn on the light.
"Morning." I say as I place her cup down on the bedside cabinet and walk back around to my side of the bed.
Anne reaches for her cup and brings it to her mouth where she takes a sip.
"Mmmm nice, thank you." She says before returning the cup to the cabinet.

"So, any plans today?" I ask.
Anne sits up in bed and rests her back against the headboard. She rubs her eyes with her hands before replying.
"I was going to pop round to see Maria after work as she'll want to know all about our plans for when we go on holiday."
"That sounds a good idea; did you want me to pick Michael up from school or will you do it with Maria?"
"I'll ask Maria to drop me round at the school. If she can't then I'll let you know."
"OK." I take a sip of tea as I relax sitting on top of the bed.

"So what are you going to do on your day off?" Anne asks.

"Not sure. I might just go for a drive."

Now that I've had time to think things through; I think it would be better for me to drop Stewart off somewhere during the day. The police are looking for the Mouthless Maniac during the weekends and particularly at night; so I should be alright to drop him off as it's daytime and midweek. Once Anne goes to work; I should have at least five hours before she arrives back with Michael after school. I try to formulate a plan in my mind of where to take him and how best to drop him off; when an idea suddenly pops into my head.

We all get dressed and washed and head downstairs for breakfast. Because Anne slept in longer than usual we don't have the time to prepare a full cooked breakfast. I fill my cereal bowl with cornflakes and pour cold milk over the top while Anne pops a couple of slices of bread in the toaster and fills two glasses with chilled orange juice from the fridge. It's not the same having cereal instead of bacon, sausages eggs and tomato's but as we're running late, it's better than nothing. Within two minutes, we all climb into the car and head off towards Michaels school.

"Did you enjoy last night Michael with Debbie being round?" I ask.

"Yes dad, can she come round again tonight?"

"No sorry son. Anyway you'll be seeing her at school so you won't want to see her again tonight as well? I ask.

"But we haven't finished our book dad."

"You and your Manga book; when you're on holiday, you'll be able to read the Manga book with Debbie all day and every day."

"OK dad."

We pull up outside the school and Michael climbs out. We remind him that his mom will be picking him up with Maria in her car later so he knows which car to look out for. He smiles and waves to us as he walks down to the main gate.

We pull out into traffic and head for the supermarket.

"So let me know if you can't pick Michael up." I remind Anne as she steps out of the car and turns back towards me.

"I should be able to, but if I can't; I'll definitely give you a ring." She blows me a kiss and closes the passenger door before disappearing inside the main entrance to the supermarket.

I know I haven't got much time so I head straight home to collect Stewart and within ten minutes pull up outside the garages.

'Now what vehicle should I take?' I think to myself. *'It's going to be much easier to drive the van as Stewart is already tied up in the back and the thought of transferring him to the car is too risky in broad daylight.'*

I climb into the cab and pull the van out before reversing the car inside the garage and locking the door. I take off my leather jacket and slip the hoodie on over my head before quickly checking the glove compartment to make sure the tazer is safely tucked inside; everything looks in place so I get in behind the wheel and drive the van out and up the side road.

Within a few minutes I'm heading out of town towards Manchester on the M62 motorway. The traffic is fairly busy on the motorway as it's the main route out of town heading for Manchester and the M6 motorway which will take me north towards Scotland. I keep the van at a steady seventy miles per hour which is the legal limit on motorways, although many vehicles are passing me with ease. I don't want to be stopped by the police for speeding at anytime and I definitely don't want to be stopped today with a captured police officer in the back.

The petrol gauge on the dashboard tells me the tank is three quarters full so it should be enough to get me to Scotland before I need to fill up. I carry on along the M62 keeping my eyes open for any police cars along the route. I don't know why I'm paranoid; but having Stewart in the back is making me nervous and the more I think about carrying this dangerous cargo; the more my hands and neck begin to perspire. I turn the radio on to keep my mind off thinking about Stewart. The song 'Roxanne' comes on by the police so I quickly change the radio station over to Classic FM and I allow the soothing 'cello suite' from 'Johann Sebastian bach' to calm my nerves.

I see a sign up ahead letting me know that I need to take the next turning for the M6 heading north towards Preston and Carlisle. I ease the van over to the left hand lane and follow the slip road onto the M6 heading north behind an arctic lorry. The lorry has a foreign registration plate and is transporting something I can't quite make out from the unusual foreign logo on the back. Keeping to the seventy miles per hour speed limit I find that I'm catching the lorry up quickly as they're restricted to a speed of fifty six miles per hour so I pull out to my right and overtake the lorry with ease.

I pull back over to the left hand lane just ahead of the lorry when I notice the lorry swaying from side to side; drifting into the middle lane and back into the left hand lane.

'That's not very good driving' I think to myself as he drifts back out and in again.

'If he's not careful, he may take out an unsuspecting driver trying to overtake. I wonder what he's doing. Is he tuning the radio in or something?' I think to myself while trying to see the driver in my wing mirrors.

I stare into my wing mirror as the cab of the lorry comes into view and I immediately see the cab is empty.

"What! You've got to be kidding, where the hell is the driver?" I ask myself.

Just then, the driver re-appears in view.

"What are you up to?" I say to myself as I continue to stare in the wing mirror at the cab. The driver bends down again to his side and disappears before re-appearing holding a can of drink in his left hand.

"Now that better not be alcohol." I say to myself as I slow down a little to keep the lorry in view.
The lorry sways again over to the left and right as he drinks from the can of beer. My mouth opens wide in shock at seeing someone driving an arctic lorry during the day while drinking.

'How many beers have you had mister?' I think to myself.
'Where are the police when you need one? This guy could kill someone if he's not stopped.'
I see his indicator light come on as we near a motorway services so I turn my indicator on and pull onto the slip road heading for the service station just ahead of him. I want to double check that he's been drinking alcohol and not coke or lemonade before I decide to do anything. Turning into the car park, I steer the van to the far end closest to the lorry park so I can keep an eye on the driver of the arctic as he makes his way to the entrance of the services.

I open my driver's door and climb out onto the hard tarmac of the car park. I can see the arctic lorry park up next to another lorry with a mattress sign on the side advertising the bedding company they work for. The man climbs down from his cab and locks his vehicle before making his way over to the paved walkway that will lead to the main entrance. I examine the man's clothing so I can recognise him when he enters the building; he's wearing a distinctive blue and white striped tee shirt under a denim jacket with white chinos. I turn towards the main entrance and stride out in an effort to get there before the lorry driver does.

Walking through the main doors to the complex; I glance behind me and notice the man is about thirty metres behind. Usually long distance lorry drivers frequent motorway service stations to have something to eat and drink as they basically live on the road. They also use them for toilet breaks and I imagine being stuck behind a wheel for hours and drinking while he's driving; he must be bursting for the toilet. I hedge my bets and head towards the toilet in the hope that he'll be calling in here first.

I walk through the open doorway first to my left and then right around a corner into the communal wash area and urinals before scanning the area for others using the facilities. A man is just finishing off drying his hands at the air blower while someone else is in one of the cubicles. I don't need the facilities myself, so I pretend to use one of the urinals whilst the man at the air blower finishes drying his hands and heads back out through the entrance.

I'm hoping my driver will be walking in any second now so I position myself by the dryer ready to turn towards the exit as he enters. The man in the cubicle must have had an upset stomach as the noise and smell from the cubicle is horrendous; I'm surprised he hasn't fainted because I'm standing at least ten metres away and the stench has already reached me.

The driver walks in through the door and I step towards him making out that I'm about to leave. We both come to a halt facing each other in the doorway and I quickly shuffle side to side to give the impression that I want to walk past and he's blocking my way. As I'm a little taller than he is, I'm hoping he'll apologise and step aside.

"Zorry Prosze!"
He says and steps to my right to allow me to pass. I immediately detect that distinctive malted barley odour from his breath as I walk past him confirming he's been drinking and driving. He staggers in to the room and heads over to the bank of urinals on the left hand wall as I step out of the room.

I stop just out of view and wait a few seconds to allow him time to reach the urinals as I know he needs to relieve himself. I pull my mask down over my face and take out the tazer ready for action before stepping back into the toilets. I see the lorry driver leaning over the urinal concentrating on what he needs to do so he doesn't pay any attention to me as I walk up behind him. His head is tilted forward with his hands in front of him directing the flow of urine into the ceramic bowl.

'That's it; concentrate on what you're doing.' I think to myself as I jab the tazer into the right side of his neck while holding the left side of his head to stop him moving away.

His body shakes for a few seconds as the 300,000 volts surges through him. I hold the tazer tight against his neck and watch the pained expression on his face, tighten and relax as he contends in the throes of agony. His eyes finally close as the pain gets too much for him and his legs buckle allowing his body to drop down and away from the wall. I quickly step to the side and watch his unconscious body drop onto the floor tiles while he's still clutching his manhood.

The sound of the lorry driver being zapped, followed by the noise of his body thudding onto the floor must have notified the man in the cubicle that an incidents taking place because the straining sound from the cubicle suddenly stopped. I figure he's either listening intently for any other sounds or he's fainted from his own smell. In either case, I'm not really bothered because I don't intend on staying long. I step back from the prone man on the floor and pocket the tazer and tuck the mask back inside the hood out of view.

'*Well I'm not going to let you drive anymore in your condition.*' I think to myself as I reach down and feel inside the man's pockets for his truck keys. I carry the keys over to the nearest empty cubicle and drop them inside the toilet and stuff half a roll of tissue on top to hide the keys from view. I step back outside the cubicle and head towards the exit when I notice the unconscious man on the floor still holding his tadger begin to urinate again, forming a perfect arc onto his chest. I quickly walk out giggling to myself.

Seeing and smelling all the food outlets is making me hungry so I walk over to the burger counter and order a burger and coffee for myself. My order arrives within a few minutes and I take my food over to a nearby free table with four chairs where I sit down facing the toilets so I can keep an eye on what happens next. A tall man dashes out from inside the toilet and heads straight for the gift shop and speaks to the person behind the counter. He turns and points to the toilets and continues explaining something to the attendant who then picks up the phone and calls for security or the police.

I finish my burger and wander over to the gift shop where I pick up a couple bottles of still water, a few sandwiches and cakes and join the short queue at the till to pay for my items. A lady in front of me pays for her items and vacates through the front entrance. I step up to the till.

"Is everything alright?" I ask the young man behind the counter.

"I think someone's been attacked in the toilets." He replies looking quite excited at the thought of something different in his daily routine to brighten up his day.

"Did the police catch who did it?" I ask.

"No; I've just called them, they should be here in a few minutes." He says.

The lad looks like he's more interested in what's happened in the toilets than serving customers; so I just pay for the stuff and head out to the van.

I'm not too worried about the man on the floor of the toilets as I'm sure he'll get whatever is coming to him. I'm hoping the police will notice that he's had too much to drink while he explains to them how he was attacked and his keys were stolen. I can just imagine his face change when the police decide to arrest him for drink driving and take his licence off him. I climb in behind the wheel of the van and start the engine; I notice a police car turn the corner down the slip road towards the car park and the main entrance. I drive out slowly onto the slip road and out onto the motorway to continue heading north for Scotland.

I check the clock on the dashboard and realise I'm on schedule to reach Scotland in plenty of time so I relax a little now that I've been fed and watered. I continue driving north at the recommended seventy miles per hour in the left hand lane while ninety percent of the traffic in the middle and right hand lanes are whizzing past me. The majority of them are breaking the law; some by only a few miles per hour whereas most are doing eighty or ninety at least. I know I'm against those who break the law; but I don't class speeding as a major offence.

'So what if they drive ten or twenty miles per hour faster on a straight road where everything is going in the same direction? Providing everyone drives sensibly, I don't expect anything would happen. I do however object to those who drink and drive or those who speed in pedestrian areas of town where someone could easily get run over and killed.'

Dropping Stewart off

I stare at the road ahead and listen to the classic radio channel again to relax. It's not long before I notice the large Scottish sign telling me I'm about to enter Scotland followed by the sign for Gretna where many romantic people have travelled to get married.

I take the next left onto the A75 signposted for Dumfries where the traffic gets a little lighter as we drive along a two lane 'A' road. I feel quite relaxed now that were near where I want to drop Stewart off; I just need to find somewhere remote to do it. Ideally I'd like to find an abandoned barn or something; it needs to be somewhere that would protect him from the elements so he's warm and dry and I can leave the food with him. I know he won't be able to walk with two broken legs but if he decided to crawl; it would possible take a day or two to make contact with someone. Hopefully by then, I'll be on holiday in Lanzerote.

I drive around a fairly sharp bend to the right and then left before I see the police car up ahead stopping traffic. My immediate instinct is to turn around and head in the opposite direction but I'm on a normal road with a stream of traffic driving towards me on the opposite side of the road preventing me from doing a u-turn and a few cars behind me stopping me from reversing. I'm stuck!

'What the hell am I going to do now? I can't turn around because the road is too narrow and the

oncoming traffic is continuous. My only option is to continue on towards the police road block.' I think to myself.

Two police cars are parked on the left in a lay-by while one officer is directing the oncoming vehicles to pull into the lay-by as a policeman leans into the car window and checks something with the drivers. "What are they doing?" I ask myself.
They seem to be saying something to the drivers before allowing them to drive away.

'Are they searching for me? Do they know my name and checking driving licences?'
I can feel my heart pounding in my chest as I draw closer and closer to the road block. Beads of sweat start to drip down my neck and back; my palms seem to be soaked from moisture making my grip on the wheel loose.

I quickly dry my palms on my thighs and return them to the wheel. I'm two cars away now and the panic within me is reaching boiling point. I can see myself being caught and once they find Stewart in the back; they're going to beat the crap out of me. I don't know whether to scream or black out. The two cars ahead pull in to the left as two officers approach their windows; the third officer now just in front of me waves his arm indicating for me to pull over to the left as the two cars ahead pull away.

My instinct is to make a run for it; I could just push my foot down hard and knock the police officer out of the way as I speed down the road. If I do that, they'd surely catch me and arrest me. Even if they don't; they'd get the registration of the van and catch me later on. Whatever I do now; I'm going to get caught. I decide to just give myself up and pull over. I steer the van over to the left and stop next to the furthest police officer who leans in towards the window. I wind the window down and wait for those all too familiar words.

"Mr Douglas, you're under arrest."

"Good afternoon sir, sorry to delay you but were asking everyone if they've seen this man." He holds up an A5 photograph of an elderly gentleman with white hair and a goatee beard.

"Sorry I haven't officer." I reply.

"That's OK; if you see him, do not give him a ride as he's escaped from the psychiatric hospital and is considered dangerous. Just make a note of where you've seen him and notify the police immediately." the policeman explains.

"OK Officer, thank you very much."

The policeman steps back from the van, allowing me to continue on my journey. I pull out of the lay-by and drive on along the A75 towards Dumfries.

I can't believe my luck. I thought I'd been caught for sure. I don't know if I can take anymore excitement today. I was hoping to continue past Dumfries and towards the Galloway forest but the way I'm feeling at the moment; I think I've had enough. I see a sign up ahead for the town of Annan and Canonbie.

"That'll do me." I say to myself.

I turn off left and follow the road around to the right to a T junction. I turn right on the B6357 for Canonbie.

B roads tend to be very quiet in Scotland as they're not the main roads travelled by tourists so you can cover quite a distance and not see anyone for miles. I continue along the road looking for anything that may be suitable. I see a stone cottage up on the left set back from the road so I slow the van down a little to have a better look; as I pass the house I notice an elderly lady in the garden hanging out some clothes on a line to dry them in the sun.

I press the accelerator and speed past focussing on the distance for any other buildings. I pass a copse of trees and then an open field to the left with cows grazing; more trees and another field to my left when I spot a stone building far in the distance.

As we drive closer I realise the building is not lived in; the windows are boarded up and the roof looks like it's constructed of metal sheeting. I slow the van down so I can take a better look; the stone wall bordering the field is a little worse for wear, not the usual well kept wall with its level top running the length of the field but one with uneven surfaces and gaps.

The wall along the edge of the roadside tapers off where the lane leading to the empty house begins up on the left. I turn the van into the lane and drive the short distance to the empty building where I pull up and turn the engine off.

The lane opens out to the front of the building with trees all around the right side of the clearing with the lone stone cottage on the left. The weathered stone wall with its lime mortar looks old. A single door in the centre with two small windows, one either side showing signs of neglect. The glass in both windows are thick with dirt and grime housing cobwebs in all its corners; the thick wooden door made out of solid oak would have been expensive when it was first bought but now with its damaged knocker and handle looks a little worse for wear.

I walk over to the door and knock.
'Bang, Bang'
I'm hoping nobody is home so I can use the building; but if someone does come to the door I'll just ask if Donald lives here. They'd probably say.
'Noo Won livs hea'r o'tha neam;' or something similar in a Scottish accent.

I wait another twenty seconds just in case someone comes to the door, but nobody does. I look in through the window to see if I can see anything but the place looks empty and unlived. I try the door handle.

The door opens to my surprise. I suppose as it's an empty house and never been lived in for years and located in the middle of nowhere. The owners probably thought there's no reason to lock the place up. Who would ever want to go inside? I step into the room of the cottage basically a three metres by four metres wide space. An old two seater sofa covered in dust with stains and rips in the fabric against the far wall to the left of a small window with a cabinet against the right hand wall next to an open fire place with a few logs stacked to the side. To the right of the room is a doorway to the kitchen area with a free standing cooker, sink and a dining table with two chairs. Another room to the left of the lounge leads straight into a single bedroom with a metal framed bed supporting a very old worn mattress. There's no toilet, no electricity or gas.

'No wonder it's not lived in; this place needs knocking down and rebuilding.' I think to myself.

I walk back out to the van to collect Stewart. Sliding the side door open, I see Stewart still arched over the workbench tied to his tethers. I step inside the back of the van and Stewart's head turns in my direction. I need to drop him off but I don't want him to see me or try and retaliate so I take out the tazer and zap him for the last time in the side.

"Arghhhhhhhhh" Stewart moans before blacking out. I pocket the tazer and pick up the marker pen from out of the box and write on Stewart's chest.
'Dirty Pigs get punished.'
I drop the marker pen back inside the box fixed to the floor of the van and pick up the scissors. After cutting Stewart's restraints, I drag him over to the side door of the van and prop him up against the door frame. I look at the gravelled drive and realise it would rip

Stewarts heels to shreds if I dragged him to the cottage.

'I think you've suffered enough for one day so I think I'll have to give you a fireman's lift.' I think to myself as I step down outside the van.

I tuck Stewarts right arm around my neck and grabbing below his right leg; I pull him up onto my shoulders and carry him into the cottage.

I lay him down on the sofa so that his back is towards the door and his head is resting on the arm. I find a couple of old blankets from the bedroom and use them to cover Stewart's naked body to keep him warm. I walk back out of the cottage and retrieve the bag of food from the van and leave it on the sofa with Stewart so that he has something to eat and drink for the next day or two. I peel the tape from his mouth and eyes and quickly walk out and close the door before he has a chance to turn around and see me.

Stewart was still unconscious when I left him, but I know he'll be coming around very soon and I don't want to be here when he does. I climb inside the cab and start the engine. I know the sound of the engine starting just outside the front door may wake Stewart from his unconscious state and being a police officer; he may wonder if the sound outside is from the vehicle that brought him here. If he thinks that, he may be tempted to crawl to the front door in the hope of seeing the registration or at least identifying the make and model of the vehicle.

'In his condition; I know it would take him at least a minute to crawl to the front door and by then I should

be a thousand metres away out of sight.' I think to myself but then something dawns on me.

'What if he crawls the short distance to the small window at the back and sees me drive down the path and right along the main road?'

"Crap, I'd better get a move on." I say to myself as I spin the steering wheel around and press the accelerator to the floor.

The van speeds around in the clearing doing a perfect u-turn while kicking up pebbles from the driveway smashing both windows at the front of the house.

'Oops that's definitely going to wake him.' I think as I speed down the lane to the junction at the main road. I don't wait to check for oncoming traffic and pull out turning right and accelerate along the B6357 and out of view.

It's not long before I'm back on the A75 and heading towards the M6 for England. I notice the change in scenery from the rural rugged countryside of Scotland to the flatter roving landscape of the north of England. I keep driving south in the left hand lane of the M6 travelling at the customary speed of seventy miles per hour. My mind keeps thinking back to when I saw Stewart last curled up on the sofa with the blanket over him.

I wonder where he is now. Has he made an effort to crawl out of the cottage in search for someone to help him; I hope not. Well I hope he does get found, but not so quickly that the police carry on their search for the masked maniac this weekend.

I don't hear from Anne so I assume she's arranged to pick Michael up from school. Looking at the time; I realise I could have picked him up as I'm just outside Liverpool now and it's only two thirty seven. I slow down and take my time driving the van towards home now that I know for sure that I don't have to worry about Michael. I pull up and give way at a roundabout to a white van as it drives past me, when I see an Artic lorry speed past with the name Pinchford on the back.

'*That name rings a bell. Now where have I seen that before?*' I think to myself as I pull out behind it.
I follow the artic lorry for a little while trying to think of where I've seen it before when it suddenly dawns on me.
"You're the idiot who nearly drove into us the other day." I shout out as my memory recalls the incident on Wednesday.
"Right, you're not getting away from me this time." I press down on the accelerator to catch up with him and ease off when I'm five metres behind.

He turns left at the next roundabout and then a right into an industrial estate. I notice the advertising board to the left of the road listing all the businesses on the estate and see Pinchford listed as the sixth building on the right. The driver of the lorry indicates right and pulls into the yard; I steer my van over to the right and park against the curb by the entrance of Pinchford's. I look across to see the driver climb out of the cab and walk into a corner office next to the warehouse. I imagine he's just finished his deliveries and is probably finished for the day as lorry drivers tend to start early to get their deliveries done. A moment later, the man re-appears and walks over to his car and climbs in. The silver Subaru revs his engine and speeds away from the car park leaving tyre marks on the ground.

"Cowboy." I call out.

The Subaru pulls up to main road and luckily for me turns right and drives past me. I start the engine and follow.

Within a couple of miles, the Subaru pulls up outside a terraced house on Shelby Road where the man gets out and walks up to his front door. He puts his key in the lock and opens the door before disappearing inside.

"Gotcha, I know where you live now." I say to myself as I pass the house and take a note of the number '127' Shelby Road. I stop the van a bit further along to jot down the address so I don't forget where this loser lives before heading for home and a well earned cup of tea.

The house is empty when I walk through the door as I expect Anne and Maria must be picking Michael up from school just about now so I head into the kitchen and put the kettle on for a drink. I take out a cup from the cupboard and put a teabag in it while I wait for the water to boil. Watching the kettle boil affords me time to think about my activities over the past week and the people I've caught and taken money from.

'Now how much did I take off George Peterson, he had eighty five quid on him and I took six hundred out of the bank. What about David?' I think to myself.

'He didn't have much from what I can remember; it was something like forty five quid on him and sixty quid out of his bank account. Then there was Leroy, now he was a good find. I remember he had a wad of money on him, wasn't it about two hundred and sixty and then I took another three hundred from his current account and another two hundred and eighty.

The girl didn't have any money or ID on her but then there was good old Stewart Grimm who kindly gave me seventy five quid and another one thousand two hundred out of his bank. So that makes it nearly three thousand in the past week. That means I don't have to earn any more; three grand is six weeks worth of wages so basically I don't need to work until Christmas.'

The kettle finishes boiling so I pour the water into the cup with the teabag in. I stare at the boiling water chase the teabag around the base of the cup drawing out the brown coloured tea from the bag allowing the water to transform from clear liquid to a light brown. I put the kettle back on its stand and give the cup a quick stir with a teaspoon to help the brewing process to speed up. I take out the teabag and drop it in the waste bin before pouring in a small amount of milk to bring the colour of the tea from light brown to a tan colour.

"Look at that; a perfect cup of tea." I say to myself before putting the milk back in the fridge and carrying my cup of tea through into the lounge. I relax in the armchair drinking my tea and thinking of what to do next.

'So what shall I do now that I have plenty of money? I don't need any more money so why take the risk of getting caught over the weekend if I don't have to. But If I don't go to work on Friday and Saturday night, what do I tell Anne? I suppose I could still go out and look for people who need sorting out; I could always just take notes of who they are and where they live for future reference. Then I could go back and sort them out in the future when it's convenient and less risky. I've already marked down the first person that needs sorting; the Artic lorry driver who nearly ran into us the other day.'

The front door opens and Anne and Michael walk in.
"Hello Darling, how are you?" Anne asks.
"Great thanks. Did you have a nice time with Maria?"
"Yes; it was nice catching up. So did you go for that drive?"
I remember as a boy going up to Crosby and spending time on the beach with my parents and younger brother. We would play hide and seek in the sand dunes.
"Yes, I took a drive up to Crosby and wandered along the beach."
"You wouldn't believe it, but I was talking to Doris at work the other day and she mentioned the beach at

Crosby and how nice it is. Did you used to go there when you were young?" Anne asks.

"Yes my mum took us when I was about ten or eleven."

"We'll all have to go sometime; Michael would love it." Anne says.

"Maybe we could all go after we come back from Lanzerote. Although it's a little cold at this time of year, maybe we could go when the weather gets better. So do you fancy a cuppa?" I ask.

"That would be nice." Anne replies.

'I don't believe it, I've just realised what a big mistake I've made telling Anne that I drove to Crosby and walked along the beach. If Anne puts two and two together she could suss me out in no time. What always happens when someone goes to the beach? You end up with sand everywhere; in your clothes, shoes, pockets, hair and especially in the car. I really need to cover my tracks a little better. Maybe I should only speak once I've worked out what I'm supposed to say instead of blurting out whatever comes into my head that could get me in trouble.'

I finish making Anne her cup of tea while she helps Michael with his homework.

"Here you are." I pass the cup to Anne as she's sat on the floor next to Michael's bed with Michael drawing something on an A4 sheet of paper.

"Thank you." Anne takes the cup from me and has a sip of tea.

"Wow that looks interesting. What are you drawing?" I ask.

"We've got to draw England and we've got to draw where we live and we've got to draw where the queen lives." Michael explains as he draws a rough outline of the country.

"Anne, I'm just going to nip out and fill up the car as I think I'm on empty if that's alright?"

"Yes that's fine. Can you pick up a bottle of wine?" She looks up at me adoringly.

"OK, won't be long." I dash down stairs and pick up the car keys.

I remember there's a hand car wash and valeting service near the supermarket. If I get the car valeted; I could tell Anne that I needed to have it cleaned as it was full of sand from the beach which would tie in nicely with the story I told of going to Crosby. I head out the door and make my way down to the garages to collect the car.

"Here you are; a nice bottle of Californian white wine for you to drink this evening and a large pack of peanuts to nibble while we watch a film tonight."

"Thank you Chris." Anne replies as she prepares dinner.

"Have a guess what film I bought?" I ask.

"Don't know. Wait does it have a pretty actress in it?"

"It might have."

"So what is it then, some hot babe's movie?"

"Actually, it has a handsome actor in; that you like by the name of Jude Law."

"Corr I approve already." Anne says.

"I saw the cover and thought it was the perfect film to watch considering were going on holiday in a few days."

"So what's it called?"

"It has Jude Law, Cameron Diaz and Jack Black and Kate Winslet in it and it's the perfect film to watch as we're going on HOLIDAY!"

"OK, so what's it called?"

I hold up the DVD and smile.

"Very funny." Anne says before turning back to peeling the potatoes.

We relax in the evening and watch the film together. Anne enjoys a couple of glasses of wine while I enjoy a few whiskies.

"That was a lovely film." Anne says as she puts her now empty glass down on the coffee table and picks up a few more peanuts from the bowl.

"It was quite good wasn't it?"

"That's the type of film I like, no sex, violence, swearing. Just a good old feel good movie. Why can't they make more movies like that anymore?"

"I think it's because there aren't that many good scripts around or maybe people in general just want sex and violence in movies"

"I don't know why, I much prefer a nice film as opposed to one where people get hurt. I want to be entertained not walk out of the cinema feeling thoroughly depressed."

"I know what you mean. I feel the same way. The thing is, this world is violent and corrupt and people tend to go to see a movie as a form of escapism. So the ironic thing is, why would you what to escape a violent world to watch something that's just as violent? It doesn't make sense."

"You're so right darling. They've got it all wrong in the entertainment business. They need to re-think what entertainment should be all about and just make movies that make people feel better about themselves. Anyway, I think its time for bed."

Anne stands up and picks up the empty glass and bowl and carries them into the kitchen to be washed up in the morning.

'I think about the conversation we've just had and wonder if my efforts are actually making a difference in the local community. The news reports I've heard recently definitely indicate that the crimes in the local area are getting fewer and fewer so I must be making a difference. I do think also that people are becoming more aware of the consequences of committing crimes now that criminals are being punished and the news clearly report what's happened so all can see. That's got to be a good thing. I think if I was a criminal, I wouldn't want to be caught by the Mouthless Maniac.'

'I think I'll continue sorting criminals out for a while; maybe until Christmas. I could re-evaluate the situation each month to see if what I'm doing is making a difference. If I'm not; then maybe I'll stop but if I am, I may just continue until the country is free of crime or until I find something better to do.

Maybe at that point I might have earned enough to retire anyway.'
I finish off the last dregs of my whisky from my glass and make my way upstairs to bed.

Friday 5th November

The alarm goes off as usual waking me from a restful sleep; again I think the whisky helped soothe my mind from the long journey up to Scotland and back. Anne must have gotten up earlier as theirs a space next to me in our king-size bed. I decide to just lay here for a few minutes to allow time for Anne to bring up a cup of tea for me. I stare up at the ceiling, not thinking about anything as men often do, before images of Stewart drift into my mind.

'I wonder how he's doing. Has he been found? Has he tried to escape from the cottage I left him in? Did he manage to eat and drink anything? Is he dead?'

Panic strikes at my heart at the thought of killing someone.

'What if he died? What if the injuries to his knees had turned septic and the poison in his blood killed him. I could be done for manslaughter.' I think to myself. I can feel my heart pound in my chest at the thought of being a murderer.

'I could end up in prison for a long, long time.' Perspiration breaks out all over my body as I contemplate the implications of killing a police officer.

'The prison officers would take it out on me; they would make a purposeful effort to make my life a misery. Making unexpected calls on me all times of the night and day to beat me up using clubs. The police would encourage them and would want reports

on what happened to me and how my life would be a living hell.'

I need to find out what's happened to Stewart and I need to know soon before my heart gives up.

"Hello darling, you're awake then?" Anne asks as she walks in with a cup of tea and places it down on the side cabinet.

"Chris! Are you alright, you look like you've got a fever?" she places her hand on my forehead.

My mind returns to the present as I stare up at Anne's concerned face looking down at me.

"Yes sorry Anne, I just feel a little faint at the moment; I'll be OK in a few minutes."

"Are you sure, you're burning up."

"Don't worry; I'll be fine once I've had my cuppa." I reach across and take a sip of tea.

"That's better; I feel much better now. See its working." I give Anne a smile.

"Do you have to do anything this morning?" Anne asks.

"No why?"

"Well you just stay in bed and relax. I'll take Michael to school and I'll bring home a thermometer to check your temperature when I get back from work. And that's an order."

"Aye Aye captain."

Anne walks back out of the bedroom and makes her way downstairs.

I don't mind chilling out today as I don't need to do anything or see anyone and it'll give me an opportunity to watch the television. I'm hoping I'll hear something on the news about Stewart and it's probably better for me to hear the bad news while Anne is not here so she won't see my shocked expression. I finish my cup of tea and just relax until I hear Anne call up the stairs to say she's just about to leave for work and take Michael to school.

"Goodbye." I shout back as they exit through the front door.

I throw back the covers and make my way downstairs to listen to the news.

I turn the television on and flick the channels hoping to find a news channel; house under the hammer, time team, come dine with me. I can't find anything that resembles the news so I switch to the main menu and scan the listings.

'Eleven o'clock on BBC2 is the news; that'll do' I think to myself.

I look at the clock on the wall which tells me it's only nine thirty.

"What! I've got ages to wait." I decide to take a shower and get dressed to help pass the time and maybe make myself some breakfast. I leave the television on for some background company as I make my way back upstairs and into the bathroom.

The hot water from the shower washes over me in a forced spray burning the top of my head and warming my shoulders and back as I feel the water race down my lower back over my buttocks and down my legs. I keep my head forward so the concentration of water is mainly on the back of my skull. The heat numbs my

senses enough to allow my body to relax; I close my
eyes to fully enjoy the experience of being warmed
through to the core. Being enveloped by water has a
total absorbing effect transporting my body and soul
to another place, washing away every concern or
worry and leaving my body renewed and invigorated
and in peace. I think to myself. *'If it wasn't for the
water and electric companies charging the earth for
the privilege of using the shower; I could definitely
stay here all day.'*

I suddenly remember the news will be on in a few
minutes so I quickly finish showering and get dressed
before making my way down stairs. I check the clock
on the wall and realise I've about ten more minutes
before the news is on.

"Time for some toast and marmalade and maybe
another cup of tea, I think" I say to myself.
I wander into the kitchen and put two slices on bread
into the toaster and press the lever to turn the machine
on. I switch the kettle on and take out another cup
from the cupboard before popping a teabag into the
cup. Our toaster is on its last legs as it tends to toast
only one side of the bread fully while the other side is
mildly toasted. I usually put the butter and marmalade
on the undone side to disguise the fact that it's not
really toasted. The toast pops up at the same time the
kettle boils. I pour the water into the cup and finish
buttering the toast before spreading on a thick layer of
marmalade; a dollop of milk into my cup and its all
done. I put the milk, butter and marmalade away

before walking through to the lounge to watch the news.

I don't know what it is. I know Stewart is alright really, but my mind is telling me other things. I start worrying about everything; making things up to worry about. They say that anxiety is the cause of most deaths and that most of the things we worry about never come to fruition, they never happen! So why do we worry about things which will never come true or effect us? I try to calm myself and relax by taking a bite of my toast followed by a sip of tea. The news report comes on.

'The bank of England has kept its interest rate the same which means good news to homeowners; there's been another bombing in Syria presumed to be a terror organisation and England win against France in Rugby.'

I sit back in the armchair chewing on the last piece of toast watching the news. The news of the bank interest rates is quite good for us as we don't have to worry about paying a higher mortgage payment for the time being. I'm not too bothered about bombing in other countries as I think this country has its own problems to solve and rugby? Again I don't follow sport that much unless its football and the reds. The national news finishes and they quickly cover the local news. Politicians are committing some crime to do with expenses; major development project being agreed on a housing estate and Tom Jones performing again in Liverpool at the end of the month.

"Now, over to Wendy and the Weather report." The screen shows a forty something woman standing next to a map of the west of England. I turn the television off and ease back in my chair.

"So nothing about Stewart then; so that means they've not found him yet or else they would have said something. Finding an injured police officer has got to be big news to report on, so as they didn't say a word must mean he's still in the cottage. I don't have anything to do tonight while I'm working. Maybe I should take another drive up to Scotland and check on him?" I ask myself. The more I think about it, the more I need to confirm in my heart and mind that he's not dead. I would feel a lot better about it if I knew for sure that he's alright. I convince myself that, that's what I'll do later tonight. I lie back in the chair and close my eyes for a nap.

I hear the door open and Anne walk in.
"Hi I'm home." Anne shouts upstairs before she realises I'm sat in the armchair in the lounge half asleep.
"Oh hello I thought I'd relax down here instead with a hot drink." I reply.
Anne hangs up her coat and walks over to me.
"So how are you feeling, did you fancy some lunch?"
"Yes please."
"I've brought home some coriander and carrot soup and beef broth; which would you prefer?"
"The beef broth."

"OK, I'll just go and make some and we can have it with a nice thick crusty roll; now just relax for a while, while I make it."

Anne wanders into the kitchen to make our lunch so I put my feet up on the coffee table and relax back into the chair.

A few minutes later, Anne walks through with our soup on a tray with a buttered roll.

"Here you are darling." She places the tray down on my lap.

"So how's your temperature?" she remembers that she's bought a thermometer which is still in her bag. "Wait a minute; don't eat any of the soup until I've tested your temperature." She dashes over to the front door where she left her bag and retrieves the item still wrapped up in plastic and card.

I look down at my beef broth soup which smells delicious. I pick up the soup spoon and scoop some of the soup up. I look over at Anne who is desperately trying to un-wrap the thermometer. Her hands are tearing at the plastic protective cover in the attempt at freeing the encased thermometer from the backing card. I slowly insert the spoonful of liquid into my mouth and return the spoon to the bowl for a second mouthful.

Anne looks over at me.

"Shan't be a moment" as she pulls the cover off and extracts the glass pencil shaped thermometer.

"Here we are." She shoves the end of the thermometer into my mouth so the end is tucked under my tongue.

"Just hold it there for a minute." She says as she places her hand on my forehead again.

Sixty seconds later Anne pulls out the thermometer and examines the mercury level.

"WHAT! YOU'RE BURNING UP!"

I give her a smile and lift up my spoon with some soup in it.

"I couldn't resist, sorry. I'm fine really"

"CHRISTOPHER you had me worried then"

"Sorry, the smell of the soup was too much for me. I couldn't resist, anyway I'm fine really."

"OK but if you feel unwell later then tell me straight away and I'll ring your work and tell them you're to sick to come in tonight."

I think to myself.

'There's no chance of that happening. Even if I wasn't well, I couldn't let Anne ring work for me as she would find out that I don't work there, never have and never will.'

We enjoy our soup together while watching a bit of television.

'Loose Women are on ITV at the moment. I'm not too fussed about what's on as its just background noise as we're chatting about our holiday.

"So do you have everything for holiday? Do you need some new swimming shorts and flip flops?" Anne asks.

"No I think I'm alright."

"I thought I would pop out to the shop later to get a new swimsuit and maybe a sarong, are you sure you don't want me to pick you something up while I'm at the shops?"

"No, if I need anything. I could always buy it on holiday. I could probably buy ten pairs of shorts there for the same price I would pay here just for one pair."

"You're probably right. But I'm not going to risk not having something that fits and I can wear on the first day. I'm not wasting any sunbathing opportunity."

"What time were you going out shopping?"

"I thought I'd go about two thirty so I could get what I need before picking Michael up. Is that alright?"

"Yes that's fine. I thought I'd get some sleep at three until eight before I have to work tonight."

"OK, so I'll wake you at eight."

The ITV news begins at one thirty so we sit and watch what's happening around the world until its time for Anne to go out shopping. There's no mention of Stewart on the news again so I try to reassure myself that it's a good thing that he's not been found yet and hopefully not dead.

"Right I'm off now so I'll see you later tonight. Try and have a good rest while I'm out. Love you." Anne says as she kisses the top of my head.

"OK, see you later." I watch her walk out.
'Time for one more cup of tea before bed I think.' I head into the kitchen and put the kettle on again.
The alarm goes off exactly at eight o'clock as Anne walks into the bedroom with a steaming cup of tea.
"Did you sleep well?" Anne asks.

"Yes thanks." I reply before taking a sip of tea.
"There's some Macaroni cheese and broccoli left
from dinner, did you want me to re-heat some for
you?"
"Yes please, I'm starving."
"Do you want me to make you a pack up for tonight?"
"Yes and as its getting colder, could you make up a
flask of coffee as well?"
"Good idea, I'll do that after re-heating your dinner."
Anne kisses me on the forehead and makes her way
back out of the bedroom and downstairs. I take
another sip of tea before deciding to get out of bed.

The plate of Macaroni cheese and broccoli is
steaming away on the dining table with a fork neatly
placed to the side. Michael is sat in front of the
television in his pyjamas ready for bed. I walk over
and take a seat at the table and tuck in to the hot food.
"Mmmm tastes delicious." I say giving my approval.
"You're welcome, I'm glad you like it." Anne replies
from the kitchen as she's preparing my pack up for
later.
"Michael! I think its time for bed. Say goodnight to
your father."

Michael switches off the television and rushes over
toward me.
"Good night dad, love you." He puts his arm across
my shoulders and kisses me on the cheek while I'm
chewing a large mouthful of macaroni.
"Mloof gu too" I reply as a piece of macaroni falls out
of my mouth and lands back on the plate. I quickly
cover my mouth with my left hand and pull a guilty

look at Michael as we've always told him not to speak with his mouth full.

Michael smiles before rushing through to the kitchen to say goodnight to his mom.

After dinner Anne and I relax for a little while on the sofa listening to some music and chatting about our holiday.

"I've made a list of everything we need to take, just so we don't forget anything." Anne says.

"Good idea, I'll make my list tomorrow although I think I can remember shorts and flip flops. I don't think I need anything else."

"CHRISTOPHER be serious; we don't want to get there and realise we left something vitally important behind"

"Oh yes; I remember seeing that film 'home alone' when they left their child behind."

"Well there's no chance of that happening; if you don't remember Michael, I'm sure I would remember him and so would Debbie. She's looking forward to spending two weeks with her best friend"

"Ooooo true love. Ooooo"

"Christopher, you're incorrigible."

"I might be, if I knew what it meant."

"Oh look at the time; its nine thirty. You'd better get going."

We both stand; I walk over to the front door to get my coat and shoes on while Anne fetches my pack up and flask of coffee for the night.

"Here you are darling, have a good night at work."

She hands me the food and drink before kissing me.

"Right, see you in the morning." I open the front door and walk out into the darkness.

As its not going to be a usual night I only change into my corset and hoodie with the mask inside. I don't bother with the gauntlets or the forearm or shin guards as I don't intend on getting into trouble tonight. I just want to drive up to Scotland and check on Stewart before coming straight back. I just feel more comfortable now wearing my corset with the flattened metal brackets stitched on. It makes me feel protected; kind of like wearing a uniform. When I'm wearing the corset it gives me confidence to walk the dark streets at night and not worry who I might walk into. I definitely feel better wearing it than not wearing it. I lock up the garage and climb into the Skoda ready for my long drive.

Return Journey to Scotland

There's one big advantage to driving at night. The roads are much less congested with fewer lunatics and boy racers on which means your journey can be a lot less stressful. I follow the same route I took the other day out of Liverpool and up towards Scotland on the M6. I check the time and quickly calculate I should get there just before midnight travelling at a steady eighty on the motorway providing I don't get delayed. Its about a hundred and sixty miles to the cottage where I left Stewart and my petrol gauge is showing three quarters full so I should be able to get there and half way back before I need to re-fuel. I try to relax a little and not think of what I might find when I get there. I glance at the speedometer as the dial flickers just below the eighty miles per hour mark; I press down a little more on the accelerator pedal and watch the dial creep up just past eighty.

Most of the traffic at this time of night seems to be heavy goods vehicles and the occasional car either in the left hand lane or overtaking in the middle lane. I stick to the left hand lane and use the middle lane for overtaking too. I don't want a speeding ticket and the police seem to be a little more lenient with those doing eighty but not to those speeding at ninety or a hundred. I watch a Porsche 911 speed past in the outside lane doing at least a ton and glance in my rear view mirror to see if I can spot a flashing blue light of a police car chasing him. No such luck, I can only see the headlights of vehicles streaming back behind me.

'Maybe the police have something better to do on a Friday night than chase speeding motorists' I think to myself.

I know from experience that the town centres nowadays are generally thriving with activity from drunkards, drugs, robberies, muggings, prostitution and most definitely fighting so it doesn't surprise me in the least at not seeing any police on the motorway.

Just then a police car shoots past me with his lights flashing.

"Wow speak of the devil, just when I was wondering where all the police were, and here they are. I wonder if they're after that Porsche" I ask myself.

The flashing lights from the police car, gets smaller and smaller into the distance until it disappears. I like it when the police arrest people; it shows that they're doing their job properly. It's a shame they can't catch more criminals, maybe then the world wouldn't be in such a mess and I suppose if they did catch more; then I would be out of a job. Not that I'm worried about losing the opportunity to prevent criminals myself as I know it just wouldn't happen. I remember Pete telling us the other week that for every single crime they solve, another four crimes are committed in the area.

I look ahead into the distance at the few vehicles on this side of the carriageway going the same way as I am leading a trail of red tail lights lighting the route up to Scotland. I spot a blue flashing light far in the distance and realise the police have pulled someone over. Within a few minutes I've caught up with the police car now parked on the hard shoulder behind a nice Porsche 911 sports car.

"Ha ha ha ha, what a muppet." I say to myself.

It gives me a smile to think that people with money sometimes think they can get away with speeding; so what if they get a ticket. What's sixty quid fine when you're earning a hundred thousand a year; Peanuts, that's what it is, peanuts. It doesn't mean anything to them. The thing is; one too many speeding tickets will result in no licence to drive. I continue on past the police and towards the sign signalling the border of Scotland and England.

I see the turning for the A75 up ahead signposted for Dumfries so I ease over into the left hand lane and continue off onto the A75.

'*Not long now*' I think to myself as I drive along.

My mind quickly imagines all sorts of scenarios.

'*Will I find Stewart still in the cottage or will he be lying on the roadside half eaten by animals.*'

Just the thought of something like that is making me feel sick to the stomach. I decide to turn some music on and try and relax. The radio blurts into life as I press the on button and I hear 'the night has as thousand eyes' by Bobby Vee which makes me feel uneasy. I like his music but under the circumstances this song creep's me out. I switch to another radio station when I hear an Elvis song.

"That's better" I say to myself.

It's not long before I see the sign for Annan so I indicate left and turn left off the main road and follow the road around to the right to a T junction. I turn right on the B6357 for Canonbie and continue along the road towards the first stone cottage I saw with the lady putting out her clothes on the line. I can just make out the copse of trees up ahead in the darkness and just beyond that should be the cottage where I left Stewart. I pass the copse of trees on my left and immediately spot a police car parked at the end of the lane leading to the cottage with its blue flashing lights strobing in the darkness. My heart begins to beat faster and faster as I'm forced to drive nearer to the parked police car as I'm on a single carriageway and it would look suspicious and dangerous if I tried to do a three point turn in the road. Through the darkness to the right of the blue flashing light I see an ambulance with its rear doors open. I slow the car down a little as I approach the parked vehicles and notice two figures carrying a stretcher to the back of the ambulance?

A lone policeman appears at the side of the police car while shining a torch down in front of him, he waves with his other hand to get me to slow down and stop. *'Maybe he's going to ask what I'm up to driving just before midnight on a Friday night down a lonely lane. He's bound to ask me where I'm headed so I'd better think of something quick.'* I think to myself.
My mind speeds into overdrive as I try to think of a logical answer as I pull up next to him and wind the passenger window down. The officer leans into the car window.
"Good evening sir, what brings you down this road at this hour?" he asks.

I vaguely remember passing a hotel on the A74 near Hollee last year when I travelled up to visit a few whisky distilleries and I know it's in the general direction.

"Hello officer, I'm on my way to The Mill Forge near Hollee, I'm meeting my girlfriend there; I should have taken the A74 but came along the A75 by mistake. Am I going in the right direction for Hollee and the A74?" I ask.

"Yes you are sir; just keep going straight on this road."

"Thank you, officer." I think it would look suspicious if I ask about the man on the stretcher so I keep my mouth closed and pull away past the police car. I glance in the back of the ambulance and see Stewart on the stretcher with an oxygen mask covering his mouth. The paramedic is injecting something into his arm.

That's a good sign; if Stewart is wearing an oxygen mask then he's still alive. Maybe the food and drink I left him helped. I stare back in my rear view mirror at the blue light getting smaller and smaller before disappearing around a corner. At least I know he's being taken care of now and he's not dead; I can start to relax a little. My stomach starts to gurgle and churn from hunger. The nearest food place has got to be a motorway services and I can't exactly turn around and go back the way I came, so I continue on towards Hollee and the A74. I know once I'm on the A74 It wont be long before I'm heading south on the M6 for England.

I take the turning for the A74 heading south and within a few minutes see a sign ahead for a 'Welcome Break' services at Gretna Green. I take the turning left down the slip road and up to a small roundabout where I have to turn right over the bridge across the A74 as the services are on the northbound side of the carriageway. I'm not too bothered because I'm hungry and I need to fill up with petrol. I follow the directions to the main car park and park next to an Audi A4. I quite like the look of the A4 but never had the money to buy one. I start to think about all the money I've made recently and reason that I could buy anything I liked within reason.

'The only problem with buying something nice nowadays; you worry that other people would try and steal it, or at least damage it so I dismiss the idea as a bad idea.'
I lock up the car and wander in through the double doors in search of the burger king.

Saturday 6th November

The nice things about motorway services and the food outlets; they're generally 24hour services so you can get food any time of day or night which is handy for my line of work. I don't mind the sandwiches and the flask of coffee Anne kindly made me but it doesn't compare to the smell of a nice burger and freshly ground coffee. I walk to the counter where a young lad takes my order. I should just say 'The usual' as I seem to be calling into these fast food outlets more frequently. I feel my stomach to see if I can feel a paunch but can only feel the hard metal brackets of my protective corset under my hoodie. The food arrives and I carry the food over to a small table and sit down to eat.

The dining area has approximately twenty five tables and only two are occupied at the moment. Two elderly gentlemen are drinking coffee on one table and three young lads are on another eating burgers and chips from the burger king counter. I sit on a table equidistant from the other two parties forming a three point triangular shape so that I can see the other occupied tables. I pick up my burger from out of its box and take a bite; I remember the last time I ate a burger and nearly choked from biting off more than I could chew.
'Now that was embarrassing and I won't be doing that again in a hurry.' I think to myself as I chew the small mouthful I have in my mouth.

The burger tastes delicious as usual as I allow the flavour to invigorate my taste buds. I lift up my drink and take a sip to wash down the burger as I observe the people in front of me. The three lads seem to be a little bit noisy with regular expletives after every second word. The older man glances over at them with some annoyance at having to listen to foul language. The lads continue their conversation which seems to be getting louder and louder. The older man looks around again this time pulling a face of disapproval.

"What are you lookin at; you gotta problem or somfink" one of the lads yells out to the older man at the other table.
"Do you mind keeping the noise down, were trying to enjoy our coffee" he replies.
The lad that spoke suddenly stands up and walks over to the elderly gentlemen.
'I don't like the look of this.' I think to myself.
'I wonder if something will happen or maybe the lad will just say something to the older gentleman and return to his table.'
I take another bite from my burger and watch intently at the young lad.

The lad steps between the two men and slaps the drinks out of their hands.
"You've finished drinking now, so get lost"
As the men stand up from their seats; the lad pushes one of them in the chest. The old man stumbles back against another table and chairs. His friend tries to intervene when he too is pushed against the railing

that divides the seating area from the shopping area. I find myself up on my feet and storming over to the lad who pushed the older men.

"Oy that's enough!" I call out.

The lad turns towards me and is quickly joined by his two mates from the table.

The two lads must have reasoned that his mate could handle two old men on his own, but may need a little help in having to deal with a younger man.

"What!.... If I were yu, I'd keep out of it or else." The lad clenches his fists indicating he's happy to take me on.

"You owe these men an apology and a fresh drink each."

"Well they're not getting one, so wot are you gonna do about it?" he asks.

I clench my fists and hold them out to the sides.

"Right, come on then!" I say challenging him as I step forward and lift my fists and forearms up to protect my head hoping he'll take the bait and punch me in the ribs.

The lad falls for it. I see his right fist fly forward and catch me on the left side of my ribcage. 'Crack'

"Arghhhhh"

He quickly pulls his broken hand back towards him while cradling it in his left hand. His two friends stare at him in confusion probably wondering why he's injured when he punched me. They're shocked expressions provide me with the opportunity to kick the nearest one to the leader right between the legs. The lad didn't see it coming because he was so preoccupied with looking at his mate's broken hand. My right foot smashes into the lad's jewels compressing them flat with the force of someone kicking a field goal at rugby; his upper body buckles under the impact and lifts up off the floor for a second before his whole body crashing down in a crumpled heap at the base of the table.

The un-injured lad must have quickly calculated he's on a losing side as his hands come up in an apologetic manner.

"Sorry mate"

He reaches inside his pockets and pulls out two five pound notes and quickly offers them to the older men.

"Here mate, sorry, take it."

The older men now recovered from being shoved replies.

"That's alright, don't worry about it." I think they think the lads have been punished enough.

I look at the older men and say.

"No, they need to pay you for your drinks, go on; take the money."

The young lad still holding out the cash passes the money over to the men.

"Thank you" the older man says.

I look at the un-injured lad.

"I suggest you take your friends out before I change my mind"

The lad helps his friend up who'd been kicked in the jewels.

"Come on Dave." The three of them make their way out of the seating area and towards the exit. I turn and walk back towards my table when I realise my half eaten burger had fallen on the floor. I bend down and pick it up before placing it in the waste bin. I take my seat back on the same table to finish drinking my coffee when the two older men walk over towards me.

"We noticed your burger was on the floor so we bought you a new one and a fresh cup of coffee."
"Oh thank you very much; you needn't have bothered really."
They put the tray down on the table with the burger and three coffees on.
"Is it alright if we join you?" One of them asks.
I look at the tray and then at them.
"Yes off course, sit down."
"Well that was exciting." one of the men says.
"Yes it may have been for you Tom but I was scared."
"Simon; you're always scared"
"That's because you're always getting us in trouble, that's why." Simon says.
"Sorry, we've forgot to introduce ourselves, I'm Tom and this is Simon." Tom reaches across the table and shakes my hand. Tom does the same.
"Hi I'm Chris."
"It's nice to meet you Chris and thanks for your help." Simon says.

"No problem; I suppose it made the evening a little exciting, so how are you two. It looked painful being pushed into that table?" I ask.
"That's alright, I've had worse." Tom says.

"So are you friends or work colleagues?" I ask.

"Tom and I have been friends for most of our lives; we were in the navy together. Tom still thinks he's twenty five."

"If I were twenty five again I would have kicked those lads to kingdom come and back." Tom says.

"See what I mean. That's why he always gets us into trouble."

I have a little laugh to myself before taking a sip of my freshly bought coffee.

"So what brings you out at this hour on a Friday night; I mean Saturday morning." I ask Tom and Simon.

"We've been to a re-union of our ex service buddies up in Aberdeen where we use to be stationed. We were the last to leave so we thought of breaking up the journey on our way down to Liverpool. And its Tom's turn to drive now." Simon announces.

"I know it's my turn, I don't mind driving."

"So do you go to the re-union every year?" I ask.

"No. usually it's every ten years but as were getting older Jack Phinigan decided to shorten it to every five years now. I guess he thought most of us wouldn't make it to the next one." Simon says.

"It's probably a wise decision." I say as I take a bite from my burger.

"So what about your; what brings you out on a Friday night by yourself?" Tom asks.

I start to panic a little as I try to think of a legitimate excuse. I continue chewing my burger for as long as I can to give me time to think. All the while pulling a face and pointing to my mouth while over emphasising my chewing in the hope they realise its bad manners to speak with your mouthful. I finish what I'm eating and say.

"I come up to Scotland regular with work; I need to visit my customers in the evening."

"You're not one of them insurance salesmen are you?" Simon asks.

I think for a minute whether to say I am, but then again; if he knows about insurance and asks me a question I'd be found out for sure. So I decide to keep to my bogus business story.

"No I do business with the pubs and clubs and I find it's easier to catch them in, in the evenings. I sell snacks; you know crisps and peanuts etcetera."

"Have you had a good day today?" Tom asks.

"Not too bad. It's been a busy week so I'm off on my way home now for a relaxing weekend."

"So where's home?" Simon asks.

"Liverpool"

"Red or Blue?"

"Red."

"Good lad, we're both reds too, shame Tom here lives in Birkenhead; I live on Salisbury Street, Islington."

"Wow, were basically neighbours, I only live a mile or so from you." I say.

"I'll tell you something; if we had that mouthless vigilante up here there wouldn't be any trouble." Simon says.

"Yes, we were just talking about him before those lads got a bit noisy. Have you heard about him Chris?" Tom asks.

"Mouthless vigilante, wasn't he on the news the other day?"

"Yes, it was terrible that they arrested him; as far as I was concerned. He was the reason why crime was on the decrease in Liverpool." Simon says.

"He was doin a great job, the news reporter said criminals were worried about getting caught by this guy so they stopped committing crimes, even the street gangs stayed at home. It was great." Tom adds.

"That's it, I remember. Wasn't he arrested for trying to attack a police officer in plain clothes?"

"Yes, that was it." Tom says.

"See that's what I don't get. He's been attacking only criminals so why would he attack a policeman? It doesn't make sense." Simon adds.

"I'm sure the truth will come out, it always does. Maybe it was a setup?"

"I wouldn't put it past the police to do something underhanded to catch him. But I don't understand why they wanted to catch someone who was doing a public service. Getting rid of criminals and making the streets safer to walk on at night. I say they should have given him a medal."

"I agree with you, I think he's been doing a good job. Anyway it's been nice chatting to you; maybe I'll see you around sometime and thanks again for the burger and coffee." I shove the last of the burger in my mouth and pick up my coffee cup.

"Have a safe journey Chris and thanks" Simon says as I turn toward the exit.

I walk out of the services and towards my car when I notice two figures over towards my right come running towards me. I look over and recognise the uninjured lad and his mate Dave who I kicked in the jewels running towards me. Dave is still showing signs of being injured as he's slightly behind his mate. I can't see the leader of the three so I imagine he's hold up in a car or van somewhere resting his hand.

The uninjured lad runs up towards me; I see his right fist pull back behind him ready to explode into a full forced punch towards my head. I pull off the lid to my steaming coffee and step to the side as the lad's fist flies across my face missing me by a few inches. I throw the contents of my cup full into his face. "Aghhhh" the lads hands quickly clutch his burning face as he bends down desperately trying to wipe away the burning hot coffee.

Dave reaches me and immediately stops and stares at his mate clutching his eyes. I take the second opportunity presented to me by kicking Dave between the legs.

Dave's body buckles and he collapses on the ground in front of me holding his groin lying in a foetal position. I quickly turn back towards his mate now with his back to me still holding his face.

'This is very considerate of you to face the other way with your legs apart.' I think to myself.

I swing my leg forward up between the lad's legs as hard as I could crunching the arc of my foot into the apex of his legs flattening his unprotected soft parts into nothing. His legs lift up while his body drops to the ground bashing his knees and head on the tarmac. I step around them and open my car door and climb in. I don't want any trouble tonight as it's only a day away from going on holiday and I don't want to end up in jail for GBH or something. I know they started the fight but you can never tell how things would work out when the cops arrive. Two of them would probably say that I started the fight and they didn't do anything; the third guy would also tell the same story so I'd rather not risk hanging around. I start the engine and pull out onto the slip road and head back over the A74 and down onto the M6 heading southbound for Liverpool.

Two hours later I find myself nearing the outskirts of Liverpool so I quickly check the time and see it's far too early to be heading home so I continue on towards my favourite resting place near Wrexham. I arrive in my usual lay-by at three forty eight and set the alarm on my phone for five o'clock to give me enough time to leisurely head for home. I adjust the seat in the car so I can lay right back for an hours sleep.
'It's been an interesting and busy night.' I think to myself.

'I've prevented a drunkard from driving his lorry, seen Stewart get treatment by the paramedics and had a fight with three yobs and made a couple of old boys happy. It's not been too bad really.'
I close my eyes and try to visualise sheep jumping over a fence to help me drop off. It doesn't take long to fall asleep and I don't believe it was the counting

of sheep that did it but the shear exhaustion from fighting with three men half my age.

News Report

My alarm wakes me up exactly on time for my return journey home. I sit up in the driver's seat and readjust my chair to the upright position. I find that having a nap for an hour doesn't do you any good; it's too long for a short nap and too short for a restful sleep. My body takes a few minutes to return from the state of slumber as I rub the sleep from my eyes and give my cheeks a slap with both hands to revive my senses. The dark sky outside is never appealing or inviting for someone to get motivated to take a drive. A bright sunny day on the other hand can get anyone motivated. My body shivers for a moment to expel any chills from the body and I grab the cold steering wheel ready for the journey.

I start the car and turn the headlights on before putting the car in first gear and pulling out onto the road with full lock to do a U-turn. The road is clear and just wide enough to manage the manoeuvre in my small car; any bigger and it would have turned out to be a three or five point turn. I look down at my lunchbox on the passenger seat and suddenly feel peckish so I take out the sandwich Anne made for me and tuck in; the flask of coffee is just warm at this point but drinkable so I pour myself a cup full to wash the sandwich down. I definitely don't want to get home without eating the food Anne prepared or else I'd be in big trouble. I finish the food off and continue on my journey home.

"Good morning Anne." I call out as Anne gets up from the breakfast table to make me a cup of tea.

"Good morning Chris, how was your night?"

"Good thanks, what about yourself, did you sleep well?"

"Yes slept like a log"

I hang my coat up and take my work shoes off before walking around to the dining table to join Michael who's still reading his manga book.

"Hello son, how are you?"

Michael glances up from his book.

"OK dad." His eyes immediately look back down to what he's reading in his left hand; his right hand scoops up a spoonful of Frosties Cereal soaked in milk to his mouth.

'Crunch Crunch Crunch.' He chews the cereal without taking his eyes off the book. A drip of milk runs down from the corner of his mouth onto his chin; he wipes it away with his sleeve.

"Must be a good book then?" I ask.

Michael doesn't hear me; he's either so engrossed in his book that he's just blanked everything else out. I decide it's probably best to let him finish what he's doing before trying to continue our conversation; which isn't going to well.

"Here you are darling." Anne places the cup of tea down on the table for me while she sits down to finish her breakfast of scrambled eggs on toast.

"Thank you." I pick up my drink and take a sip.

"I'll make you something to eat in a moment, just want to finish my eggs before they get cold." Anne says.

"That's alright; I'm not that hungry this morning. It wasn't long ago since I had my midnight snack." Anne looks at me suspiciously.

"What time did you eat?"

"Oh I don't know, maybe an hour or so ago."

"Wow you must have been starving all night. How did you manage not eating anything until five thirty this morning?"

"I…er had a burger earlier."

"A burger! Where did you get that from; you know it's bad for you eating burgers in the middle of the night. Christopher, you've got to be more careful with your health, it's not good for you."

I knew it was a bad idea telling Anne about my midnight snacks.

"Sorry, I'll try to be good." I look at her with apologetic eyes.

"At least you only have one night left for work; you have booked Sunday night off haven't you?"

"Yes darling, I couldn't exactly work through the night until six o'clock and then go on holiday on Monday morning exhausted."

"Good; so promise me no burgers tonight?"

"I promise." I say.

I decide to finish my tea in the lounge while watching some television. The early morning news comes on discussing the rise in petrol prices for the third time this year which has angered most people in the country and especially the small business men who can't afford to deliver their goods to customers. I sometimes wonder how the oil companies can charge such exorbitant prices when they're making so much profit.

'Breaking News Report' appears on the screen and a reporter is seen standing outside the Merseyside Police headquarters.

"David, what can you tell us about the recent attack made to a police officer?" the news reporter in the studio asks the on site reporter.

"Thank you Kelly. A local police sergeant was found injured and naked last night suffering from pneumonia after becoming the next victim to the vigilante, know to us as the mouthless maniac. Police were called to a cottage in Scotland where a naked man was seen crawling along the road partially covered over with a thin blanket. Ambulances were called and the man later to be identified as a police sergeant with the Merseyside constabulary was taken to Dumfries County Hospital for treatment."

"We thought the masked maniac was caught a few days ago and is in custody. So how could he attack someone in Scotland?" Kelly asks.

"It turns out Kelly that the man suspected of being the masked maniac was in fact a mental patient escaped from a local hospital and not the real masked maniac."

"Why would the masked maniac attack a police officer, his record of attacks have mainly focused on criminals; so why attack a police sergeant?"

"That's a good question Kelly; apparently when the sergeant was brought into the hospital suffering with pneumonia and leg injuries the words 'Dirty pigs get punished' was written across his chest and as we know, the masked maniac has written across his victims chests identifying the reason why they were attacked. So the question we need to ask ourselves is; what does the masked maniac know about this police sergeant? Is he a dirty pig as described by the writing across his chest? This was the question we tried to raise with the Chief Constable who declined to answer our questions at this point pending an investigation."

"So if this sergeant was as the words describe him; a dirty pig. We have the masked maniac to thank for revealing a rotten fruit within the barrel of clean honest and brave police officers we have in the police force."

"All we know Kelly is the masked maniac has always been right with regards to his victims and although the chief constable at this time doesn't want to comment. The truth will always come out in time."

"Thank you David; and now over to Sarah with the weather."

I turn the television off and carry my empty cup out to the kitchen where Anne is washing the dishes.

"Right, I'm off to bed now. See you later about two."

"OK darling; have a nice sleep." Anne kisses me while taking the dirty cup and dunking it in the washing up water.

I make my way upstairs and into the bathroom for the usual ablutions and a quick wash before getting undressed and climbing into bed.

I start to think about the news report.
'*Everyone will know the masked maniac is still on the loose so will the police be out in force tonight in a massive sting operation to catch me I wonder.*
What about Pete and Jenny, will they have their holiday cancelled now that they know the vigilante is still at large?'
I close my eyes and try to free my mind from any distractions as I visualise sheep jumping over a fence.

A loud bang wakes me from my sleep as I sit up quickly in bed. Its dark and I feel a little disorientated not being able to focus on my surroundings. I hear the sound of glass breaking downstairs; it sounds like a window then shouting from what appears to be a group of people. I flick the bedside light on and jump out of bed; my feet find my slippers quickly as I make my way around the bed towards the bedroom door. Its strange that Anne's not in bed with me and I'm not sure what the time is. Where is she? Did she make the banging sound and what's all that shouting I can hear from men downstairs. I open the door and step out onto the landing. Two men in dark uniforms run up the stairs and head straight for me.

It seems to happen in slow motion seeing the men grab both my arms and lift me up in the air. Suddenly I'm pushed down onto the bedroom floor and pinned down with the weight of one of the men sitting on my chest while the second man hooks around my right wrist a metal shackle of some sort. I can't quite see as my head is forced over to the side as the man sat on my chest is pressing his left hand down hard on the side of my head squashing my face in the carpet.

'*What's going on,*' I think to myself.

'*Who are these men?*' My right wrist is pulled up over my head and twisted pulling my right shoulder up and across my face. The man on my chest slides off me allowing my body to roll over onto my stomach before my right hand is swung back and down to the base of my spine. Someone grabs my left wrist and pulls it towards my right wrist before I feel the metal shackle folds around it when I hear someone call out.

"Chris Douglas you're under arrest!"

My eyes spring open wildly staring through the dimly lit bedroom for the darkened figures only to see an empty room. I sit up in bed and the realisation that it's all been a dream makes me give a sigh of relief. My heart beat still beating fast from the shock of being caught by the police with my breathing matching my heart rate. I close my eyes with relief at the sudden realisation that it's not real.

'*I desperately need a holiday*' I think to myself.

I wipe the sweat from my brow with my hands and give my eyes a quick rub before checking the time. The clock face tells me its 1:56pm; time to get up. I reach over and turn the alarm off and climb out of bed.

I can hear Anne downstairs in the kitchen and the soft noise from the boiling water in the kettle. I wander into the bathroom to wash my face in cold water. The image in the bathroom mirror looks tired and a little older than the last time I looked. I notice a few laughter lines around the eyes and a sprinkling of grey hairs just above my ears. I brush my wavey blonde hair neatly back behind my ears with my fingers to make myself more presentable; although Anne knows what I look like after a night on the town so a little ruffled hair isn't going to matter much. I wander back out onto the landing and into the bedroom to find Anne placing a fresh cup of tea down next to the bed for me.

"Hi darling, did you sleep well?" she asks.
"Good thanks."
"Jenny has invited us over to theirs for dinner tonight so we can make plans on what to do on holiday. Is that alright? Pete will be there so you can chat to him for a bit before you have to get off to work."
"Yes that's fine, what time do they want us there?"
"Jenny said about six"
"I could drop you and Michael off home after dinner about nine thirty before I head for work if you want?"
"That sounds good. I'm just making an apple pie to take over for pudding."
Anne makes her way downstairs to carry on her baking while I rest on the bed and finish my cup of tea.

'*What to do tonight?*' I think to myself.

'It's my last night tonight before we go on holiday so I don't want to do anything stupid and get caught. I could always just drive over to my favourite lay-bye and sleep for the night; although it's getting cold in the car when you're stuck in the middle of nowhere. I could always book a room somewhere and sleep in a comfortable bed for the night; I've got the money and I don't need anymore money this week. If I do that, I would be wide awake in the morning and Anne might wonder why. I remember that lorry driver who nearly ploughed into the front of us the other day who lives on Shelby Road. I could always give him a visit tonight in the car. I wouldn't want to miss him out as he nearly killed Anne and Michael and that's unacceptable. I think I'll pay him a visit tonight just so it ties up all the loose ends.'

We all watch a black and white movie on the classic channel during the afternoon which we find really entertaining. It's the first time Michael has seen John Wayne in a film before.

"That was a good film wasn't it Michael?" I ask.

"Yes dad, is that really how the west was won?" Michael asks.

"I don't think so."

"I wish I could be a cowboy dad?"

"There are some cowboys living not to far away, one of them came in our house and fixed our kitchen window."

Anne starts to laugh. "Christopher, don't be horrible. He did a good job."

"I'll tell you something Michael; did you know John Wayne in the film, you know the big guy. His real

name was Marion. Isn't that funny having a girls
name although I don't expect many people told him
that to his face."
We look at the time and see its time to go to Pete and
Jenny's.
"Come on you two lets get some food." I say.
Anne heads into the kitchen to fetch the apple pie and
Michael and I put our coats and shoes on.

We arrive five minutes early outside Pete's house and
I park the car on the road at the end of their drive. We
all climb out and make our way up the drive towards
the house when I glance over at the garage and see a
police car parked up on the drive.
*'That's interesting; deja vu. This reminds me of the
first time we came here for dinner seeing the police
cars in the drive.'*

In my heart I know its nothing but my brain is telling
me the police are here to arrest the masked maniac. I
slow my pace a little and try to calm my nerves with
some deep breathing which Anne notices.
"Are you alright Chris?" she stops and looks at me
looking a little concerned.
"Yes sorry, I think I've got a little indigestion or
heartburn or something. Maybe I just need to eat
some food, that's all"
We carry on to the door and knock on the door
knocker.

The door quickly opens revealing Jenny dolled up to
the nines with a short evening dress and high heels

and hair tied up displaying tear drop diamond earrings.

"Anne, Chris, come on in." We step through into the hallway and give Jenny a kiss.

"You look fabulous; you didn't say we needed to dress up for the occasion?" Anne says.

"No, of course you don't. I just felt like putting on something nice as were on holiday soon." She gives a little excited scream.

Anne screams too in approval and they both hug each other.

"Well, dinner smells lovely Jenny. Oh, I've baked an apple pie for pudding if that's OK?" Anne asks.

"That's lovely, thanks Anne; sorry Pete won't be long, something has turned up which needs sorting out. Come on through to the lounge." She closes the front door and we all wander into the lounge where Debbie is sat reading her manga book.

"Debbie, Michael's here." Jenny says.

Michael makes his way over to the armchair to join Debbie. Anne and I take a seat on the sofa.

"Drinks anyone?" Jenny asks.

"I'll have a white wine if that's alright." Anne says.

"Any soft drink for me thanks Jenny." I say.

Jenny makes her way into the kitchen to fetch the drinks while we wait on the sofa for Pete to finish with the Police officer in his study.

"Oh hi Chris and Anne, you remember Mark." Pete calls through from the entrance hall as he and Mark make their way to the front door.

"Oh hi Pete, yes you played on our team last week in defence?" I ask.

"Hi Chris, yes you're right. I was the one who saved that shot on goal from Stewart and I've still got the bruises to show for it on my thigh." He points to his right leg.

"Ouch, it did look painful." I add.

"Not as half as painful from the tackle you took from Stewart; how are you, will you be playing again tomorrow?"

"Yes, I'm fine thanks and I will be playing."

"Great, so I'll see you tomorrow. I'm off to work now; on the late shift again."

Mark waves as he makes his way to the door, Pete says a few more words to him before he walks out and the door is closed behind him.

"So! We're on holiday on Monday. What time is your flight?" Pete asks.

"I think our flight is at ten in the morning, what about yours?" I ask.

"Great were on the same flight as well. What if we drove there together, we could pick you up at eight in the morning so we can get through customs and maybe have some breakfast at the airport?"

"Wow that would be great thanks Pete." Anne says.

"Great, well that's sorted. So where's Jenny with the drinks?" Pete asks.

"Here I am." Jenny calls though from the kitchen as she walks in with a tray carrying our drinks.

We sit and chat for a little while in the lounge making small talk before Pete gets up and turns the television on for the local news.

"Sorry guys; just got to listen to this for a moment." Pete says.

The anchorman begins his report. 'The masked maniac is on the loose again, hurricane Betty expected on our coast and Liverpool win in the Derby game against Everton.'

Pete sits back in the armchair and turns the volume up a little on the television.

'The masked maniac who has been attacking criminals is still on the loose. Police arrested a man thought to be the masked maniac only to realise later when the real masked maniac attacked a local police sergeant who was found last night crawling along a road in Scotland having been attacked and injured. Over to Beveley, for the full report.'

The television screen shows a brunette reporter standing outside a cottage on a darkened lane. 'Thank you Trevor. She continues. Police and Ambulance services were called to this property late last night where they found a naked man crawling along the side of the road with a small blanket wrapped around him. The man now believed to be Sergeant Stewart Grimm of the Merseyside police had been attacked by the masked maniac and left here in this deserted cottage with a few provisions of food and water. We spoke to the chief constable earlier today who had this to say."

The screen flicks onto an earlier recording outside the Police headquarters where the chief constable made a statement to the press.

"One of our officers was attacked by the masked maniac and left in an abandoned cottage in Scotland. The officer is receiving treatment and is in a stable condition. We do not tolerate any attacks on any of our officers and this mouthless maniac will be prosecuted with the full weight of the law for his violent and criminal actions against someone in a position of trust and someone with impeccable credentials within the force. I intend to find this villain personally and bring him to justice."

"Thank you Chief Constable Grimm." The news reporter says.

I notice the name of the chief constable appear on the television screen. 'P Grimm.'

"WHAT!" I cry out.

Everyone turns quickly to see why I shouted.

'I can't believe he's related to Stewart Grimm, the Chief constable is related to the man I attacked. That means the chief constable is going to throw everything at finding the masked maniac.'

I look at Pete's face and then Jenny's and Anne's who all seem shocked that I cried out.

"What is it Chris. What's happened? Anne asks.

I look at their concerned faces and realise I need to explain myself.

'What can I say?' I try to quickly think up some plausible reason for calling out when I just say the first thing that comes into my head.

"Did anyone see the guy in the distance? He was only there for a second. I think it was my uncle walking out of the Police station."

"I didn't see him" Pete says.

"No I didn't, I was looking at the chief constable." Anne says.

"Oh it doesn't matter; it just shocked me seeing him on television. He was always in trouble when I was a lad."

"Was he the black sheep of the family then?" Jenny asks.

"He wasn't just the black sheep, but the charcoal burnt black sheep." I say showing a look of disapproval at being related to someone bad.

"Well I'm glad I married the good one in the family then." Anne says.

We all have a giggle at the thought.

Pete switches the television off and Jenny tells us its dinner time.

We all sit around the dining table and Jenny serves up the food. Lamb chops new potatoes and broccoli with onion gravy and mint sauce.

"Thank you Jenny this smells delicious." I say.

"Thanks Chris."

"So Pete, the news said that the masked maniac is still on the loose. So wont you have to cancel your holiday as you're in charge of the investigation?" I ask.

"I would normally, but because I've already booked and paid for it; they've said I could go but I have to return after a week, Jenny and Debbie can stay for the two weeks but unless they find the masked maniac before the weeks up, I'll have to get back and continue with the search for him, sorry guys." Pete says.

"That's terrible Pete; can't someone else look after things while you're on holiday?" Anne asks.

"Sorry, it's my case. I'm lucky to be getting any holiday as it is."

Are they related?

"I noticed the chief constable has the same surname as Stewart; are they related?" I ask Pete.
"Yes, he's Stewart's father."
The new potato I have in my mouth gets lodged at the back of my throat as I begin to cough and turn blue.
'Hugkkk' a small round shaped potato flies out of my mouth and lands in my drink sending coke splashing over the sides of the glass.

"Chris, are you alright?" Anne calls out.
I hold my hand to my mouth to stop any more bits of potato falling out and indicate with my other hand that I'm alright.
Everyone stares at me for a moment looking concerned. I manage to swallow the remains of the food before replying.
"Sorry, I think I was rushing my food as it tasted so nice."
"That's alright Chris, just take your time and enjoy it." Jenny says.

My heart begins to sink and I start to feel sick just thinking I've attacked the son of the Chief Constable; what bad luck on my part.
'*I'd assume the Chief Constable is going to concentrate all his efforts in trying to catch me now that I've attacked his son. If he intends on doing that; it won't be long before they find out who I am. So what do they know about me? I don't know; I've been pretty careful at not leaving clues. I've burnt all the evidence from what I can remember so they shouldn't*

*have DNA or fingerprints to track me down and the
victims have all been blindfolded so they wouldn't
know what vehicle I've been driving.'*

*'Maybe they know they've been tied up in a van but
some of them have been put in a suitcase in a car, but
do they know that? Maybe they think they may be in a
van, I'm not sure. Surely you could tell the sound of a
van to a car; but some cars sound like vans,
especially the diesel type cars. So let's assume all
they really know is; all the victims have been tied up
and transported in a van but they don't know what
van or the registration. I think if I don't use the van
for a little while that would help.'*

*'As I'm on holiday in two days for two weeks means
the van won't be used while I'm away and the search
for me would go cold. I've got to go out tonight so if I
use the van for the last time tonight, I should be
alright as I don't suppose the police could set up a
sting operation that quickly. It would also mean that
when I catch the lorry driver and transport him in the
van; he would definitely know what vehicle he's in
and tell the police when I release him. Hopefully the
police will only be looking for a transit van of some
description in the future. When I get back from
holiday, I could resume my work using the car for a
little while and with a bit of luck, the unit in
Birmingham will be available and I could focus my
crime prevention services in a totally different city. I
may even own a box van by then so that would
definitely confuse the police. I think I should be*

alright for now. Just think; one more night working and then holiday time in the sun.'

"He has another son in the armed forces, looks just like Stewart but with shorter hair. I think he's in the Marines or something." Pete adds.

"So why hasn't the police caught this guy, surely they must have plenty of evidence on the guy already as he's attacked at least ten people?" I ask Pete.

"Sorry, I'm not supposed to discuss the case, but I can tell you we don't have anything substantial. The guy's been really meticulous about not leaving clues."

"What about fingerprints, surely he must have left something, somewhere?"

"We did have a partial fingerprint in a house where he attacked a suspected paedophile but it wasn't enough of a print to find out who he is."

"What about eye witnesses. Surely someone must have seen something and then there's cctv cameras?"

"I know Chris, but this guy is very professional. He doesn't attack anyone where there are cameras and he doesn't leave clues. To be honest, since he's been attacking criminals; the crime rate has dropped significantly in the Liverpool area. I hope that we never catch the guy because he's doing a great job, but don't tell anyone I said that."

"No off course not." I say.

Pete smiles as he takes a mouthful of food.

"I was talking to a couple of old boys the other day and they said the same thing. If the crime rate is decreasing in the area because of this guy then why not let him continue what he's doing and maybe crimes in Liverpool will stop altogether; Liverpool would be the safest place to live in the country." I say. "That would be nice, wouldn't it Jenny to live in a crime free society to bring up our children?" Anne asks.

"Yes, now that would be nice." Jenny replies

I feel a little bit better knowing the police have no evidence on the mouthless maniac. I just need to keep it that way. My mind quickly jumps to what I need to do later on this evening.

'*As it's my last night for two weeks, maybe I could leave a red herring for the police to follow to take them totally off the trail. What if I planted my mask and maybe some clothing from a victim in someone's house for the police to find? That should keep them busy for a while. What if I plant the stuff in a known criminal's house; someone who needs to be put away, maybe someone in a high profile position.*' I think to myself.

I begin to remember reading about a local gangster who opened a strip club in town a few years ago.

'*The locals complained about it but nothing ever was done about it. People did suspect that the gangster must have paid the police off or at least the local council. I do remember some of the people who complained to the council had their cars damaged and petrol bombed. It was all over the news but yet again, nothing was ever done. A lot of people thought there was something dodgy going on inside the club; it was more than a strip club because there was a quick turnaround of dancers in the club and no one knew why or knew where the girls had disappeared to? It all sounded a bit funny. Maybe the boss was involved in human trafficking or prostitution or something. Now that's the type of person I'd like to put down and maybe tonight's the night to do it.'*

I notice everyone had finished eating their main meal while I still had quite a bit of food left; I'd managed to eat half my lamb and only two potatoes with half the broccoli.

"Are you alright Chris? Don't eat it if you really don't like it; I wont be offended" Jenny says.

"No, no sorry, it's lovely. My mind was on something else. This is lovely." I pick up a large piece of Lamb on my fork with a whole new potato covered in onion gravy and shove it in my mouth.

"Mmmmm gnize" I try saying with my mouth full.

"CHRISTOPHER! Don't be such a pig." Anne screams across the table.

"GZory" I try to apologise as I put my knife and fork down until I've chewed the food in my mouth to a satisfactory degree in order to swallow the huge mouthful.

"Anyone for pudding, we have Trifle or Apple pie and ice cream?" Jenny asks.

We all give jenny our orders for pudding and I slowly finish off the rest of my main while the others chat across the table.

After dinner we all make our way into the lounge to relax on the more comfortable chairs. Jenny brings through more drinks. Anne has her second glass of wine while I stick to drinking coke.

"So it's your last night tonight, what is it that you do Chris?" Pete asks.

"Just boring old distribution stuff; you know sending stuff here there and everywhere. It's not as exciting as your job." I reply hoping to re-direct the conversation onto something totally different.

"Do you know if there are any jobs going for Alex as he's out of work at the moment and I thought working at your place would be ideal, you know loading and unloading vehicles would keep him out of mischief?"

"I'm not sure, but I'll keep an eye out for you and let you know as soon as something turns up."

"That's great thanks Chris." Pete replies.

"Do you ever have to deliver stuff yourself, or are you office based?" Pete asks.

I start to feel a little nervous at being asked about a job I have no idea about. I look up at the clock to see its just gone nine.

"Sorry Pete I think we need to go. I have to drop Anne and Michael off before getting to work for ten." I stand up and look at Anne so she gets the hint.

"Thank you very much for a lovely evening and great food again. So we'll see you tomorrow for football and then Monday morning at what time are you picking us up?" I ask.

"Eight o'clock we'll pick you up on Monday and thanks for coming over, so see you tomorrow at three" Pete says.

We shake hands and give the women a hug and kiss before Anne, Michael and I make our way down the drive to our car. Jenny and Pete wave to us from the open front door as we drive away.

"That was nice and it was really nice that they've volunteered to pick us up on Monday to take us to the airport" Anne says.

"Yes that is really nice of them. It means I won't have to pay for airport parking which will save me thirty quid; I could buy a bottle of whisky with that."

"Oye more like five bottles of wine for me." Anne exclaims.

"Yeah whatever!"

I drop Anne and Michael off at the door and drive off as they enter our house. I quickly turn down the lane leading to our garages and pull up to the right of my garage. I open the garage door and drive the van out before parking the car inside the garage. It takes me ten minutes to get changed into my protective gear and lock the garage up again. I sit in the driver's seat and stare out through the windscreen thinking through what I need to do tonight.

'If I'm going to get the lorry driver at this hour, he's going to be home and in front of the television watching the news or the football so I don't imagine he's going to answer the door when someone knocks after ten o'clock at night. So how am I going to get him to come outside at this hour?' I think to myself.

'He lives on a terraced row so if I make too much noise outside his house the neighbours would look out and see me. What if I damage his car and get him to chase me down the street; the neighbours wouldn't see me in the dark so I could plan to get him round a corner out of the way from prying eyes.' That's what

I'll do. I begin to visualise the events in my mind so I'm clear about everything.

"OK just need to pick up a couple of things first." I say to myself.

I start the engine and pull out of the garages and up the side lane to the main road. I turn right in the direction of the supermarket.

I park the van near the entrance to Tesco's and climb out of the van; the car park is fairly empty this time on a Saturday night as most people are in the pub or at home watching the football highlights on TV. I grab a basket and head for the alcohol aisle where I pick up the cheapest bottle of vodka before heading down to the food aisle where I pick up two large bottles of vegetable oil and then make my way to the express checkout. The girl gives me a strange look as she scans the items and then asks for the money.

"Don't even ask; I have no idea what my son wants with these?" I say to her.

She laughs and says. "I know what you mean, I have a son myself."

I give her the money and she passes back the receipt and change.

"Thank you." I say as I carry the items out with me.

I drive towards Shelby Road which is only a few minutes away and turn into the road at the higher number end. I notice on the right a house displaying the number 195 on its door so I've got a little way to drive before I reach 127. I notice a stream of cars parked against the pavements along the whole length of the street belonging to the residents. I slow the van down to a steady twenty miles per hour so I can keep an eye on the vehicles parked next to the kerb as I need to identify the silver Subaru belonging to the truck driver. I inspect each vehicle as I drive past, Mini, Audi, Ford, Ford, Renault, Ford, Subaru. That's it; the silver Subaru is correctly parked outside number 127.

"Perfect" I say to myself as I drive past. I notice further up the road a turning on the right about fifty yards away from the guy's house. I pull up to the turning and stop the van, looking right to see if I can spot a parking space; nothing.

"This is ridiculous." I say to myself.

I look at the corner of the road and calculate I could just about fit the van on the end. I want the side door of the van against the pavement so I reverse the van into Wilson Street and park against the curb.

I'm parked with my back end right up against a cavalier estate car parked on Wilson Street with my bonnet towards Shelby Road; it's definitely not legal but who cares, its night time and I've got a job to do. I don't expect to see any traffic wardens around at this time so I should be alright for the next twenty minutes or so. I turn the engine off and climb out and walk around the front of the van and onto the pavement. The streets are quiet but for the faint sound of some road traffic in the distance travelling along the main road. I glance down Shelby Road towards number 127 with the silver Subaru parked outside between a boxed white van and a Ford Fiesta behind; I need to get the guy to come out of his house and chase me along the pavement so I look around for a stone or brick to smash his car window and set the car alarm going.

It's not easy to find when you're looking along pavements and streets that are regularly cleaned. I don't see any as I make my search along Wilson Street so I resort to looking over the small garden walls on the front of the houses. Most of the gardens are neat and tidy with a central patch of lawn with bordering flower beds that have been pruned and cleared of stones. I reach a run down house where the garden is overgrown and find a metal rusted door hinge.

'*That'll do*' I think to myself as I pick it up from among the weeds.

I make my way back around the corner into Shelby Road. The road is still void of people so I wander back to the van and take out a bottle of vegetable oil. I open the side door to the van and leave the door slightly ajar for quick access when I need to get inside quickly.

I begin my slow walk down the road towards the man's house occasionally checking windows along the route to see if anyone can see me. Most of the houses have their curtains closed blocking out most of the light from inside the houses but for a small slither of light around the edges of the windows as the light tries to escape. I reach the house belonging to the lorry driver with his parked car outside and stop.

'*I need to formulate my plan beforehand so things run smoothly.*' I think to myself.

I run the scenario through in my mind.

'*I smash the window of the car and pretend to rob it, as soon as I hear the front door to the house open I make a dash to my right along the pavement to the corner of Wilson Street where I empty the contents of the oil on the pavement. I pull down my mask and wait for the man to come running around the corner; he'll be so shocked to see my mask that he'll not notice the oil and slip on the ground, stopping against the van. I tazer him and shove him in through the side door.*'

"Right lets do this." I say to myself.
I lift up the rusty hinge and throw it against the side window of the Subaru with all the force I can muster.
'Crash! Wah, Wah, Wah.'
The alarm begins to wail with side lights flashing. I step towards the car door and bend forward to make out that I'm stealing something. Clenching hold of the bottle of oil, I begin to unscrew the lid when I hear the front door start to unlock. I turn right and begin my run towards Wilson Street while looking back to see the lorry driver appear at the door.
"Oye you.." he sprints out of the door after me followed by another younger man desperately trying to put on a shoe as he hops down onto the pavement.

"Crap! Here we go again" I say to myself as I reach the corner.
I turn into Wilson Street and immediately begin to pour the oil on the pavement with my left hand while pulling down my mask over my face with my right. The bottle quickly empties covering most of the pavement in vegetable oil. I look up at the corner and

see the man rush round towards me; his eyes lock onto my face and I see his expression change from rage to horror. His left foot steps out to slow his speed down but as his foot lands on the oily pavement; he immediately loses traction and his foot begins to slide across the pavement. His right foot tries to assist his failing left foot as he steps down hard on the same slippery patch of pavement sending him flying through the air towards the side of the van.
'Crash'
The man's head smashes against the wheel arches knocking himself out cold. His body lays motionless in a crumpled heap against the vans wheel. I realise I don't have much time because his mate is closely following behind; I look up at the corner as his younger mate arrives.

Deja vu seldom happens during a lifetime but in this instance the man following seems to be wearing exactly the same clothes as the first guy only a younger version. He rushes round the corner in exactly the same fashion stepping on the oil with his left foot and doing the exact same manoeuvre as his dad. His right leg steps in and then slips while his body takes a kind of head dive towards the van.
'Thud.'
This time the lad dives head first into the crumpled body of his dad cushioning his fall somewhat.
"Arghh" the lad calls out as he regains his footing from his crouched position as he tries to stand. I notice his body is leaning to one side with his right hand holding the left side of his ribs. I expect he's winded himself when he crashed into his dad still

unconscious on the ground. I don't waste anytime on waiting for him to make his move, so I step forward and jab the tazer into his chest. He stumbles back over his father and down onto the ground as I continue to push the electric charge into his torso. His body shakes and spasms for a few moments and then I see his eyes close.

I pocket the tazer and grab the lad's wrists and drag him towards the side wall of the house on the corner. I sit him up so he's propped against the wall before turning my attention to the lorry driver crumpled against my front wheel. I open the side door and lift him into the back. Within seconds I've secured his hands behind his back and secured his feet. I tear off two strips of duct tape and fix one over his eyes and the other across his mouth. He starts to come around as he's lying on the floor of the van. I tazer him in the chest until he's out for the count before closing the back sliding door; I make my way back around to the cab and climb in behind the wheel.

I look over at the lad propped against the wall; I haven't any gripes against him, he hasn't done anything wrong except trying to protect his dad so I think he's been punished enough. The dad however nearly killed me and my family and needs to be taught a lesson so that's why I'm taking him and not his son. I start the van and drive away.

Horrace

I continue to drive south out of town along the A533 towards Widnes and then over the bridge towards Runcorn; I have plenty of time on my hands at the moment as the gangster I want to attack later wont be around until his club closes at around 3am in the morning so I've got nearly five hours to play with before then. I continue along the A533 when I see a sign for Whitehouse Industrial estate on the left; I turn into the estate in search of a quiet location. The business units are all very big with security gates and private parking; I continue driving around on the Aston Fields road in search of somewhere to pull over. Its not long before I see a smaller unit with a 'For Sale/For Let sign, I drive into the empty car park and pull up along side the building tucked away from prying eyes where I turn off the engine and switch off the light to the van.

Some of the business that I saw on the way in looked like they work twenty four hours a day so I imagine lorry's drive in and out all night for many of them. Where I'm parked comprises of a few smaller businesses that are all closed which suits me just fine. I take a few moments to compose myself before I climb out of the van and make my way around to the side door. I can hear the guy inside banging in an attempt at breaking his bonds and freeing himself. I slide the door open and the lorry driver stops dead; he senses his time is up and braces himself for another bolt of electricity. I tazer him in his stomach until his body becomes limp. I climb into the back of the van and lift him up onto the workbench where I connect the karabiner around his ankles and wrists. I step back out of the side door and pull on the other end of rope as his body is pulled into position arched over the workbench; I tie off the end of rope to hold him in place.

Looking around the industrial area, I quickly check the coast is still clear which happily it is. I step back into the back of the van and take out the scissors from the box and begin cutting off all his clothes and placing the bits in an empty bin liner. I keep the mans wallet and phone to one side and pocket the change he has in his pocket which amounts to three pounds and sixty seven pence. The man begins to stir again; he tries to twist and pull at his restraints but finds it too painful so he refrains from his efforts and remains still in his arched agonising position. I put the scissors back in the box and pick up his wallet to see what's inside.

A photograph tucked behind a plastic window reveals a picture of his son and himself leaning against his truck. There's no other picture so presumably he's divorced from his wife and probably lives with his son. I find a debit card and credit card with a driver's licence and seventy pounds in cash. I pocket the cash, driving licence and cards and dump the empty wallet in the bin bag with his clothes. I pick up the hammer and smash it down on the man's right kneecap. 'Crack! Mmmghhhhhhh' the man moans before blacking out. I don't like smashing a persons kneecap with my hammer, and to be honest; if I think about what I'm doing would make me physically sick. I just try to focus on the hurt and pain these men have caused others; I try and recall the day when I awoke in hospital after being attacked. When I think of the pain and discomfort of being hit on the head and being stabbed in the leg gets me so angry. I know its wrong to attack others, but in my case I'm preventing these individuals from attacking innocent men and women. That's why I can do what I'm doing without any feelings of guilt or remorse. I pick up the phone and climb back out of the van, close the door and climb back in the cab for a rest.

I place the phone in the glove compartment before examining the drivers licence and cards. The man must be in his fifties as he's been driving for thirty three years. The name on the licence is Mr Horrace Cleavedon.
"Horrace Cleavedon! Who in the world would call their kid Horrace? What a stupid name." I say to myself.
I look at the clock and see that it's 10:47pm.
'*I'll give him fifteen minutes to chill out before I ask him for his pin number.*' I think to myself.
I turn on the radio and press the button for Classic FM to chill out; the soothing sounds from a full orchestra's violin section relaxes my mind and body as I close my eyes and elevate my thoughts along waves of restful music.

The orchestral tempo's transition from the calming tranquil tones to a full on brass section disturbs my tranquil relaxation. I open my eyes and glance at the time on the dashboard which tells me its now 11:22pm.

"Wow that went quick." I say to myself.

'I can't believe it, it only seemed five minutes since I closed my eyes.' I think to myself.

I quickly rub my eyes to wipe away any sleep before turning off the radio.

"It's about that time I think to ask old Horrace for some money." I say to myself as I open the driver's door and climb back out of the cab ready to do business.

Horrace jerks within his restraints as I enter the side door of the van. The interior light comes on illuminating the naked man arched over the workbench. I step closer and lean my head in towards Horrace's left ear.

"Horrace!"

Horrace's body jerks and moans from the pain from moving.

"Horrace, you've been a naughty boy haven't you?" I ask.

He shakes his head.

"Listen Horrace, I know you've been a naughty boy because I've seen you drive like a lunatic nearly killing innocent people in your massive lorry. This has to stop before you hurt someone. Do you understand?" I ask.

Horrace nods profusely.

"Good, I'm glad to hear it. Now as you may understand, when a person is forced to work overtime; he's generally paid extra for working, isn't he?" I ask.

Horrace just listens.

"In my case, I've had to work longer catching naughty people like you when I could have been sat at home relaxing. So in a way of remuneration I need you to pay me. I'm going to remove the tape from your mouth and I want you to tell me the pin number to your debit card. If you lie to me or say anything else; I'll use my hammer and break something else on your body. If you tell me the truth, I'll let you go without any further injury. Do you understand?"

Horrace nods.

I peel back the tape from off his mouth.

"Six, six, eight, two." A coarse voice calls back his reply.

I replace the tape across his mouth.

"Good lad" I say.

I step back out of the van and slide the side door shut. Looking around at the industrial estate and visualising my journey here, I recall seeing an 'ATM' cash point about half a mile away. I climb back in the van and drive off towards the cash point.

Within a few minutes I pass the ATM attached to the local bank on the high street. I take the next left and park the van on a side street. The air feels a little cold around me so I pull the cord on my hoodie to pull in the material around my neck to keep the chill out. I step out of the van and lock the door behind me as I take a slow walk to the cash machine at the bank.

I enter the card into the slot of the cash machine and wait for the prompt to enter the pin number. The prompt appears on screen and I enter the numbers six, six, eight and two before pressing enter. The information on the screen disappears for a moment before reappearing with the balance of £3,877.45.
"Well now that's what I call a healthy bank balance." I say to myself.
I press the numbers three followed by two zeros. The machine churns away as it counts out the notes out before dispatching the debit card followed by a handful of notes. I pocket the card and cash and make my way back towards the van.

As I walk I try to think where I could find another cash machine as I'm not familiar with this part of town.
'I remember seeing a sign for 'Halton General Hospital' just off the A533 as I drove here; it's probably about a mile away. They must have a petrol station near the hospital I could try.' I think to myself.

I don't intend on taking all of Horrace's money; but I do want him to remember he's been fined for being a wreckless driver and when he looks at his bank statement; it will remind him. I climb back into the van and head in the direction of the Hospital and in search of a petrol station. It's not long before I see the sign for Halton General Hospital so I take the slip road off the A533 and turn right at the top of the slip road for the hospital. I see blue flashing lights behind me and realise it's an ambulance speeding towards the hospital obviously carrying someone in dire need of medical treatment. I pull over to the left and allow the ambulance to drive past.

Half a mile later I notice the petrol station on the other side of the carriageway. I take the slip road on my left which takes me across to the other side of the carriageway and towards the petrol station; I pull into the service station and stop the van next to a petrol pump. I figure it's worth my while to fill up with petrol at the same time as withdrawing money from the ATM as it kills two birds with one stone.

The forecourt is empty except for my van so I walk straight over to the cash point and withdraw the same amount I had previously taken. After filling up with diesel which costs me sixty three pounds I head straight into the shop and purchase a hot coffee and sandwich, cake and a packet of gingernut biscuits to dunk in my coffee. I pay the cashier for the fuel and food before heading back to the van.

I sit back in the driver's seat and quickly calculate my takings for the evening.
'*So Horrace has paid me seventy three pounds and sixty seven pence in cash. I've just taken six hundred out of his account and paid sixty eight pounds for fuel and food. That means I've earned a grand total of six hundred and five pounds sixty seven pence I think.*'
I pick up the coffee from the cup holder and take a sip of the hot liquid.
"Mmmm Nice Coffee" I say to myself.

'*I think that'll do just nicely for tonight. So what shall we do next?*' I think to myself as I look at the time on the dashboard.

'*I may as well take a drive around to see Mr Don Urchoni at his* 'Hot Girls - Just Men' *club to see what mischief I can cause for our local gangster.*'

I look back at the time to see the clock display change from midnight to 00:01 am; a new day.

Sunday 7th November

It takes me just over half an hour to arrive at the nightclub as I notice the clock telling me its 12:37am as I drive the van past the entrance and park further along the road on a side street. I position the van on the corner of the side street so that I have a clear view of the entrance to the club just in sight about a hundred metres down to my left. I want to keep the van far enough away from the entrance so as not to be noticed by anyone and not too far away that I can't walk to the club. I want to wait for closing time when everyone has left and Mr Don Urchoni leaves the building with his chauffer stroke bodyguard.

Just thinking about taking on such a big man in town with his body guard is causing me some stress even now. I take a few deep breaths to try and calm my nerves as I think through my strategy. I begin by visualising each step in my head so that I'm completely clear about what's going to happen later on. I run the scenario through over and over again until I'm happy and confident with my strategy. I know it's never a guarantee that a plan will work; but the more you prepare the better you're chances of achieving a successful outcome. I look down at the bottle of vegetable oil and vodka.

'I hope this is going to work' I think to myself. I set the alarm on my watch for two fifty in the morning to give me time to wake up ready for my attack on Don. I close my eyes and rest back into my seat.

The next two hours fly bye quickly with the occasional moments when a noise from further down the street awakes me from my slumber. The alarm burrs and vibrates on the dashboard informing me its time to wake up. It takes me a few moments to clear my head and return to the present; where I've planned to take on the most violent and most powerful man in Liverpool. I start to feel sick with the realisation of what could go wrong; if I make a mistake, not only would I lose my life but I'm sure Don would get my wife and son too.

'What the hell am I doing?' I think to myself.

Feelings of doubt pour over me and I start to wonder if this is a good plan or not. I could always back out; no ones forcing me to attack Big Don Urchoni. Who in their right mind would ever think of attacking Don unless they had an army behind them? I rub my face with both my hands to try and clear my thinking and stare out into the darkness along the main road towards the Hot Girls – Just men club. There's a couple of men outside the club chatting away when a taxi pulls up and they climb in; the taxi pulls away and drives past me taking his passengers to their destinations. I expect they were the last of the customers to leave the building so only the staff next and then big Don himself.

I watch the front door and within ten minutes a group of men and girls leave through the front door and walk around to the side car park where there are three cars parked. I watch them all saying goodnight to each other before they climb in their respective vehicles and drive out of the car park; one car drives past me while the second car drives in the opposite direction. The car park is now empty except for a white lexus LS460 saloon car with the personalised registration of B16 DON. If you left a nice car like that around Liverpool it would end up with the wheels missing; not the case with Big Don; everyone knows who he is and knows not to touch anything of his, else your life wouldn't be worth living. Just seeing the car there confirms he's in the building and will be coming out soon. My heart begins to pound loudly in my chest and my anxiety level is on par with the most stressful situation I've ever experienced.

"Come on Chris, if I've decided to stop criminals I can't be choosey about who I want to stop; you can do it." I say to myself.

I check the tazer in my pocket is still working and take out the gauntlet gloves from the glove compartment and put them on. I check the protective corset is snug around my chest and the protective shin and forearm guards are firmly in place. Everything feels OK; I reach back and feel the mask safely tucked away in my hoodie. I know it's still there; I just need to reassure myself that I'm fully prepared for the job I'm about to embark on. I pick up the bottle of oil and step outside the van and close the driver's door behind me. I look down the street towards the night club and focus my attention on the front door in anticipation of the bodyguard walking out to fetch the car from the car park as I wouldn't expect Don to walk the thirty feet to the car when he has a driver that'll fetch the car and bring it straight to the front door for him. I need to get there before the bodyguard leaves the building so I step out towards the club.

It's not long before I reach the point on the kerb on the opposite side of the road directly across from the club and stop to check no cars are coming before crossing. I know there's no cars and even If there were I would be able to hear them coming so why did I stop at three o'clock in the morning when most people are tucked away in bed; I put it down to something I've always done ever since being a kid and watching the Green Cross Man on television and his Green Cross Code.

'Now what did he say?' I think to myself.
'That's it. Always use the Green Cross Code because I won't be around when you cross the road.'
The image of Dave Prowse in his green cross uniform really stuck in my mind for years and I suppose it worked because I'm still doing it at the age of forty nine. I laugh to myself as I look both ways down the road when I notice the front door open to the club.

I'm a little surprised and shocked to see the bodyguard step out from the front door and look both left and right to see the coast is clear. I was hoping to be in position hid away somewhere around the side of the building. My body tenses as I expect him to see me standing by a bus shelter. The six foot three bald head thick set bodybuilder turns around and acknowledges to Big Don that the coast is clear before walking to his left to fetch the car.

'*I can't believe he didn't see me. I know its dark and I'm wearing dark clothes and I am on the opposite side of the street so I suppose that helped but call your self a bodyguard?*' I think to myself.

I think I would give him the sack; but then again, if he's been doing this work for years its no wonder he's missed me. He's probably getting bored of doing the same old thing over and over again and again. I'm not complaining because it's now presented me with the opportunity I needed.

I watch the bodyguard walk over to the car park to fetch the car while Mr Don Urchoni steps out of the front door with a briefcase obviously containing the takings for the night and turns to lock the front door. I cross the road as quickly and quietly as I can and reach the other side without anyone noticing. Don is just finishing off shutting the metal shutters to the main door which is lowered from a key switch that operates a winch. The metal shutters fixed above the door inside a metal boxed casing churns away as the shutters slowly lower down sealing the door space.

Don's concentration is focused on the base of the shutters as it gradually eases its way lower and lower. The burring sound of the winch must have drowned out any sound I made crossing the road; so it's not surprising that I'm able to creep right up behind him without being noticed.

I lift the mask from inside my hoodie over my head and into position over my face before taking out the tazer and jabbing it into Don's side. His body is pressed forward against the shutters with his left hand still holding the briefcase while his right hand gripping tightly onto the key operating the electronic switch. I hold the tazer firmly in his side until his legs give way and he drops in a heap on the ground. I can hear the car start up around the corner in the car park so I expect to see the Lexus pull out very soon from the car park. I open the bottle of vegetable oil and splash it all around the pavement in front of the club before stepping back around the side of the main entrance where I crouch down in the darkness tucked in the corner.

The light mounted above the doorway of the club illuminates the narrow path leading to the entrance; I position myself around the side of the doorway in a darkened corner. I hold tightly on to the tazer in readiness to attack the body guard as soon as he runs to help his boss. The lexus pulls out onto the main road and drives the short distance to the main entrance where it comes to a stop.

'I can just imagine the body guards expression when he sees big Don Urchoni slumped on the ground. He'll probably imagine that he's had a heart attack or something as his brief case is still in his hand.'
I see the door to the car fly open as the bodyguard notices Don. He's quickly out and standing beside the car looking across the roof of the car at Don's body on the ground when he calls out.

"Boss, are you alright?"
Not getting a response confirms his worst nightmare.
He runs around the car leaving the driver's door wide
open and sprints the short distance from the road to
the front door of the club. I watch him carefully as he
steps on the vegetable oil.

His left foot slides along the pavement towards the
door while his arms fly out to the sides to aid his
balance. He quickly steps forward with his right foot
to support his upper body falling over to the side. His
right foot steps firmly down on another oily section of
path sending his right foot back behind his left leg;
twisting his upper body into a spiral dive head first
towards the front wall of the building.
'Crack.'

The bodyguard's bald head hits the corner of the
brickwork knocking his head back while his whole
body crumples to the ground. I quickly step out from
the hidden corner and move towards the body guard
lying flat on the ground. He must have sensed me
coming out from the corner because his powerful
arms automatically push his upper body back up from
a press-up position into a semi crouched position
staring right at me. Blood from a gash in his bald
head starts to run down his forehead

He sees me move out from the shadows towards him
holding my tazer. In military response; still leaning on
his left hand and both knees, I see his right hand
quickly reach inside his jacket pocket for something
which I can't quite make out as the front of his body

is now in darkness. The metal reflective nozzle flashes out from under his jacket sends me into a panic at recognising the tip of the browning pistol pointing directly at my head.
'*I'm dead!*' I think to myself.

'*I picture my wife's face looking at me with tears rolling down her cheeks while Michael is sobbing with his face buried in her bosom.*'
'*What are they going to do now, without a father or husband to take care of them?*' Flashes of past events, memories of getting married and the arrival of a baby boy jump into my mind as I await the sound of the gun shot. Time must have slowed down immensely because the shot never came.
'*Why hasn't he fired yet?*' I think to myself.
I look back at the bodyguards face.

The blood from his forehead runs into his eyes blurring his vision. He tries to wipe the blood away with his left hand but the continuous stream of blood prevents him from opening his eyes. I step quickly around him pushing his gun hand away from me with my left hand while stabbing the tazer hard into the back of his neck.
The electric charge surging around his body causing his muscles to contract and release at great speed not only makes his body spasm and collapse; it automatically affects his hands causing them to do the same. The explosion next to me is deafening as the 9mm bullet is fire out to the side and hitting the brickwork of the club. I hold the tazer in place until I'm happy baldy is not going to do anything once I let

him go. His body flattens out along the pavement and I see his eyes close. I stand up and walk around him towards Don still crumpled on the floor with his hand still clutching his briefcase.

I lift him up under his arms and drag him to the car where I open the passenger door and sit him inside. His body is limp and his head has drooped over to the side resting on his left shoulder. I fix the seatbelt and return for the briefcase which I place in the foot weld between Dons feet. I close the door and make my way back around to the drivers side where I climb in and close the door.

I can just make out the bodyguard trying to move but lacking the energy. I put the car in gear and press the accelerator as hard as I can to get out of there as quickly as possible. As soon as I'm far enough down the main road to be out of view from the club; I take the first left and work my way back towards where I parked the van. I look again at Don who is still out for the count. I expect because of his age and unhealthy lifestyle, his body just couldn't recover as quickly as someone younger and fitter.

Within five minutes I pull into the gap behind the van and a mini cooper and turn the engine off. Don begins to stir in the passenger seat as I notice his head slowly lift up from its resting place on his shoulder. I don't want him to see me because I haven't got my mask on at the moment so I quickly grab the tazer with my right hand; while pressing my left hand against his face to push his gaze away from me I jab the tazer into his chest. His hands try to reach for the tazer but due to his suppressed state his arms drop to his sides as the next surge of voltage is delivered to his motionless body. I watch his aging body oscillate in the chair until I know he's had enough. I replace the tazer back inside my hoodie pocket.

"Right, that should knock you out for another ten, or fifteen minutes. So the question is; what shall I do with you now?" I ask myself.
I'd thought of how to capture him which worked out alright but my plan didn't go as far as this; so I've got no idea of what to do next. I sit quietly in the lexus trying to think through the next stage of my plan to get Don arrested for being the Masked Maniac. Immediately an idea pops into my head.

"That's it! The local police station is situated on the main road directly opposite a road that runs uphill. If I get Don to drink the vodka I've bought and get him to sit behind the wheel of his car while it rolls down the hill towards the police station. Hopefully, his car might run into the side of a parked police car; that should do it!" I say to myself.

'I could plant some evidence in the car so the police will have no doubts that they've caught the Masked Maniac and I'd be in the clear for the time being' I think to myself.

'The first thing I need; is to put Horrace in the boot of the Lexus.' I step out of the car and close the driver's door behind me. I slide the side door open to the van

and see Horrace in his usual position stretched over the workbench. Horrace flinches and moans as the pain in his leg must be now unbearable.

"Horrace, I'm going to let you go now but I want you to remember something."

Horrace stiffens and his head turns to the side to listen intently to what I'm about to say.

"Horrace. If you ever do anything wrong in the future, I'll find you and I'll break more body parts. Do you understand?"

Horrace nods in agreement.

"Good, now I'm going to transport you to my car just for a few minutes while I take you to somewhere safe."

I don't want Horrace to struggle or refuse to get into the boot of another vehicle so I decide it would be best just to tazer him for the last time. Horrace blacks out within a few seconds of being tazered in the side. I use the marker pen to write across his chest. 'Commit a crime and be punished.'

I put the marker pen in my hoodie pocket with the pair of scissors before unhooking the Karabiners from Horrace's ankles and wrists. I hold him up under his arms and manoeuvre him over to the side door of the van where I lay him down. I step out and check the coast is clear. The streets are empty so I grab Horrace again under his armpits and pull him out and along the pavement to the parked Lexus behind. I reach the back of the car and lay Horrace down on the road just behind the bumper so I can shut the van door and open the boot to put Horrace in.

I step back towards the side of the van and slide the side door closed and turn to walk back towards the car when I hear voices coming towards me. I glance around desperately trying to see where the noise is coming from when I see a boy and girl walking towards me about a hundred metres along the pavement. They seem to be looking at each other and chatting as they walk.

'Crap! They're bound to see the naked white body of a man lying on the ground between two cars as they walk past' I think to myself.
'What am I going to do? I wont have time to pick Horrace up and put him in the boot, they'd surely see me.'
I decide to do the next best thing. I quickly dart between the Lexus and the mini cooper and lay on top of Horrace to cover his naked body. I position my body perfectly mirroring Horraces body with my arms down by my sides and my face resting on his face. It all seems a little bizarre to be lying on a naked man at 3am in the morning but I don't have any other option.

The voices get louder and louder until the sound of their voices is right behind me and then it stops. I can sense they've noticed us lying on the ground between the cars. I close my eyes desperately trying to think of what to do; when I hear my voice speak.
"Wodger, ooh wodger do that again. Oh Wodger, can I take my clothes off now?"
I hear footsteps of the couple dash away along the pavement followed by giggling as they run to the

corner of the street and disappear left along the main road. I jump to my feet and look left and right. *'They've gone; thank goodness.'* I think to myself. I press the key fob to the car and the boot of the Lexus opens slowly revealing an empty boot compartment.

Horrace is still on the ground out cold. I reach down and lift him up and into the boot before pulling my mask down over my face to hide my identity. I lean into the boot and remove the tape from Horrace's eyes and mouth before shutting the boot.

I climb back into the driver's seat and start the car. Don is still out for the count so I pull out and drive towards the police station. I don't see any other vehicles for the whole journey to the top of the hill leading to the police station. I pull up next to the kerb and turn the engine off. Don starts to show signs of recovering so I quickly tazer him for the last time in his side until he blacks out again. I take out the bottle of vodka and steadily pour the clear liquid into Don's mouth while his head is pressed back.

The half litre bottle of vodka slowly disappears down his throat. I wipe the bottle on my clothes to remove any fingerprints before inserting my left index finger into the neck of the bottle to hold it up. I press Don's right hand around the bottle making sure his fingerprints are pressed down nicely on the glass before letting the bottle drop into the foot weld.

Holding onto Don's arms, I pull him across the car and into the driver's seat where I position his body in the correct position for driving. I take out the marker pen and again wiping it clean on my clothes I use Don's hand to hold it for a second before letting the marker pen fall inside the door panel. Finally I take out the pair of scissors and cut the bra straps holding my mask in place inside my hood. I cut off any remaining strands attached to the edge of the mask before placing the mask on Dons face. At this point Don's mouth is wide open which allows me to insert the mouthpiece nicely into Dons mouth so his saliva covers the plastic mouth hold inside the face mask. I remove the mask and place it nicely on the passenger seat before picking up the briefcase and placing it on the pavement behind the parked car.

"Right, I think that's everything" I say to myself standing on the pavement looking at the evidence before me. I walk back around to the driver's door and start the engine. I pull across the seatbelt and click it into its locking mechanism holding Don securely in place. Luckily for me the road ahead is clear of cars and is perfectly straight with the Police station right in front of us about a thousand metres where two police cars are nicely parked right outside the station right ahead of us. I lean my left foot into the foot weld and press the brake on the automatic car. I grab the gear changer and put the controls into drive before releasing the brake and stepping out of the car. The car starts to move forward in the direction of the police station. Running along side the car with the door open; I make the necessary adjustments to the steering so the Lexus is pointed directly at the parked police cars. When I'm sure the

car is on a collision course for the parked police cars;
I quickly close the driver's door and stop to watch the
Lexus slowly pick up speed towards its final
destination.

The Lexus with Don and Horrace travelling in is only
moving about ten miles per hour when it hits the side
of the police car on the right.
'CRASH! WEH WAR WEH WAR' the alarms to the
Lexus and Police car both go off together. Within
seconds the front door of the police station opens and
an officer runs out to investigate the noise. He stops
for a second and raises his hands in the air as to say.
'What the hell is going on!' as he assesses the scene
before him. He runs around to the driver's door of the
Lexus to see if the driver is hurt. The police officer
opens the door and leans in to the vehicle. It's not
long before he realises Don is driving while under the
influence of alcohol because I see the officer drag
Don out of the car and slap a pair of hand cuffs on
him. I think I've seen enough so I turn and head back
up the road to collect the briefcase I'd left on the side
of the road.

I continue walking for a good ten minutes before I
spot a taxi driver just dropping someone off at a block
of flats. I still have a few miles to go before I reach
the van so I decide to take a taxi as I'm tired and in
need of something to eat and drink. The taxi driver
was pleased to take me to where I needed to go as it
was his last drop of the evening and the van was
parked not to far from where the guy lived. I wait
until the taxi driver drives away before walking

across the road and climbing back into the cab of the van. I put the briefcase down on the seat next to me and start the engine. The clock in the cab tells me its nearly four o'clock in the morning so I quickly calculate that its not worth driving out to my favourite lay-bye for a nap as it would take me a good hour to get out there which would mean basically turning around and heading home again. My stomach starts to make a noise, telling me its time to eat. I pull the van out onto the road and head straight for a service station on the Motorway.

I arrive at the services within twenty minutes and park up near the entrance. As per usual the car park only has a speckle of vehicles parked up comprising of work vans and about two sales rep cars probably on their way home from some convention or training weekend. I take a quick look at the briefcase that I took from Don; the brown leather case is beautifully made with the initials DON embossed in the leather next to a silver combination lock under the handle. I know Don must have locked it before he left the club, so it's probably futile to try and open it now. I really can't be bothered at the moment as I'm physically and mentally tired and my stomach is in desperate need of coffee and a burger. I tuck the briefcase under the seat and exit the van; after locking the door, I make my way into the services and straight to the burger kiosk where I order a half pound cheeseburger with fries and an Americano coffee.

I find a seat at an empty table and tuck in to the food and drink. My mind starts to recall the events of the evening of how I was nearly killed by Don's Bodyguard which sends shivers down my spine. How I had to hide Horrace's body from the young couple walking bye and how it all could have gone wrong. *'I really need to take more care of myself in future'* I think to myself.

'I must have over ten grand in cash from all the victims I've attacked so far so I don't need to keep pushing myself and taking chances that I cant really afford to take. What if the bodyguard had shot me tonight?' I think to myself.

'Anne would be a widow and Michael wouldn't have a father to bring him up. That would be unthinkable and it upsets me knowing that could have been the reality of tonight's escapades.'

I take another sip of coffee to help me think straight. *'Ten grand is plenty to keep us financially secure for a couple of months. I could just take a long holiday and not worry about any of the bills or the need to work. But what would I tell Anne?'* I wonder. *'Oh, hello Anne, I don't need to work for a while because I've robbed people and have ten grand in a box in the garage.'*

'No, that's not going to work.' *'I suppose I don't need to think about it for a little while as were on holiday on Monday for two weeks. Maybe I could think about it when I'm on holiday. I know I'd be more relaxed then and have clarity of*

thought. I don't want to start making rash decisions and regret it later on.'
I finish off my burger and fries before returning to the kiosk and ordering another.

"Good morning Anne." I call out as I enter the house.
"Good morning darling." Anne says as she walks through from the kitchen with my cup of tea.
"So how was your last night at work?" she asks.
"Not too bad thanks, I can finally relax now and not think about work for a whole two weeks."

"I know, isn't it wonderful. We're on holiday in less than fifty hours. Yippee!" Anne puts the drink down on the dining table and gives me a hug.
It's nice to hold my wife tightly, pressing her ample breasts against my chest while I inhale the subtle scent of her perfume and natural body smell.
Moments like this remind me of how important Anne is to me and how I would do anything to keep her safe and happy.

I finish drinking my cup of tea before heading off to bed for a sleep. I set the alarm for two o'clock so I've got plenty of time to wake up and make it to the football game at three o'clock. After snuggling down under the duvet, I close my eyes and try to relax. I try to visualise lying on a sun lounger next to a swimming pool in Lanzerote watching young sun tanned women walk past me in small white bikinis. I keep my head fixed in the same position on the sun lounger but follow the women with my eyes, ogling their athletic female form behind dark sunglasses to avoid detection from the passing women and my wife lying next to me. I notice an exceptionally beautiful blonde woman glide past me heading for the pool as she disappears behind a parasol and a palm tree. I'm conscious of my wife noticing every movement I make but I don't want to lose sight of the gorgeous beauty that had just walked bye. I turn my head in the direction of where she went; when I spot Anne glaring at me. I blink for a second as she's transformed into someone in uniform holding out a set of handcuffs.

The shock of seeing Anne in a police uniform coming to arrest me wakes me up with a start. I sit up in bed breathing fast.
'What does that mean?' I think to myself.
'What does dreaming about the police coming to arrest me mean? Is it a warning? Are they on to me and I should expect someone to turn up to arrest me?' I don't like having nightmares about being arrested. I'm so desperate to go on holiday and just relax and re-energise from all the stresses and strains I've had to endure over the past few weeks.
I rub my face with my hands and check the time on the clock.
'13:55' shines the display on the clock face.
"That went quick." I say to myself.

I jump out of bed and head for the bathroom for my usual ablutions. Anne brings up a cup of tea and places it on the bedside cabinet while I get changed into my football gear comprising of Adidas shorts and Nike tee shirt and sweat top. I finish my cup of tea while sitting on the bed and carefully deliberate which colour socks to wear. I decide on the red sports socks that matches the colour of my favourite football team; Liverpool.

I wander down stairs and see Anne and Michael sat patiently on the sofa all dressed in their coats and shoes with Anne holding a bag.

"I've made a cake and a flask of coffee for half time and I've put in two small bottles of water in case you need to re-hydrate yourself." Anne lets me know.

"That's great, thanks. So shall we go?"

We all head out of the front door on our way to the game.

Football

We pull up next to the pitch and park the car. Everyone seems to be already here again so we climb out and wander over to the pitch where Jenny and Debbie are standing with some other wives and children.

"Chris!" I hear my name being called; I look out towards the players on the pitch and see Pete running over to meet me.
"I did wonder if you were really coming after last week."
"Of course, I said I would."
Angela Green sees me and wanders over with Edward Pickles.

"Hi Chris, you've met Eddy haven't you?" Angela says.
"Yes, we spoke last week."
"Yes, how are you doing? Are you fit to play again?" Edward asks.
"I think so."
"That's great! Can I be in your team?" Edward asks.
"Don't worry Eddy I've worked something out already so the three of us can be in the same team." Pete adds.
"You must be good then, if everyone wants to play with you?" Angela asks.
"You should have seen him last week he played like Rooney." Edwards replies.
"Who's Rooney?" Angela asks.

We all laugh. "It doesn't matter Love, just watch the game and see how many goals we score." Edward says as Pete and I walk onto the pitch to meet up with the other players ready for the team selection.

Sergeant Chris Miller replaces Stewart Grimm in choosing for his side. Luckily for us; he's been on holiday for the past two weeks so he's out of the loop, you could say regarding whose good and who's not. Pete chooses first and I'm selected for his team. Miller picks Dave Redhouse and then Pete selects Edward which makes Edward happy. Once the selections have been completed we make our way to the respective ends of the pitch to formulate our plans before were called to the centre to kick off.
Andrew Hill tosses the coin to decide which team will kick off.
"Heads, Right Chris your team will kick off; Pete, what side do you want to play on first?"
"We'll stay this side." Pete replies.
We all take our positions ready for kick off.

The whistle blows and Chris passes the ball to Tom on his left near the centre of the pitch. I move in quickly and snatch the ball from his feet. Stepping around him I notice Pete's already making his move forward with Edward in support. I kick the ball hard and straight past the midfielder and just ahead of Pete. Edward darts to the right of the penalty box as Pete feeds the ball through to him; Edward catches the ball with his right, then a tap with his left takes him past the last defender before striking the ball hard and low

with his right foot straight through the goalies legs
into the back of the net.
'GOAL'

Screams of excitement comes from the rest of the
players on Pete's side with a high pitched scream
especially from Angela on the side line. We all run up
to Edward to congratulate him.
"Well done lad; that's got to be the fastest goal we've
ever scored." Pete says.
"I know; I can't believe it. That was a brilliant pass;
thanks Pete and what about Chris stealing the ball off
Tom." Edward says.
"Yes well done sticky." Pete compliments me.
We all pat each other on the backs before heading
back to the centre to restart the match. I notice Angela
jumping up and down on the side line in jubilation of
her boyfriend scoring the first goal.

Chris and Tom are a little bit more cautious the next
time they kick off, they pass the ball back to their
midfielder to give themselves a chance to move
forward towards our goal. Colin Frey wellies the ball
forward towards Chris as he makes his run into the
goal box to head the ball. Daniel Hucknell catches the
ball with ease and quickly throws the ball out towards
our midfielders who pass it forward to me just above
the halfway line.

I feel quite confident now that I've tested my leg so I
stride out towards their goal, dribbling past the first
player then a second and finally a third before kicking

the ball hard and curved around the goalie into the top right corner.

'GOAL'

Everyone screams.

I look over to the side line where Anne and Michael, Jenny and Debbie are waving frantically and jumping up and down.

Pete and Edward catch up to me.

"Wow that was pure class, I tell you." Edward says.

"Thanks, let's give Pete a shot on goal next." I reply.

"Sounds alright to me, can't let you two score all the goals." Pete adds.

Chris starts the game again with a pass back to Colin in midfield who quickly passes to Adrian Smith on his left. Edward is quickly on him and slides in with a tackle; Adrian jumps to the side and knocks the ball past Edward before running down the wing towards our goal. He sees Chris and Tom running into the box to receive a pass; Adrian kicks the ball high and across to the penalty spot just as Tom gets there; he volleys the ball with his right foot at the goal. Daniel dives for the ball but can't quite make it as the ball skims off his fingertips and crashes into the cross bar bouncing back out towards our defenders. Ian Quinn collects the ball and hoofs it forward towards me in midfield.

"Chris!" Pete shouts to me as he's positioned himself in space to the left of their left back defender. He starts to make his run diagonal past the last man. I see his run and kick the ball straight towards the goal with just enough pace to stop in front of Pete as he runs towards goal. Pete collects the ball at the end of the goal box and takes it around the goalie before tapping it in the back of the net.

'GOAL!'

After the game we shower and get changed into clean clothes before meeting the girls in the clubhouse for some refreshments. Pete and I head for the bar while Anne, Jenny, Debbie and Michael take a seat at a table.

"That was the best game ever, who would have thought we'd win ten goals to three." Pete says.

"It was a good game. I think everyone watching enjoyed it as much as we did." I say.

"I think you're right there Chris. I don't think poor Chris Miller's team thought it was a great game with losing ten, three though. I think he'll remember this game for a long time."

"At least he'll have a couple of weeks to forget about his defeat as we'll be on holiday tomorrow."

"That's right. Oh by the way; I'll be able to stay the whole two weeks now."

"That's great news. But I thought you had to come back to catch that masked man?" I ask.

"No not anymore. Apparently he crashed his car into a police vehicle last night whilst under the influence of alcohol."

"That's a bit stupid of him. Are you sure it's him?" I ask.

"Yes, it's definitely him. We found the mask he wears in the car and his next victim in the boot. Case closed. So I can relax and enjoy my holiday now without worrying about having to come back and catch this vigilante."

We order our drinks and food at the bar before making our way back to the table where Anne and Jenny are chatting; Debbie and Michael are also engaged in conversation about Japanese stuff.
"Here you are; white wine for the girls and coke for Michael and Debbie. We've ordered the food." Pete says.

We take our seats at the table with the others.
"Did you hear about the good news?" I ask Anne.
"What good news?"
"Pete can stay on holiday with us for the whole two weeks now." Jenny says.
"Wow, that's brilliant. But I thought you had to come back to catch that criminal." Anne asks.
"They caught him last night and you wouldn't believe who he is." Jenny says.
"Jenny! We can't say at the moment until he's attended court and convicted." Pete advises.
"Sorry Pete. Anyway, I'm glad they've caught him and we can all enjoy our holiday together."
"So any thoughts of what you fancy doing in Lanzerote?" Anne asks Jenny.

"I thought we could do a bit of shopping and a lot of drinking and dancing but mostly lazing by the pool and working on our tan." Jenny says.
"That sounds like a great idea. What about you lads?" Anne asks.

"I fancy a tour round the island and maybe check out some to the local bars, see a bit of the night life. What do you think Pete?"

"I'm with you Chris. We can leave the girls by the pool and go off somewhere by ourselves." Pete adds.

"Oye it's supposed to be a family holiday; not a boy's holiday, and a girl's holiday." Jenny says.

"I suppose you're right, how about staying by the pool and eating in the hotel one day then the next day explore other parts of the island together?" I suggest.

"That sounds like a good plan, but the essential thing is; I don't want to think about work at all." Pete adds.

"Hear Hear!" We unanimously all call out as we raise our glasses in a toast.

The food arrives and we all tuck in without saying a word. I think it's because Pete and I are exhausted from all the running around and the girls are exhausted from all the jumping and screaming they did after every goal. We chat about general things during the next hour or so before heading home for an early night. I drop Anne and Michael off at the door before driving the car down to the garages to park up for the night. I turn of the engine and step out of the car when something dawns on me as I look at the garage door.

"I haven't checked what's inside that briefcase" I say to myself. I remember putting it under the seat in the van but can't remember ever taking it out.

I open the shutter doors to the garage and step around to the side of the van. I use the fob to unlock the doors and open the driver's door which only opens partially because of the width of the garage so I have to squeeze myself through the gap and onto the seat behind the wheel. It's dark in the cab at this time so I have to turn on the interior light to see what I'm doing. The light is just bright enough to see all around me so I reach down and pull out the briefcase and place it on the seat next to me. Don must have set the combination before he left the club so it's basically impossible to guess the combination. I try to think of a way to open the briefcase when I remember the claw hammer in the back.

'That's it, I'll claw the sides open' I think to myself. I squeeze back out of the cab and around to the side door where I retrieve the hammer. Climbing back into the cab I position myself so I'm half facing the centre seat with my back against the driver's door so I'm facing the briefcase.

Holding the briefcase with my left hand so the handle and combination blocks are facing me; I raise the hammer with my right hand and swing it down hard against the metal combination block.
'Crack!' the lock explodes as the cover and circular discs fly out. I grab the case and try to pry the lid away from the base but realise; although the combination block has been knocked off the latch within the briefcase remains intact.
"Stupid locks! Why didn't Don buy a briefcase from china instead? The whole briefcase would be in bits by now." I say to myself.

I turn the briefcase over so the other combination block is uppermost on the case and swing the hammer down hard against it.

'Crack!' the same thing happens as I watch the metal casing fly off.

I lay the case flat and use the claw part of the hammer to prise up one corner of the case. 'Crack!' the latch breaks on the right side.

"Brilliant, just one more" I say to myself.

I turn the case around and do the same to the left hand corner. 'Crack!' the left hand latch breaks and the lid lifts up a little before dropping down again.

I put the hammer down on the dashboard and using both hands, I slowly open the lid to the briefcase.

I look inside the case and can't believe what I'm seeing.

'What have I done? I'm definitely a dead man for sure. Don's never going to forget this. My hands begin to shake and my heart feels like its motoring. Beads of sweat cover my forehead and neck from the anxiety I'm feeling right at this moment. My mind feels like it's just frozen in some sort of outer world experience, not quite knowing if this is real or a dream. The increased stress causes bile to rise up in my oesophagus making me feel nauseous worrying about the implications this could have on my family. At the time I thought it would be a good idea to implicate Don in this plan of mine. It was supposed to take him out of the picture for a little while and maybe make him think that he's not beyond the law. But looking at the contents of the case means I've hit

Don hard and he's not going to forget the masked maniac ever until he's personally killed him and his family.'

I look down at the stacks of money nearly filling the briefcase. I don't know how much money there is, but at a guess I would estimate there's maybe £60,000 or more. I slowly close the lid and tuck it back under the seat of the cab. After climbing out and locking the garage shutters, I slowly walk up the side road to the front of my house.

'I can't let Anne know there's something wrong, were on holiday tomorrow. I don't want to spoil it for her or Michael. I'll just have to pretend nothing is wrong. Anyway; Don's in jail at the moment pending a trial so I'm safe for the time being but I know when Don wins his case and is freed; I'm going to be the first thing on his menu. 'KILL THE MASKED MANIAC' is going to be his main priority.'

Monday 8th November

The alarm goes off at six thirty and I immediately switch it off. I've been awake for the last two hours worrying about last nights find, I slip out of bed and make my way down stairs to put the kettle on. My eyes still feel heavy and my mind is in a fog probably from lack of sleep. I pour some water in the kettle and place it back on its base before switching it on. I open the top cupboard and take out two cups and place them down on the work surface before putting a teabag in each. My mind seems to be working at a snails pace at the moment so I take the opportunity to wash my face in cold water from the sink. The cold water revives my senses and wakes me up just as the kettle comes to the boil; I pour the boiling water into each cup and replace the kettle back on its base.

Looking out of the back window as the morning light begins to illuminate the garden and garage rooftops reminds me that we'll be on holiday in Lanzerote in a few hours. I try to visualise the hot sun and ocean views lazing by the pool with a cool refreshing pint of lager in my hand. I start to feel a lot better already. "Come on Chris, focus. Were on holiday in less than four hours, forget about Don." I say to myself.
I take out the milk from the fridge and pour a small amount into the cups before removing the teabags and placing them in the bin. I hear movement from upstairs as Anne and Michael make their way downstairs and into the kitchen.
"Hi Dad." Michael says.

"Hello son, what do you fancy for breakfast?" I ask.
"Frosties!"
I reach up and take out the cereal box and a bowl for Michael and hand it to him.
"Good morning darling, I was just about to bring up a cup of tea for you."
"That's alright; I'm too excited to have my drink in bed. I'll make some bacon and eggs for us."
Anne opens the fridge and takes out a pack of bacon and the carton with the eggs in.
"I'm just going to get washed and dressed if that's alright with you."
"Yes, that's fine; breakfast will be reading in about five minutes. Oh and thanks for my tea." Anne says.
I pick up my cup of tea and make my way upstairs to get ready.

It only takes me a few minutes to wash and shave and get dressed. I take out my suitcase and throw some clothes into it for our holiday. I notice Anne's already packed her bag as I see it next to her coat and passport.
'She's so organised' I think to myself as I search my bedside drawer for my passport which I find tucked away under several letters and bills. I lay the passport next to Anne and Michael's and finish off putting the last of my clothes in my bag before zipping the sides up. I think I've packed everything, although if I've missed something, I could always buy what I need when were there. I make my way back down stairs to see Anne carrying two plates of food over to the dining table.

After finishing breakfast; Anne washes the dishes while I collect the luggage from the bedrooms and bring them down and place them by the front door. Anne puts our passports and holiday details in her hand bag for safe keeping.

"So is there anything else we need? Have we forgotten anything?" Anne asks.

"I don't think so."

"Is everything switched off, Michael did you unplug your television and Xbox?" Anne asks.

"Yes mom."

"Are all the doors and windows locked?" She asks.

"Yes, I've checked them twice already. It's only the front door that's unlocked to allow us to leave." I sarcastically say.

We all sit silently on the sofa while staring out the window for our ride to pick us up.

"What time did Pete and Jenny say they were going to pick us up?" Anne asks.

"Eight o'clock." I reply.

We all look at the clock on the wall which tells us its five to eight.

"What time does you're watch say? Is the clock slow?" Anne asks.

I've never seen her looking so anxious, but as it's our first real holiday in a long time; I'm not surprised.

"My watch says its seven fifty five, six now. Don't worry; Pete will be here in four minutes. He's a policeman, and they're always punctual." I reassure her.

We all stare back out of the window at the empty street.

I see Anne look back at the clock and then at the window. If we were not married, I would have strangled her by now.

"What time is it now?" she asks.

"The same time the clock is displaying." I reply.

We hear a faint sound of a car pulling into the street which causes us to all stand and move towards the window.

The sound gets louder and louder until we see a vehicle pull up outside our house with 'POLICE' stencilled on the side.

My knees start to buckle as I step back in horror at seeing the police.

'Has Don told the police who I am? How did they find out so quickly? Was it Horrace who worked it out? What gave me away? Did they find some piece of evidence somewhere? Maybe the mask I left had my fingerprints on it and they've been working through the night desperately trying to find out if the fingerprints matched Don's.'

I step back and collapse on the chair when I hear a knock on the front door.

'BANG, BANG, BANG.'

"Chris! Are you alright?" Anne asks as she notices me slumped in the chair.

I look up at her, not knowing what to say. How can I tell her our lives have ended, within seconds I'm going to be taken away in handcuffs. Don's going to find out who we are and Anne and Michael will be murdered very soon; but it'll all look like an accident of some sort. Me! I'm just going to be put in jail somewhere with a bunch of criminals; friends of Don no doubt, whose going to make my life a misery.

Michael runs to the door and opens it. A dark figure steps into the lounge.
"Come on guys, were on holiday. I arranged for Edward to pick us up and drop us at the airport; saves on parking. We're travelling in style in a police minibus." Pete says.

"That's great Pete, were all ready, except Chris doesn't look so good at the moment." Anne says.
I'm so relieved to know I'm not being arrested.
"Sorry, I think I ate my breakfast a little too quickly. That's all, I'm fine really." I reply.
"Great, so let's get going." Pete encourages us to get a move on by shooing us out with his arms.
We carry the bags to the minibus and store them in the back with Pete and Jenny's luggage.
"Morning Jenny, this is different." Anne asks.
"I know, isn't it exciting." She says.
I quickly dash back to the front door and lock it with my house key.
"OK let's go." I tell Edward in the driver's seat. We all get in and Edward pulls away heading for the airport.

We check our bags in at the airport and make our way through security into the departure lounge where we all sit down and have a drink to relax while we wait for our flight to be announced. The morning news is on the television which we can just about hear amongst the hustle and bustle of holiday makers and commuters moving like a swarm of bees from one location to the next. The constant drone of voices mingling between the multi national arrays of people is never ending. Pete notices something on the television and tells us to watch.

The Chief Constable appears on screen making a statement regarding the recent arrest of the Masked Maniac. The bottom of the screen scrolls a bulletin report stating 'Masked Maniac Arrested.' The Chief Constable comments to one of the reporters. "We are pleased to announce that the mysterious Masked Maniac has been apprehended by our diligent officers in the early hours of Sunday morning. His next victim was found alive and well in the suspects car together with further corroborating evidence proving beyond a doubt that we have finally caught this vigilante whose been terrorising the local community"

"I can't say anything at the moment but I'm really surprised to find out who this guy really is. It doesn't make any sense, but hey. Its all done and dusted now pending a court hearing." Pete says.
"Why doesn't it make sense?" I ask.
"I don't know. If you have lots and lots of money and property; why would you risk it all by attacking petty criminals?"
"I see what you mean. Maybe he just likes hurting others?" I say.
"The thing is; this masked maniac was only attacking people who have committed a crime. But if you're a criminal yourself; then why would you attack

someone who does exactly the same as yourself? It just doesn't make sense." Pete explains.

"Don't worry about it Pete, we're all on holiday now. Let's just forget about work and enjoy the next two weeks with our friends." Jenny says.

"Yes, let's forget about England and think about getting a blooming good tan in Lanzerote." Anne adds.

The tannoy informs us that our boarding gate is open.

We make our way down to the gate and board the plane in an orderly fashion. Pete, Jenny and Debbie are seated two rows behind us on the other side of the aisle which is nice. We wait for the rest of the passengers to board the plane before the stewardess's walks along the cabin closing all the overhead lockers before returning to do a final head count while the captain informs us of the flight details including the height we will be flying and the expected time we will be landing in Lanzerote. The stewardess finally closes the cabin door and the plane begins its taxiing to the runway ready for takeoff.

She stands next to our row and begins the pre-flight demonstration showing us where the nearest exits are and the use of our inflatable life vests in the event of an emergency which Michael really enjoys as he's sat right next to her as she waves her arms pointing in all direction. She finally takes a seat near the front of the plane as the plane comes to a halt pointing down the runway. The engines begin to roar and there's a surge of power as the plane propels itself along the tarmac.

I look over at Anne whose rigid in her seat clinging
on for dear life to the arm rests with her gaze directly
forward. Just beyond her I can see Michael on the
aisle seat looking round with a grin on his face;
obviously enjoying his first experience of flying. I
glance out of the window and see the ground drop
away from us as the plane begins to lift into the air.
The buildings and roads below get smaller and
smaller as the plane rises higher and higher eventually
disappearing into cloud before rising out of a blanket
of cloud to see the bright blue sky clear into the
distance. I lean my head back against the head rest
and close my eyes. Finally I can now relax as we
leave Great Britain and head for Playa Blanca Resort
in Lanzerote.

The End

20544014R00249

Printed in Great Britain
by Amazon